WAR OF THE ARCHONS

SPEAR OF MALICE

R·S·FORD
SPEAR OF
MALICE

BOOK THREE of WAR OF THE ARCHONS

TITAN BOOKS

Spear of Malice
Print edition ISBN: 9781785653124
E-book edition ISBN: 9781785653131

Published by Titan Books
A division of Titan Publishing Group Ltd.
144 Southwark Street, London, SE1 0UP

www.titanbooks.com

First Titan edition: January 2021
10 9 8 7 6 5 4 3 2 1

A CIP catalogue record for this title is available
from the British Library.

Printed and bound by CPI Group (UK) Ltd, Croydon CR0 4YY.

PROLOGUE

The Ramadi Wastes, 107 years after the Fall

THE wastes were silent but for the occasional snort of oxen, the relentless squeaking of the wagon's wheels and the flapping of its hide cover in the breeze. The sounds had been Byram's constant companions for endless leagues of sand. It was enough to drive a man mad and brought to mind the Lament of the Ramadi. *The Seven Deserts calling myriad names, Calling thy despair.*

Byram had much to despair about.

They were on their way to Kragenskûl, that vast city in the desert, and must have journeyed for a hundred leagues. Byram so hated to travel. The poorly secured covering allowed the sand to constantly encroach on the wagon's interior and despite the welcome breeze, the cart stank of unwashed bodies as the other Priests of Wraak sat sweating in their robes. It was intolerable, but Byram knew he had no choice. At least he could take solace that he was not out riding in the sun like Kraden's men.

Byram glanced ahead, past the wagon driver, past the lumbering oxen that pulled them along, to see Lord Kraden riding at the head of the column. He looked perfectly happy despite the elements, sitting proudly, bald head exposed to the sun. His mount was much less content, white froth covering its hide as it plodded along, close to death.

Dragging his eyes away from the warlord, Byram glanced across at his travelling companions. They were nondescript, their hoods pulled over their faces, hands hidden in sleeves. Only one other stood out. She sat towards the rear of the cart, shaven head focused on the column of soldiers marching in their wake. There was a look of longing on her scarred face. Byram knew the Carpenter yearned for only one thing – to inflict pain – and she was empty without it. Sadism brought her to life, and to most men that would have been anathema. But Byram had long ago learned to appreciate her talent for torture as one might admire a fine painting or sculpture. Beneath the smock he knew she wore close-fitting leather, buckles secured tightly, pinching her flesh, causing her constant discomfort. It was as though the pain was her captor and she its willing prisoner. He was so glad she had come.

A sudden bark from Kraden diverted Byram's attention. Looking ahead he saw what had caused the warlord such instant mirth. The desert city of Kragenskûl loomed on the horizon and Byram felt relief wash over him that this hellish journey was almost at an end.

The city grew larger and Byram thought back to the last time he had seen the place. It had been on some long-distant campaign when one of the Legion's long-forgotten lords had seen fit to besiege the city. Naturally they had failed – the white walls of Kragenskûl were all but impregnable – but as they drew closer, Byram could see much had changed.

As impenetrable as those walls might have been, clearly they were not strong enough for the city's new ruler. Earthworks had been built all around the perimeter and new fortifications were being constructed, but that was not the most striking change. Where before the city's spires had peered menacingly from behind the city wall, now a colossal tower had been built in its centre, stretching up to the heavens and dwarfing the buildings that surrounded it.

The flags that now fluttered on the battlements no longer bore the black skull on red of the Qeltine Brotherhood. Now the Qeltine and every other cult of the Ramadi Wastes were gathered beneath a different banner. The white desert songbird flew on every pennant. It had once been the symbol of the dead god Eranin, a deity worshipped by a cult long since lost to history, but now it was reborn as the symbol of Innellan – queen of the Seven Deserts.

Nobody stood in their way as they passed the earthworks and trundled through the vast open gates. Byram could see members of the Bloodguard standing sentry but they made no move to stop Kraden as he led the way, nor did they try to inspect the contents of the wagon.

Once inside the city Byram caught sight of the tower in all its majesty. It was a vast monument dedicated to the White Widow, and he could only imagine the effort required to build such a thing in such a short space of time, but then he was sure Innellan could motivate even the most lacklustre servant to the greatest of labours.

The wagon came to a stop at the base of the tower and

Byram wasted no time in climbing down from it. His back was stiff from the journey and his legs unsteady, but still he was in better condition than the team of bulls that had pulled them across the desert.

Kraden had already dismounted and stood staring up at the massive building like a child in awe of a giant. He turned, regarding Byram with a huge gap-toothed grin.

'Isn't it magnificent,' he boomed. 'We are here, at the heart of Kragenskûl. I had always dreamed I would fight my way in at the head of an army, but instead we just ride right through the gates like we own the place.'

Ignoring Kraden's exuberance, Byram made his way inside. If the others were already there it meant he had been tardy. It would be unwise to keep the White Widow waiting.

As soon as they entered through the arch at the base of the tower they were attended by thin figures dressed in white. Their faces were wan, eyes sallow, but the most unnerving thing was their mouths; sealed shut with strands of wire. The Silent Sons beckoned Kraden forward and led the way up the vast, winding staircase.

Byram was in no mood for such a climb after their long journey, but what choice did he have? He slogged his way up the stairs and before long his breathing became laboured. For his part, Kraden practically bounded up the endless flights, his armour doing little to encumber him.

When finally they reached the summit, Byram was sweating profusely and he paused to catch his breath before ascending the final stairway to the throne room. Gathered below it were the warriors of various Ramadi cults. They

8

stood in stony silence, tension hanging in the air like an executioner's axe. The hatred these men and women bore for one another was visceral – they had fought for generations and now they were thrust together as a single tribe. Only the threat of Innellan's wrath kept their violent natures at bay.

When Kraden approached the stairs, the Bloodguard barred his way. Before he could protest, Byram stepped forward. Immediately the guards stood aside and allowed him to pass. Kraden growled as he was left behind, but there was little the warlord could do. Both men knew it was Byram who held the real power within the Legion of Wraak – it would have been pointless for Kraden to protest.

When he reached the summit, Byram could see the rest were already gathered. They stood within the dark room, illuminated by warm red sunlight that shone through a huge arch making up one half of the chamber.

The High Chieftain of the Hand of Zepheroth stood in one corner having travelled the relatively short distance from Gortanis. He was every inch the savage, dusty animal hides covering his muscular shoulders, his face a brutal mass of barely subdued hatred.

From the once beautiful city of Mantioch had come the Hierophant of Katamaru's Faithful. He lingered by the archway, his gold-banded arms folded as he stood impatiently.

The Reverend Mother of the Daughters of Mandrithar was from distant Isinor, her black garb covered in empty sheaths for her myriad knives.

There were also representatives from the Doom of Haephon, the Eye of Honoric and even Duchor's Blades –

their delegate looking more like a seasoned pirate than the lord of a Ramadi cult.

Byram could feel the discomfort in the air. As below, there was a palpable tension. Old vendettas still burned like raw wounds and Byram felt at any moment the unspoken hatred might boil up into violence. All that was dispelled as a door opened at the far end of the chamber. A warm wind blew past them in a single swift gust, all threat of violence was replaced by an overwhelmingly malevolent aura, and every one of these lords of the desert dropped to their knees.

Byram risked a glance upwards, instantly regretting it as he saw her appear from the dark. Her red gown trailed behind her, white hair flowing down to a wasp-thin waist. As her black-eyed gaze scanned the gathering before her, Byram felt suddenly sick at the sensation of utter evil she cast.

Gracefully Innellan mounted the stairs to her onyx throne and sat gazing down at the Ramadi warlords, each kneeling in fealty.

'Thank you for attending,' she said, her words dripping with insincerity. None of them had any choice in this. They were slaves to her will, for now and always. 'Who will begin?'

The Hierophant stood. It seemed he truly was impatient for this to be over.

'My queen,' he said, keeping his head bowed. 'The invaders to the east are proving ever more troublesome. The Shengen forces have liberated several mines in the area. The Lords of Byzantus have been all but destroyed. Before long the enemy will arrive at the gates of Mantioch. We have done everything we can to repel the invaders but their general is a cunning tactician – always two steps ahead of us. They also have a warrior among their ranks – a woman invincible on the field. We need help in the east, my queen. You must send reinforcements to aid us before the city falls.'

Innellan didn't answer, but instead simply stared at the Hierophant. The man hadn't given a great account of himself and Byram half expected the White Widow to strike him down where he stood. Instead she cast her eye across the rest of the kneeling warlords.

'Next,' was all she said.

The Hierophant reluctantly sank to his knees as the veteran pirate of Duchor's Blades rose to his feet. Understandably, he spoke with a nervous edge to his voice:

'Our spies in Kantor have reported Queen Suraan still holds onto her neutrality. She will neither pledge her loyalty to you nor the Suderfeld king until her son is of an age to take the throne. However…' He paused, as though afraid to relay the news. Byram didn't envy him the task. 'We have learned a Suderfeld contingent is already making its way north and are about to meet with her. I do not know what they might offer her for an alliance, but even if we sent envoys with a counter-proposal now, they may well be too late. Now united, the Suderfeld is strong, their armies mighty, and the resurgence of magic there gives them a distinct advantage. It seems unlikely Queen Suraan will be able to resist their influence for long.'

Innellan rose from her throne and the pirate took a step back. Relaying such news might not be good for him, and Byram even felt a touch of sympathy for the man.

'On your feet,' she said. 'All of you.'

The compulsion to stand coursed through Byram's every fibre and he stood with the rest. He was overwhelmed with the yearning to obey Innellan's word and he had long since learned not to resist.

The White Widow walked among them. When she passed close to him, Byram felt a heady mix of emotions battling for supremacy – yearning, loyalty, revulsion, fear. He almost shook as these feelings overwhelmed him.

'The Suderfeld is of little concern,' she said. 'Its king is a puppet. There is a power behind that throne that I will deal with in due course. The true enemy lies to the east.'

As she spoke, Innellan walked past the weathered figure of the Reverend Mother. The old woman became agitated, the perspiration that ran down her temple making tracks across her dust-stained cheeks.

'Each one of you will pledge a tithe of troops to march east and relieve Mantioch,' Innellan continued. 'The city must not be allowed to fall. This enemy must be destroyed at all costs.'

As she spoke, Byram saw the Reverend Mother reach a hand behind her back, producing a blade from a hidden sheath in her waistband. He suddenly felt a spark of excitement – of hope. The Reverend Mother was so close, and Innellan's back was turned. Could this nightmare be about to end? Could one of them at least resist Innellan's allure for long enough to strike her down?

The Reverend Mother snarled as she lunged forward, blade raised to plunge into the back of Innellan's neck.

Byram heard the feral cry, his heart pounding as he realised they were about to be freed.

Innellan didn't move, simply gazing out of the arched window, as the Reverend Mother froze. She stood transfixed, knife raised high, every muscle trembling as she fought against the White Widow's glamour.

Slowly, Innellan turned to face her would-be assassin, a curious look to her pale features.

'Brave,' she whispered. 'Your resolve is only to be admired. How long have you harboured such a defiant heart, I wonder?'

The Reverend Mother gritted her teeth against Innellan's enchantment. Byram almost felt sorry for her; this woman he had fought against for decades, this deadly warrior who had seen fit to defy a goddess.

'No matter,' Innellan continued, 'clearly you have a formidable strength of will. It will be a shame to lose you. But defiance cannot be tolerated.' She turned dismissively, lazily gesturing with one hand. 'Cut your throat.'

The Reverend Mother continued to tremble, and Byram could see a single bloody tear drip from her eye. The knife in her hand drew closer to her neck but the woman fought against it, refusing to obey to the last.

With a shriek, the Reverend Mother dropped the knife and ran towards the open archway. With a last cry of defiance she pitched herself over the side and into oblivion.

Byram watched in amazement. In the end the Reverend Mother had chosen her own way to die. She had defied Innellan's command. She had disobeyed the god who reigned over them all.

In that instant Byram realised Innellan could be resisted. That someone with enough determination might be able to strike her down. He also knew that it most certainly wasn't him.

Innellan stared after her rebellious servant. It was as though she too understood her own vulnerability. For the first time Byram saw doubt draw over the White Widow's visage, but it was gone as soon as it appeared.

'You have your instructions,' Innellan said quietly. 'Send your levies to Mantioch. The city must not fall.'

Every one of them bowed low, backing out of the throne room before making their way down the stairs.

After rejoining Kraden below, Byram ignored his questions while the Silent Sons led them back down the tower. He spoke to no one as they followed an emaciated servant to a chamber near the foot of the stronghold. It was bare but for a single window, while a plain wooden bed stood to one side and a mirror hung on the wall.

Standing in the centre of the room, Byram tried to clear his mind of what had happened. No matter how he tried to purge himself of Innellan's influence he knew it would be impossible. There was no way he could ever rid himself of her allure, but neither could he blindly follow her into oblivion. She had to be stopped, but what could he do? He did not possess the will to resist her glamour. The Reverend Mother had shown a strength he had never witnessed before and still she had perished.

Opening his eyes, Byram caught sight of himself in the mirror. The serpent tattoo that encircled his eye had long since faded. It was still visible though, an indelible part of him, much like his loyalty to the Legion of Wraak. A Legion that was no more. A Legion Byram wanted back with every fibre of his being.

He knew he had to fight these seditious ideas. There was no way to resist the White Widow and even the most fleeting thought of betrayal might lead to his death. Before he could begin to purge himself of those feelings, his chamber door creaked open.

The Carpenter entered, her robe discarded, her shaved head now concealed beneath a leather hood. In one hand she held a whip, and on seeing it Byram loosened his robe and let it fall to the ground. All thought of defiance had to be scourged from his body.

As the Carpenter began to minister to him, the sting of the lash cutting his buttocks so exquisitely, Byram felt the sudden release of his burden. He could only hope the pain would be enough to quell any further notion of disobedience. It was the only way he would survive.

1

ADAALI stared at the ceiling, too afraid to close her eyes. For the past three nights her dreams had woken her well before dawn but the memory of them was scant. Try as she might to piece them back together she could only gather brief flashes – disparate images and scenes, as though she were trying to remember a mummers' play from years ago.

She had seen gods in a distant land. A faraway place and a faraway time where the sky was the bluest she had ever laid eyes on. Or was it the blackest? Had there been a storm raging? The tighter Adaali tried to grasp the images the more they slipped through her fingers. All she knew for certain was that she had been surrounded by titans. Myriad gods with myriad faces, angels and demons with immense power, and she had been nothing but an ant scurrying about their feet. It had been enthralling until they had turned their eyes upon her and then, when she was locked in their inscrutable gaze, she had found herself falling – the wind in her face, her gut twisting with the thrill and terror of it – but she woke before the shock of any impact. What it all meant she could not say, but Adaali knew she would not find any answers wallowing in her bed.

She pulled back the sheet and stood, feeling the chill through her nightslip. It was damp with sweat and clung to her as she moved towards the open window and leaned out, gazing at the dark city. Beacons burned all along the walls of Kantor, and she could just make out sentries patrolling the battlements. The guardians were vigilant, but it did little to reassure her. Only recently a great warlord had been defeated in the east, but to north and south powers were beginning to stir; powers that threatened to consume the entire Cordral. Kantor was caught in the middle, and there was no telling what catastrophe might befall the city.

Shaking her head, she tried to dislodge the feeling of dread. She was still plagued by the memory of her dream and needed something to clear her senses and make her focus.

After peeling off the slip, she donned a plain red tunic. Still in her bare feet she made her way down through the sleeping palace. She trod carefully just as Dragosh had taught her, leaving no sound as she passed by the servants' quarters and the guards standing at their posts. Eventually she reached the ground floor of the palace and came out into the central courtyard. It was a wide open space that had once been an ornamental garden. On Dragosh's insistence it was now cleared of all foliage and a thick bed of sand had been laid across its length.

'If Princess Adaali is to be her brother's sworn protector she will need her own training yard,' he had said. The Queen Regent had taken little persuasion.

Naturally the yard was empty. A brazier stood in each of the four corners but they had long since burned down to embers. The encroaching dawn light began to cast long shadows but Adaali could see enough to train. A couple of servants walked at the periphery of the square carrying chamber pots and somewhere, someone was baking bread. The smell of it on the morning air made Adaali's stomach rumble with longing, but she had not yet done enough to deserve a morning meal. She would earn it first.

Weapon drills were her favourite. When Dragosh arrived he would most likely work on her physical conditioning, which was something she hated. He had told her she must get stronger, that her slight frame would need much development, but this time before dawn was her own. She could fill it how she pleased.

The weapon rack to one side of the yard held spears, axes, swords, maces and other, more exotic weapons. Dragosh had once told her that when she mastered them all she would no longer need him. Adaali knew she was years away from that and should probably pick something she was weak with like the axe. Instead, she reached forward and plucked a spear from the rack.

As soon as she held it in her hand memories of her dream were gone, threats from north and south forgotten. It was just her and the weapon.

She ran through the drills Dragosh had taught her – low sweeps, swift jabs, deep thrusts. As she moved through the forms she considered how perfect the weapon was for her. Its superior reach meant she could attack a more powerful sword-wielding opponent and stay out of their range. Her speed meant she could dart in without fear of being struck and outmanoeuvre even the quickest armoured enemy.

The longer Adaali practised, the more she knew this was her true purpose. Not that she had ever had any choice. She was Queen Suraan's eldest, but her younger brother was rightful heir to the throne of Kantor. In years past she would have been married off to the heir of another city state or foreign court, or perhaps to seal an alliance with a Suderfeld lord, but this was not that time. The other great cities of the Cordral were gone, and Queen Suraan would never have allowed Adaali to be wed simply to secure an alliance. Instead, in this time of mistrust and uncertainty, Adaali was to be her brother's guardian. Prince Rahuul's most trusted shadow. She would never sit on the throne of Kantor or any other, and Adaali had long ago learned to accept it. Or had she? Had she come to terms with the fact she would be nothing more than bodyguard to her younger brother? Never have any ambition other than to ensure his safety?

Adaali span on her heel, ending the combat drill, and let fly with the spear. It soared twenty feet across the training yard, and embedded itself in a wooden target. She heard the wood crack and splinter, shocked at her own strength. She had flung the weapon in anger, the injustice of her position making her throw it all the harder.

'Your form is good,' said Musir Dragosh. Adaali started, finding him watching from the shadowy extremities of the training yard. He stepped out into the growing light of dawn, his muscular figure moving lithely as a leopard. 'But your throw was wild.'

'But accurate,' she replied, gesturing at the wooden target, cracked down the middle where the spear had pierced it.

Dragosh considered the broken target as though trying to find fault, but couldn't quite manage it.

'You are here before sunrise again. So that is something,' he said, as though it pained him to grant her any kind of praise.

For the past few days, Adaali had risen before the sun and made her way to the training yard, trying to wash the troubling dreams from her mind. She would have liked to accept Dragosh's compliment, but it was not diligence that had brought her there, more necessity.

She made to retrieve her spear, but Dragosh halted her with a raised hand.

'Your adherence to the discipline of the spear is impressive, but you rely on it too much,' he said. 'Your other forms are weak.'

'But the spear is—' she tried to say but was silenced when he motioned with his finger.

'Sword and shield,' Dragosh pronounced.

It was her least favourite of all the weapon forms, but Adaali knew better than to protest. She might have been a princess of Kantor, but Musir Dragosh didn't care. Any sign of petulance or defiance and he would punish her. Once punished by the leader of the Desert Blades, the lesson was learned in full.

Adaali took a sword and shield from the rack and tested the balance of the blade in her hand. It was a well-crafted weapon, much like those used by warriors of the Desert Blades, save for its dulled edge.

Dragosh waited in the centre of the square. He carried

no shield and his blade was drawn. This was no training weapon but his sword of office. The ornate hilt was crafted in the shape of an eagle and the razor-sharp blade gently curved to a point.

Adaali advanced purposefully. Experience had taught her Dragosh would rarely take the initiative and she wanted this over with so she could move on to a more favourable weapon. She feinted to the left before slicing in from the right. Dragosh easily parried her attack and she took advantage of his lack of shield, shoving her own forward. Dragosh dropped his left shoulder, leaning away from the attack, and she missed by several inches.

Her teacher countered, sweeping his blade at head height, and she ducked. He cut downward and she raised her shield, feeling the power of his blow rock through her arm. Gritting her teeth against it, she thrust in again, and with one simple sidestep Dragosh avoided the attack.

She let out a slow breath, anticipating the inevitable counter as Dragosh hacked down diagonally. Knowing he would expect it, Adaali lifted her shield in another feint, then dropped and rolled beneath the strike instead of blocking it. She heard the blade pass by her head and swiftly rolled to her feet, yelling in victory as she struck with the sword.

However, Dragosh had already moved, altering his stance and striking a final killing blow. His keen-edged blade rested beneath her chin and Adaali froze.

'Don't claim victory until the enemy is dead,' Dragosh said.

'Yes, Musir,' she replied.

'Now, again.'

Adaali risked a longing glance towards the spear protruding from the wooden target board before hefting her sword and shield once more. This was going to be a long morning.

She had washed and eaten hastily after her session with Dragosh before going to her lessons. The airy room in the eastern wing of the palace was a far cry from the intensity of the training yard, but as much as Adaali resented being beaten daily with sword, spear and axe, it was still far preferable to the stultifying dullness of the classroom.

She sat beside her little brother Rahuul, her mother standing before them both, reciting some treatise on ancient history from a suitably antique tome. Rahuul gave their mother his rapt attention, spellbound by her words, but Adaali did not share his attentiveness. The histories bored her as much as mathematics, languages, geography or wordcraft, and Adaali made no attempt to mask her contempt. In years gone by she had worked her way through a dozen tutors, each one giving up due to her ambivalence or often open disdain. It was one of the reasons their mother had taken to teaching them herself. Only she and Musir Dragosh could hold Adaali's attention.

But there were other reasons Queen Suraan had taken to tutoring her children personally. Since their father's death, threats to the royal family had come from every quarter, creeping from every stinking lair and darkened corridor. Where assassins were not lying in wait, self-serving courtiers and city aldermen lurked ready to pour their poisonous influence into the ears of the fledgling prince. The Queen Regent would have her children influenced by no one but herself.

As her mother spoke, Adaali ignored the words, instead thinking about the burden this woman was under and how serene she seemed despite the weight of it. There was war to the north where a new queen had risen – a witch queen if rumours were to be believed. She had united the cults and threatened to invade the south, but fortune had favoured the Cordral when invaders had come along the Skull Road from the Shengen Empire. Instead of turning their eye to Kantor they had instead struck north to take war to this new queen and her army of fanatics. For now, the north was not a priority – more pressing was the threat from the south.

There had been conflict there since before Adaali was born, but now that war was over. Since then, the King of the Suderfeld had pressured Queen Suraan for an alliance. So far she had resisted, desperate to keep Kantor and the Cordral free of further conflict, but how long she could hold out only time would tell.

Suraan's voice suddenly stopped and she looked up from her tome, past her children to the far end of the chamber. Adaali turned to see a man standing at the open door. She hadn't even heard it open, not that it was surprising given the newcomer.

Egil Sun was silent as a serpent and just as slender, his dark blue robe covered in scraps and rolls of parchment. He entered the room with his usual solemn expression and as much as Adaali refused to fear him, she couldn't help but feel it creeping up within her, threatening to overwhelm her every faculty. He was Keeper of the Word, said to know forbidden things, said to have done hideous crimes in service to the crown of Kantor, and he carried the stink of dread wherever he went.

'Apologies for the intrusion, my queen,' Egil said. 'But we must speak further about the impending visit.'

Adaali looked back to her mother, seeing she was trying her best to control her anger.

'Can you not see my children are at their lessons?' Suraan replied.

Egil regarded Rahuul, choosing to ignore Adaali altogether, which she was more than thankful for.

'Indeed, my queen. But the delegation from the Suderfeld will not wait. And neither must we. They are due to arrive on the high moon, and we still have much to prepare for.'

'Then prepare for it,' Suraan said, unable to disguise the impatience in her voice. 'You are vizier to the crown. Is that not one of your duties?'

'Yes, my queen, but we must discuss what you are to say when you meet their envoy. We must have a united front. Kantor must know its mind – all the possibilities must be prepared for.'

'I have not yet decided whether I'll meet with them personally, Egil.'

A stony silence as Egil considered her words. 'But you must. This is no time for neutrality, my queen. Kantor must decide who it will stand with. And who it will oppose.'

'Kantor has always stood alone, Egil. We are a free

people; we do not have to pick sides. Sometimes inaction is the only course of action.'

'Now is not the time for worthless epithets.' Egil's tone had lost all its reverence and he practically sneered down his hawk nose. Adaali felt herself bristling at the lack of respect, but it was not her place to challenge him. 'We did nothing when the Shengens passed through the gates of Dunrun and we were fortunate not to have suffered the consequences.'

'You were the one who ignored the warnings, Egil. Don't presume to lecture me—'

She paused, glancing down at Adaali and Rahuul as though suddenly remembering they were present.

'Children,' she said, her voice calm once more. 'The vizier and I must speak. Your lessons are over for the day.'

Rahuul needed no further encouragement and scrambled from his seat. Adaali was less keen to leave her mother alone with Egil, but she obeyed nonetheless. But then what choice did she have? Adaali had long since learned her duty was to obey.

'Let's play seeker,' Rahuul said as soon as they left the room behind them. He ran on ahead down the corridor.

Adaali walked after him, in no mood for his games. When she reached the end of the corridor he was awaiting her around the corner, hiding behind a big pot plant, but still in plain sight. He leaned out from behind the plant and gave her a mischievous grin.

That brought a smile to her face, but also filled her with sadness. All her little brother wanted was to run and play. He had no idea what awaited him in a few short years. Assassins already hid in every alcove and the rulers of the

Cordral's other provinces coveted Kantor's throne. Adaali's purpose was to keep her brother from danger, and the only way to do that was to see him mature before his years, not indulge his childish games.

'Come on, let's play,' Rahuul urged.

Adaali would have much preferred it if he had children of his own age to run and play with, but the Prince of Kantor could never be afforded such a simple luxury. All he had was her.

'All right. I'll seek,' she said.

Adaali watched as he scurried off to hide. She knew she had to cherish these moments of innocence. They would not last much longer.

2

JOSTEN was beginning to think this was a mistake as he struggled on through the desert. The sand stung his eyes despite the cotton scarf tied tight around his head, and the desert wind howled in his ears, threatening to send him mad.

The rest of his men seemed to be weathering the conditions more resolutely, and Josten was forced to plod on in silence rather than look weak. There was no way he was about to complain while surrounded by twenty taciturn Shengens. They were staunch to a man, every last one the veteran of a dozen campaigns. A more professional bunch of soldiers he couldn't have wished for, and here he was, in charge of them all. Josten Cade, mercenary and pirate, leading the best fighting men in the world. It was strange how things turned out.

But then, everyone got what they deserved.

When they reached the top of the next windswept ridge he felt palpable relief. In the distance was their rendezvous point – an old temple half buried in the sand, its central tower listing dangerously as though the desert were trying to swallow it whole. He crouched down, shielding his eyes as he tried to make out details of the site, wary of signs of ambush.

'Is this the place, you think?' Retuchius asked.

Josten nodded. 'Looks like it, though there must be hundreds like this littering the Ramadi.'

As he spoke something glinted from the tower protruding from the centre of the ruin.

'That's our man,' said Retuchius.

'All right, let's move,' Josten shouted above the din of the storm.

On his order, twenty men made their way down over the ridge, sticking close together as they crossed the sand to the ruin. At the gate they paused warily, but as Josten peered into the courtyard he saw a single scout already waiting for them. He was tall, face hidden within a headscarf, but when he gave the signal of the Shengen legion Josten relaxed.

The walls of the ruin offered them shelter from the howling winds and Josten led his men inside, glad of the respite. He pulled the scarf from his face and when the scout did likewise Josten recognised the stern features of Kyon, former praetorian to the Iron Tusk himself.

'Glad to see you alive,' said Josten.

'Likewise,' Kyon replied. 'I was beginning to wonder if you were going to make it.'

Josten patted the scout on the shoulder. He was a good man, solid, dependable. Considering they had fought on opposing sides not a year before it was a surprise they'd become close. Kyon harboured a deep shame that he was desperate to atone for. The Iron Tusk's hold on the Shengen legions had been a strong one, a devotion only a god could command, but Kyon still felt responsible for his own actions.

'What do you have for us?' Josten asked.

'They are on the way,' Kyon replied. 'The party set out from Mantioch yesterday. About a dozen riders on horse, but I managed to stay ahead of them – the storm helped with that.'

'How long do we have?'

'An hour, maybe less.'

Josten turned to the rest of the men. 'Right – you all know the drill. An enemy patrol is on the way. We need at least one of them alive. If our luck holds they'll want to take shelter here. That'll be our chance.'

Retuchius looked uncertain. 'A dozen riders would be hard enough to take down even if we didn't need prisoners,' he said. 'And what if there's more than that? If we try and take them on here we'll be trapped. We're stuck in the middle of the desert with no way to send for help.'

'There's no more than a dozen,' Kyon said.

'According to you,' Retuchius snapped.

There was no love lost between the two of them. Retuchius had been loyal to Emperor Laigon even before he defeated the Iron Tusk. Kyon had ordered the slaughter of men of the Fourth Standing; Retuchius' old legion. As much as Josten could understand his mistrust of Kyon, he knew they had no choice but to fight together.

'We need information on their movements,' Josten said. 'Short of asking nicely this is the next best thing. We all know the dangers.'

That was enough for Retuchius and he nodded his

assent. Josten wasn't worried, he knew Retuchius was being overly cautious. He'd seen these men fight, had faced their shields and spears, and would rather be fighting at their side than with a hundred death cultists.

'Right then,' Josten raised his voice above the din of the storm. 'I want men ready to block the entrance, there's only one way in and out. The rest of you take flanking positions, we need to hem in the riders and take them down before they can manoeuvre, shield walls to either side.'

The Shengens obeyed him without question, carrying their shields and hunkering down amongst the fallen masonry.

'What about me?' said a voice behind him.

Josten turned to see Eyman. He was a young lad of the Cordral, an ex-militiaman who'd decided to follow Silver and the Shengens when they struck north from Dunrun so many months ago. He was inexperienced but keen, a combination that would either see him become an asset or a right royal pain in Josten's arse. Which one remained to be seen.

'Why don't you take the tower?' Josten gestured to the crumbling monolith that looked over the entire temple. 'Keep an eye out for us.'

Eyman looked up at the crumbling building uncertainly. 'Er... sure. I can do that.'

Josten watched as he scurried away. With any luck Eyman would give a good account of himself. In a perfect world he'd only have experienced fighters at his side, but that was a luxury he'd had to forego.

Once the men had taken their positions, Josten joined the shield wall at the gate. He crouched down, pulling his

30

scarf around his face. There was no more to say now. They knew their jobs. All he could do was wait.

His hand strayed to the sword at his side. Idly he flicked up the cross-guard with his thumb, loosening the blade in the sheath. Old habits died hard.

As time passed, Josten noted that the cover offered by the swirling sand and deafening gale was now abating. Why did nothing ever go right? Before he could lament further, Eyman waved from the tower, gesturing back west through the open gate.

Josten peered out, seeing horses appear through the dying swell of the sandstorm. Quickly he moved back, flattening himself against the crumbing wall, holding his breath as he waited for the first of the horses to come trotting into the courtyard. The riders were covered in the yellow dust of the storm, their horses' eyes covered to shield them from the stinging sand. Josten watched, slowly unsheathing his blade as the last rider entered through the gate.

'Now!' he yelled.

On his order, half a dozen men rushed to block the entrance, their shields locking together, spears jutting forth to form a deadly barrier. The rest of the Shengens rushed in from the riders' flanks, crouching behind tower shields, advancing with surprising speed.

Josten ran forward, trying to locate their commander. Whoever he was he'd have the most information and with any luck Josten could subdue him before one of the Shengens impaled him on the end of a spear.

A horse reared as he rushed past, its pained whinny

rising above the sound of the storm. To the front of the column, Josten spied his target. The man's headscarf had slipped, revealing his olive-skinned face and the iron band about his head that marked him as a Hierophant of the Set.

He raced past the line of attacking Shengen warriors, grabbing the bridle of the Hierophant's horse and pulling it towards the ground. The beast was strong, but it couldn't resist as the bit tightened in its mouth. The Hierophant took a wild swipe at Josten with his sword but missed, unbalancing himself. He slipped from the saddle, hitting the ground and rolling aside.

The Hierophant came up on his feet as Josten advanced. The man glanced back along the column as it came under attack and it was clear his men were losing the battle. The Shengens had them penned in, and though they had the advantage of being mounted, their swords could do little against the spear-wielding legionaries.

'There's nowhere for you to go,' Josten said. 'Put down your weapon.'

The Hierophant took no notice, snarling as he darted forward, curved blade raised. Josten hadn't expected him to do as he was bid, and he parried the incoming attack. Before he could counter, another horse bolted in between them. Josten barely had a chance to dodge out of the way before the rider took a swipe at him.

The Hierophant leapt up behind the man, screaming the order to retreat. As one, the remaining riders bolted for the wall of shields barring the way out.

Josten rushed after the Hierophant, but the high priest

dragged the rider from the saddle in front of him, flinging him to the ground. The cultist hit the dirt at Josten's feet then leapt up to attack. Josten parried the frenzied assault just before the fanatic was skewered on a Shengen spear.

Only three cultists remained in the saddle now – the Hierophant one of them – and they spurred their mounts towards the Shengen shield wall. Josten fully expected the horses to pull up short when faced by the wall of spears, but cursed when he remembered they were blindfolded. The first horse smashed into the shield wall, its screeching whinny pealing out above the storm as it took two spears to the chest. The impetus of its charge smashed a gap in the shield wall, scattering the Shengens and allowing the other two horses to gallop through the breach.

Josten cursed again, eyes darting around for an abandoned steed. He saw one, milling in a panic, but before he could grab the reins he heard a voice from above.

'I've got it,' shouted Eyman, dropping the few feet from the tower overhead. Deftly he landed in the saddle of the horse, and before Josten could shout at him – whether to congratulate him for his dumb luck or tell him not to be so bloody stupid – the lad had kicked the steed after the escaping cultists.

'Bollocks!' Josten gave chase. One more horse milled about the courtyard, its rider slumped over its back. He pulled the corpse to the ground and climbed up into the saddle.

'Try not to kill any more of them,' he bellowed at Retuchius, though it was clear he was already too late for that. Putting heels to the horse's flanks, he raced after Eyman.

The storm was abating with every passing moment, and Josten could see Eyman just ahead. He tried to shout after him, but the wind was still too strong for his voice to carry. As they galloped across the sands in pursuit, the cultist pulled his steed up, turning to face his pursuers. His sword was drawn as he charged towards them and Josten held his breath, expecting Eyman to be cut from the saddle when the two riders clashed.

As they drew level, Eyman ducked, hanging off the saddle as the cultist's sword slashed overhead. It was a feat of horsemanship Josten had not expected – maybe he had underestimated the young militiaman all along. But he didn't have time to wonder on that as the cultist continued the charge straight at him.

Josten raised his sword high. There'd be one chance at a strike as they galloped past one another. He could see the cultist's wide eyes now, peering desperately from within his headscarf. He looked wild, or was it scared? Didn't matter either way, Josten had to kill him quick all the same.

At the last second the cultist jumped up, bracing his feet against the saddle, then leapt. Josten cursed as the cultist barrelled into him, knocking him from his horse's back. They both hit the ground, rolling in a torrent of sand. Josten tried to get to his feet, but the fanatic was on him, clawing at his face as he pulled a curved knife. Josten barely managed to grab his attacker's wrist before that blade was plunged into somewhere vital.

They were wrestling now, spinning in the sand. A flash of fear in the fanatic's eyes, and Josten smashed his forehead into the man's face. The cultist fell back, dazed enough for Josten to take the initiative and stick the curved blade into his chest.

There was no time for gloating. Josten was on his feet and running after Eyman. Through the eddying storm he caught sight of tracks in the sand. Quickening his pace he raced up the side of a dune, at any moment expecting to see Eyman's decapitated body lying in the sand. As he neared the top he saw a riderless horse standing there, still blindfolded, waiting patiently like it was in a stable.

Josten's heart sank as he slowed, approaching the top of the ridge carefully, fully expecting the lad to be dead. As he gazed down the other side he almost laughed. Eyman sat atop the prone body of the Hierophant, the priest lying unconscious beneath him.

Eyman looked up at Josten and smiled. 'Took your time,' he said in his thick Cordral accent.

Josten smiled, suppressing his laughter. It looked like he had underestimated the lad after all.

3

THE palace was in upheaval as servants and maids prepared for the impending arrival of the Suderfeld envoys. Adaali could only marvel at their industriousness as they swept and polished the corridors and reception rooms to a fine mirror sheen. She had never seen the place so busy.

Likewise, she had never seen her mother so preoccupied, barking orders as though she were a battlefield general. Everything had to be perfect and Queen Suraan was determined to impress their guests, whenever they deigned to arrive. For Adaali it was a welcome relief. With her mother's attention focused wholly on the aesthetics of the palace, Adaali and her brother were all but ignored, if not actively encouraged to stay out of the way.

Musir Dragosh was equally busy, ensuring his Desert Blades were prepared for the southerners. Every warrior shone like a bright gem, having lacquered their arms and armour, trimmed their beards and oiled and braided their hair. They each looked as beautiful as they were deadly.

As a consequence, Adaali's weapon master had no time to train her, and she could spend her time on less vigorous pursuits for a while. This meant keeping the prince entertained. Not that she could complain. Adaali was her brother's protector, but having some time to simply play was a welcome relief from the usual formality of her duties.

She had already lost count of the number of times they'd played seeker today, but as the afternoon wore on Adaali was still not losing her enjoyment of it. As always, she was the one doing the seeking, but it gave her a great deal of pleasure to hunt through the old forgotten hallways of the palace. She also took encouragement that her brother seemed to be improving in his role as hider.

The tower at the southwestern extent of the palace complex was long disused, but the pair knew several ways inside. It was full of clutter – abandoned tapestries and paintings, elaborately crafted furniture left to rot, threadbare sofas that would once have seated emperors and sorcerers long dead. Forgotten trinkets and treasures from all over the world had been gifted to the palace when Kantor had sat at the centre of a huge empire. Now that empire was no more, and the memory of it was as decayed as the tower itself.

Adaali had already searched the bottom levels of the building, her bare feet easily navigating the uneven and broken floor tiles and the rusted detritus that lay strewn all about the place. As she worked her way up, she began to get a sinking feeling that Rahuul had ignored her order not to hide at the summit of the tower. The further she went, the more certain she became.

A rickety ladder led to the uppermost level, the staircase having rotted and collapsed. She had warned Rahuul that the observatory was forbidden but as she climbed up into the vast chamber, roof pitted with holes and housing a loft of nervous pigeons, she saw him waiting for her.

He sat at the edge of the room, back to her, legs dangling over the side. One entire wall of the observatory was open to the elements. Decades previously a gigantic telescope had stood there, mounted atop its frame. Now only the rusted metal of the frame remained, the telescope itself long gone.

Adaali felt her heart skip a beat. One slip and Rahuul would plunge to his death, but he seemed heedless of the danger.

She made her way towards him, not wanting to call out and startle her brother lest he slip from the edge. A sudden gust of warm wind blew across the observatory, stirring the dust on the ground and shaking the rafters.

'I know you're there,' Rahuul said as she approached.

Adaali let out the breath she was holding.

'I thought we agreed. You were not to come up this high. It's dangerous up here.'

'You agreed,' Rahuul replied as she moved closer. 'Not me.'

'If Mother finds out we're up here she'll murder us both.'

'Then don't tell her,' Rahuul said.

Adaali was both surprised and impressed at how rebellious he was getting. He had been coddled all his life, brought up surrounded by advisors and protectors, yet he still had a fiercely independent streak that none of them had noticed. Adaali had often been accused of similar traits but she guessed her brother was just better at hiding them.

She carefully sat down beside him, letting her own legs dangle over the edge but resisting the temptation to look down. Rahuul stared out across the city, his expression

38

serious, surveying the domain that he would one day inherit.

As Adaali regarded her baby brother, she realised how fast he was growing and with it, how clever and regal he was becoming. He was certainly much cleverer than she had been at his age.

'What are you thinking about, little prince?' she asked as he watched Kantor and the deserts beyond.

The slightest of smiles rose on one side of his mouth. 'I am wondering who will help me rule when I am king,' he said.

Adaali sucked air in through her teeth. 'Oh, I would imagine Mother will find you a wife. A most suitable one, who smells of perfume and wears fine silks.'

Rahuul screwed up his nose at the thought. 'I don't like the sound of that. It will be just like having another mother – only this one will be younger.'

Adaali giggled. 'If it makes you feel better, little brother, you will always have me. I will always protect you.'

As she gazed out across the city, she knew how true that was. She was destined to always stand by his side. To never leave this place nor live her own life, no matter how alluring that might seem.

Rahuul looked across at her, the smile dropping from his lips. His eyes turned sullen and the sad look on his face almost broke Adaali's heart.

'But who will protect you?' he asked.

Adaali thought on it, and went for the easy answer. 'We will always have Mother,' she replied. 'And Musir Dragosh. He will protect both of us.'

Rahuul shook his head. 'We will not always have them.

They are old. They will both die soon while we have many years ahead of us.'

Adaali almost laughed at her little brother's wisdom, but she realised he was right. One day she would be his only protector and there would be no one left to watch over her.

'I will take care of us,' she replied, trying to convince herself as much as him. 'Do not think on such things. It will be many years before you should worry about who protects whom. For now you should worry about what Mother might do if she finds out we're up here.'

Adaali leaned back away from the ledge, rose to her feet in a single graceful movement, and held out her hand to Rahuul. He took it, and she pulled him to his feet, leading him out of the ancient observatory and down through the ruined tower.

He might have been clever beyond his years, but his hand still felt tiny in hers as they walked the ancient corridors. Adaali felt the burden of her responsibility more than ever. She could only hope that he would grow strong and powerful, in stature as well as in mind. That he would command loyal armies and lead a faithful nation. Maybe then he would not need his elder sister to watch over him. Perhaps then she would not feel so shackled to her duty.

The maidservants and groundskeepers were still hard at work as Adaali led her brother back to the palace. Their mother scurried from one great hall to the next, barking orders at anyone who would listen, and it became obvious she would have no time for her children. Adaali felt some relief when the royal maids came to take Rahuul for his evening bath and she was finally left alone.

But what to do?

She could not remember the last time she had not been given some task by either her mother or her weapon master. She had spent the morning at exercise before taking care of her brother, and heading to the training yard seemed a waste of this free time.

As she wandered the halls, passing the servants vigorously polishing the silverware for the hundredth time, she spied a familiar face. She had not known Ctenka for long, since he had been at the palace for only a few months, but she had spoken to him a number of times before. He was younger than most of the palace guard, and much less strict in his duties. Even now he was picking at something on his uniform, as though he had spilled food down himself and was now panicking in case a superior officer found him in a state of dishevelment.

'Stand to attention, Ctenka,' she said in her best impression of Musir Dragosh.

The young guardsman turned with a start, his face a picture of panic until he saw who had spoken to him.

A smile of relief crossed Ctenka's lips. 'Princess, my apologies. I appear to have something on my uniform.'

'Then it's a good job you're not on parade,' she replied.

'Indeed. I'd be in for it if I was.'

'Don't worry,' she whispered, 'I won't tell.'

Ctenka flashed her a conspiratorial wink, before glancing around to see if there was anyone else watching.

'I'm afraid I am on guard, princess,' he said. 'As much as I'd like to talk—'

'You have your duty to perform,' she interrupted. 'I understand. More than you know.'

'We all have to do what we are tasked with, princess. Even you.'

'Yes, I know. But some of us have no choice in what that task is.'

Ctenka shrugged. 'Sometimes we discover our true calling. Sometimes that calling finds us.'

'And you decided your true calling was to guard this corridor?' she asked.

'It is an honour,' he replied without hesitation. 'Given the choice I would be nowhere else.'

Adaali glanced up and down the hallway. There was nothing to guard but the tapestries and a few ornamental urns. 'I find that hard to believe.'

'And I can understand why,' Ctenka replied with a shrug. 'I know you never chose to be a princess. I know you are destined to protect the prince until his dying day. Perhaps it is easier for me. One can easily dedicate oneself to a cause when you choose it yourself. But it does not lessen the honour I feel. Nor should it lessen the honour you have been gifted. You might be your brother's keeper, but you are still a princess. I will always be a lowly servant.'

Adaali suddenly felt a little guilty for questioning Ctenka's choices, but she couldn't let him off the hook that easily.

'At least you get to leave this place, once in a while. At least you are free to go where you choose.'

'Trust me,' he said. 'You're not missing much. You are far better off here than elsewhere in the city. If I had the choice, I would rather have my lodgings in the palace.'

'I'm not sure I believe you,' she replied, a wicked plan

formulating in her mind. 'I think that is something I would like to judge for myself.'

'What?' Ctenka asked, looking a little worried.

'I know almost nothing of the city beyond these palace walls. I think you would be the perfect guide to show me something of Kantor.'

Ctenka shook his head vigorously. 'I think that would be more than my life is worth.'

'Nonsense,' she said, folding her arms in a determined manner. 'You will show me the sights, Militiaman Ctenka.'

He suddenly straightened, standing to full attention as Musir Dragosh appeared at the far end of the corridor leading three warriors of the Desert Blades. Adaali had enough time to offer Ctenka a sly wink, then scurried off before she was spotted.

She gathered a cloak from her room before waiting near the main gate for the rest of the afternoon. As night fell, groups of palace guardsmen came and went, some heading out into the city and some arriving to perform their duties for the night. Ctenka eventually walked from the palace, laughing and joking with two maids as they ambled their way across the gardens towards the gate. Adaali picked her moment, walking out from behind the cover of a neatly trimmed hedgerow and joining close behind them. No one even gave her a second glance as the four of them made their way through the gate, acknowledging the guards with a cursory farewell.

Adaali felt a sudden thrill, as though she had escaped a prison cell. She had never left the confines of the palace unattended and here she was, free as a desert bird to explore as she wanted.

Ctenka led the way through the streets, bidding goodnight to the two maids at a crossroads by kissing them both on the cheek. Adaali would have been shocked at his lack of propriety, but she knew commoners were far less beholden to formality than the courtiers she was used to.

The further they travelled through Kantor, the busier the streets got, and the grimier the buildings became. Adaali had only ever seen the tree-lined promenades and the spectacular avenues of Kantor's main thoroughfares. She had never been through so many dingy back streets, and the change in environment was unnerving.

Before panic could overcome her, Ctenka ducked into a side-street tavern. Outside a man was leaning against the wall, head down, desperately trying not to retch. A rat scurried in front of her feet, and Adaali began to think this was a bad idea. But she was here now. This was what she had wanted – a moment of freedom. If she lost her nerve now she would always be left wondering.

Gritting her teeth she walked to the door of the tavern and pushed it open. Immediately she was assaulted by the sound of raucous laughter and the stench of pipe smoke. No sooner had the door swung shut behind her than her eyes began to well from the thick mist that filled the air.

Thankfully, no one gave her a second glance as she made her way inside, looking for Ctenka amidst the throng. It was with some relief that she heard his laugh, loud and joyous, from one side of the room.

Adaali moved closer, swerving lithely between the chairs and tables, managing to avoid the boisterous patrons until she reached Ctenka. There she stood for a moment, cloak still drawn about her head, until he noticed her.

'Oh no,' Ctenka said, as the look of mirth fell from his face.

Adaali slipped into the chair beside him with a grin. He was with three other men she vaguely recognised from the palace. Each of them looked as startled and worried as Ctenka, one even rising from his seat and making for the door.

'I told you,' she said. 'You would show me the sights.'

Ctenka's mouth hung open for a moment before he spread his arms wide. 'Here are the sights, princess. Drink them in. I hope you like them?'

She took in the revelry all about her before turning back to him. 'I must admit – not so much.'

'You cannot be here,' he said leaning towards her. 'It's dangerous.'

'Life is danger,' she replied. 'I would have but one night of freedom. Is that too much to ask?'

'You're not the only one at risk,' he said. 'I could be in serious trouble for this.'

'Show some heart, Ctenka. Have you never been in trouble before?'

A grave expression fell upon the young militiaman's face. 'Yes, I've been in trouble.'

'And was it worse than this?'

He fixed her with a serious look. 'I was at Dunrun,' he replied.

Adaali did not need to know any more. She had heard tales of the siege, the sacrifice the men of the Cordral had made to hold the gates of the eastern bastion against the Iron Tusk. She

45

could barely imagine what horrors Ctenka had experienced.

'I am sorry,' she replied.

Before they could speak further, another off-duty militiaman sat with them, slamming a handful of glasses down on the table.

'Get this shit down your necks, you bunch of ugly fuuuu—'

He stopped when he saw their uninvited guest.

Adaali gazed in amusement at the militiamen gawping at her, then down at the glasses on the table filled to the brim with some pale liquor. Carefully, she reached out and took a glass, before knocking the contents back in one. The liquor burned as it went down, and Adaali fought to keep a neutral expression, despite the instinct to gag.

One of the militiamen smiled at her show of bravado, quickly followed by a second. Then one of them picked up his own glass and downed it before slamming it back on the table. The rest were quick to follow... all but Ctenka, who shook his head in dismay.

With the ice broken, Adaali's new companions began to relax, and she sat listening to them talk as the night wore on. It was a boorish and mundane discussion, but a welcome change from the usual stuffy conversation of the palace. One of them lit a pipe, and she was allowed to try it, despite Ctenka's protestations.

Music played well into the night, and Adaali found herself tapping her foot along to the rhythm. These were not the formal orchestrated songs performed in the palace, but tunes that were raw and played from the heart.

The tavern grew more raucous, but she chose to stay no matter how many times Ctenka begged her to leave. She watched as men and women argued, only to grip one another moments later in an ardent embrace, and kiss their differences away.

They laughed and loved despite the harshness of their existence, and Adaali realised she had never experienced such freedom within the confines of the palace. This was life, with all its cold reality and rare beauty, and it was doubtful she would ever get to experience it again.

Eventually she stood, feeling a little sadness that she had to leave.

'I have to go. I will tell no one of this, Ctenka. Do not worry yourself.'

'I must insist I escort you back to the palace,' he said, rising from his seat.

'No, you must stay,' she replied. 'Besides, you could never keep up with me.'

She smiled at him as he wavered on drunken legs.

'But it is my duty,' Ctenka slurred.

'Goodnight,' was her curt reply, before she left him in the corner of the tavern, and ventured out into the night.

Adaali hid in the shadows of a nearby alleyway and paused for a moment, watching the tavern entrance. When Ctenka stumbled out into the night glancing this way and that for her, she felt a flutter of admiration for him. Was he duty bound to protect her, or did he watch over her from genuine affection? Either way, she appreciated the gesture as she turned and made her way back to the confines of the palace.

4

THE sandstorm had subsided, but there were still ominous skies to the west. As they made their way back to the Shengen encampment, Josten allowed himself to relax, letting the relief wash over him, allowing the fatigue of the past few days to creep into his bones.

On the edge of a huge canyon sat the camp of the Shengens. It had seemed a foolhardy place to set up, but Laigon had explained the sense in it. They could not be ambushed from the rear – no enemy could have scaled the sheer cliffs of the canyon. And should they come under attack, the Standings would have no way to flee. It would make them fight all the harder. Laigon had seemed to relish the idea, his eyes lighting up as he explained it. All it did was make Josten realise what a circus he had become part of. He was lost in a desert full of madmen – so mad they had made him one of their leaders. Josten would have laughed at the insanity of it, had he any strength left to laugh with.

He hailed the sentries as they approached, and the legionaries greeted them like old friends. The Hierophant was bound at the hands, an old sack covering his head. Eyman had taken it upon himself to safeguard the prisoner, taking pleasure in dragging him along by a rope. It was a little sadistic, but Josten didn't see the point in discouraging him.

They led their prisoner through the camp. Few of the

Shengen troops batted an eyelid. Most were busy sharpening their weapons and cleaning armour of the dust that infested everything. The recent sandstorm would have seen the entire encampment covered in a thick yellow layer, but credit to the men of the Standings, the place was already cleared and looking pristine. Josten felt a rumble in his stomach as they passed a fire with meat spitted above it. The desert creature slowly blackening above the fire might have appeared fearsome when it was alive, but right now it looked delicious.

Dotted throughout the camp walked individuals who were clearly not Shengen. Men and women both, of all colours and creeds; slaves liberated from the numerous mines in the east of the Ramadi who had thrown their lot in with Silver and her growing army. They had made the progress of Silver's forces that much easier, taking little persuasion to rise up against the cults who had enslaved them. Many of them were native to these lands and had taught the Shengens how to forage and hunt in the barren desert. Without them, they would never have advanced through the Ramadi so quickly.

Silver led a seasoned army. After months of fighting in the desert they were yet to be defeated, even though they had faced a fanatic zeal from every cult on every battlefield. But each time the staunch discipline of the Shengen Standings had prevailed. Despite their devotion to Innellan, the armies of the cults were simply no match for Silver's forces, and each one had been defeated and forced to flee into the desert. Now her army approached Mantioch, the huge fortress city barring the way to the west. They could not progress while it still stood defiant. It would be their most difficult test, and

Silver was leaving nothing to chance.

'Take him to the prisoners' tent,' Josten said to Retuchius. 'I'll tell the emperor we're back.'

The legionary nodded, and he and the others dragged the Hierophant across the encampment.

Laigon stood at the edge of the canyon discussing manoeuvres with his centurions. They were gathered around a small table, analysing the rudimentary maps they had cobbled together. As Josten drew closer he heard them talking of the imminent assault on Mantioch. The desert city was a huge monolith, and they had no idea how many troops lurked within its walls. They could not simply bypass the place and leave untold numbers of Innellan's faithful at their rear. It had to be taken before they could carry on their crusade against the White Widow.

Laigon spotted Josten and a smile spread across his face. His centurions moved aside and the two men embraced.

'It's good to see you still alive,' said Laigon.

'I'm not gonna lie, it's getting harder to stay that way,' Josten replied.

The two had fought side by side in more battles than they could count. As Emperor of the Shengen, Laigon had his praetorians to protect him, but still he chose to fight in the vanguard of every conflict they faced, and Josten had chosen to fight right alongside him.

'Did you find what we were looking for?' Laigon asked.

'Kyon came through. The Hierophant is here, in one piece.'

'Good work. Though how much we will get out of him remains to be seen.'

'He'll talk. They all do.'

Laigon took Josten by the shoulder. 'Come. You must be thirsty after so long in the desert. Let's have a drink.'

He led Josten back to his tent as the centurions continued to discuss their plans. Josten was looking forward to a drink, he was parched, but these Shengens didn't quite know how to slake a thirst like they did back in the Suderfeld. Josten followed Laigon to the command tent and watched as the emperor made tea in a battered pot. Wine would have done the trick far better, but if tea was all there was, that's what he'd have to drink.

'How long before we attack Mantioch?' Josten asked, taking the chipped porcelain cup Laigon offered.

'Not long, I hope. Our stores are dwindling, the supply route along the Skull Road has become more difficult to traverse with these storms. If we don't launch our assault soon, morale will dwindle.'

'I find that hard to believe. These men would follow you with empty bellies into the depths of hell.'

Laigon didn't seem so convinced. 'They are only human, my friend. Even their loyalty will wane when hunger gets the best of them.'

The flap to the tent opened. Silver entered, those cold blue eyes regarding them both. She looked tired, but still resplendent in the armour forged for her by the Shengen smiths.

'I heard you were back,' she said. 'Success?'

Josten shrugged. 'Was it ever in doubt?'

'I'll take that as a yes,' she replied.

Over the past months of fighting Silver had become even more humourless, if that were possible. Though their

51

victories had been numerous their casualties were high, and Silver seemed to feel every one physically. Her own wounds, inflicted by the Iron Tusk so long ago, had been slow to heal and every battle took more of a toll on her. Josten knew she was more than human, more powerful than any of them, but no amount of attention from the apothecaries and field surgeons seemed to remedy her ills.

'I'll take you to him,' Josten said.

They made their way across camp to where a lone tent stood away from the rest. As they did, every legionary showed his fealty not only to Laigon but also to Silver, bowing before her, some even making religious signs, as though worshipping her like a saint. She ignored them all, unwilling to acknowledge the gestures.

Inside the tent the Hierophant was still bound, though the sack had been removed from his head. He sat impassively, sweat running in rivulets through the filth that caked his bald pate. Kyon, Retuchius and Eyman stood around him, waiting patiently.

'He won't speak,' said Kyon as they entered. 'Won't even take a drink of water.'

Josten looked at the priest who stared back defiantly. His skin was tanned but for the pale band across his brow where he had worn an iron circlet. That was now lost to the desert after his struggle with Eyman.

'Not talking?' Josten said, crouching beside the prisoner. 'You can save yourself a lot of pain if you just tell us what we want to know. How many defenders do you have in Mantioch? Are reinforcements on the way? Give us something and we can get you fed and watered.'

The Hierophant stared back at him. Josten got the impression the man would have spat in his face if he'd had any spit left.

'Looks like we'll have to do this the hard way,' said Retuchius. He seemed to be looking forward to a bit of torture. 'This fanatic will be a tough nut to crack.'

Josten looked to Silver. 'Maybe you should talk to him?'

Josten knew she would rather have done this her way than see a man, even one of the enemy, brutalised for information.

As she took a step forward, the Hierophant seemed suddenly fearful. He shook his head, still not willing to speak, but it was clear just the sight of Silver made him terrified.

'You know who I am?' she asked.

The Hierophant nodded. 'I know who you are,' he said, voice croaky and dry.

'You are afraid?' she said.

'I am more afraid of Her,' the Hierophant replied.

'But Innellan is not here. There is just us.'

'She will come. She will kill all of you. There is nothing—'

Silver reached out a hand, placing the tips of her fingers against the side of the Hierophant's head.

'The Stone,' he screamed suddenly. 'We are moving the Stone. The Set of Katamaru hid it from the Widow, but she knows. She covets it. If you take it first it will grant you great power.'

Silver took a step back. 'The Stone of Katamaru?'

The Hierophant nodded feverishly. 'It will be transported from Mantioch to Kragenskûl when the storms have abated.

One day, maybe two. If you are swift you could take it for yourself. It will grant you great power, no?'

Silver didn't answer. She stood, considering the Hierophant's words before turning and leaving the tent. Josten and Laigon followed.

'Didn't take long for him to start singing,' Josten said. 'Just how important is this stone?'

'It is a powerful artefact,' Silver replied, brow furrowed in thought. 'It is a beacon between worlds.'

'So what's it for?' Josten asked, in no mood for her riddles.

She shook her head. 'That is not important. All that matters is that it does not fall into Innellan's hands.'

'Then I will take one of the Standings,' Laigon said. 'We will claim this artefact and bring it to you.'

Silver shook her head. 'No. The warriors of Mantioch will spot your men from miles away. This must be done with stealth.'

She paused, still deep in thought. Josten could see where this was going. 'All right. I'll do it,' he said.

'I am grateful,' said Silver.

She didn't sound it. To Josten it sounded as though she had fully expected him to do it out of duty. When she turned without another word and walked away, he knew her gratitude was only offered begrudgingly. He had followed her in this crusade north because he believed in her, but even his loyalty was starting to be tested.

'She is exhausted,' Laigon said, as though reading his thoughts.

'I know. We all are.'

'No one is forcing you to do this,' Laigon said. 'I have other men, just as capable.'

Josten raised an eyebrow. 'Just as capable?'

Laigon offered a rare smile. 'They would not perform the task with your natural charm and grace, but they would see it done.'

Josten laughed. 'No. I can handle it. I'm just keen for all this to be over.'

'Once Mantioch has fallen, the way to Kragenskûl will be open. Then we can face Innellan.'

'That'll do us no good if Silver's dead on her feet.'

'I will see to it that she rests. Don't worry. Just make sure you are safe, my friend. This could be a dangerous mission.'

Josten clapped Laigon on the shoulder. 'I've got the easy job. Robbing some travellers on the road? How hard can that be?'

'Somehow I feel it will not be so simple.'

'I used to be a pirate,' Josten said with a wink. 'I robbed people for a living.'

'Just come back alive,' said Laigon, grasping his forearm in the warrior's way. 'We need you. May the trickster god protect you.'

Josten appreciated the sentiment. But no amount of well-wishing and relying on gods was going to get the job done. After they had embraced once more he left Laigon to the business of besieging Mantioch.

Later, as night drew in, he sat by a fire with his men. They'd eaten well and rested after days in the desert. It never ceased to amaze Josten how they managed to stay so resilient, even out here in the wilds of the Ramadi, surrounded by thousands of fanatics whose only wish was to slaughter them all.

'This could be a tough one,' he told them as the fire crackled away. 'If anyone wants to stay behind I won't think any less of you.'

'They're all tough,' said Kyon. 'Tough or easy doesn't matter as long as you don't get killed.'

'Then you're in?'

Kyon nodded.

'I'm in too,' said Retuchius.

The other men around the fire all gave their assent. The legionaries of the Fourth Standing were a brave bunch and Josten had known deep down none of them would say no.

'And you won't be going without me.'

The last one was Eyman. Despite his words, Josten could hear the trepidation in his voice. Part of him thought he should have let the young militiaman sit this one out, but the lad was as brave as the rest, perhaps braver. Josten would never have embarrassed him by making him stay.

Their loyalty hit him hard. He'd led men before, but most of the time they'd fought for the money. This bunch did it for loyalty. Not that loyalty would keep them safe. If they ended up dead that loyalty would have all been for shit.

Josten would just have to make sure they lived. Keeping himself alive would only be a bonus.

5

ANOTHER night plagued by nightmares, only to wake and have Dragosh push her harder than ever on the training yard. He seemed to take great relish in demonstrating her weaknesses. Despite the hardship, Adaali had done her best, quelling her frustrations and fighting until she was exhausted. When it was over, Dragosh had dismissed her without comment, and she had no idea whether he had been pleased with her tenacity or merely disappointed at her lack of progress.

Now she was in her room, resisting the desire to rest. Dragosh had made it clear she was weak, her scrawny frame far from what was needed if she was to carry the mantle of her brother's protector. He had taught her many ways to improve, how to build her muscles using her own meagre bodyweight. A hundred push-ups to strengthen chest and arms, two hundred squats until her legs ached, three hundred sit-ups so her stomach was like iron. Then the exercises to keep herself supple, stretching until it felt like every muscle and tendon might snap.

As Adaali stood, heels planted firmly, bending at the waist until she could lay her palms flat on the floor, she heard a commotion from the courtyard below her room. She moved to the window, shielding her eyes from the sun as she looked down. Through the palace gates rode a procession of warriors and Adaali felt her heart flutter with excitement. Their steeds were huge beasts, larger than any horse Adaali had ever seen. Atop each one sat a southern soldier, a knight of the Suderfeld, encased in plates of steel armour. Across their chests were tabards of bright crimson, each one emblazoned with a rearing lion of gold.

This was the foreign delegation they had been expecting. In all her wildest dreams Adaali had not expected them to make such an impressive and fearsome sight. They must have been baking inside their armour, but not one of them showed any sign of fatigue as they trotted into the courtyard carrying their banners.

Her door suddenly burst open. Rahuul raced up beside her, almost toppling through the window in his eagerness to view the newcomers.

'Have you seen them? Look at them down there. Are they giants?' He jumped from one foot to the other in his excitement.

'No, they are not giants,' Adaali replied. 'They are just men. Knights, they call them. Warriors just like ours.'

But Adaali knew these were knights cut from a different cloth to the Kantor militia. The martial reputation of the Suderfeld was one to be respected. It was a land that had been stricken by war for decades. She knew every one of these visitors was a veteran who had survived a dozen battles. These were men to be feared, not that she would have told Rahuul as much.

'Can we go down and see? I want to meet these knights.'

Adaali laid a hand on his shoulder in the vain hope it would stop him hopping about. 'All in good time,' she said.

They watched as one of the riders dismounted. He was different to the rest, wearing opulent yellow silks instead of armour. His hair was the colour of straw and he might have been handsome but for the jewelled patch he wore over one eye. Behind him was another southerner who was also without armour, but this one looked fearsome. His body was heavily muscled, more so than even Musir Dragosh, and his face was covered in a fiery red beard. Where his arms weren't covered by thick iron bands they were adorned with swirling tattoos and he held on tight to the broadsword at his side as he climbed down from his horse.

No sooner had the men taken in the sight of the courtyard than they were greeted by the rake-thin figure of Egil Sun. Adaali watched as he greeted the men like old friends, the one with the eye patch smiling widely as he took Egil's claw-like hand in his own.

'Why have they come?' Rahuul asked her.

Adaali shook her head. 'I don't know for certain. But I think Egil would like there to be an alliance between the Suderfeld kingdoms and Kantor.'

'What does Mother say?'

It was good that he realised who was really in charge. From the way Egil acted it was he who was regent of Kantor and not Queen Suraan. Adaali was thankful her brother had not fallen under the vizier's spell.

'She is not so sure.'

'When will I get to meet them? I should meet them, shouldn't I?'

She looked down at her little brother. So young and yet so much weight on those narrow shoulders. Adaali had never wanted to protect him from the world as much as she did now.

'You will,' she replied. 'Later. For now, see to your breakfast. A king cannot meet his guests on an empty stomach.'

At the mention of breakfast, Rahuul rushed off towards the dining room. Adaali turned back to the courtyard, seeing Egil standing close to the hulking warrior. They spoke in hushed tones as the man with the eye patch gazed around the courtyard once more. As he looked up he caught Adaali's eye. She looked back at him, and when he raised his hand and smiled at her, she waved back, before catching herself and taking a step away from the window. It would not do to be so informal with a guest of the palace, but there was something disarming in that smile.

She put the visitors to the back of her mind, and returned to her exercises.

Later she had dressed in her plain tunic once again, ready to continue her training, but Dragosh was not awaiting her in the yard. It did not take Adaali long to find him, following the sound of his voice as it echoed through the palace corridors. He was instructing his men of the Desert Blades as she approached, making it clear that they were to be more vigilant than ever as they patrolled the palace grounds. As he dismissed them he saw her approach.

'There will be no more training today,' he told her, before she could even speak.

'But I am ready,' she said, unable to hide her disappointment. She was keen to redeem herself for her earlier failures.

'With so many strangers in the palace I am needed elsewhere,' he replied. 'We will continue later. There is much I have to do.'

Adaali should have done as she was told, but curiosity got the better of her. 'I would like to meet these foreigners,' she said. 'They seem a curious bunch. I'm sure we can learn much from them. Rahuul would also like to—'

Dragosh shook his head. 'No. Stay away from them. We know little enough about them as it is. Your job is to protect the prince. Keeping your brother safe should be your only concern. Make sure Rahuul stays in his room – he is not to mix with these people unaccompanied.' He seemed adamant, and Adaali was not about to argue with her weapons tutor.

With a final nod, Dragosh left her to see to his duties. She watched him go, thinking on his words, but she could not get the image of that one-eyed southerner from her mind.

Nevertheless, Adaali obeyed, making her way back through the palace, taking the opportunity to slip by the scurrying servants and vigilant guards unseen. Dragosh had taught her how to use the shadows and the environment to conceal her passing and she had taken to it better than any of his weapons training. When she reached the royal chambers though, there was no hiding from what awaited.

'Adaali,' her mother called as she reached the top of the stairs. 'Come, there is much to do.'

She saw her mother standing in the vestibule, surrounded

by handmaids she recognised and a couple of men she didn't.

'What is it, Mother?' she asked as she entered, a feeling of dread slowly creeping up inside her.

'There is a feast to attend to,' her mother said. 'We must all look our best. We must show the people of the Suderfeld what they are dealing with.'

'Dealing with?'

Queen Suraan shook her head. 'Never mind. Just go with the maids and have your bath.'

Adaali lifted her tunic and sniffed. The smell wasn't that bad. 'But I don't need—'

'Just go.' Her mother's tone brooked no argument.

Adaali went with the handmaids and let them strip her tunic. A bath had already been prepared with rose petals and oils and Adaali reluctantly climbed in. At first it was a relaxing experience until the handmaids took to scrubbing every inch of her. By the end it felt as though they had scraped her skin raw, and she was pulled from the bath and dried off with soft towels. All this went against Dragosh's lessons. He had taught her to endure hardship, to hone her body into iron, and here she was being primped and powdered like some prize animal.

When they led her out into a dressing room her mother and brother were already there. Rahuul was taking great delight in trying on an array of magisterial robes in red and blue silk, shot through with gems of green and yellow, but when it came to her turn Adaali struggled to muster the same enthusiasm. Eventually she was dressed in a bright blue gown, the sleeves so long they covered her hands. Her head was covered with a scarf that draped in front of her eyes and she was forced to wear velvet sandals that pinched her toes. It was beautiful, and she hated every inch of it.

Adaali was a warrior. It had been made clear to her for as long as she could remember that she was no princess, but here she was dressed up like one of those snivelling courtiers her mother so often complained about. How was she to protect her brother when she couldn't see, walk or hold a weapon properly due to this ridiculous dress? Nevertheless, she had her duty to perform, and if this was her mother's wish then she would have to obey.

When finally Adaali and her brother were ready, their mother came to lead them to the feast. She was dressed in her finery, head covered in a silken veil, the crown of Kantor on her head. Adaali had never seen her look so beautiful.

The queen led them down to the dining hall. Dragosh was waiting for them, and he opened the doors. Adaali could hear the sound of conversation hush from within as Dragosh led the procession. All eyes were on Suraan as she walked to the head of the huge feasting table and Adaali could see that there were dozens assembled. Aldermen from the outlying regions sat in their respective places. The two Suderfeld envoys were positioned side-by-side, one hulking and bearded, the other all charm and smiles. Egil Sun had taken the seat opposite them, leering like a vulture about to feast.

Suraan took her place at the head of the table and Adaali sat on her left-hand side, Rahuul on her right. Even with Dragosh standing vigilantly behind them, Adaali still felt exposed. All eyes were on the royal trio and she had never felt so conspicuous.

No sooner had Queen Suraan seated herself than Egil Sun was on his feet.

'Your Royal Majesty, may I present our esteemed guests from the Suderfeld.' The two southerners rose, the bearded brute some inches taller than his blonde counterpart. 'This is Duke Bertrand of Canbria, envoy of Stellan, King Regnant of the Suderfeld.' The man with the eye patch bowed in respect. 'And this is Manssun Rike, champion to King Banedon of Arethusa.' The bearded warrior gave an almost imperceptible nod, stark in its contrast.

'Our pleasure, Your Majesty,' said Duke Bertrand. 'And may we take the opportunity to thank you for such generous hospitality.'

The queen acknowledged him with a nod as Egil continued. 'They are here on behalf of the King Regnant who wishes—'

Queen Suraan raised a hand for Egil to be silent and he duly obeyed.

'I am willing to listen to any entreaties,' she said. 'But these envoys should know that Kantor has remained a neutral power for many decades. We are not willing to become embroiled in a treaty that will see us at war.'

Egil glanced towards the duke, who smiled wider, inclining his head at Suraan.

'A wise policy, Your Majesty,' said Bertrand. 'But it is not the treaty that will see you at war. The Ramadi invasion of your lands is inevitable. The White Widow is a threat to both our realms and the only way to defeat her is for our nations to unite. King Stellan suggests an alliance of marriage. A union of hearts and minds.'

'And armies?' Suraan asked.

'Why of course. The military might of all the Suderfeld would be at your disposal.'

The queen seemed unmoved by the prospect. 'And who would my son be marrying? King Stellan has no daughters.'

'But King Banedon of Arethusa does,' said Manssun Rike in his gruff voice. It cut through the air of the dining hall like an axe.

The queen regarded him coolly. 'So you would have us marry the heir of Kantor to a minor noble?'

'The son of King Banedon is no—'

Manssun Rike stopped when Bertrand laid a hand on his meaty arm. 'This will still be a powerful alliance, Your Majesty.'

'The answer is no,' Suraan said.

Egil Sun rose to his feet. 'Majesty, you must consider—'

'I must consider nothing,' she said. 'Now, let us feast.'

Before anyone else could speak the doors to the dining hall opened and the first of many courses was brought in. There was no more talk of marriages or alliances as the gathering ate. Adaali picked at her food as she watched the envoys talk to one another. Duke Bertrand seemed to be going to great lengths to keep his burly companion calm. When they had finished, Queen Suraan stood.

'It is time for me to retire,' she said. 'I hope you have enjoyed our hospitality.'

'Indeed,' said Duke Bertrand rising to his feet. 'And I hope you will later allow me some time to discuss matters further?'

The queen considered his words for a moment. 'Perhaps,' she replied.

Dragosh led the way for the royal procession and Adaali stood, ushering Rahuul after them as he took one last bit of a sweet cake. They left the dining hall behind and returned to the royal chambers. Adaali watched with concern as handmaids helped her mother to her bedchamber. It seemed the public engagement had taken a toll, but there was little Adaali could do about it. Once she had kissed her brother goodnight, she returned to her own chamber and wasted no time in stripping off the bothersome gown.

She should have gone to bed, but then she remembered how Dragosh had been so preoccupied with palace security. With so many strangers he would surely be too busy to train her in the morning. Now would be a better time than ever to take advantage of that.

After changing into her plain tunic she slipped from her room and padded down the corridor from her chambers. The palace was still well lit, but she managed to pass unseen as she slipped out into the dark of night.

It was silent in the training yard but for the sound of distant crickets. Adaali regarded the weapon rack, knowing it was pointless even pretending to choose. Before she could reach out for a spear she started at a voice behind her.

'Good evening.'

Adaali span, feeling her heart pounding as she saw a stranger in the shadows.

'My apologies, I didn't mean to startle you,' said Duke

66

Bertrand as he walked out into the moonlight.

'You did not startle me,' she lied.

He smiled knowingly. 'Of course not. A little late to be training, isn't it? And in such darkness?'

'Musir Dragosh says a warrior should not rely on her senses or her environment. A warrior should be prepared to face her enemy at any time, day or night.'

'Musir Dragosh is very wise. But I am no enemy.'

She looked him up and down. In his fine clothes and with no weapon he was far from threatening. 'No, I suppose you're not.'

He seemed friendly enough and wore an easy smile, but she could sense a sadness to him. His brows were furrowed and there was a melancholy present in his one blue eye.

'Do you often practise so late?' he asked.

'Not often. Only when I am told.'

He nodded his understanding. 'I hear that. I too have to do what I'm told.'

'But you are a duke. Surely you can do as you please.'

Bertrand laughed at her answer. 'If only that were true, my princess. Above me there are kings. Above them is the King Regnant. Above him...' He trailed off, as though he was reluctant to speak further. Adaali couldn't imagine who could possibly be above the King Regnant.

'So even you must do your duty,' she said. 'I have my duty too.' She looked back at the training rack, at the weapons laid out there, thinking on the hours of pain she had endured.

'I'm sure. It can be a burden.'

She looked back at him, thinking about the miles he

had travelled to broker his alliance only to receive Queen Suraan's rebuttal.

'Will your king be angry you have failed?' she asked.

Bertrand shrugged. 'I have not failed yet,' he said.

'But you may well have to give him sad news.'

He fixed her with another mournful look. 'It is not the news that will be the sad part.'

Before she could answer, she heard a palace servant talking nearby and realised it would not do for her to be caught alone with one of the palace guests.

'I must go,' she said. 'Good luck to you, Duke Bertrand of the south.'

'And to you,' he replied.

With that she left him in the training yard and made her way back inside. When she finally reached her chamber it was empty. As she ducked under her covers she thought on the duke and how sad he had been. She almost felt sorry for him, but sorrow did no one any good. Everyone had their burdens, and no one else could carry them.

6

EYMAN looked nervous as they rode their horses west. Josten knew he should never have let the young lad come, but he'd been too keen to be refused the chance. Now he looked about ready to shit his saddle.

Why did this always happen? Why did he always find himself watching over the weak link in the group? Nobody had ever watched over Josten Cade when he'd been young and green and as much use as tits on a bull. He'd had to learn quick what it meant to be a soldier. He'd been flung in the sea and forced to swim or drown. Eyman would just have to learn the hard way like everyone else.

'You'll be all right,' he said reassuringly.

So much for the hard way.

Eyman grinned. 'I know. What's the worst that could happen? Right?'

'Capture and torture,' Kyon said from behind them.

'It won't come to that,' replied Josten.

Eyman didn't say anything else. It was obvious he was considering the notion. Josten just hoped the prospect of death or torture would make him more careful, fight that bit harder. He hoped it wouldn't fester and turn to fear – that would make the lad less than useless.

Putting it from his mind, Josten squinted northeastwards. He could just make out the spires of Mantioch in the distance. They had given the place as wide a berth as they could, keeping a wary eye out for scouting bands of cultists, but so far had been lucky enough to avoid any roaming patrols.

'How much further?' Retuchius asked. 'We've been riding for a night and a day.'

'Another few leagues and we should pick up the road west to Kragenskûl,' Kyon answered.

Retuchius remained silent. Despite all they'd been through he still hated Kyon. As long as it didn't stop them doing their jobs, Josten wasn't about to get involved.

Kyon's words were proven true no more than an hour later when their horses came to a road, if Josten would have called it that. It was more a dusty trail where the endless desert flattened out, east to west.

'No place for an ambush,' said Retuchius.

Josten nodded in agreement. 'We'll keep moving west, hopefully the road will cut through another forgotten town or temple. With any luck we'll be ahead of whoever's transporting this stone.'

'Did we ever find out what it's for?' Eyman asked as they took the road west at a trot.

'No idea,' Josten replied. 'All I know is Silver wants it kept out of Innellan's hands. That's good enough for me.'

'So it could be useless?'

'Useless to us, maybe. But if Innellan's demanded it be taken from Mantioch to Kragenskûl she must want it for something.

Anything we can do to disrupt that gives us an advantage.'

'So it's some magic bauble?' Eyman said.

Magic. Josten still hadn't got used to that word, despite all he'd seen. 'It could be a lump of useless rock, for all I know. But we have our orders and we're going to see them through.'

They continued along the road as it swept up the side of a steep bank. At the top Josten reined in his mount. Looking down on what lay beyond, he allowed himself a smile.

In a shallow valley sat the remains of an abandoned mine. Several tunnel entrances were held up by ageing timbers and tracks for mining carts could still be seen snaking along the ground. Here and there stood abandoned huts. The road ran straight through the middle of it.

'This is the spot,' Josten said as his men reached the brow of the hill.

'Perfect,' said Kyon as he looked down onto the broken valley. 'We can block the exit on the other side of the quarry, pen them in.'

'How long do you think we have?' asked Retuchius.

'Not long,' Josten replied. 'The Hierophant said they'd be moving the stone as soon as the storm stopped. That was yesterday.'

'Then we'd best get a move on,' Kyon said, urging his horse down into the quarry.

Josten ordered Eyman to stay up on the ridge and keep watch over the road back to Mantioch. The rest of them entered the quarry and made cover on either side which they could hide behind. Retuchius took the horses ahead, tethering them out of sight. Then they waited.

Concealing himself within the entrance to a collapsed mine, Josten took his position. Most of his time these days was endless hours of boredom split up by moments of extreme violence and terror. But he'd known what he was letting himself in for when he followed Silver north to the Ramadi. He was a fighting man, always had been. This was his life. Granted, he'd always been paid a decent wedge of coin for his trouble, and now he was offering his services for free, but nothing much else had changed. At least now he had a cause. Now it felt like what he was doing mattered. Best not to dwell on that too much lest he persuade himself he'd made the wrong decision. As Eyman galloped down into the quarry, Josten didn't have to think on it any longer.

'They're coming,' Eyman said. 'Less than a league back.'

'How many?' Josten asked.

'Half a dozen riders. One wagon.'

'All right. Tether your horse with the rest and get yourself behind the barricade.'

Eyman nodded, urging his horse on down the road.

Josten drew his sword, pressing himself up against the wall of the tunnel entrance. Time seemed to stretch. It always did before the fight, before the killing. Less than a league shouldn't have taken that long, but it was an eternity when you were about to risk your life. When you were about to run charging at someone with a sword, hellbent on killing them and they hellbent on surviving. He should have been used to it by now, but Josten reckoned no one could ever get used to a thing like that. Not unless they were mad.

He glanced out across the quarry, seeing the Shengen

hiding, waiting. At least he wasn't alone. These easterners were forged in iron – strong, tough, loyal. A thousand like these and Josten could have ended the War of Three Crowns years ago.

At the sound of hooves tamping against the hard ground, the time for daydreaming was over. Josten squeezed himself tighter against the side of the mine entrance as he peeked down the road. Eyman had been right – half a dozen riders, three in front and three behind a wagon. It trundled down into the quarry, wheels kicking up dust as it drew closer.

Across the quarry the wagon drew level with him. Retuchius crouched behind an upturned cart, his men were further down the road, hiding behind the rocks and ridges, and inside the carcasses of derelict huts. As Retuchius nodded his way, waiting for the signal to attack, there was movement behind him. The ground rose up, as though the side of the valley was coming to life. Josten could only watch in horror as he realised it was all too human – a man hidden beneath his cloak, half buried in the dirt.

They were already lying in wait.

Josten was about to sprint from the mine entrance, about to shout that this was a trap, when something came at him from deeper in the tunnel. He just had time to raise his blade as the shadows came alive; a hulking figure lurching forward from the dark.

'Ambush!' Josten cried, but the shout was lost beneath the ring of metal as he parried a sword thrust.

His attacker was a brute, flesh covered in charcoal, naked but for a kilt around his waist. The giant's hair was

73

greased back, eyes two white pools of hate, and he charged at Josten with all the fury he'd come to expect from these mad cultist bastards.

There was no room to swing his sword in the tunnel, and Josten staggered back, just managing to parry another thrust as he stepped out into the open. From the corner of his eye he barely had chance to register the mad battle going on across the hill as Retuchius and the rest of the Shengens were forced into a desperate fight for their lives.

The warrior came at him again, swinging that curved blade with precision. Josten parried as he backed away, stumbling all the while, desperate to keep his footing.

Below him the doors to the wagon burst open, more cultists teeming out, taking the fight to the Shengens.

The cultist swung again, thick arms wielding that blade like it weighed nothing. Josten ducked, countering with a thrust of his own sword. He struck the cultist in the guts, blade driving in halfway to the hilt. It was a thrust that would have felled any normal man, but these cultists were far from normal. They were slaves to the White Widow, in thrall to a god, and they would strive to do her bidding even if every limb was severed.

Ignoring his grievous wound, the cultist raised his blade once more. Josten could only stare up at it, his own weapon lodged in the enemy. Before that blow could land, another sword hacked into the side of the cultist's head. Blood spattered Josten's face as the cultist was felled like a tree. Eyman stood there victorious, a look of grim determination about his young features.

Josten planted a foot on the dead man's body and wrenched his weapon free. A glance around at the battlefield and he knew they'd already lost. On the opposite hill Retuchius lay face down, blood pooling in the sand around his head. The other Shengens were fighting valiantly but with the reinforcements who'd burst from the wagon and a dozen more springing from beneath the dirt of the quarry they were sorely outnumbered.

'Get to the horses,' Josten shouted. Eyman just stared back at him in shock. Josten grabbed hold of his collar. 'Fucking run!' he bellowed.

That was enough to light a fire in the young militiaman, and he turned, racing west along the road to their hastily erected barricade.

As battle raged around them, Josten could see more men fighting up ahead. The cultists seemed to be appearing from nowhere, their camouflage hiding them beneath the ground until the moment was right to attack. Kyon swung his weapon expertly, cutting down two cultists, but more were streaming from the hills on either side. As Josten raced towards the battle he knew this was all his fault. How had he missed the sign of the ambushers? How had this turned into such a fuck-up?

There'd be time to chastise himself later, if he managed to get out of there alive.

Josten charged into the enemy, smashing the back of a skull open. He swung again, taking another in the shoulder. Kyon moved to position himself by Josten's side as Eyman stumbled to a halt, unsure of what to do.

'Keep running,' Josten barked, as he and Kyon retreated from their attackers, the barricade at their backs.

They were surrounded. More cultists were advancing from down the road, a good half dozen. An arrow streaked past Josten's head, embedding itself in the wooden barrier behind him. Archers were all they needed.

Kyon picked up a fallen shield and Josten joined him behind it. More arrows struck the steel. There was a shrill yell beside him as a kilt-wearing fanatic charged. Josten swung, taking down the attacker with a solid blow.

'Get out of here,' he shouted at Kyon.

The Shengen turned to make a run for it, just as an arrow hit him in the shoulder. He dropped his shield, stumbling in the dirt as two more arrows struck him in the chest.

Josten glanced back over the barricade in time to see Eyman on top of a horse, kicking it for all he was worth, leaving the quarry behind. Good for him.

Turning back to the cultists, Josten gritted his teeth. Time to hate. Time to fight. Time to die.

They were surrounding him now. Maybe a dozen. None of them seemed too keen on attacking though. They still had that zeal in their eyes but something was stopping them from ending this. More warriors came from the quarry and over the ridge down into the mine complex. There must have been more than a score hidden all about the mineworkings. Josten realised he and his dozen men had never stood a chance.

A huge warrior pushed his way to the fore, curved sword in hand. Blood spattered his charcoal-covered face and dripped from that blade.

'Drop it,' he said, motioning to Josten's sword with his own.

'Do I look fucking stupid?' Josten replied. 'I'll go down fighting, if it's all the same to you.'

There was a sharp hiss before Josten felt a burning hot pain stab through his thigh. He yelped, losing his balance as he grasped the arrow someone had just fired into his leg.

'I warned you,' said the big cultist.

That was fair enough, but Josten would be damned if he'd let these bastards take him alive. He tried to push himself back up, but the pain shooting through his leg wouldn't let him. Instead he had to kneel, brandishing his sword as best he could, ready to take the first one of them that approached in the groin.

The big one came forward, swung his blade and knocked the sword right out of Josten's hand. So much for going down fighting.

'What do we do with him now?' said one of the cultists. 'Back to Mantioch?'

The big one shook his head. 'No. We have our orders. Get him in the wagon.'

Josten tried to fight them off as they rushed him, but there were too many. He didn't even get a decent shot at one of them before his hands were tied behind his back and he was bundled towards the waiting wagon.

He grunted and snarled as they threw him inside, but he knew it was pointless. No amount of defiance was going to save him now.

7

THE world was roiling in a storm of red and death. Teeth gnashing, flesh tearing, bones cracking in a never-ending nightmare from which she could not wake. She was trapped in this hellish vision, a foetus wrapped in the belly of some unseen horror.

Above it all, voices whispered malevolent words, hate-filled curses just beyond her understanding, a thousand screeching mouths assailing her all at once. And yet, behind it all, one voice was with her, whispering words of hope, a beacon in this fog of terror. She tried to reach out to that voice, to grasp it and hope it could pull her free like a fish from the sea, but it was too distant, too weak. It could not overcome the wave after wave of bile.

She would have screamed but she had no voice, would have run but she had no legs, would have fought but she had no arms. If only she could open her eyes...

Adaali woke panting in the cool night air. Once again the linen sheet clung to her legs, holding her fast. She unpeeled it from her cold wet flesh and cast it aside, rolling from the bed and crouching down, the voices fading. At the back of her mind she could still hear the distant clashing of weapons. Those voices raised in anger.

The moon shone bright through her open window,

bathing the room in silver light. She glared at it, taking some relief from its welcome glow. It was as though the shining beacon were bringing her back to reality. She suddenly felt foolish, scared by a dream. That was for children, not for a warrior.

But as she crouched she realised a shade of her nightmare was still with her, echoing in the distance. The ringing of steel. A man shouting in anger.

This was no dream. Something wasn't right.

The door burst open, casting her room in bright lantern light. Adaali shielded her eyes against it as she adopted a defensive stance, all she could see was a dark silhouette framed in the doorway.

'We have to go,' said her mother. 'Put something on. Quickly.'

Adaali barely had the chance to register her relief. She didn't question her mother's orders – with the door now open the noise of combat was louder. She could hear the distant sound of fighting as she hastily grabbed her tunic and pulled it over her head.

'What's going on?' she asked, noticing Rahuul clinging to his mother's skirts.

'We are under attack,' Şuraan replied, leading them from her room. 'The palace is not safe.'

Out in the light of the corridor Adaali saw that her mother held a knife close to her side. The guards who would normally have stood vigilantly in this wing of the palace were nowhere to be seen.

'The southerners?' Adaali said, visions of marauding

knights flashing through her mind's eye.

'Not just them,' her mother replied as she took Rahuul's hand and led him down the stairwell. 'We have been betrayed. We can trust no one.'

Adaali tried to process that thought. They could trust no one? But how could this be? The Desert Blades were loyal, the militia of Kantor had protected the royal family for generations.

'Where is Musir Dragosh?' she asked.

The queen shook her head. 'I don't know.'

The sound of combat grew louder as they made their way down into the lower levels of the palace. As they turned a corner, Adaali glanced back down the corridor and in the wan light she caught sight of someone lying on the ground. She didn't recognise who it was but it was clear they were quite dead. The sudden gravity of their situation began to dawn on her. All thoughts of bad dreams were gone – now the nightmare was all too real.

When they made their way down another flight the sound of fighting grew louder. Queen Suraan stopped, pulling Rahuul closer to her side. Her little brother looked bewildered, though to his credit he showed no fear. The queen turned, placing the lantern down on the ground.

'Stay close to me, both of you. We will carry on from here without a light to guide us. Stay close, do you understand?'

Rahuul and Adaali both nodded and the queen grasped her son's arm, pulling him after. A woman screamed somewhere in the distance. More men shouted. They made their way down another stairwell and found yet more bodies.

In the scant light of the lower levels two men fought. They grunted and groaned, rolling on the tiled floor, but the queen did not wait to see who might win. She pulled her children on, out into the gardens and towards Adaali's training yard.

Fires burned in their braziers and with the moonlight, Adaali could see the fighting clearly. The Suderfeld knights were gathered in force and opposing them were the Desert Blades. The warriors of the Cordral fought valiantly, their curved swords flashing in the moonlight. Despite their skill, there was little their weapons could do against the stout shields and armour of the southern knights.

Around the perimeter of the training yard was a path to the front gate but it was blocked by the melee. Queen Suraan paused in the shadows for a few short moments with her children as she decided what to do. Adaali was mesmerised by the fighting. She could not see Dragosh, but recognised some of his warriors. Someone screamed and she saw one of the Desert Blades fall, clutching a wound in his side. His assailant raised a straight-edged sword and brought it down on the warrior's head, crushing his skull.

Before Adaali could witness any more violence, her mother dragged her back inside the palace. They moved through an arch into an anteroom and Adaali could tell her mother was leading them down to the kitchens. If they could reach them it would be their only chance of escape.

They entered the dining room through a side door, but before they had moved five paces, the queen stopped. In the dim light Adaali could see someone sitting at the head of the table. Other figures lingered in the shadows.

81

There was a sudden flare of light as a taper ignited, and Adaali recognised the corpse-thin face of Egil Sun.

'I've been waiting all evening,' said the vizier, lighting the candles on the table before him. 'So glad you could finally join me.'

Suraan pulled Rahuul closer. Adaali could see her grip tightening on the knife at her side.

'This is treason, Egil,' she replied. 'You cannot hope to get away with this.'

Egil spread his bony fingers. 'But I already have.'

'The Desert Blades will hunt you to the ends of the earth. The people of Kantor will never accept you as their ruler.'

As she spoke, Egil rose to his feet, moving from the other side of the table. Adaali wanted to scream, to rush forward and claw out the old bastard's eyes, but she dared not move.

'I don't expect them to. I am no king. Merely the kingmaker.'

Suraan pulled Rahuul behind her. 'You will leave my son—'

'Please. I intend nothing so wicked as murdering a child. I will treat him as my own... once you are gone.'

Suraan screamed, raising the knife and throwing herself at Egil like a wild beast. Before she could reach him, one of the vizier's bonecasters rushed from the dark. Adaali saw a glint of steel in his hand and her mother's scream was cut short as he plunged it into Suraan's ribcage.

Adaali felt the world end. Something broke in her chest as she watched the queen's body go limp, the knife dropping from her grip to clatter on the stone floor. Gently, the bonecaster laid the queen down. All this Egil Sun witnessed without emotion, before looking up at Rahuul.

'Come, my prince,' he said, reaching out a hand. 'Let us get you to safety.'

Rahuul took a step away from the vizier as Adaali laid a protective hand on her brother's shoulder. Though he had seen his mother murdered he did not weep, but raised his chin in defiance. She could feel him trembling at her touch, holding back his grief and anger. Adaali had never been so proud of her brother's nobility in the face of such horror. But she had never been taught the same restraint.

She rolled across the floor, grasping her mother's knife as she rose, and in one swift motion opened the bonecaster's throat. She turned to face Egil, but he staggered back from her attack before she could make it, knocking into the table and sending the candles toppling. The room was suddenly bathed in darkness.

Adaali could hear the bonecasters moving as one, desperate to defend their master and slaughter Adaali where she stood. She leapt back, picking up her brother, relieved he had not moved a muscle.

'Careful,' Egil hissed through the dark. 'Do not harm the prince.'

They began searching the dining hall for her, but Adaali had trained long and hard not to be heard, to leave no sign of her passing. Rahuul was silent as she carried him through the black, clinging to the edge of the room as she made her way to a door at the far end of the chamber.

With a swift motion she wrenched it open, allowing

83

light to flood in. As the door closed behind her she let her brother go and grasped a six-foot brazier, wedging the door shut with it. Egil's bonecasters smashed themselves against the door, but she had already grabbed Rahuul's hand and was rushing away down the passage.

Adaali's heart was pounding, and she felt a lump growing in her throat. She had just witnessed her mother's murder, but she had to put that to the back of her mind. It was her duty to protect Rahuul. That was all that mattered. There would be time enough for grief later.

The kitchens were mercifully empty as she raced through them and she dragged Rahuul along to the side exit, pausing for a moment before opening the door out onto a pathway to the rear of the palace.

Adaali paused again, checking her brother over to see if he was all right. When she was satisfied he was unharmed she looked him in the eyes, seeing that expression of bewilderment.

'We need to run,' she said. 'We need to get far from here. Do you understand?'

He nodded, too overwhelmed to speak. Adaali hugged him to her, feeling his body tremble. All she wanted was to hold him, to keep him safe in her embrace, but she knew that would be suicide. No one was coming to help them now. They had to flee or die.

She took Rahuul's hand and led him out into the night. All about them were the sounds of clashing steel as the battle raged on. As she passed through the gardens at the side of the palace there was movement in the main courtyard thirty yards to her right. She hunkered down behind a bush of intricately trimmed topiary, pulling Rahuul down beside her. Peering through the undergrowth she saw the bearded giant they called Manssun Rike. He was surrounded by red-clad knights, the bodies of Kantor militia littering the ground all about him. Adaali had never truly feared anyone before, but seeing that warrior's glare filled her heart with dread.

A knight came staggering from the palace, clutching a wound at his side. Manssun grabbed him by the arm, seeming unconcerned that he was injured.

'Did you find them?' he demanded.

The knight shook his head. 'The vizier says they've escaped.'

'Well they can't be far. Take more men and spread out. And find Bertrand. This is no time for him to be fucking cowering in his chamber.'

Adaali had seen enough. It was obvious who they were looking for and she had to put as much distance between Rahuul and the palace as possible.

Under the moonlight, they stole across the gardens to a little-used side gate. There lay two corpses, one a warrior of the Desert Blades, the other a Suderfeld knight. Adaali pulled Rahuul past the bodies and out into the city.

Compared to the din of the palace the streets were deathly quiet. Adaali clung to the shadows, wondering what next. She remembered her mother's words – *we can trust no one*. She couldn't even go to the militia. Or could she? Egil had clearly betrayed them but did his plot go all the way to the watchmen on the street? The only one she could really trust was Musir Dragosh, but he was nowhere to be seen.

Adaali glanced down at her little brother. She had to

keep him safe. This was no time to take risks. She would have to see him out of the city and away, and worry about which direction once they had left Kantor well behind them.

'You have to be silent now, Rahuul,' she said. 'Not a sound until we have left the city. Understand?'

He nodded obediently, and she kissed his cheek before leading him further into the city, clinging to the shadows all the while. Rahuul played his part, keeping silent, staying close to her. Adaali was proud of how brave he was, especially after what he had witnessed. For her own part, she felt devastated – each step was a labour. All she wanted to do was collapse and weep and rage at the night, but she fought the urge, pushing herself on.

Eventually they reached the edge of the city. Beyond the market square was the gate northwards. It was barely used, the trade to the north having dried up in centuries past. Hopefully it would not be well guarded.

Adaali struck out across the open ground to the far end of the square, instantly regretting it as she heard the snort of an approaching horse and the grunt of a rider urging it on. Their way was suddenly barred, and in the moonlight, she could see the rider was young, wearing the uniform of a militiaman.

'Stop there,' he demanded.

Adaali obeyed, pulling her brother behind her.

'We are just going home,' she lied. 'My brother ran away and I—'

'You're the princess,' he said. 'And that's the prince.'

His horse became agitated, snorting once more as he pulled on the reins.

'No, we are no one,' she said, unable to disguise the panic in her voice.

'They're here,' the militiaman cried at the top of his voice, wrenching his sword from its sheath. 'I've found the royal bastards, they're here.'

In the distance she could hear voices shouting out in reply. More militia responding to the horseman's yell.

Adaali grabbed Rahuul's hand and tried to race for the edge of the market, but the militiaman steered his horse to block their path. There was nowhere to go as the voices beyond the marketplace grew louder.

She heard a whisper from the night, a dull metallic ring that came to a sudden halt. Glancing up she saw the haft of an axe protruding from the horseman's chest. He slumped in his saddle, blade falling from his hand before he slid from the back of the horse and landed in a heap.

Adaali turned to see a giant approaching from the dark. Relief washed over her as she saw framed in the moonlight a face she recognised. Musir Dragosh walked with purpose, grasping the reins of the horse before it could bolt.

'Get on,' he ordered.

Adaali wasted no time in jumping up into the saddle. Dragosh lifted Rahuul up behind her and he grabbed her around the waist. As the distant voices grew closer, Dragosh led the horse north. Adaali glanced back, seeing men running after them. Voices yelled for them to stop but Dragosh was in no mood to heed their words.

The north gate was just ahead of them now and, in the light of the lanterns hanging from the city walls, Adaali could see her weapon master was gripping tight to a wound in his side. He stopped at the edge of the marketplace, glaring across at the guards on the open gate before glancing back at their pursuers.

'You have to go,' he said, handing her the reins. 'Just ride. Don't stop for anything.'

With that he pulled his huge curved blade from its sheath.

'Come with us,' Adaali begged. 'There is room on the horse for all of us.'

Dragosh shook his head. 'You will be swifter without me,' he replied. 'And you must be swift, girl.'

Adaali looked back again. In the dark she could see the silhouette of Manssun Rike crossing the marketplace, surrounded by his knights.

'Go,' Dragosh hissed, slapping a hand against the horse's flank.

The steed bolted, setting off at a gallop. Adaali had no time to turn back, to see her weapon master face the Suderfeld warriors. No time to watch him die.

As she rode towards the open archway, the militia rushed to block her path. She did not heed their demands for her to stop as her heels beat against the side of the horse, urging it on faster. An archer rushed down from the parapet, taking a shot at them, but the arrow flew by harmlessly. The militia barring her way did not have the stomach to face down a galloping steed and they scattered as she rode by. In an instant she was under the arch with nothing but the sound of their angry cries in her wake.

The sun was rising on the distant horizon as she urged

the horse onwards. Adaali did not dare allow it to take a breath until she'd left the city in the distance. The road rose up to higher ground that looked down on the city and Adaali was more than a league distant before she reined the horse in, turning to take one last glance back at Kantor. It seemed quiet in the dawn light, as it would have on any other morning.

'We will return here soon, Rahuul,' she said. 'We will find a way to reclaim your crown.'

Her brother's grip loosened on her waist and he began to slip. Before she could catch him he fell from the horse, landing on the ground with a sickening thump. Adaali jumped from the saddle, crouching beside him. When she saw the arrow protruding from his ribs she clamped a hand over her mouth.

'I was silent,' he whispered. 'Just like you told me.'

She tried to speak, to tell him everything was all right, but all she managed was a strangled sob. Reaching out she grasped her brother's hand as he stared back at her. But he wasn't staring at her any longer. He was staring at nothing.

Her entire life had been dedicated to keeping her little brother safe, and now he was gone. She had failed.

Despair began to swell in her heart as she looked up to see riders leaving the northern gate of Kantor. The longer she watched them approach, the more that despair began to contort. It smouldered, catching alight, bursting into flame until it raged. Until she raged.

Let them come. She would fight them. But not here, not now.

She would avenge her brother, but first she had to run.

8

NIGHT had fallen over the Shengen camp and a blanket of stars shrouded the huge canyon. Siff breathed in the night air as she watched the constellations paint their slow journey across the black canvas sky. The realm of mortals had its own mundane beauty, and she was determined to appreciate every brief moment while here. But Siff knew she did not belong in this place. Before long this would all be over, and one way or another she would return home.

A twinge of pain in her side dragged her from the reverie. How many battles had it been now? How many enemies had she slaughtered to get to Innellan? And how many wounds had she suffered on the journey? Wounds that would have slain any mortal. Wounds that were all too slow to heal.

She knew that all she need do was stand atop a promontory, hold up her hands to summon her troops and accept their eager worship. Their benefaction would see those wounds healed in an instant. She only had to welcome their devotion and she would become more powerful even than Innellan.

But Siff refused. She was here to stop Innellan, to see an end to this perpetual cycle of worship and war. To stop the suffering that it inevitably led to. If there was one thing she could not compromise on it was that, and so she would have to suffer the pain. She would not succumb to the same temptations as Innellan and Armadon. Laigon would be the one her armies followed – let him be their figurehead and she his faithful lieutenant. It was the only way.

Siff closed her eyes, breathing deeply, trying to control the pain with her strength of will, but it did little good. She turned from the edge of the canyon, heading back to the encampment. Perhaps if she threw herself into planning the coming battle it would help take her mind from her injuries.

When she reached Laigon's tent she was relieved to see he was still awake. The flickering light of a candle was visible through the entrance and she passed the praetorians guarding the way to see him still poring over the Shengen attack plans. The coming siege would be difficult, but Laigon had marshalled dozens of campaigns in service to the Shengen emperor and the Iron Tusk after him. If there was any man who could overcome the defences of Mantioch it was he.

'Still awake, Valdyr,' she said as she looked down at the plans. 'Do you never rest?'

'I could say the same to you,' he replied, still staring at the map of the outlying terrain.

Siff could see he had laid out plans for the siege. Small wooden blocks represented his troops, the city of Mantioch had been hastily sketched at the centre of the map. There was only one way in across a raised bridge.

'Are we ready?' she asked.

Laigon nodded. 'Siege ladders will be hoisted at the

eastern wall to cause a diversion. Then the ram will be pushed across the bridge to the main gate.'

Siff looked down at the plans. Even from the rudimentary sketch she could tell they would suffer great casualties. More sacrifices. But they would be necessary if Innellan was to be stopped. If she was allowed to continue her reign in the north this whole realm would eventually suffer much greater loss.

'Are your men ready?'

'My men are always ready. They have not failed you yet.'

Siff felt the pain of that more keenly than any wound she had suffered. Despite her refusal to accept their worship she knew they held her in as high regard as their emperor.

'And I will not fail them,' she replied.

Laigon regarded her with sympathy. 'You should sit this one out. You need rest. It would not—'

'No. I will be in the vanguard as always. I cannot ask them to risk their lives while I stand aside and watch.'

Laigon was about to argue when there came a shout from outside the tent. When they both walked outside to see what the commotion was, Siff saw a rider entering the camp.

The horse was exhausted, snorting loudly as it came to a stop. The rider was in a worse state and he tumbled from the saddle to be caught by two of the Shengen warriors, who gently lowered him to the ground.

Siff approached, seeing it was one of Josten's scouts. The man gratefully accepted a waterskin, drinking deeply from it.

'What has happened?' Siff asked. 'Where is the rest of your troop? Where is Josten?'

The man tried to rise but he was too fatigued. 'Ambush,' he managed to say.

Siff knelt beside him. 'What is your name?' she asked gently.

'I am Eyman,' said the scout. He was no Shengen, but one of the Cordral militia who had joined them at Dunrun.

'Tell me what happened to you.'

He knelt on the ground, taking another drink before saying, 'They were waiting for us. They knew we were coming. It was a slaughter. Everyone...'

'Josten?' she said.

He fixed her with a sorrowful gaze. 'Everyone,' he repeated.

Siff stood as the camp surgeon came to see to the scout. Josten was lost. As much as Siff tried not to feel the grief of it she still suffered the loss keenly. She clenched her fists, nails digging into her palms as she tried to shrug off the pain. Josten had agreed to join her even though this was not his fight. She had persuaded him to come along on her crusade and he had sacrificed himself for the cause. But then, so had so many others. Blaming herself would not bring him back. She had been tricked. Innellan had deceived her into chasing the Stone of Katamaru and she had fallen for it like a fool.

She marched through the encampment to a tent surrounded by sentries. None of them stood in her way as she lit a torch from a nearby sconce and entered. The Hierophant was still tied to his chair, asleep. As she entered he awoke, blinking in the brightness of the torch as he saw her standing, watching him. It pleased her to see the fear that crossed his features.

'You must have known this moment was coming,' Siff said.

'I had no choice,' the Hierophant replied. 'The White Widow demanded prisoners. That was my sacrifice.'

'And the Stone of Katamaru? Was that also a lie?'

The Hierophant could not hold her gaze. It was clear he did not want to answer, conflicted by his fear of Siff and the terrifying prospect of betraying Innellan.

'We still have it… in Mantioch. But Innellan cares little for it.'

'What do you mean, she cares little for it? The Stone is an artefact of supreme power.'

The Hierophant shook his head as Siff took a step forward. It needed all her will not to crush his head in her hands.

'Please, I am but a servant. I know nothing of—'

He stopped, his face reddening. As Siff watched his features went slack, his body convulsing, white froth gathering at the corners of his mouth. Before she could move closer, his eyes flipped open revealing two dark black pools.

Siff knew she was no longer in the presence of a mortal. This was her sister Innellan in all but flesh.

They regarded one another across the tent. Slowly her sister smiled in that wicked way that so many found alluring. It sickened Siff to her stomach, and it took all her willpower not to pull the Hierophant's head from his shoulders and fling it into the night.

'You are determined to stop me,' the Hierophant spoke with the voice of an Archon. 'That much cannot be denied. But I wonder; are you sure you're strong enough, sister?'

Siff didn't want to answer. She knew she was being goaded, but simply couldn't help herself.

'We will meet soon enough,' she replied. 'And you will see exactly how strong I am. You have betrayed the covenant. You do not belong here.'

Her sister laughed, dry and hoarse through the Hierophant's throat. 'Of course we belong here. This is our purpose – to rule over these chattels. And it is their purpose to serve. To worship us.'

'No. That is not the way. We agreed. We all agreed.'

'*You* agreed,' said Innellan. '*You* dictated. *You* ordered and enforced. None of us believed it. Without benefaction what are we?'

'We cannot—'

'*You* cannot,' Innellan snarled. 'You refuse it, but it taunts you. I can sense your weakness… and your yearning. You want their worship more than I do. Why deny yourself any longer?'

'Because I am stronger than you. More powerful than you will ever be.'

Another wicked leer. 'Then you should prove yourself, sister.'

'What do you—'

Before Innellan could speak another word, the Hierophant's eyes rolled back in his head, the black turning again to white. Blood began to trickle from their corners as he sobbed dark rivulets down his cheeks.

Siff took a step back as the Hierophant began to choke, spitting gobs of red from his throat, convulsing as though stricken with a palsy. Within moments his body went limp, head lolling to one side.

Then you should prove yourself, sister.

What had Innellan meant? Cold dread welled up inside her as she left the tent. The camp was calm, surrounded by the quiet of night, but something was wrong.

Siff rushed to the highest point of the camp, to the ridge looking over the surrounding desert. There she closed her eyes, feeling the bodies among the encampment, every soul within it – some resting, some anxious, some hopeful.

With ethereal fingers, Siff reached out, stretching past the limits of the camp, spreading her essence beyond any mortal boundaries. She crossed the desert, feeling with her consciousness in every direction, snaking her way along the desert floor. She was half blind in the darkness, but still she could feel her way, every inch filling her with a growing sense of foreboding until…

They stood tall and silent in the blackness of the desert. Row upon row waiting at Innellan's behest less than a league away from the Shengen encampment. It was a horde – countless warriors of the Ramadi, a host made up of fanatics from every cult.

Siff opened her eyes, feeling the cold breeze chill her to the bone. Innellan's army was coming in overwhelming numbers. Her sister had been right – it was time to prove herself.

9

THE drumming of hooves on the hard dirt road were all she concentrated on as she urged the horse further north. It was getting tired beneath her, but what could she expect after galloping the steed for a day and a night? As the sun began to rise on the desert she could feel the beast becoming less surefooted, its breath coming in ragged gasps, but still Adaali kicked its flanks, pressing it harder. It was the only chance she had to survive this.

Despite digging her heels into its flanks the horse ignored her, slowing every few yards. She glanced back, peering through the morning haze at the distant horizon. They were still there. The riders who had dogged her trail for a day and a night were not yet ready to give up the chase and she could just make out their dark cloaks billowing as they forced their own steeds on to greater exertion. It was not enough that they had murdered her mother and brother, they would only be satisfied when she too was dead.

As Adaali focused north once more, memories of the slaughter in Kantor began to plague her. The vision of her mother raging, flinging herself at Egil Sun only to be cut down by the bonecaster's knife. Adaali gritted her teeth against the memory, forcing it from her mind, only to have it replaced by the dying face of her brother, those eyes of his filled with such innocence.

'I was silent. Just like you told me,' he'd whispered, moments before taking that final breath.

Adaali's eyes welled, the tears streaking her face as she rode. The anger at such injustice burned inside her, the fire of vengeance raging. There would be a reckoning for this and she would start with her pursuers, but she knew she could not face them on open ground. Were she to stop and confront them here she would be cut down in an instant. Then who would avenge her family? Not Musir Dragosh, for surely he was already dead. Not the militia of Kantor, for they had done nothing to stop this massacre in the first place. She was the only one left now, and she was determined that Egil Sun would die by her hand before she perished. All she had to do was live long enough to see it through.

That prospect seemed a distant one as her horse faltered beneath her. Its rhythmic hoofbeats grew more unsteady, but in her desperation Adaali kicked it on all the harder. It stumbled, and she felt cold panic grip her chest. With a final pained whinny the horse reared, then collapsed to the ground. It hit the earth with a thump, but Adaali had already cleared the saddle and rolled clear, despite her fatigue. She rose to her feet in a cloud of dust, and approached the prone horse. It was still alive, but barely. Exhaustion had finished it, the bulky warhorse was not bred for long flights through the desert.

Adaali knelt by its side, laying a hand on the horse's neck. She would have to leave it here to die alone and suffering.

With no weapon she could not help relieve the animal's pain.

'Thank you,' she whispered. Then she was on her feet once more, running north as the dawn sun began to illuminate the desert.

It beat down on her intensely as she fought her way north across the sands, across the dust, over dunes and rocky outcrops. Every now and again she would allow herself a glance back into the distance, and every time she would see those dark-cloaked riders gaining on her. It wouldn't be long before they ran her down.

There was nowhere for her to flee. This far north, this close to the Ramadi border, there was no civilisation, no towns or cities had existed here for decades. Since the Fall they had all been consumed by the desert. Her only chance was to keep going, to put one foot in front of the other until she could find somewhere to hide, or at least make a final stand.

Thirst clawed at her throat, her muscles cramping, her legs burning from the endless flight. She crested one last ridge, ready to give up the chase, when she saw something below that restored her vigour.

It was a settlement – or at least it had been at one time or another. A sorry collection of buildings was arranged in a wheel formation, narrow streets forming the spokes that led to a central hub. Most of the buildings were in ruins, with those to the east all but consumed by the sands, though a few remained intact.

As she stumbled down the side of the ridge, Adaali wondered if there might at least be someone alive here. Someone eking out a meagre living in the desert. The closer she got the more she abandoned the notion. There was no one alive here, there hadn't been for centuries. Besides, no one could help her even if the place was inhabited. The bonecasters would slaughter anyone who stood in their way.

Still, there was nowhere else for her to run. If she were to strike out further into the desert she would be easy prey. This was as good a place as any to stand and fight and die.

Adaali moved further towards the centre, her search becoming more desperate as she tried to find some hiding place or anything that could be used as a weapon. In one crumbling two-storey building she found the broken handle of a sword, the blade long since rusted away. Just as she was about to abandon any hope of finding something useful she noticed the haft of a spear lying in the dirt. As she picked it up, the wooden shaft crumbled in her grip, but the rusted steel head was still in one piece. Adaali allowed herself a smile. At least she would not go down easily – she would show these bonecasters the viciousness of her bite.

Pressing on, she reached the centre of the settlement. Here a few of the buildings were almost intact, though there were still no signs of life. A dried-up well stood in the centre of the town, and across from it was what looked like the ruins of an ancient temple. Adaali crossed the central square, tentatively peering inside. The door had rotted away, and she crept through the open arch. Inside was but a single chamber, high ceilinged and relatively undamaged. As the sunlight beamed through the gaps in the roof, Adaali gasped at what she saw.

Someone had been there recently, at least in the past few weeks. Every inch of the walls was covered in script.

101

Markings, cyphers and litanies covered the place. As Adaali peered at the words, she realised they were little more than the ramblings of an unhinged mind. 'I am the betrayer,' seemed to be a common theme, repeated again and again. 'No justice for the damned,' and 'She has cursed us all,' were also repeated again and again, scrawled alongside pictures of mighty fortresses and scenes of torture and death. On one wall was the depiction of a giant hag, leering and cruel, her hands distended to stretch out over a legion of stick warriors, like they were marionettes and she the puppeteer.

Adaali became more unnerved the longer she stayed in the place, and slowly she backed out into the open air. Glancing around the central square she realised she didn't have long. She must find somewhere to hide, to lie in wait for her pursuers.

Only one other building looked suitable, and she rushed towards it. Once inside she was relieved to find the staircase still standing, and she carefully made her way up, hearing the rotting timbers creak under her weight. There was one room on the upper floor, and Adaali crouched by the window. It gave her a good view of the square and the road that led to it from the south. There she knelt, gripping the spearhead in her hand. It was a pitiful weapon but it would have to do.

Before she could lament the weaknesses in her poorly planned ambush, she heard riders approaching from the south. There were five of them, steeds lean and swift, where her own had been broad and powerful. No wonder it had perished, pursued so hard through the desert by these long-ranging beasts.

Each of the riders wore a black cloak but the hoods were drawn back. Adaali could see the pale, emaciated faces of the bonecasters as they came to a stop at the centre of the settlement.

The riders jumped down from their steeds, quickly hobbling them before they began their search of the settlement. Adaali pressed herself against the wall of the ruined hovel. It was only a matter of time before one of them found her.

She gripped the spearhead tightly, feeling it cut the flesh of her palm, but she didn't make a sound as she heard a creak from the stairs below. Gritting her teeth, she peered from behind a broken section of wall, her eyes fixed on the open archway. The bonecaster's curved blade slowly appeared as he tentatively crept into the room. Adaali was stunned by fear, but she knew she had to overcome it. She could not just crouch there waiting to be discovered – waiting to be murdered like some coward in the desert.

Silently she leapt. The bonecaster saw her from the corner of his eye, but he was too slow to raise his blade and defend himself. Adaali plunged the spearhead deep into his chest, jamming it between his ribs.

They both tumbled to the floor, the timbers cracking beneath their weight. Adaali looked down, expecting the bonecaster to fight, but he just stared back at her, bloodshot eyes wide and pleading. Blood trickled from the corners of his mouth, and for the first time Adaali noticed how young he was. Not much older than a boy. Not much older than her.

A sudden commotion below sparked her into action. She grasped the boy's fallen blade and turned to face the door.

Two more bonecasters had rushed up the stairs and the first one came at her, sword raised.

Adaali ducked the blow, lashing out with the blade and opening a wound in the first attacker's shoulder. She was not swift enough to stop the second smashing into her cheek with the butt of his blade. Adaali reeled back, unable to stop them as they rushed her. The fight was swift, but ultimately futile as she wrestled against two much stronger opponents. The relentless flight north had left her weak and now she stood no chance. As the two bonecasters disarmed her, another joined them, hastily tying her ankles and wrists with a rope.

'You will die,' she cried as best she could through her dried throat. 'I will kill you all for this.' Adaali knew they were empty words but still she struggled as they dragged her down the stairs and dumped her beside the well like an animal. As she screamed at them, one knelt on her back and secured a thick knotted rope across her mouth to gag her.

It was useless. There was nothing she could do to stop the inevitable. Egil Sun possessed the crown of Kantor now. He was never going to let some whelp take it from him. Adaali's fate was sealed.

She lay there defeated as one of the bonecasters unhobbled the horses and they prepared to leave. Before they could haul her onto the back of one of those steeds, the men stopped, frozen in place.

Adaali craned her neck to look along one of the sunken streets. Down it came a shambling figure. Matted hair and a thick dirty beard covered his features, a torn and battered tunic hung from his body, the original colour now hidden beneath the dirt and dust of the desert. His bare legs were sunburned and filthy and he ambled into the centre of the town as though blind to the scene before him.

Warily the bonecasters drew their weapons, but none of them moved to stop the hermit as he made his way towards the ruined temple Adaali had entered earlier. As he moved past the well his eyes met Adaali's. Despite his filthy appearance and shambling gait, Adaali could see a keen intelligence burning in those dark eyes of his, though they bore the aspect of a wolf more than a man.

The hermit slowed, and for a moment she could see there was conflict in him. She didn't allow herself to hope that he might intervene; what could one man do against four bonecasters? But still, as he came to a stop she thought that perhaps there was still a chance.

He looked around at the bonecasters, at their naked blades, then he let out a long sigh.

'Why do you torment this creature?' the hermit said in a quiet voice, gesturing to where Adaali lay.

The bonecasters looked at one another uncertainly, but did not reply. Adaali had never heard any of their ilk speak before. For all she knew, Egil Sun had ordered their tongues removed. She wouldn't have put it past the old bastard.

'No one is speaking?' said the hermit. 'Not one of you?' He glanced at them all in turn. 'That is a shame, for I have not spoken to another soul in such a long time.'

They still stood in silence until the closest bonecaster moved forward, his patience run out. He raised that sword high as he rushed at the hermit, and as much as Adaali wanted to shut her eyes against the horror she forced herself to watch.

At the last moment, as the blade came crashing down to cleave the hermit's filthy head in two, he moved aside. His hands darted out like snakes and somehow the bonecaster was disarmed. Then the hermit countered with one swift movement, hacking off his attacker's leg at the knee.

The bonecaster howled, collapsing to the dirt next to his severed leg, clutching the stump. His scream rose like a braying animal as his blood pumped across the sand.

'I am sorry, my friend,' the hermit said, holding out a hand in apology, as though he had just spilled the bonecaster's drink rather than taken a limb.

The remaining three rushed in as one. Those curved blades slashed at the hermit as Adaali watched in amazement. The ring of steel rose over the screams of the wounded bonecaster as the hermit stepped from the path of their attacks. Before Adaali knew what had happened the fight was over and she was staring at three corpses.

The wounded bonecaster still screamed as his fellows lay dead all about him, and the hermit approached him gingerly. 'Again, my apologies,' he said, before sinking the tip of the blade into the wounded man's throat. His screams were replaced by a sickening cough as he drowned on his own blood.

Adaali struggled to sit up, her back against the crumbing well as the hermit approached her. She felt panic rise within her as he came forward, unsure of what he might do. Without another word he put down the bloodied blade and untied her wrists and ankles. Adaali quickly pulled the gag from her mouth.

'Who are you?' she asked.

He raised his hands, encompassing his bleak surroundings. 'Out here, I am no one.' Then his brow furrowed as though he had made a mistake. 'Or perhaps I am everyone.'

She stood, regarding him as his eyes turned to the ground. It was obvious he was the one responsible for the mad ramblings written on the temple interior. But it was also obvious he was much more than some insane hermit. She had never seen such skill with a blade. Even Musir Dragosh was not so swift and deadly.

'What now?' she asked, as much to herself as to this madman.

'Now I suggest you flee,' he said, gesturing to the horses still milling at the edge of the plaza. 'Far away from here.'

Adaali considered it. She could ride from here. No one was chasing her now and she could go anywhere she wanted. But where? Deeper into the desert? Surely she would die of thirst before she reached an inhabited settlement. Or worse, she would reach the Ramadi Wastes and whatever horrors they might contain.

'What if I wanted to stay here?' she said, almost regretting asking. This was a madman, and yet he had rescued her. If she was to survive perhaps he was her only hope.

'Do as you wish,' he said, turning to make his way back towards the temple.

'Will you help me?' she asked, annoyed at his sudden indifference. 'You can't rescue me, just to abandon me now.'

The hermit shrugged. 'The way I see it, I rescued myself. But I suppose it's been a long time since I had any company. What could it hurt?'

Adaali sighed in relief. 'Thank you. I am Adaali.' She didn't feel the need to expand. What good would it do explaining her heritage to this crazy man in the desert? 'Who are you?'

The hermit thought on that for a moment, as though he'd forgotten. 'I had a name a long time ago. It's been so long since anyone has had reason to use it.'

'I have to call you something,' she said.

'Very well.' He turned to her and she could see the keenness once more in those dark wolf eyes of his. 'I am Dantar.' With that he turned and made his way to the temple.

With nowhere else to go in this ruin of a settlement, Adaali followed.

10

THE noise was deafening as the cultists battered themselves against the Shengen shield wall. They were a relentless mass of hate, but Siff had learned that lesson well after months of fighting her way west across the desert. But where before the Shengen army had trampled over the cultist bands, cutting them down like wheat, now the enemy was present in overwhelming numbers.

Innellan had summoned a horde. Warriors from every cult in the Ramadi had flocked there to end Siff's crusade. She could see them now, sensing their hate, their loathing for these invaders and their unwavering devotion to Innellan.

There was fear in the air certainly, but also excitement – a strange joy hanging over the desert... the prospect of slaughter. It sickened her to the core while filling her with an ecstasy undreamed of.

Men and women were already dying. Even those slaughtered far across the battlefield left their mark on her, their pain, their despair. It was visceral, like manna fuelling her, bringing her to life, showing her a purpose she had long since abandoned.

There was a time – millennia ago – when Siff would

have taken pleasure in this. She would have bathed in the sensation, fed on it, revelled in the glory. But that time was long past. The memory of those glorious aeons only served to remind her of why she was there. Of how important it was she put an end to this perpetual warfare.

But for now, the only way to do that was to fight.

North, across the rows of Shengen helms, Siff could see Laigon marshalling his men for war. He stood tall and proud, every inch the emperor. The Shengen Standings obeyed his every barked call, each order carried out to the letter. He showed no fear despite standing on high ground, prominent above his warriors even as arrows plunged past him. Such bravery moved Siff. In all her time in the mortal realm, from aeons past to now, she had never met a braver mortal. Not even her faithful Bezial had shown such courage. It shamed her to be standing back among the auxiliary troops, only able to witness as her servant led the main body of their defence.

She and Laigon had agreed that her role should be secondary. It was important that the troops follow him, and that she not overshadow him with her divine presence. So there she stood with auxiliaries, positioned to the south near the edge of the canyon.

Siff sensed their unease. They were freed slaves who had chosen to join her crusade against the cults. Though they were strong men and women, good fighters all, they could never match the discipline of the Shengens.

Perhaps now would have been a good time for an inspiring speech, but Siff was still wounded and oh, so tired. Despite the keen sense of expectation that surrounded her, all Siff wanted was to find a lonely corner of the desert and rest. But this was no time for weakness. This was a time to fight or die.

It would have been so easy for her to rise up and claim what was rightfully hers – to have these warriors worship her like a god. That would have healed her festering wounds and she would have been born anew. The cultists would have fled before her might and those who refused would have been crushed beneath her fury, but that was just what Innellan wanted – for Siff to succumb to the temptation. If she did so all would be lost and she would become that which she sought to destroy. Siff had to resist, had to be strong.

The din of battle drifted over from the north where the cultists had dispatched their cavalry to assault Laigon's shield wall. Armoured warriors rode giant steeds, slamming their war mauls and hammers against the tower shields of the Shengen. Their attack was relentless, the sound of it booming across the desert, but still Laigon's men held. Siff felt only pride at their stubborn refusal to be beaten. They thrust their spears, bringing down their foes one by one, dragging them to the ground where their armour and steeds would do them no good.

So focused was her attention on the battle to the north that Siff almost didn't hear a cry go up from one of the auxiliaries. She turned west, peering though the haze.

Siff cursed. A red-armoured host was charging across the flats. She shouted above the sudden panic of the auxiliaries, ordering them to remain steady, to brace their shields. The men and women surrounding her obeyed, but Siff could feel the doubt creeping in. The red horde looked fearsome and it

111

seemed inevitable her motley division of troops would break beneath the onslaught.

She would defend her position. Would stand side by side with these mortals and show them how to face down such impossible odds. Despite her fatigue, her wounds, the opposition she faced, Siff would show them they had made the right decision to follow her.

'Hold!' she shouted, as the enemy closed. They were a red wall of might, charging with all the hate and fury Siff had learned to expect.

She stood front and centre. To her flanks she could feel her army begin to waver in the face of the armoured tide. Her own forces were poorly equipped, having salvaged what weapons and armour they could from their defeated enemies. It would be a slaughter.

'Hold!' she cried again, and despite their fear, her warriors refused to break.

Then there was no more time for words.

The red-armoured legion crashed into the auxiliaries, smashing them down, hacking them apart like meat.

Siff screamed, charging into the midst of her enemies, a sword in each hand. With a single slash she severed a head, another and she took an arm. In an instant she was showered with blood, consumed by the din of slaughter. Her army was being destroyed around her, but she had no time to save any of them, no time to rally them, to spur them to greater effort. Lost in the frenzy of battle, Siff gave herself over to the ecstasy of killing.

Each slash of the blade filled her with strength. Each

death was a ritual benefaction to feed her Archon's craving. Despite the size and strength of the behemoths she faced, Siff could not be stopped. She cut a swathe through their ranks. They had expected this to be a murder, and murder she would give them.

Another swift flurry of blades and she had cut a furrow in the massed enemy. The armoured warriors shied from her weapons now. No one would face her and she stood at their centre, breathing heavily from the exertion, feeling her enemies' warm blood running down her flesh.

'You are cowards all!' she screamed. 'Who will face me?'

'I will!' a deep voice shouted from within the crowd.

A huge warrior, a head taller than the rest, pushed his way forward. Below his shaved scalp his face was a mass of scarred and broken flesh. This was a general if ever she had seen one.

'I am Kraden,' he announced. 'Known as the Fist. High Lord of the Legion of—'

Siff leapt forward before he could finish, both swords flashing, slicing that huge battered head from its red-armoured shoulders. As his body toppled to the ground, she stared at the remaining enemies, daring anyone to step forward, demanding another challenger.

Instead her troops rallied. A flung spear embedded itself in the chest of the nearest warrior. The auxiliaries surged forward, falling on the armoured troops. With their leader defeated, the cultists were lost, dropping beneath the swords and axes of Siff's army.

She watched as they pushed the enemy back, hacking away in a frenzy until the army of Lord Kraden was routed.

113

But there was little time to appreciate the victory. No sooner had the legion of warriors fled than Siff heard cries to the rear of her troops.

There came the familiar sound of blades clashing, of men and women crying in pain and alarm. Siff pushed her way back through the ranks, back towards the camp, and she could see figures running, the flash of blades in the sun.

She sprinted through the camp, hunting the next foe, desperate for the fight. Butchered bodies lay strewn across the centre, dismembered limbs lying in the blood and muck. She found them on the edge of the canyon. Six figures, decked in black and red, a single blade held by each. Sword Saints, peerless warriors, Innellan's elite. From the look of it, they had managed to scale the sheer canyon wall to attack the auxiliaries from the rear. A courageous move. Siff would show them the folly of it.

Ignoring the pain in her limbs, she rushed forward, twin blades flashing. The half dozen swordsmen spread out, none of them in haste to engage. Though these men were as fanatical in their devotion as any of Innellan's faithful they still fought with a keen intelligence. The first backed off, parrying Siff's swords, allowing his fellows to move around to flank her. Once she was surrounded they attacked as one and it was all she could do to fend off the onslaught of steel.

The sound of their blades rang out above the roar of the distant battle, a chiming song of death. Siff rolled, avoiding the sweep of a sword by a hair's breadth. These were incredible warriors, the most gifted mortals Siff had ever faced, but still no match for her.

Parrying one strike she took the head from a Sword Saint as he span to engage her. Ducking a sweeping blade she hacked off a leg, feeling the ecstasy of combat grip her in its tight embrace. Memories of endless battles fed her, the experience of a hundred lifetimes filling her as she dodged and parried, dancing in between those flashing blades. Another thrust pierced a heart, a sweep of steel opened a throat. With every death she felt stronger, every spatter of blood an anointment.

When finally she stood alone, her earthly body panting for air and surrounded by corpses, she felt the elation abate. Her auxiliaries surrounded her, awestruck at what they had witnessed. Worshipping this paragon of the sword. Siff wanted nothing more than to stand and accept it, but in the aftermath she suddenly felt her side go numb. The sword she held in her right hand fell from her grip and she looked down to see one of those enemy blades impaled in her side.

Grasping the razor steel she pulled it free, feeling every inch of it slide from her flesh. Her teeth ground together as she tried to fight the pain but it was no easy feat. Looking up, she saw Laigon pushing his way through the crowd, and felt relief overcome her as he approached.

'We have the day,' he said, his brow furrowed in concern at her grievous wound.

She wanted to congratulate him, wanted to share in the elation of victory, but instead she stumbled, falling into his arms. He held her up, calling for a surgeon, but Siff could already feel the wound healing.

Over Laigon's shoulder she saw her army falling to its

knees. The surviving auxiliaries, those men and women who had witnessed her defeat six of the most skilled warriors in the land, offered their praise. Some bowed their heads, others looked to the sky, their lips moving in silent prayer.

Their worship nourished her, brought her back from the brink, empowered her. It was exquisite, and she wanted nothing more than to lie back and accept it.

'No,' she whispered to Laigon. 'Get me away from here.'

He made to protest but she squeezed his shoulder. 'You have to get me away. They cannot pray to me. It's too dangerous.'

Laigon looked into her eyes, seeing something there that convinced him to obey. More of his warriors appeared, taking Siff and helping her through the crowd.

As they carried her away, all she could do was look back at those kneeling worshippers, feeling the power of their prayers receding even as she longed for more.

11

*S*HE *was being hunted, the terror of it spreading through her body, and the certainty that if she did not flee she would be slaughtered fuelled her flight through the night.*

The desert was cold, the darkness cloying, but still she plunged on through the black, heedless of the unseen dangers all around, for there was terror in her wake. Shapeless nightmares that would not give up, would not relent until they had run her down and slaked their thirst on her lifeblood.

Her feet thumped against the desert floor, but she cared little for stealth now. Speed was all she needed, hoped for, craved as she fled into the night. But no matter how far, no matter how fast, she could not seem to lose these hunters.

Her ankle turned on the uneven ground and she cried out in pain, cursing the blackness surrounding her. She stumbled, the flesh of her heel pressing against a sharp rock, the pain lancing up her leg, but still she staggered on.

They were closer now, she could hear the drumming of their tread on the hard ground, the relentless rhythm pounding in her ears. She risked a glance back, peering through the dark for any sign of who or what was chasing her down.

As her vision fell on them she knew it had been a foolish thing to do.

The riders were a manifestation of every night terror, every imagined horror. Black hoods masked their faces, leaving her to picture the horror of their visages. Their night-black steeds blew hot steam, hooves driving through the darkness, kicking up the dirt beneath them. Her heart raced as they grew ever larger, as their pursuit made a mockery of her flight.

She sobbed, immediately hating herself, cursing for showing such weakness, but there was little else for it. No matter how far and how fast she fled there was nothing she could do to escape the approaching doom.

Somewhere off in the distance she heard someone shout. It echoed at her through the night, minuscule but familiar. Another shout, this time closer, and she recognised her brother's voice.

She tried to call back to him, to try and find him through the gloom, but her own voice was lost. Before she could look for him she stumbled again, this time her legs gave way as she fell to the earth, sprawling in the desert.

Another voice in the night – a single wail of anguish, of loss. A woman crying out one last lament.

'Mother!' she screamed.

The riders fell upon her.

Adaali's eyes flicked open. The interior of the temple was lit grey by the moonlight lancing in through a broken roof. As she lay there she could just make out the writing on the walls, the crazed symbols, the ranting of a broken mind.

In the opposite corner lay Dantar. She couldn't hear him breathing, or see any movement beneath his blanket. He was nothing more than a pile of old rags lying in the corner of a dilapidated building.

Gently she pulled back her own blanket and sat up gingerly, at pains not to wake the hermit. Had this been the wisest move? To fall in with a wild man of the desert? Looking around at the walls of the temple it seemed not.

The more she looked at those walls, the more she read those ravings, the more Adaali thought she had made a mistake. Perhaps it was the eerie aspect cast by the moonlight, perhaps it was her recent dream that unnerved her, but either way she knew this was wrong. Dantar had shown her a kindness in rescuing her, and he showed no sign of doing her harm, but still – remaining here would be foolish.

Making no sound, Adaali stood. She carefully padded across the floor and ducked through the broken door and out into the night. The full moon cast everything in a gentle glow, and she felt a twinge of excitement as she made her way to the tethered horses.

Adaali moved up to the waiting steeds, not wanting to spook them as they stood silently beneath what was left of an ancient stable. Gently she laid a hand on the first animal's neck and its muscle twitched, hooves clapping against the ground.

She whispered to it, trying to calm it as she stroked the long black mane. The horse snorted, shying away, but Adaali stayed close, speaking soothingly, trying to convince the animal that she was no threat, until it calmed enough for her to untie the reins. It followed obediently as she led it from the stable and out onto the road.

As she led the horse away from the half-buried settlement,

she glanced back half expecting to see the mad hermit watching her, but no one was there. If Dantar was awake, if he knew she was leaving, then he did not care.

When she had led the horse far enough along the northern road she mounted and placed her bare feet in the stirrups, nudging it on. At first they walked, then when she was satisfied they were out of earshot of the temple she kicked the mount harder, urging it into a trot, then a canter, taking the road northwards through the desert. Before long there was nothing surrounding them but empty sands and Adaali felt the excitement of freedom, of escape.

She rode the horse until daybreak. Her heart was still pounding when eventually it carried her up into the hills. When they reached the summit she could see for miles in every direction. Not a soul in sight, and Adaali allowed herself to stop, to breathe in the freedom. There was no one coming after her now, no sign of pursuers, and she patted the horse's neck. The beast shook its head as though in answer.

'We've done well, my friend,' she said. Her steed had no opinion on the matter.

She climbed down from its back and the horse ambled over to chew lazily on the desert scrub. Looking south, Adaali began to wonder if this had been such a good idea. She was free, yes. But free to go where? To do what? No one was pursuing her, but her dream remained all too vivid. The cry of her brother, her mother's wail in the dark. It had been horrifying, but the reality had been much worse.

Her mother had been slaughtered before her eyes, cut down as she tried to defend her family. Rahuul had died in her arms, bleeding out his last as she looked on helplessly.

As she stared to the south, Adaali knew that somewhere beyond the horizon, Egil Sun was presiding over the kingdom of Kantor. He had done this, he had usurped the throne and now Adaali was riding away from him as far and as fast as she could.

The shame of that hit her all at once. She was running away from what was rightfully hers. Hiding in the desert like a lizard. What would Musir Dragosh have thought of that? Would he have been proud of her escape? Or would he have chastised her for her cowardice?

Adaali knew the answer. Running was no option. She had to ride south. Had to reclaim what was rightfully hers. To take the crown and take her vengeance on Egil Sun no matter if it cost her life.

Adaali was the princess of Kantor, but she had never been raised as such. Rahuul had been the rightful heir, and she nothing more than his guardian. Was the crown even hers to take? Would the people of the Cordral follow her as their ruler?

'People of the Cordral be damned,' she growled to the night.

What did she care if they considered her the rightful queen, this was not their affair. Let them follow her or not, all that mattered was that she kill Egil Sun. The throne might not have been hers by right, but she had a right to avenge her mother and brother. Just let them try and stop her.

Now all she had to do was return to Kantor, kill Egil Sun and take the throne. The thought of it twisted her insides.

There was no way she could do such a thing alone, and what help did she have? A man driven mad by loneliness. How could she even begin to think she would succeed? There was little chance she would even get close. But little chance was still better than none.

She glanced over at the horse, still chewing on the brush.

'What do you think?' she asked. 'Is this madness?'

The horse didn't seem interested.

'No madder than asking a horse for answers.'

Taking the reins, she climbed up into the saddle again and rode the long path back to the town. When it was within sight she could see smoke rising up from the centre, and as she made her way through the buried streets the smell of cooking meat assailed her.

In the centre of the main square a fire had been lit in the dried-up well. Over a rusty grill, Dantar was cooking meat. It didn't take a genius to work out what kind of meat it was, and Adaali patted her horse's neck reassuringly.

The hermit didn't bother to look up from his cooking as she tethered the mount and came to stand by the well. A huge slab of haunch was slowly blackening, and the smell of it made her stomach rumble. They both stood watching the horsemeat cook, until Adaali grew tired of the silence between them, and sat in the shade of a nearby building. Dantar made no attempt to ask where she had been. It seemed curious that for someone who had spent so long alone he didn't seem to care for conversation. Adaali observed the silence for as long as she was able.

'What does the writing mean?' she said eventually.

At first he didn't answer, and she began to regret asking the question. Dantar was clearly isolated for a reason and it was likely his rantings only made sense to his troubled mind. Eventually he glanced back towards her, the iron blacksmith tongs he was using to turn the meat held loosely by his side.

'What markings?' he said.

'In the temple. The writing on the walls. The pictures. What do they mean? I know it must have been you who drew them.' Despite the man's unpredictable nature, she couldn't stop herself asking.

'They are… just reminders,' he replied.

'Reminders of what?'

He turned back to the grill. 'Of another life.'

She meant to pry further when he produced a knife from inside his rotting clothes. That was enough to quell her curiosity.

With swift sure strokes he carved some of the meat away and skewered it on the edge of the knife. She stood as he approached, wary of the weapon in his hand, but all he did was offer it to her.

'Thank you,' she said, carefully taking the knife.

She hadn't realised how hungry she was, and she tore the meat in half with her teeth, chewing swiftly and barely even tasting it. When it was gone she handed Dantar back the knife.

'Is there any water?' she asked, instantly chiding herself. He had rescued her, taken her in, fed her and here she was demanding even more.

Dantar nodded. 'There is water. But we'll have to go and collect it.'

Without another word, Dantar entered the old temple and returned with two empty goat bladders and a couple of torches. Handing one of each to Adaali, he gestured for her to follow him.

Dantar led them down one of the streets that radiated from the central square. She followed him to a ruined dwelling, the door long since rotted away. They both ducked under the lintel and Dantar led her down a flight of worn stone stairs into the dark. There he struck a flint, lighting his torch and offering Adaali the flame. A passageway led them from the cellar further into the darkness beneath the sunken town.

They followed the tunnel as it sloped further into the depths, the air growing damp as they went. Eventually it came out into a huge subterranean chamber, tunnels and tributaries running off from the cavernous interior. It was constructed from crumbling brickwork, all that remained of an ancient maze of sewers from before the Fall.

'I love what you've done with the place,' Adaali said, seeing the rows of weaponry and armour stacked against every wall. 'Very homely.'

Dantar had clearly busied himself unearthing every piece from the derelict town. The stash was more bountiful than any armoury Adaali had ever seen.

Her attention was caught by a soft noise in the distance, the sound of gentle trickling. Adaali had never appreciated the sound of running water so much in all her life. She hurried further into the cave, leaving Dantar behind as she came to a shallow stream flowing across the cave floor. Falling to her knees she dropped the torch, cupping her hands and scooping up a drink of water. It tasted awful, but she drank deep, cupping up handful after handful of the tepid liquid.

When she was done, she picked up the torch and rose to her feet. In the light of the fire she could see there were more markings on the wall. If Dantar's scrawling on the temple wall had been but a small glimpse into his thoughts then here was an epic tome writ large.

A war amongst the heavens was played out across the interior of the cave. As Adaali moved her torch she could see a story of epic battles, of titans ruling over the earth, of death and sacrifice. What was it Dantar had said of those drawings in the temple?

'Are these reminders of another life, too?' she asked, turning to see he was watching her intently.

Slowly he shook his head. 'These are a vision of what is to come,' he replied.

Adaali looked back at the wall. She couldn't tell what frightened her the most – the prospect that these were the ravings of Dantar's sick mind... or that somehow he was telling the truth. That somehow he could see what would come to pass; that the world would be consumed by an apocalyptic inferno.

She took a step back from the etchings, trying to put the images out of her mind. Dantar was on his knees now, filling one of the goat bladders from the stream. He was clearly a troubled individual, but he had shown her nothing but kindness. From his appearance, no one had shown him any.

'Maybe you could use that water for more than drinking?' she asked.

As soon as the words came out of her mouth she regretted it. How stupid. She had meant it as a friendly suggestion, but on her lips the words were simply cutting. Luckily Dantar ignored her.

Adaali knelt close to him. 'I mean we could probably both do with a wash.'

When he didn't answer she reached out a hand to him. 'I can try and repair your clothes if—'

As she touched his arm, Dantar flinched, dropping the goatskin and backing away from her touch. Adaali was shocked by his reaction – surely she was the one who should have been scared, but Dantar cowered from her touch as though it burned his flesh.

'It's all right,' she said gently. 'You can trust me.'

Dantar backed away to the wall, and Adaali approached, hands raised. He was like a wounded animal, and she had to show she meant him no harm.

'We're friends, Dantar,' she said. 'We have to help each other.'

She reached forward again, trying to lay a soothing arm on his shoulder, when he suddenly lashed out. He planted a hand in the centre of her chest, shoving her back across the cave. Adaali lost her footing, slipping on the slick ground and stumbling into a pile of stacked weapons.

As she foundered, Adaali felt the white heat of anger well up within her. Immediately she tried to quell it. Dantar had only reacted on instinct. It was her fault after all, but the white-hot rage welling up within her would not abate. It rose, consuming her as she got to her feet, hand moving of its own accord to grasp a spear stacked against the wall. Her eyes were focused as though Dantar stood at the end of a tunnel shrouded in red. He was all she could see as she aimed, pulling her arm back to launch the weapon at his heart.

At the last moment her sense won out over the rage.

A crack echoed through the cave as the spear hit the wall beside Dantar's head, shattering along its length. As Adaali stood shocked it was Dantar's turn to move, as he too grasped a spear. She wanted to dodge, or to cross the distance between them and stop his throw, but instead she stood transfixed. Was she frozen? Or did she merely want to stand and wait – to let him throw that spear and impale her where she stood?

Dantar's throw was fluid, his form perfect. He did not miss.

Adaali stood stock still as the spear skewered the ground between her legs. The two of them stood for some moments, the only noise their breathing and the gentle trickle of the stream. They were like two wounded animals facing one another, too injured to fight, too proud to back down.

Then Adaali began to laugh. It echoed through the cave, growing more shrill. She dropped to her knees, unable to stop laughing, as though she had been told some cosmic joke, the secret of the universe finally revealed and it was the most hilarious thing she had ever heard.

The laugh turned into a sob, her chest heaving, and her heart felt like it would burst as she began to weep onto the dark earth. Her grief poured out until she felt Dantar lay his hand gently on her shoulder.

Looking up she saw sympathy in his dark eyes.

'Will you teach me?' she asked. 'Will you show me how to fight? How to control my rage?'

'Why?'

'Because I have to kill a man,' she replied.

Dantar did not take long to consider it. 'Yes. I can do that.'

12

*E*VERY *facet of the cracked and broken Heartstone was alive with a different image. Durius watched them all, seeing and feeling everything at once in a chorus of violent imagery. The sights and sounds of the battle were alive in his head, filling his senses as though he were among the thick of it. He could smell the stink of blood, feel the sting of every sword blade, sense the grief at every death, and at the summit of the Blue Tower he knew his fellow Archons could feel it too.*

It was eerily quiet as they all stood and viewed the carnage. Mortana watched with rapt interest, still cradling the tiny goat-like form of Armadon, who was asleep in her arms. Badb looked down from the rafters with those black eyes, crow wings folded around her armoured body. Hastor and Ekemon stood side by side, the burning king impassive in his molten armour. The rheumy eyes of old Hastor watched, a tear rolling from the corner of one to make its way down the haggard landscape of his face.

Durius took a step back, averting his gaze from the Heartstone despite the dramatic scenes playing out within. Instead he watched the gathered gods, trying to work out what they were thinking. Some of them would want an end to this, some to throw themselves into the fray. Who was who would become clear soon enough, and Durius did not have to wait long until the first of them revealed his real feelings.

'We must go,' said Kastion, his red eyes glaring from that beautiful porcelain face. 'Look what is happening. Our sister, Siff, is weak. It won't be long before she perishes and only Innellan is left. There is no time to waste, we have to go through.'

'No,' Durius replied. 'We have to let this play out. We have to give Siff a chance.'

Kastion regarded him with a look of contempt. 'The longer she refuses the worship of mortals the weaker she becomes. Then what? We let these apes decide the winner? Our fate is to be chosen by mortals?'

'If that is what it takes—'

'No!' Kastion's voice boomed, destroying the tranquillity of the tower. 'By our inaction we are gifting that realm to Innellan. Soon there will be no one to stand against her. Soon she will rule the mortal plane unchallenged. We must enter and level the playing field.'

'And that is the only reason you would enter?' Durius asked. 'To level the playing field?'

'What other reason is there? We all agreed to the covenant. But it has been broken now. We have no choice but to—'

'But to help Siff. And we do that by giving her more time.'

'She is beaten,' Kastion gestured a slender arm at the Heartstone. 'Anyone can see that. Were I to enter I could win this war for her.'

'And then what?' Durius asked. 'You would return Innellan to us and destroy the Heartstone behind you, I suppose?'

Kastion stared at Durius. It was obvious his true intentions had been found out and his hesitation spoke louder than any of his words. 'I am bound by the covenant, as are we all.'

'I'm sure,' Durius replied.

Kastion scowled. 'You doubt me?' he snarled. It was just the *reaction Durius had expected from his impassioned brother.*

'Enough,' said Mortana, walking forward to stand between them. 'Durius is right, we must give Siff more time.' Armadon stirred in her arms, whining at the arguing voices.

'The more time we waste, the more powerful Innellan becomes,' Kastion said. 'Soon she will control the whole realm, and then where are we? It will be impossible to remove her. She will control the mortal plane like a tyrant and we will be powerless to stop her. Reduced to wallowing here like animals in a cage while she rules like an empress.'

Durius could see his brother Kastion was spellbound by the Heartstone, his desire overcoming his reason. 'But Siff has won the battle,' he pointed out. 'She has routed Innellan's forces.'

'And at what cost?' Kastion snapped, gesturing to the Heartstone and the scene playing out on its myriad facets. 'The dead have been piled high on both sides, but Siff's alliance of crusaders is now dwindling.' He turned, glaring up at the roofbeams. 'Badb, you must see the sense in this? Join me. And you, Ekemon. We can waste no time. Let us pass through before it is too late. Let us lay claim to at least a portion of the mortal realm before Innellan consumes every league of it.'

Badb cawed from her perch and Ekemon made a furtive glance at Hastor before taking a tentative step towards the Heartstone.

'No,' said the wizened figure of Hastor. 'We must not act rashly. The prudent thing to do is wait. Siff is the victor, the momentum is with her.'

'See,' said Durius, trying to quell his panic. 'Hastor the Wise is with me. We have to wait. Give Siff the time she needs.'

'And what about my time?' Kastion cried, his white angel's face twisting into an ugly parody of its former beauty. 'I have been caged here for centuries. Forbidden from claiming what is rightfully mine. And for what? To save the lives of apes? This is my destiny, none of you have the right to stand in the way of it. You think I should just accept my fate while Siff and Innellan tread the lands of men, their power growing? You cannot deny my right, none of you.'

Durius stepped in front of his brother and Kastion stared at him with those baleful red eyes. For the first time in an aeon, Durius felt fear, but he could not back down now. It was to his relief that Mortana stepped up beside him.

'I suggest you cool your temper, brother,' she said to him. 'We all agreed to the covenant. Innellan has broken that pact. She is guilty of apostasy. Would you want to be found guilty of that crime? To be an outcast?'

Durius could see Kastion's rage bubbling beneath the surface. 'I will have what is mine,' said the seraph. 'None of you will stand in my way. When I return I will be at the head of an army. Should any of you try to stop us you will be destroyed.'

Before anyone could answer, Kastion took to the wing, sweeping from the tower and into the dark skies that surrounded it.

The silence was broken by another deafening caw from Badb, who also spread her wings and took flight. Before she was gone from sight there was a crackle of superheated metal and Durius felt molten heat emanate from Ekemon before he burned like a forge fire, disappearing in a billow of acrid black smoke.

'I think their feelings are pretty clear,' he said.

Neither Mortana nor Hastor answered him as they glared from the tower into the distance.

'So what now?' Durius asked.

'Perhaps we should gather our own forces,' said Mortana. 'If the others are about to return at the head of a horde we cannot stop them alone.'

Hastor nodded his agreement. 'That would be a wise response. We must protect the Heartstone at all costs.'

'Even if it means war?' Durius said. The prospect filled him with dread, not least because he was the only one of their number without an army. 'Think on the slaughter. The deaths. Perhaps we should have more faith in our sister.'

Mortana looked to Hastor, who in turn stared into the Heartstone. They could see the wounded being treated, the dead being burned, and through it all Siff's army was still in good spirits after its victory. Their sister was gravely wounded however, still refusing to succumb to the temptation of worship.

Hastor gave a long, wheezing sigh. 'Durius is right. We should give her time. We all put our faith in Siff's wisdom before. We should do so again. She will do her utmost to end this.'

'And if her utmost is not good enough?' asked Mortana.

'We must hope that it is,' Hastor replied. 'Time is our ally. Let us hope it does not run out before Kastion and the others return in force. For then, war is inevitable.'

Mortana's expression darkened as she regarded the events in the mortal realm. Armadon reached up a stubby arm and tugged on one of her braids and this time her patience was done. She pulled his childlike arm away from her hair then cast him aside. The embryonic form hit the marble floor with a thud, but rather than mewl in protest Armadon crawled off to one corner. Durius could see his brother begin to commit some obscene act upon himself and quickly looked away.

133

There was a cry of pain from the other side of the tower, and Durius turned to see Hera curled into a ball by the stairs. Her eyes were closed tight and her teeth gritted against the agony that wracked her body. He approached, kneeling down beside her. Now more than ever, he should not have concerned himself with the suffering of a single mortal, but he had to admit the woman had grown on him over the past days. She was brave, stalwart, her current suffering was no fault of her own. Hera had been caught up in a wicked game played over millennia – its latest victim.

Siff had taken her body, and now Hera was feeling every wound the Archon suffered in the mortal realm. As soon as Siff's crusade was over and she returned to the Blue Tower, Hera would simply cease to exist. It would be a cruel end, one that even Durius could not help but regret.

'The pain will pass,' he whispered gently, laying a hand on her arm.

If she heard his lie she did not answer. He knew the pain would not abate. If Siff chose not to accept the worship of her followers, and if her wounds continued to fester, then Hera would suffer like this until her end.

Hera's eyes suddenly opened and she stared at Durius with frightening clarity. Reaching out she grabbed his shirt, pulling him close. 'End it,' she whispered. 'Please end it now. I cannot stand this agony. I cannot do it myself. Send me after Mandrake, let me follow my lover, I beg you.'

Durius tried to muster a look of sympathy.

'This will be over soon,' he whispered.

That did little to placate Hera, who closed her eyes once more trying to shut out the pain.

Durius stood, leaving her to the torture. There was nothing else he could do for her. Hera's only hope was that Siff could act quickly and defeat Innellan. Because if she failed, it would not only be Hera who suffered.

13

THEIR staffs clacked together in a rhythmic beat and it was all Adaali could do to parry the incoming blows. Dantar was far faster than Musir Dragosh, that much was obvious, but where her old weapon master had always seemed to be pushing her to her limit, she couldn't help but think Dantar was holding back.

They repeated their drills over and over – a blisteringly fast sequence of thrusts, dodges, swings and parries. Adaali had mastered each one quicker than she would ever have thought possible, even learning the names of the unusual stances Dantar taught her – the Mantis, Spider and Scorpion.

In turn, Adaali felt she was having something of a rejuvenating effect on her tutor... or perhaps it was just his newfound joy for tutelage. Either way, she had finally managed to persuade him to crop his filthy matted mop of hair and beard. Clean shaven, Dantar somehow managed to look even more like a wolf. His sharp, lupine features were handsome, his whole demeanour much more youthful. He was a far cry from the mad hermit who had saved her life.

They stood at the top of a dune as they practised, nothing but open desert surrounding them, no distractions, no interference. Their training had been the same for the past few days, though this time it was different. Always they had carried sticks, but today Dantar had ordered her to bring a large bundle. Adaali guessed from its weight and feel it was a bale of weapons, and as they practised the stick-drill she found herself furtively glancing to where it lay, hoping they would soon move on to the real thing.

Eventually Dantar ordered her to stop, and no sooner had he gestured to the waiting bundle than she fell upon it like a hunting hawk, opening the haul of weapons.

'Swords,' said Dantar, before she could even think about reaching for a spear.

Obediently, Adaali picked up two blades, handing one to Dantar.

As they squared off she felt some trepidation. She had seen how good he was, and in all her previous training she had fought with dull-edged weapons. Now she was fighting with a real sword, feeling the weight of it in her hand, the danger.

As though sensing her reluctance Dantar said, 'I won't hurt you.'

Adaali felt annoyed. 'As if you could,' she replied, stepping back to adopt the Mantis stance with wide bent legs, blade pointing down.

Dantar gave nothing away as he gracefully slid into the Scorpion, legs square, sword in the air pointed at her heart. And there they stood as the sun beat down, neither moving. She did not want to be the first to attack, the first to give away their intention. Adaali began to think this a test of patience the longer it went on, the heavy blade beginning to weigh on her as she squinted in the bright daylight.

Eventually she succumbed to her impatience, and rather than retreat and recover, she rushed in, yelling for all she was worth, forgetting everything Dragosh and Dantar had taught her about messaging your intentions to the enemy.

With a single ring of steel Dantar disarmed her, flicking out his foot and tripping her to boot. As Adaali went sprawling in the sand she growled in anger, but resisted the temptation to pound the dirt with her fist.

'If I had a spear you would not have such an easy time of it,' Adaali said as she stood, and retrieved her sword from the sand.

'Take your pick,' Dantar replied, casually gesturing to the collection of weapons lying on the ground.

As she stomped towards the weapons she tried to calm herself. Adaali knew that if she let her emotions lead her she would always fail. She had to keep control of her anger, not let it control her.

She placed the sword down and took one of the spears. It was reassuring in her hand, despite being several ounces too heavy at the head. Still, she would make for a much more formidable opponent with an unbalanced spear than a perfectly weighted sword any day.

Facing him, she decided to ignore the drills and stances Dantar had taught. Instead she adopted one of the positions she had learned from Dragosh in those long endless sessions in the training yard. The Desert Blades were peerless weapon masters, their knowledge of the spear as extensive as any blade, and now she had the added advantage of reach.

This time Adaali didn't wait, didn't stand for endless moments in a game of who-moves-first. She struck as Dantar squatted down into Spider pose, his blade held in two hands, pointed at the ground.

The first thrust he dodged easily with an almost imperceptible drop of his shoulder. Adaali pulled the spear back and thrust again, this time Dantar parried. Before he could counter, she danced away across the sand, but he merely stood, waiting for her to attack.

Slowly she circled him, expecting the warrior to turn and track her movement. Instead, Dantar remained still as she moved to his rear, not even looking at her. He was exposed, vulnerable.

Well, damn him – if he was going to be so bloody stupid...

She thrust the spear towards his broad back. Dantar span, blade flashing in the sun, hacking off the tip of the spear and sending it spinning away. Adaali was left standing with nothing but a useless stick in her hand.

'It's been a while,' Dantar said. 'I wasn't sure if I still had the speed.'

'I'm glad to have helped allay your doubts,' Adaali replied, throwing the useless stick over her shoulder in frustration. 'I think that's enough for now, don't you?'

'As you wish.' Dantar shrugged.

Had this been Dragosh he would not have relented until Adaali was a sweating quivering mess. But Dantar was different; it didn't seem to matter to him one way or the other whether she learned or not.

Once they had gathered the weapons into the bundle

and made their way towards the town, Adaali began to feel regret. It had been she who had asked for Dantar's help, and now she was squandering what he might teach her. She had vowed revenge, and here she was, giving in at the first sign of frustration. But surely that was only natural? She yearned for vengeance, and practising for days in the desert with what amounted to a stranger wouldn't achieve that. Or would it?

She looked at Dantar, not for the first time wondering who he was, and how he had learned his peerless talents with a blade. Surely it had to be worth knowing?

'Who were you?' she asked as they walked.

Dantar did not turn to look at her. 'Who was I? That seems a curious question.'

'You haven't always been a man of the desert. Wild nomads don't learn such skills from desert foxes. So who did you used to be?'

'What does it matter who I was? Surely all that matters is who I am now.'

That didn't help at all. For all that Dantar's past was a mystery, Adaali had little idea of who he was in the present.

'You have the pale complexion of a Suderfelder. But your hair is dark like a northerner. Perhaps a mix of the two?'

Dantar almost imperceptibly shook his head.

Adaali persisted: 'You don't know or you don't want to tell me? If you don't know that means you must have been an orphan. Now, we are getting somewhere.'

Dantar stopped and turned on her, regarding her with cold dark eyes. 'Your curiosity might one day bite you like a snake,' he said.

Adaali realised she had gone too far. 'I'm sorry,' she replied. 'I just wanted to know who you are.'

'I don't know who you are,' he replied. 'And yet I don't badger you with questions. I assume that if you wish to tell me, then you will.'

'What are you so afraid of—'

'Very well. See that tree over there.' He pointed to the east. Adaali squinted, seeing a dried-up tree stump protruding from the desert. 'Hit the target and I will tell you all you want to know.' He pulled a spear from the bundle and handed it to her.

As she held the spear Adaali regretted raising the subject, but she had waded in up to her neck now and the only solution was to wade back out again. The tree stump looked too far away, but if she had learned one thing over the last few days it was not to underestimate herself or what she could overcome.

Drawing back the spear, she focused. The image of the stump was painted in her mind and she visualised the spear hitting it dead centre, splitting the wood asunder. Adaali held her breath as she pulled back her arm, then let fly. As she released the weapon she gave a cry of exertion. The spear flew true, and she counted two heartbeats as it soared through the air… and hit the ground five feet from the target.

'Close,' said Dantar.

It was nowhere near close.

'Very well,' said Adaali. 'Keep your secrets if you wish.'

'I might,' he replied. 'But it's obvious you won't. So tell me, Adaali of the south. Why have you come here? What are you running from?'

'That was not part of the bargain,' she said, turning back towards the south.

'What are you so afraid of?' he replied.

'My mother and brother were murdered,' she snarled, all the pent-up grief spitting forth with venom.

Dantar was unmoved. 'It is obvious you have suffered loss. So that is why you would have me help you take revenge?'

'That was not all I lost.' And she continued, telling Dantar, this stranger in the desert, who she was, who her mother was, her brother, how she had been raised as his protector and how she had failed in that one solemn duty. She told him of Egil Sun, of the southern envoys, of the night of treachery. In the telling the tale became more real, burning itself into her mind. Rather than purge her rage it stoked the fire within her, until by the end she stood before Dantar barely able to control herself. She no longer trembled with grief but with fury.

'You are the princess of Kantor?' Dantar said, if only to break the silence.

This she had expected. What now? Would he try and gain some kind of leverage? Would he try to take her back south, to gain some reward now he knew the truth?

'I am,' she replied, as though daring him to try.

Dantar nodded, then turned away and continued back towards his home.

'Wait,' she said, hurrying after him. 'Did you not hear what I told you? Do you not care?'

He shrugged. 'What difference does it make?'

She thought on that. The throne of Kantor was lost to

usurpers. In reality, she was no longer a princess, but a lost child in the desert. She was no one. 'None, I suppose.'

'There you are, then.'

They carried on, and Adaali began to wonder if Dantar really was as ambivalent as he seemed.

'So will you still help me? Even though you know the truth?'

'I can teach you to fight,' he replied.

'And what about helping me reclaim what is mine? Once I am strong enough, will you come with me to Kantor? Will you help me kill Egil Sun? Will you help me retake the throne?'

He shook his head. 'That would be foolish. For both of us. The pursuit of justice is a noble errand, but this would be futile. I could train you for a thousand years but you will still not succeed.'

'You don't understand,' she snapped. 'Did you not hear a word I said? They murdered my mother. My little brother.'

He stopped, turning to face her. 'I know loss,' he said, those dark eyes of his looking sullen for the first time. 'I had many brothers once. One of them I held most dear, though I never let him know the truth of it. We grew up together, suffered much side by side. What we shared no one else could ever understand, and he too died as I watched. He told me one thing before he took the eternal sleep. *Do not be a slave to your past.* The path to vengeance is a road to prison, Adaali. Do not let your thirst for revenge put you in a cage.'

Adaali knew she should have been sympathetic. Dantar was opening up to her, it was what she had asked of him, but all it did was anger her further.

'I am not so pathetic,' she spat. 'What do you think I should do? Hide in the desert like you? Run from my past? Become a mad hermit? I will not hide from the world. And I will not rest until I have slain the bastard who took everything from me.'

She stormed away, leaving Dantar behind. Her walk turned to a run and she sped along the path back to the deserted town. When she reached it she was quite breathless. Night was falling, and rather than head back to Dantar's temple, she found another empty shell to sleep in.

As she lay in the dark she was too angry, too bitter to weep any more. But the fury that raged within did not stop her drifting off to sleep...

She was hunting.

The palace burned around her, the heat of it was intense as she ran through the corridors. Tapestries and curtains blazed, the floor was hot beneath her feet, but she would not be stopped.

A figure appeared in her path, his robe smouldering, curved blade flashing. Adaali ducked the blow, spinning the spear in her grip, striking fast and true. As she impaled her attacker there was a shriek and the robes dissolved to nothing.

She ran on. Still determined to finish the hunt, teeth clamped in a rictus grin, eyes wide despite the heat and smoke. She could smell him, that stink of perfume to hide the rot, he was close, the aura of fear that surrounded him almost palpable.

Leaping through a wall of flames she found him kneeling at the centre of a burning chamber, his robed acolytes surrounding him.

Tears ran down his hollow cheeks, bony hands clamped tightly as he prayed for mercy. But she had no mercy left.

The dark-robed guardians raced to intercept her, swords flashing as they moved with expert precision.

They were no match for her.

The spear moved in her grip as though guided by a divine source, piercing the robes, sending each one back to the hell from which it was spawned. As the fire burned brighter around her, the last of them collapsed to the ground and she was finally alone with the praying figure.

He opened mournful eyes as she approached. They pleaded for clemency, but if he thought she would show any mercy he was looking in the wrong place. Her thrust was swift and true. She stared down at his corpse, watching as it turned to ash, drifting away on the hot air. If she had expected there to be some kind of revelation, some kind of epiphany at the end of the hunt, she was sorely mistaken. Instead, she heard the resonant tread of heavy footfalls.

She retreated to the centre of the room, feeling an oppressive sense of foreboding. From beyond the flames came a huge armoured figure – a behemoth in gold – huge sword resting over one mighty shoulder.

The flames shied away from the warrior as he walked through the wall of fire. He took a mammoth step towards her, raising the sword high. She ducked, darting below the arc of the blow, jabbing at the behemoth with her spear, but the weapon glanced off his impenetrable armour.

He swung again, and this time she leapt over the blade, landing deftly, jabbing in. Another swipe of the blade, another skilful evasion, but this time she had spotted a weakness – below the armpit a narrow gap, just large enough to exploit.

She stood tall as the warrior laboured to raise his sword high. Before he could bring it down she darted to the right, thrusting the spear into his chest, pushing for all she was worth.

Silently the armoured warrior staggered, the sword falling from his grip before he toppled backwards. There was the sound of a tree being felled as the warrior hit the ground, his helmet rolling clear. She leapt up into his chest, staring down in victory, but the face that glared back at her was no enemy.

Musir Dragosh looked on with accusing eyes. Horror filled her when she realised she had slain her mentor. As the room collapsed in flames around her she tried to cry out in anguish, but made no sound.

Her eyes flicked open. Daylight encroached on the dilapidated hovel, but still she felt tired. And she was famished to her core.

The morning sun was bright as Adaali made her way to the centre of the town. She had hoped to see Dantar cooking more meat on his grill when she arrived, but instead she found him waiting patiently for her.

'What's for breakfast?' she asked.

'First we practise,' he replied.

'No. I am half starved. First we eat, then we practise.'

'You eat when you have earned it,' Dantar said, motioning to the bundle of weapons.

'No,' she snapped. 'I've had enough. This place stinks. You refuse to help me and all the while Egil Sun tightens his grip on the throne of Kantor. All-Mother knows what he could be doing, how my people are suffering. I need to return before they forget who I am.'

'I would advise against it.'

'Advise all you want,' she yelled. 'I will take one of the remaining horses. You can have the other. Consider it a parting gift.'

'You are not ready for this.'

She stopped, glaring at him, her hands balling into fists. 'Who are you to tell me whether I am ready? A madman in the desert. A crazy hermit lost to the wilds. Why should I take any notice of anything you say?'

'Because you know I am right,' he replied. That much she couldn't argue with. Adaali was not ready but neither did she care. 'But perhaps you can show I am wrong.'

'How?' she replied, determined to prove as much to him, as to herself.

'Take a weapon,' he said, rolling out the bundle and showing her the selection of spears, swords and axes. 'Take it to the far reaches of the town. Then hunt me down before I find you.'

She considered it, the desire to show him how wrong he was almost burning her up inside. 'You have the advantage. This is your territory.'

'And Egil Sun will have the advantage, he controls Kantor. I never said this would be easy.'

'Very well,' she said, taking a spear from the bundle. 'I will find you.'

With that she made her way from the centre of the town. A quick glance over her shoulder as she went and Dantar had already disappeared. Once at the edge of town she turned, looking back at the maze of derelict buildings. Dantar could be anywhere, but she was sure she would be able to track one madman. Dragosh had taught her how to use stealth, how to go unseen, how to track an enemy. And Dantar was but one man.

Sticking close to the buildings, Adaali made her way back along the streets. It was eerily silent, a slight breeze blowing through the crumbling masonry. Every now and again she would stop, listening intently, peering into every shadow, probing for the merest sign. Each time there was nothing.

Eventually she made her way back to the well at the middle of town, staying close to the side of the building, spear held tight in her grip. Five streets radiated from the centre – which one should she choose? Looking at the ground she could see tracks from earlier. Dantar's were obvious, his larger feet giving him away. From the freshness of the sign, she tried to guess which street he had moved along, but it appeared he had not made his way along any. Instead he had entered a building overlooking the well.

Adaali darted across the open to the base of the building. Her stomach fluttered, whether with hunger or excitement she couldn't tell. She tried to keep her breathing shallow and even as she peered in through the open archway. The ground floor was littered with debris. Broken furniture and ornaments lay all about, giving the interior the eerie look of a looted sepulchre.

Holding her breath, she entered, carefully placing each step lest she crush something beneath her foot and give herself away. Everything was aslant, the house having listed to the side as it was gradually consumed by the sands, and Adaali was at pains to keep her footing. She managed to reach the base of the stairs without making a sound. Glancing up a sandy slope to the second floor, she could see no sign of Dantar, but as she began to make her way up she noted a single footprint in the dirt.

Gripping her spear tighter, she crept upwards, peering over the lip of the banister. There, hunched just below the window, was the worn tunic he always wore. Dantar was unmoving, as though he were asleep, and Adaali was at pains to hold back her excitement. Steeping out onto the floor she crept forward, stalking like a lion, reaching out with the tip of her spear. Ever so gently she prodded the figure... only to find it was nothing but an empty tunic laid over a pile of sacks.

She felt cold steel pressed against her throat. Looking to her left she saw Dantar, stripped to the waist, naked blade in his hand.

'I told you that you weren't ready,' he said. 'If you cannot even hunt down one mad hermit in the desert, what hope do you have of returning to Kantor and killing your enemy?'

Adaali flung the spear down in frustration, pushing the blade away from her neck, and stormed out of the dilapidated building. She'd had enough of tests, enough of humiliation. She was going to climb on a horse and ride south and the consequences be damned.

'They will kill you,' Dantar called after her. 'And we had a deal, remember?'

There was no reproach in his voice, just quiet certainty, but still it served to infuriate her. 'I don't care what you think,' she said, stopping in her tracks. When she turned he was standing right behind her. 'I don't care about you, or about deals. I only have one promise to keep. And I intend to honour it.'

'Don't be a fool,' he said, laying a gentle arm on her shoulder.

She shrugged him away. 'Don't touch me.'

He reached out, this time gripping her arm tightly. 'I won't let you die. I won't let you sacrifice yourself for nothing.'

She knew he simply wanted to keep her from harm. But Adaali did not care any more, the need for vengeance was eating her from the inside like some parasite. She struggled against his grip, feeling it tighten on her arm.

'Let go,' she snarled. She would have her revenge and Dantar would not stand in the way of it.

Adaali reached out a hand, placed it in the centre of Dantar's chest, feeling the energy build up between them. Power welled up in her palm before he was flung back across the square.

She stood watching, mind still writhing in a fury, as Dantar struggled to find his feet. He glared back at her, and despite the power she had wielded he showed no fear.

Gradually the heat of anger subsided within her, and Adaali sagged. It was as though all the strength had been suddenly wrenched from her being and she no longer felt powerful, but weaker than a child.

'What is happening to me?' she asked, as Dantar knelt beside her.

'Is this the first time this has happened?' he asked.

'Yes. But I have felt the power before, only... only in dreams,' she replied. 'I have dreamt of it for weeks now. But I never meant to...'

'I know,' Dantar said, and he held her close. It was a

strange feeling to have the taciturn hermit show such concern, affection even.

'I don't understand,' she whispered.

'I have seen such power before. The gods have returned, Adaali of Kantor. And it seems they may have bestowed a blessing on you.'

'Then why don't I feel blessed?'

For the first time she saw a smile creep onto Dantar's face. 'The gods are a strange breed indeed.'

'I can feel it,' she replied. 'Inside me. There is something inside that is not... me. It is not natural.'

'Something malevolent?' he said.

Adaali could understand little of what burned within, but she knew one thing – it meant her no harm.

'No.' She struggled to stand and he helped her to her feet. 'Whatever this power is, it does not want to hurt me. It just feels strange, that's all. An alien thing inside.'

'Strange?' said Dantar, looking south, beyond the edge of the town. 'Any stranger than a girl riding to take on the might of a city?'

'I'm sorry,' she said, suddenly ashamed. 'You were right. It was stupid of me to insist on riding south.'

'Perhaps not. A power has returned to these lands. One not seen for over a century. And it is clear you can wield it. It lives within you, Adaali. Maybe taking on the might of Kantor is not such a foolish idea after all.'

'Do you mean that?'

Dantar turned his head and peered north. 'I once saw a girl not much older than you command an army to its knees

151

with but a word. She had spirit, just like you. If anyone could succeed at this, then you can.'

'And will you come with me?' she said without thinking.

He didn't take long to consider it. 'I would be nowhere else,' Dantar said. 'For too long I have been a slave to my past. The least I can do is help release you from yours.'

Adaali smiled back at the hermit. 'I'll saddle those horses.'

14

H<small>E'D</small> lost count of the days. Being locked in the back of a solid wagon, buffeted around like cargo for endless miles does that to a man. Not that Josten cared about the confusion, it was the thirst that was driving him insane. His throat was parched, his stomach long since emptied, and the only relief he'd had was the occasional cup of stinking water handed to him through a hatch.

The wagon had rarely stopped moving. On one occasion they had stopped, he'd been set upon by a handful of cultists, thinking they might beat him to death in the back of that wagon. Instead they'd snapped the end off the arrow in his leg and pulled it out, before treating it with some foul-smelling unguent. They'd bound it neatly enough before leaving him alone. Clearly they wanted to keep him alive for the journey.

All the while he had been forced to endure the baking hot sun or the freezing cold of night. There was no in between. Sleep had become a stranger, and he was beginning to think they were going around in circles.

When the wagon finally came to a stop, he felt cold dread clawing at his insides. This was it. There was nothing good waiting for him when they unlocked those doors, that much was obvious. Bit of torture for sure, and if he was lucky the execution would be quick. Despite the way he felt – dry as a bone and weak as a kitten – there was no way he'd go out without giving them a show.

A key in the lock. Josten managed to get himself in a crouching position, waiting for the door to open. His hands were tied behind his back but he could still do some damage with his head and his teeth. A decent kick to the bollocks might inconvenience one of these bastards at least. Anything to show them his mettle before they went at him with burning tongs and flaying tools.

The wagon door swung wide. It was night, but there was light from a few torches. Enough to see by – enough to kill by.

Josten rushed out, leaping from the back of the wagon with a holler, but days cramped up in there and the wound in his thigh had done him no good. Rather than jumping into the midst of the enemy he landed in a crumpled heap, his shoulder hitting the stone paving hard. And there he lay like a sack of steaming shite as the guards surrounding him looked down curiously. Anywhere else and he'd have been greeted by raucous laughter, men taking the piss at his misfortune, but not here. The Ramadi bred a different kind of fighting man altogether.

As he was pulled to his unsteady feet, Josten had a chance to look around. He was in unfamiliar surroundings. This was a city, but the dry air told him he was still in the desert. In the torchlight he could make out dark, ominous buildings surrounding him, but these were dwarfed by a huge tower looming over them. Josten barely had a chance to take it all in before he was bundled along the street towards it.

The closer they came, the more terrifying that tower looked. He realised it was time to stop admiring the place and start working out how to get himself out of this.

As they dragged him inside and down to the cells, Josten got a good look at the men who held him. These weren't the wild-eyed fanatics he'd fought back at the quarry – these were warriors he recognised, warriors he'd fought before. Back in Kessel he'd faced these red-clad soldiers by the thousand and here he was in their clutches again. Just his luck.

On hearing the squeaking hinges of a cell door, Josten knew he was home at last.

'What time's dinner?' he managed to croak, just before they threw him inside.

He had to admit, he'd been caged in better cells. This one didn't have a bed, a window or anywhere to shit. Not that shitting would be a problem since his belly had been empty for days. So he did what any normal man would do in the situation. He sat against the wall and waited to die.

There was no customary length of time to leave a prisoner rotting before you questioned him, so it came as something of a surprise when he'd barely shut his eyes, before keys jangled in the lock and the door was heaved open. A robed figure entered, pulling back his hood to reveal a face Josten recognised. Around his right eye was a serpent tattoo and he had one of those expressions the nobility normally wore – that simpering superiority you just wanted to smack off their face.

'You remember who I am?' asked the man.

'It's coming back to me,' Josten replied. 'You were at Kessel, when High Lord Kraden led the attack. Only it seemed to me at the time you were running the show. Was I right?'

'Let's just say you weren't entirely wrong.' The man moved forward, producing a goat bladder full of water from his robe and pressing it to Josten's lips. He drank as deep as he could before the man backed away.

'I am Byram,' he said.

'Josten Cade.'

Byram nodded, staring with cold empty eyes. 'I know who you are. A slave of the Archon Siff.'

'I don't know who that is, but I'm nobody's slave,' Josten answered.

'I think you know her as Silver. And of course you believe you have free will, the same as anyone. And I, in my turn, am no slave of Innellan.'

'Fuck that. You're all slaves to that bitch.'

Byram nodded his agreement. 'I suppose in our way we are. As you soon will be.'

There was no malice or threat to his words, just a statement of cold hard fact. Josten determined that even though he was a prisoner, he would never become in thrall to her.

'I won't kneel,' he said.

'They all believe that,' Byram said. 'But you will. In the end we all kneel before the White Widow or we perish. No one can stand against her. Your fate is sealed – if you accept it, your pain will be less before the end.'

Guards entered the cell before Josten could argue further.

They bundled him along the corridor. Still bound as he was, Josten could do little to stop them. Byram followed behind as he was half dragged, half carried up through the tower. The staircase seemed endless as he made his way up, until finally they reached the summit.

A huge chamber awaited. Through a vast window he could see the sun rising over the distant desert. Byram lurked in one shadowy corner, as though he feared drawing attention to himself. There was a sweet smell coming from somewhere that reminded Josten of the flowers they used to disguise the stench of corpses. Then he saw her.

She was smiling as she made her way from the shadows. It was a face he recognised, but much changed over the past year. Livia Harrow had smiled with those eyes, that genuine kind-hearted expression innocent girls often bore. This was most definitely not her; Innellan was no innocent.

'The prisoner,' she said, moving closer.

Josten lost his breath. In any other place, with any other captor he might have thought about saying something clever. Not now. There was nothing clever to say in the face of this.

Innellan ran a finger down the side of his face then looked closely at it, rubbing it against her thumb to clean away the dirt. 'You are one of her most prized,' she said. It was not a question. 'One of her most trusted. And soon you will be one of mine.'

'Not fucking likely,' he managed to say through gritted teeth. Just being close to her was making him tremble. He could feel the power emanating from her, and he fought the urge to satisfy her every whim. It took all his will to resist falling to the floor and licking her feet.

'Crude. Curious that she would take someone so base into her confidence. But of course you must keep that edge of irreverence – it will help with the subterfuge.'

'What are you talking about?' Josten asked.

Innellan laughed and it tinkled like a stream that would drown anyone who dared brave its waters.

'You are mine now. There is no question of that. You will be my tool. My blade in the night, and you will do it willingly.' She spoke matter-of-factly.

'Never,' Josten growled. 'But give me a knife and I'll be happy to introduce you to it.'

She laughed again as she walked around him, running her fingers through his matted hair. It was as though someone were tearing at his brain with a white-hot blade. Josten could feel his mind about to collapse beneath her ministrations, but just before he was reduced to a blubbering wreck she lifted her hand.

'You think me cruel, Josten Cade?' Innellan said.

'It had crossed my mind,' he gasped.

'And you think her good and kind and virtuous?'

'Silver? I know she's not evil. I know I'd follow her wherever she wanted me to go.'

Innellan laughed, but this time it was booming, almost loud enough to shatter Josten's ears. 'You have no idea the aeons we have lived, the things we have seen... and done. Every one of us has experienced a myriad ages and we have all been cruel and kind, benevolent and malicious. There was a time I was a nurturing empress and my lands were bountiful. There was a time *she* ruled like a tyrant.'

'I don't believe you,' Josten said.

'I could show you. But even then you wouldn't believe it. So let me show you something else, Josten Cade. Let me show you the reward that awaits if you abandon her and follow me.'

She reached forward with claw-like fingers. Josten just had time to scream before that talon grasped his face...

He rode a dappled horse. Its barding shone in the bright sunlight as he trotted through the trees, while summer blossom fell all around, adorning his golden armour with petals of every colour. Behind him was an army riding triumphant, returning home to celebrate their great victory.

There was a cacophony in his ears, cheering as they rode the main thoroughfare of the city... his city. The crown upon his head was light, the burnished metal fitting his brow as though it belonged there. He was adored, the streets lined with the joyous throng. Every man looked upon him with respect – all his past sins were expunged, all his iniquities forgotten.

The scene twisted before his eyes, his stomach lurching as he was transported to a vast summer villa, a veranda looking out to a clear blue sea lapping against the coast. The sun was bright but he was in the shade of verdant wisteria threaded through an intricately carved awning. He felt fulfilled, rested. There was no weight on his shoulders as he looked to a woman standing looking out to sea. Her back was to him, hair dark and blowing gently in the sea breeze.

Before he could step towards her there was laughter, high and innocent and untouched by malice. Looking down he saw two children frolicking on the veranda. His children. The children he'd never had.

It brought a smile to his face, filling his heart with uncompromising love. A sensation he'd never experienced.

Something tried to pull him away but he resisted. Steely hands tried to grip him, to pull him out of this vision, but Josten would not be swayed – this was his deepest fantasy, his yearning, and he would not be robbed of it.

He took a step forward, reaching out to his bride, yearning to touch her soft skin, to hold her close, to kiss her gently as their children played about them.

Again he felt himself being torn from the vision, but he refused to be swayed. This was all he wanted, all he had dreamed of, and he would live out his desire for as long as he was able.

The woman turned. Livia Harrow smiled at him, and he smiled back. She reached out, brushing his cheek with her fingertips, and he felt his skin tingle at her touch. In turn, Josten reached out, wanting to lose himself in her embrace…

'Enough!' Innellan's scream echoed in his ears. 'Not her. You will never have her. Livia Harrow is gone forever.'

Josten was torn away, the shade of Livia's face fading, to be replaced with the hateful gaze of Innellan. They looked identical, but at the same time so very different.

'You cannot resist me!' she shrieked, as much to herself as to him.

Josten could feel her rage in the air, the atmosphere of the high chamber thickening with malice, but he would not be cowed. 'Kill me if you like, show me whatever visions you can conjure, but I'll be fucked if I'll ever dance to your tune.'

His own defiance surprised him, and he expected Innellan to reach out and rip his head clean off with those talons of hers. Instead she grinned at him, impossibly white teeth gleaming.

'Kill you? No, Josten Cade, you will live.' She reached out her hand again to touch his forehead. 'You will live to see everything.'

He stood atop a blasted wasteland. The ground crunched beneath him, the hard desiccated earth cutting into his bare feet. Through the gloom, Josten could see ruins all around, the trees burned to ash, towers reduced to rubble.

There was silence, the soft breeze causing the dust to swirl, revealing more and more devastation. He took another step, feeling another crunch beneath his tread, and looking down he saw it was not the crumbling earth beneath his feet but shattered bones. He walked across a charnel house, a bed of skulls, an army of the damned, and he the last of them.

In the distance a cry... animal, tortured. Josten looked for the source but he could not see through the mirk. The noise began to echo, growing louder, consuming the air around him. He clamped his hands over his ears but he could not block out the sound. His own cry of anguish mixed into the cacophony and he clamped his eyes closed, begging for mercy from the tumult...

He opened his eyes to see her standing before him, solemn, judgmental.

'When I have reduced this land to a sepulchre, you will be the last, Josten Cade. I will make you watch, I will parade you before my armies like a totem. You will watch every last child slaughtered, see every innocent thrown on the pyre in worship of me, and you will beg for death after the horrors you witness but I will refuse to grant it.'

Josten knew he was doomed, but there was still that seed in the back of his mind. No matter how indomitable Innellan's will, he yet hid that tiny kernel of defiance. He grasped it, holding tight as he asked, 'What would you have me do?'

She moved closer. Her eyes bored into his very soul.

'I would set you free to return to Siff. Then, when the time is right, you will plunge a knife into her heart and sever the head from her shoulders. You will be my assassin and you will end this conflict. You, Josten Cade, will pave the way for my ascension, and I will see you rewarded beyond imagining.'

It seemed such a simple task. And he would gain everything he had ever wanted, of that there was no doubt. But still he grasped onto that last shard of free will, holding it like a drowning man to a piece of flotsam. It was all he needed.

Josten spat in her face. It wasn't much, his mouth was parched and he could barely spare the wet, but it was enough to demonstrate his defiance.

Innellan took a step back, tracing the line of spit with her finger. She looked at it, then licked it off her finger like spilled cream.

'Siff's faithful puppet to the end. I should tear your heart out, but that would be too easy. That would give me satisfaction for only the briefest moment. You will be mine, and there is nothing you can do to stop it.'

'If that's what you think you're in for a—'

He could feel her in his mind, probing for weakness, seeking the seed of rebellion so she could crush it. A hungry worm picking its way through his innermost thoughts, hunting, hungering, destroying.

'You are mine, Josten Cade. You have always been mine.'

Josten clenched his teeth against the onslaught. It was tearing him in two. He wanted to collapse, to beg, to give himself to her completely, but he knew that would be the end. Instead he held onto one single thought – to Silver. He filled his mind with her. The experiences they had shared, the strength she gave him, until all he could think of was her. And in return he felt Silver filling him with the power to resist.

It was a sensation he had never experienced before – one of complete faith. He knew now, more than ever, that he could rely on Silver, that he could give himself over to her, that even should Innellan choose to slaughter him here and now it did not matter, for Silver was the one thing he could worship without doubt or fear.

'You think she loves you?' Innellan whispered in his ear. 'You think she can give you what you desire? She will use you up and abandon you as she has with all the others. Forget her. Cast aside this false idol and follow me, Josten Cade. I will give you everything.'

Despite his newfound faith, he could feel himself weakening. Silver was strong, but Innellan was so close. And willing to give him anything just to follow her.

He closed his eyes, feeling the tears stream forth. This was hell, caught between what he knew was right and the lure of this temptress. He bit down hard, tasting blood in his mouth, knowing he had to resist, that if there was to be anything resembling humanity left inside him he had to reject Innellan completely.

'Give in to me!' Innellan screamed.

In that instant, Innellan had lost. Josten's mind was free and he gasped for air, just in time to see the White Widow glaring down in fury. Her eyes blazed, and as they seared with an unholy fire he felt himself begin to burn from the inside. It started as a single flame in his chest, burning outward, seizing hold of his organs, his bones, his muscle and flesh until he was immolated by an unseen conflagration.

Josten screamed, collapsing to the ground and writhing, desperate to put out the flames, but there was no fire to extinguish. Then, as soon as it had come, the flames were gone.

He looked up, desperate for air, sucking in each laboured breath as though it might be his last. Innellan stood over him, her eyes too spiteful to look upon.

'You will be mine eventually, Josten Cade. No one can resist forever. Soon you will abandon my sister and realise I am the only way. Siff cannot win. It is only a matter of time before she is crushed beneath the weight of my armies and I stand victorious over her burning corpse.'

Josten was grabbed by the guards and pulled away. All he could do was stare at the ground as they dragged him along, too fearful to look back in case Innellan was still holding him in that hateful gaze.

When he was finally thrown into his cell again he managed to look up before the door was slammed shut. Byram was watching him from the corridor beyond. If he'd expected pity from the tattooed cultist he was sorely mistaken. Instead it was a look of abject confusion that greeted him, before the guards slammed the door closed and locked it behind them.

As he crawled to the side of the room, leaning against the wall and trying to piece together his shattered mind, one thought coalesced in his head. Whether he liked it or not – Josten Cade was just a puppet of the gods. All that remained was for him to decide which one would pull his strings.

15

AFTER two days and nights on the road, the city of Kantor came into view on the horizon. Adaali did not know what the hour was, but she was thankful for the darkness as they approached. The closer they got, the more the doubt began to creep in. Had this been a mistake? Was her rashness going to get her and Dantar killed? If she was recognised at the gate this whole game would be over. She was delivering herself right into Egil Sun's hands.

But surely that would be the last thing the vizier would expect? Besides, who would recognise Adaali from any other girl? She had always been in her brother's shadow – no one had ever paid her any mind. She'd been raised as a bodyguard, a loyal servant to the future king. Who would recognise such an insignificant member of the royal entourage?

Still, Dantar had managed to find them disguises from his stash in the town sewer and they both wore the white robes of penitents. They had also taken the precaution of shaving their heads to the scalp, though that was a poor disguise for Adaali, who had always worn her hair short. As they approached the city gate she could only pray their subterfuge would work.

The gate lay open, the torches hanging in their sconces illuminating a group of guards checking an overladen cart as it made to leave the city. Dantar led his horse towards the gate and for a fleeting moment Adaali thought they might be able to enter unchecked.

'You there,' came a voice from the dark. 'What's your business?'

Dantar stopped his horse as a guard appeared from the shadows. He took hold of the reins, glaring up at Dantar.

'We are monks, headed for the Penitent Path,' Dantar said from beneath his hood. 'My brother and I seek shelter before we continue our journey.'

The guard looked Dantar up and down before glancing towards Adaali. 'Don't often see monks on horseback. Don't you lot walk everywhere?'

'A gift from a pious merchant to speed our journey,' Dantar replied. 'We could not refuse such generosity.'

'Who could?' said the guard. 'Well, you've got no weapons, so what harm could you do, I suppose.' He beckoned them in. 'Avoid the western quarter after dark. Some of the ruffians down there don't hold much store by religion, and you might find yourself donating those horses against your will.'

Dantar offered a cursory salute as he urged his horse through the gate. Slowly Adaali let out the breath she'd been holding as they left the gate behind them and rode deeper into the city. The streets were quiet, but not abandoned. There was clearly no curfew. It seemed that nothing had changed.

Where was the mourning? The wailing crowds lining the streets in protest at the loss of their beloved queen and prince?

Adaali gritted her teeth, angered at the normality of it. There should have been a full-scale rebellion by now. The masses should have risen up against the usurper Egil Sun but instead they went about their night-time business, carousing and cavorting like nothing had happened. Where was the justice in this? Where were the voices raised in fury at such atrocity?

She realised she was gripping the reins so tightly the leather had bitten into her palms. As they rode past a group of off-duty militia outside a tavern all she wanted to do was leap from her saddle and fling herself into their midst. Damn the consequences. These could have been the very men who betrayed her mother and helped slaughter her household.

Adaali let go the reins, slipping her feet from the stirrups. How dare they laugh? She would kill them all…

Dantar's hand closed tight around her wrist.

'We need to find shelter for the night,' he said quietly.

Adaali glanced back to the militia. They had not noticed the pair of them yet. She could easily be among them before they knew what was happening, but Dantar's strong grip spoke its own words of persuasion.

'I should murder them all,' she whispered.

'They are not who we're here to kill. They are meaningless. Don't let them sway you from your path.'

Adaali nodded, taking up the reins once more and urging her horse onwards. When they had left the militia behind she said, 'If we are to take shelter we need to find an inn.'

'Very well,' Dantar replied. 'Where would we find such a place?'

'I have no idea,' she replied. 'I've never stayed in one before.'

Dantar shrugged. 'Neither have I.'

'We'll need money, I know that much.'

'I have coins,' Dantar said. 'Though whether they are of your currency I don't know.'

He handed her a small bag hidden at his waist. Adaali looked inside, amazed to see it was full to the brim with gold coins of all sizes. She did not recognise the symbols minted on them, but she knew gold was gold.

'These will do just fine,' she said. 'Where did that guard tell us not to go?'

'The western quarter,' Dantar replied.

'Then let's head west. It sounds like the last place a princess would go.'

Dantar agreed, and they rode along the main thoroughfare. Adaali fleetingly remembered the night she had followed Ctenka back to his tavern. If they were heading in that direction, it was indeed the last place a princess would, or even should go.

The buildings became more careworn the further they travelled and Adaali noted a distinct change in the dress and demeanour of the few people on the street. There was a palpable air of tension, a rough look to the men and an even rougher look to the women. Not that it scared her, but the last thing she wanted was trouble. They had to be discreet, despite her desire for revenge.

The western gate stood in the distance, the road to Tallis beyond it. Here were inns and taverns for the many traders coming from there, mostly pirates and privateers selling their ill-gotten wares. The influx of such coarse traders had long since transformed the western quarter into Kantor's roughest district.

'This one will do,' Dantar said as they reached a large building with stables.

Adaali was more than happy to jump down from her horse and hand the reins over to a tired-looking stableman. He gave them instructions to go inside and pay for their night's stay, flashing them a look of suspicion. Adaali could only hope it was their monks' garb that made them so conspicuous.

When they opened the door to the inn they were hit by the musky scent of strong liquor. Late as it was there was still something of a crowd gathered in the gloomy confines, and Dantar led them inside warily. Adaali followed and they crossed the room trying to blend in as best they could, but perhaps disguising themselves as monks and heading straight to the most insalubrious part of the city had not been the best plan.

Dantar approached the man who most closely fitted the description of the innkeeper. He wore a headscarf, a heavy golden earring making one earlobe droop much lower than the other. He drummed his fingers on the bar he was leaning against, the gold rings on each digit flashing in the candlelight.

'A room,' said Dantar.

The innkeeper looked him up and down as one might if confronted by a beggar or a waif.

'We don't do charity, brother,' the innkeeper replied.

Adaali was quick to move forward, offering the innkeeper a handful of the coins from Dantar's purse. Immediately she regretted the move as she saw the innkeeper's eyes light up.

'But clearly you're not begging,' he said, eyes fixed on the gold.

Adaali could have kicked herself. Obviously she'd offered too much, but then how would she know the going rate for a night at an inn?

'We're in a generous mood,' she said, slipping the coins into his open palm. 'And we appreciate discretion.'

The innkeeper gave them a knowing wink. 'Of course. Make yourselves comfortable and I'll see to it your rooms are prepared.'

With that he slipped away into the gloom, leaving Adaali and Dantar to mix with the locals. Not that they had any intention of that.

They found the quietest corner they could, keeping their hoods raised, watching the comings and goings. Adaali watched the unashamed revels, as women sat on the laps of men, feeding them grapes, sharing their hookah pipes. Some were kissing openly, while others gambled for piles of coin.

One such group seemed louder and more boisterous than the others, and Adaali focused her attention on them as soon as she heard one of them mention the recent coup.

'It failed,' said one of the men, before taking a long draw on his pipe.

'Then why has no one heard from the queen?' said another.

'She doesn't make her own proclamations. That's what she's got the vizier for,' said a third.

The hairs stood at the back of Adaali's neck at the merest mention of Egil Sun.

'He said there's nothing wrong, and who are we to argue.

If there's been a coup the city would be under lockdown, but here we are – business as usual.'

She wanted to leap from her seat and sweep that pile of coins from the table, to grab them by their gaudy robes and scream that her mother had been murdered, her brother left to die outside the city gates. But there was no way she could reveal the truth. If anyone knew she was there the militia would be on them like vultures.

'What would it matter anyway?' said one of them. 'So the prince might be dead? Who cares, he was never going to be able to protect the Cordral. What use is a boy against what's brewing in the north?'

'And the south,' said his fellow. 'You're right. Egil Sun has been running this city since the king died and he's not done us wrong so far. Better him than some woman and her infant.'

Once more Dantar laid a hand over hers. Adaali realised she had dug her nails into the table. She relaxed her hand, feeling it throb, but the fire still raged within.

'We have to leave,' she said. 'We never should have come here.'

'Very well,' Dantar replied.

'Just like that?'

'I don't like this any more than you do,' he replied. 'And I did not like the manner of the innkeeper one bit. This was a mistake.'

He stood, and led them from the dark corner towards the door. As Adaali followed him, trying her best to ignore the prattling traders, she noticed someone watching them intently from the opposite corner of the inn. The man was unaccompanied, his face half hidden in shadow, but his focus was on them alone. That nagging feeling clung to her even when they made their way outside.

'I've been recognised,' she said, desperate to quell the panic rising within her.

'How do you know?' Dantar asked.

'I don't know for sure, but we can't take the risk. We have to get out of here.'

'Very well,' he replied, heading towards the stables.

When they reached the building, they found the door to the stable locked.

'How do we get in?' Adaali said.

Dantar was about to answer when a burly figure moved from the shadows nearby. Before they could react, more men appeared. No one made a move, but it was obvious they weren't here to welcome the two of them like long-lost relatives.

'I think we should—'

'No killing,' Adaali said, before he could suggest anything but running. If they made a scene there the whole city would be after them.

'Very well,' he replied, grabbing her arm.

Adaali didn't need any encouragement to flee, and she and Dantar sprinted for the nearest alleyway. In the periphery of her vision she could see the street ruffians moving to intercept them, but they weren't quick enough.

The street wound through the backs of houses, the ground sloppy with sewage. A dog barked from behind a low wall and Adaali ducked grimy sheets hung up to dry.

A glance behind showed they were still being pursued and Adaali's heart began to race all the faster. More men were joining the chase as they went, silently following, hounding their escape. Though she could not make out the details of their appearance, they were too determined for mere street robbers – perhaps these were agents of Egil Sun, perhaps she had been spotted at the gate and now they were hoping to murder her without a fuss, quietly slitting her throat in a back alley, the crime hidden from sight.

'This way,' said Dantar, turning a corner. Up ahead, Adaali could see their way was blocked by a high wall. Dantar didn't stop, racing towards it, using his momentum to spring from an adjacent wall and stretch up to reach the top. As he pulled himself over, Adaali used the same trick, but wasn't quite strong enough to pull it off. Her fingers stretched for the lip of the wall but she just missed, falling back down to the street and landing in a heap.

Dantar made to climb back over the wall but she shouted at him to stop. 'You have to run,' she said. 'I'll find you.'

Before he could argue, she leapt over a low fence, heading through the yard of a tenement building and straight in through the back door. Behind she could hear the sounds of pursuit getting closer as the men raced along the alley.

She rushed through the house. There was no use in attempting stealth, she would be gone before anyone woke. In the shadows she managed to find the front door, hearing the grumbling of someone stirring in an adjacent room. Grabbing the handle she pulled, rushing out onto the street only to be faced by three men. Glancing back she saw two others following her through the house, blundering their way in the dark.

'It's her,' said one of them.

Adaali looked around desperately for any way to escape but there was none. In the distance she heard someone shouting at the commotion they had caused.

'The militia,' said one of the other men. 'We have to go, now.'

'Princess, you have to come with us,' said a voice she recognised.

As a familiar young man pushed his way to the front of the group surrounding her, it was all Adaali could do to stop herself leaping into his arms.

'Ctenka,' she said. 'You're alive.'

'For now,' he replied. 'But if we don't get out of here, we'll all be for the gallows.'

She glanced up the street, seeing the militia making their way closer.

'Very well,' Adaali said. 'Let's go.'

Ctenka led the way, and she followed across the street and through a low archway and into a series of labyrinthine passages where she soon became lost within the maze. The sound of the militia faded, and the men followed Ctenka in disciplined silence. Where before he had been a lowly militiaman in the employ of the crown, now it appeared he was a leader of men.

Eventually they came to a small stairwell leading to a cellar. Ctenka ushered her down and she passed a woman already holding the door open. Inside the place was dry with a sweet smell of spice. A couple of candles illuminated a gloomy room in which stood a table and a few chairs.

'Please, princess. Sit,' said Ctenka.

The door was closed behind them as Adaali did as she was bidden. It had been a long night and she was glad to rest. Despite being mostly surrounded by strangers this was the safest she had felt for days.

'What is going on?' Adaali asked, glancing around at the motley group watching her from the gloom.

'We are still loyal to the crown and Queen Suraan,' said Ctenka. 'A resistance, if you will.'

'Then you know what has happened?' Adaali asked.

He cast his eyes to the floor and nodded. His sadness was touching. 'We know she and the prince were murdered and that you escaped. Coming back here was foolish. You are the last of the royal line. Your survival is—'

'Not as important as justice for my family,' she said.

'I understand,' he replied. 'But that will be difficult. Most of the militia are in the pay of Egil Sun. The coffers of the Suderfeld bought their loyalty months ago. All are forbidden to speak of the murders. Anyone who tries to reveal Egil Sun's betrayal will be killed.'

'And how do you know of it?' Adaali asked.

'We are not all of us so easily bought,' he replied. 'Those who remain faithful have gathered in the shadows of Kantor, determined to right the wrong that has been done. Rest assured, Egil Sun's treachery will not go unpunished. He and the southern foreigners will pay for their crimes.'

'And how many are you?'

Ctenka looked around the room. 'This is pretty much

it. I know there's not many of us, but the officers behind the coup still think we obey Egil Sun. It won't be long before we rise up and punish them for their betrayal.'

She was about to ask how he hoped to start a revolution with half a dozen unarmed men when there was a commotion from behind the door. Before any of them could move, it burst open and a white-robed figure raced into their midst.

Two of the men were flung across the room. Ctenka barely had time to face the intruder before he was grabbed by the throat and flung across the table.

Dantar raised his fist, but Adaali yelled at him to stop.

'These men are our allies,' she said. 'They mean to help us. I know this one, we can trust him.'

Dantar had a wild expression to him, and he glared around at the men with those animal eyes.

'We cannot trust anyone,' he said, still holding tight to Ctenka's throat.

His face reddening, Ctenka patted Dantar's arm. 'You can… you really can,' he gasped through his constricted windpipe.

Reluctantly, Dantar released him and stepped back. Ctenka rose to his feet, rubbing his sore neck. 'My thanks,' he said. 'But I mean it, princess.' With that he knelt before her. His men all did the same. 'It is my honour to serve. And I vow that I will bring you the head of Egil Sun or forfeit my life to the task.'

'I appreciate the offer, Ctenka,' Adaali replied. 'And I gladly accept your help.' She looked around at the other men. 'But if anyone is going to take the head of Egil Sun, it's going to be me.'

16

JOSTEN gazed down at the slop he'd been given to eat. He guessed it was supposed to break his will, to make him reconsider trying to resist Innellan's temptation. Fact was, he'd eaten a lot worse over the years. He put another spoonful in his mouth and swallowed it down. It was disgusting all right, but years on the road fighting for mercenaries and kings had given his stomach a resistance to what most people considered inedible.

The prospect of seeing Innellan again filled him with more dread than the thought of starving, but he refused to give in. If Josten was going to make it out of this in one piece he'd need to keep his strength.

Before he had the chance to force down another spoon of slop, there were footsteps outside the cell and the noise of a key turning in a rusty lock. His stomach lurched. This was always the worst part – when they came for you and you didn't know what was going to happen. Were they just going to run in and kick the shit out of you? Drag you off for a bit of old-fashioned torture? Or would it just be questions?

As his heart smashed out a drumbeat against his chest he knew it wouldn't be that last one. They didn't care what he knew – all they wanted was an assassin, and if he wouldn't do it then he was no use to them.

The door opened and the priest Byram walked in, hands tucked into the sleeves of his robe. Behind him came a woman, with a haircut like it had been hacked off by a blind sheepshearer, eyes staring wildly like she'd been smoking too much poppy. She immediately moved out of the light, scuttling into the shadows like a cockroach.

'Making the most of your stay?' Byram asked.

'The food's exceptional,' he said, holding up his half-eaten bowl of shit. 'But the décor needs a bit of work.'

'I witness much. Since our queen united the Ramadi I have borne witness to all nature of things. Miracles, atrocities. I have seen her perform unspeakable acts on man and woman alike. She has torn minds apart and left the strongest warrior a dribbling wretch. No one has ever resisted her.' He removed a hand from his sleeve and pointed an accusing finger at Josten. 'Until you.'

Josten shrugged. 'What can I say? I'm just stubborn I suppose.'

'How did you do it?' Byram demanded. Josten was surprised at the sudden flash of emotion, but he didn't react. 'Tell me how you managed to resist.'

'I have no idea,' Josten said, spooning another portion of gruel into his mouth.

'Are you some kind of sorcerer? Is that why you were sent here?'

Josten thought for a moment as he chewed on the foul mouthful. 'No, I'm just as ordinary as the next man. And I

179

wasn't sent here, remember? I was brought by your people.'

Josten knew he had resisted Innellan because of Silver. She had been the one to give him the strength to resist. As far away as she was, as caged and weak as he was, Josten knew his faith in her gave him strength even Innellan could not break.

'I doubt you are ordinary at all,' Byram said. 'But that matters little. If you want to live you'll do as I ask.'

'I will? Do tell.' Josten put the bowl down, not that he had the least intention of going along with any demands.

'Innellan has brought us all low. She has united the cults. That in itself is a blasphemy, but she will lead us all to our doom. I cannot allow that to continue. I will grant you your freedom, but first you must do something for me.'

'And what's that?' Josten was beginning to get a sinking feeling.

'You must kill Innellan.'

Josten looked up at Byram for a moment, before bursting into fits of laughter. He laughed until he started to cough up half-eaten gruel.

'Are you fucking mad?' he managed to say. 'You forget, I've also seen what she can do. That woman can't be killed by someone like me. You can't just murder a god.'

Byram was unmoved. 'You can and you will. If any of us have a chance to accomplish such an act, then it is you, Josten Cade. Accept my offer or you will die.'

'Then I'll take death,' he said. It seemed the easiest option.

Byram shook his head. 'It won't be quick, but of course it's your choice. So let me show you what awaits before you die.'

The priest took hold of the chain connecting the manacles

around Josten's wrists. He passed them through a bracket in the ceiling and before Josten could protest the Carpenter had slithered from the shadows and pulled it taut. Josten was forced to his feet, dangling from the ceiling by his arms, toes barely touching the ground.

'All right, what about we talk this through?' he managed to say, before the woman appeared at his shoulder. She made a low hissing sound in the back of her throat as she tied a leather muzzle to Josten's mouth. Her garb was made of worn leather that fitted her slender figure like a second skin. For all intents she looked like a giant snake, and even moved like one.

'This is the Carpenter,' Byram said. 'She has plied her trade since childhood. Decades of learning how best to make men scream.'

Josten wanted to tell Byram that none of this was necessary, but from behind the muzzle he was mute. He could only watch as the woman reached into one of the many straps that wound around her body and pulled out a single iron nail. From a sheath at her hip she took a hammer.

Her expression was blank as she came closer, ringing the hammer and nail off one another to make a flat monotonous tune. Josten started shaking, contemplating all the places she could drive that nail. For a moment she wafted it in front of his face and he thought he was going to lose an eye before she grabbed a handful of his hair. The Carpenter was surprisingly strong, yanking his head to one side. He felt her press the tip of the nail against his skull, then with a single blow of the hammer she drove it home.

It felt like someone had split his head in two. He

convulsed, wanted to scream, but all that rose in his throat was bile and half-digested gruel. The Carpenter took a step back to view her handiwork as Josten writhed, hanging on the chain like a fish on a hook, squirming desperately for some release from the agony.

He tried to breathe, to stay in control, but all he could do was snort through his nose, desperate for the pain to subside. It was as though he'd been torn in two from the top of his head to his balls.

As his eyes eventually began to focus he saw Byram standing in front of him. 'This will be your life for as long as I wish it,' said the priest.

He made a casual gesture with his hand and the nail was wrenched from Josten's head. Immediately the pain stopped and he sagged from the chain in relief. The Carpenter removed the muzzle from his mouth and all he could do was sob.

'Have we reached an accord?' Byram asked.

What choice did he have? Hang here and spend the rest of his miserable days in excruciating pain, or try to kill a god and face whatever she might do to him when he inevitably failed.

'I'll do it,' Josten managed to say.

The woman released the chains. Josten almost fell to his knees but managed to keep his footing. Raising a hand to his head he could feel the wound in his scalp where the nail had been driven in. The echo of the pain still rattled through his skull.

'Wear this,' said Byram, handing him a bundle of clothes. Josten dressed in a daze. It wasn't until he'd donned the clothes that he realised he was wearing the garb of Innellan's bodyguard. The red tunic fitted him like a glove and if he hadn't had such a daunting task ahead he might have been grateful for the clean outfit.

When he'd finished he also saw the Carpenter wore an identical uniform.

'What's this?' Josten asked.

'She will accompany you,' Byram said. 'I wouldn't expect you to find your way alone. Consider her your second shadow.'

Josten glanced over at the mad-eyed woman who had just hammered a nail into his skull. If that was the best he could do for a guardian angel he knew he was deep in the shit.

'Now go,' said Byram, opening the door. 'Act swiftly, Josten Cade, and this will all be over. Have faith in yourself. You are the only one who can accomplish this task.'

As rousing speeches went, it wasn't the best, but it was all Josten was going to get.

'I'll do my best,' he replied and followed the Carpenter out into the corridor beyond his cell.

Once outside they both donned the red headscarves that went with the uniform, pulling them up over their faces. Moving through the corridors Josten expected them to be challenged at every turn, but they proceeded unhindered. It was as though everyone inhabiting this place walked along in a daze – each man under Innellan's spell, every mind in thrall to her.

The higher upward they went, the more sentries they passed, but no one said a word. If anything the warriors set to guard this place seemed in more of a stupor the further they progressed. They were a useless bodyguard, but then Josten had to wonder who would try and kill Innellan in this place anyway. Could she even be killed by a mortal hand? Josten guessed he would find out soon enough. And if he could kill her, what then? Would her spell over the tower's inhabitants be broken, or would he have a legion of angry cultists after him?

One thing at a time, he supposed.

As they reached the top of the tower, Josten's stomach was tied in a knot. The Carpenter led them through an access corridor and there were no guards here. A breeze wafted in through an open window, curtains billowing gently, and Josten began to wonder if he'd be easier on himself to make a run for it; throw himself out into the night and let the fall take him. Before he could think to do it, the woman grasped his arm.

He looked down at her, and she was holding a knife out to him. For a moment he considered taking it and cutting the Carpenter's throat. Who was there to stop him? But this might be his only chance to end all this. Innellan lay but a few feet away. Kill her and this war would be over. Thousands of souls saved with one sweep of the blade.

He took the knife without a word, and the Carpenter beckoned him on through a maze of drapery, up smooth marble stairs toward a dais in the centre of the tower's summit.

Josten gripped the knife tight in his fist and swallowed as quietly as he could. He could hear gentle breathing from atop the dais and knew they'd reached Innellan's bedchamber. But was she asleep? Did a god need to rest? Whatever she was doing, he hoped she didn't wake before he had a chance to plunge his knife into her heart.

Slowly Josten approached the dais. The Carpenter hung

back, obviously this was as far as her help stretched. Every tiny sound he made seemed cacophonous as he made his way up the stairs. Once at the top of the dais he saw Innellan sprawled on a huge bed, white hair spread about her, red silks adorning her body. The knife suddenly felt heavy in his hand and all he could think was that any moment she would wake and regard him with those cold black eyes of hers.

But Innellan did not wake. Josten moved to the head of the bed, standing above her exposed throat. She murmured in her sleep, hands grasping the dark satin sheets. It seemed even a god could be stricken with night terrors.

Josten shook his head. He was here to do a job – one that might save everyone on this continent. This was no time for his mind to wander. He raised the knife, grasping it in both hands, making ready to plunge it down into the sleeping figure. A figure with the face of a young girl.

For the first time since they had been parted, Josten saw Livia Harrow lying there. That innocent girl, asleep, troubled by terrible dreams. Rather than murder her where she slept he wanted to shake her awake and tell her it was all right. To hold her close and chase away the nightmares for her. But inside he knew this was not Livia. It had her face but that was all. The girl he had known was dead and gone… or was she?

If there was even the smallest chance that he could save her, Josten would take it. Cutting this woman's throat would shatter that one chance into shards. He knew there were thousands relying on him. That he could save the world with one final act of violence… but buried within this shell there might still be something left of Livia Harrow.

185

Josten took a step back from the bed, unable to take his eyes from the sleeping girl. As much as his head was screaming at him to finish the job he just couldn't.

He crept away from the dais, back through the shimmering drapery, back to where the Carpenter awaited. She stared at him, then looked up at the dais. All Josten could do was shake his head.

The woman didn't speak, just regarded him with a baleful look. Josten had failed. He'd been given a chance, fucked it up, and now would have to face the consequences. Well, once you were in a hole you couldn't get out of, may as well keep digging.

Before she could make any more faces at him, Josten plunged the dagger in her throat. He grabbed her, held her close while she squirmed for a bit. Every other time he'd killed someone so intimately he'd looked in their eyes, but not now. He just wanted this over with. Eventually the squirming stopped and he lowered the Carpenter gently to the ground. The place was silent – no guards coming, no angry gods rising from their slumber. For now.

Josten moved quickly while everyone remained in a stupor. It wouldn't be too much of a test to make his way back down through the tower and away into the night. As he descended, he passed by sentries in the shadows, but not one paid him any mind as he kept moving, ever downwards. Eventually he reached the bottom, and was out through the huge arch and into the wide open courtyard.

He stopped to take a breath. The knife shook in his hand and he realised he'd been holding it in his fist all this time. Josten blinked up at the stars – he had to get a hold of himself, just get a grip and keep moving. Anyone gets in the way and they get stabbed in the face.

Clinging to the shadows he put as much distance between himself and the tower as he could, at any moment expecting an alarm bell to ring. As he heard the sound of a snorting horse he felt excitement begin to unravel the knot in his stomach.

The stable had three horses, lean beasts by the look of them, built for speed. Could his luck really be changing that much? Best not to count any chickens yet.

Quiet as he could he saddled the one that looked the least trouble, taking hold of its reins and leading it out of the stable. Dawn was breaking as he walked it towards the main gate of the city, hooves making far too much noise for his liking, but still no one seemed to care. But why would they? What kind of enemy would come to this place voluntarily? That would be suicide. It might still be if anyone thought to question him.

He could see the desert now, stretching away beyond the open gate. Half a dozen sentries were manning it and, brazen as you like, he nodded at one of them as though it was the most normal thing. To his relief he got a nod back. No one raised a finger to stop him as he walked right out onto the road. Before he could mount up, a figure moved from the shadows to block his path.

The tattoo on Byram's face was just visible in the shadows. He moved like a spectre to stop Josten, grasping the reins of his horse.

'What have you done?' he hissed in the dark.

Josten glanced back over his shoulder at the guards on the gate. They were watching curiously.

'I did what I had to. Now, if you don't let go and fuck off, we're both dead.'

'You had a chance to end this. A chance to set us all free. Why didn't you take it?'

Josten didn't have an answer for that. What he did have was a knife in his hand and a gang of suspicious guards behind, just waiting for him to make the wrong move. If he stabbed Byram he could probably mount and be on his way before they could shoot him down, but then he'd be dogged all the way back east. He needed a head start or he'd never make it alive.

'I need to go now,' he said through gritted teeth. 'But rest assured I'll be back. And when I do, it'll be at the head of an army.'

'What good will that—?'

Josten touched the blade of the knife to Byram's belly.

'Get out of my way.'

It was a risk. He was gambling on Byram valuing his own life above getting Josten killed. There was a moment as the hooded priest considered his options. Then Byram slowly backed away and left the road clear. Josten silently thanked whoever might be listening.

He didn't look back as he mounted the horse and kicked it to a trot. And he didn't wait for the walls of Innellan's city to be too far distant before he urged that horse into a gallop. By the stars he could see he was more or less headed east, but whichever way he was going, it was to a damn sight better place than what he was leaving behind.

17

DISGUISED as commoners, they made their way through the
night-dark streets of Kantor. Adaali carried a short stabbing
blade concealed beneath a cloak. She would have preferred a
spear, but that was the weapon of a soldier or hunter – there was
certainly no need for an ordinary citizen to be carrying one in
the dead of night, unless they had trouble in mind. But a sword
was better than nothing. Adaali kept hoping she wouldn't have
to use it before they reached their destination, but as they turned
into the northern quarter, that hope died.

Militia lined the thoroughfare, standing by in an
undisciplined gaggle and blocking the only route to the palace.

As Adaali's group moved closer, she resisted the temptation
to place a hand to her blade. She had to keep her head, had to
trust her companions to do their job. Ctenka and his fellows
had pledged themselves to her – she just had to believe their
words had been genuine.

'Ho, Pellas,' Ctenka greeted one of the guards.

'Ctenka. Out late, aren't we?' the militiaman replied.

The group slowed, and Adaali tried her best to remain at
the back, out of sight.

'You have to use your time off wisely,' Ctenka slurred.

'That you do,' Pellas replied. 'On your way to lose your wages in some gambling hole?'

Ctenka shrugged. 'Maybe tonight I'll surprise you.'

Pellas laughed. 'Not likely, Sunatra. Not likely.'

Ctenka laughed, clapping Pellas on the shoulder before bidding him goodnight. The men seemed in high spirits as they moved off, and Adaali wondered what contribution Pellas had made to the coup at the palace. Had he been complicit or merely a bystander? How she would have relished the chance to make him tell her.

Before she could think further on it, Dantar blocked her line of sight, ushering her onwards.

'Remember we have a task to do,' he whispered.

She knew he was right. If she was to have her vengeance and any chance of reclaiming the crown that was rightfully hers, she had to find Egil Sun and send him through the Bone Gate. Killing a few disloyal militiamen would never sate her thirst for revenge.

It didn't take long to reach the palace, and as soon as she saw it memories of happier times rushed back to her. Adaali regarded the place with a sudden longing, but she knew those days were dead and gone.

'The main gate's heavily guarded,' said one of Ctenka's men, gesturing to Dantar and Adaali. 'We won't get through with these two in tow.'

'We won't have to,' Ctenka replied. 'We'll use the eastern entrance.'

'But we can't get in that way. It's always barred from the inside.'

'We'll just have to open it from the inside then,' Ctenka

said, his frustration getting the better of him. Adaali wondered just what kind of men she had chosen to help her in this task. Then again, she didn't have many options.

'We'll wait at the eastern gate,' she said, knowing well the entrance he was speaking of. 'All you need do is open it from the inside. We can do the rest.'

Ctenka nodded his acknowledgement, and she and Dantar slipped around the palace wall, hugging the shadows as they went. When they reached the eastern gate they hid in the dark and waited. The wall was sheer, glass shards cemented into the cornice. There was no way in but through that gate.

Time passed slowly while she and Dantar lurked in the shadows. The longer they waited the more nervous she became, until eventually she caught Dantar's eye in the dark.

'I am sorry for bringing you here,' she said.

'Why are you sorry?' he whispered back.

'Because this is not your fight. You are risking everything for me. And you owe me nothing. If anything I owe you.'

'That's not how I see things,' he replied.

'Why? Why would you do this? Why join me and risk your life?'

Dantar shook his head. 'It just... It just seemed—'

They were both distracted by a sudden noise from the other side of the wall. They heard a bolt being drawn and the side gate swung open on rusty hinges.

Adaali dashed across the street to the gate. There she saw Ctenka and his men waiting. At their feet were three palace sentries lying on the ground. Whether they'd been subdued or murdered Adaali could not tell.

'See,' said Ctenka with a smile. 'Nothing to it.'

'You've done well,' she said.

'So what now? Do we storm the palace? Find Egil Sun and murder the bastard?'

'You've done enough,' she said. 'Dantar and I will go from here. We will have a better chance alone.'

'No,' said Ctenka. 'We have to come with you.'

'The two of us will move more quietly than a half dozen. Besides,' she laid a hand on Ctenka's shoulder, 'we may need you to help us escape the city later if anything goes wrong.'

'Very well,' Ctenka nodded. 'I'll send men to arrange it. But I will wait here for your return.'

Adaali was buoyed by his devotion. If only the palace had been filled with more men as loyal on the night her family was murdered.

'Thank you,' she said. 'And if we do not return, I only ask that you remember my family. Don't let the people of Kantor forget them.'

'Of course,' Ctenka said. 'As long as I have breath you will all be remembered.'

Adaali and Dantar left them at the gate. They moved across the grounds in shadow, easily avoiding the few sentries dotted around the palace. It seemed that with Queen Suraan and Rahuul gone there was little need for the robust bodyguard that usually patrolled the place. It made entering the palace building easy, and it took no time for them to reach the first floor.

Making their way through the familiar corridors, Adaali couldn't help but feel out of place. She had been raised here, spent her whole life in these grounds, but now it felt alien to her. With her mother and brother gone, the soul of the building had been stripped out. It was no longer her home, just cold stone and mortar.

They paused as a two-man patrol made its rounds. Adaali knew she had to reach the rear of the palace – the eastern annexe was where Egil Sun and his bonecasters dwelt, if they were even here.

She led Dantar through the corridors, down passages hardly anyone used. With no royal family it seemed clear the servants had been dismissed, and they went unchallenged as they moved silently in the dark.

When finally they reached the eastern wing of the palace, Adaali paused. Two bonecasters knelt in silent prayer on the landing outside the vizier's quarters. A brief glance between Adaali and Dantar was all that was needed before they rushed forward.

On hearing them advance, both bonecasters rose to their feet, blades in their hands. Adaali ducked the first swipe of the curved sword, bringing her own across in a counter that opened her opponent's belly. He staggered back, clutching his guts as Adaali cut across again, opening his throat, and he collapsed in a bloody heap.

Looking over, she saw that Dantar had already dispatched the other bonecaster. Neither of them had made a sound.

She approached the door, pausing to listen. It was silent, no one had been roused by the brief combat, and Adaali placed a hand against the door and gently pushed. The chamber beyond was shrouded in darkness, a single candle burning in the centre of the room. Before it knelt the rake-thin figure of Egil Sun.

He was stripped to the waist, his ribs showing vividly through the taut flesh of his chest. It turned Adaali's stomach to see his loathsome form lurking there like a vulture. Surrounding him were the tiny scrolls he kept fastened to his robes. Each one had been unrolled, laid out in a concentric pattern and he at their hub. The Keeper of the Word had his head bowed in silent prayer and he did not look up as Adaali and Dantar slipped into the room.

She paused, drinking in the silence. This was the moment she had waited for, the opportunity to avenge herself upon her enemy. She should have leapt forward to strike, but she couldn't do it. A feeling of doubt began to overtake her, a strange sensation rising up inside. Some crippling fetor hung thick about the place, filling her with a morbid dread.

As Adaali forced herself to step forward, Egil Sun looked up at the intruders. He said nothing as he rose to his feet, and Adaali was rooted to the spot, unable to act. Likewise, Dantar seemed unwilling to do anything on her behalf, and they both waited as the vizier regarded them without surprise.

'I wondered how long before assassins would intrude upon my chambers,' he said. Egil almost seemed amused, showing not an ounce of fear.

'You are the assassin,' Adaali spat. 'Betrayer. Murderer.'

'Don't be so dramatic, child. It was always meant to be this way. It was foretold.' He gestured to the parchments spread out before him.

'Prophecies?' Adaali spat. 'I'll show you how meaningless prophecies are, you bastard!'

She strained against the miasma, struggling towards him. It was like wading through mud, and when she tried to lift her weapon, Egil raised a hand. Adaali was gripped in an incorporeal fist, unable to move or speak.

From the corner of her eye she saw Dantar lurch forward. Egil regarded him with contempt as he barked a single word.

'Kneel!'

The weapon dropped from his hand as Dantar fell to his knees, powerless to resist.

Fear grasped Adaali, cold and relentless. Egil Sun had managed to manifest magic. One hundred years after the death of the last sorcerer and now, of all the people who should be forbidden to wield such power, Egil Sun had managed to find a way.

'How?' she spat.

'It is not important,' said Egil. 'All that matters is I have the power, and you have none. You were the only threat to me, child, and now you have delivered yourself at my feet. In gratitude, I can at least make this quick.'

He grinned as he raised a hand. Immediately, Adaali felt her throat constrict under the power of Egil's will. She shook, trying to fight it, trying to breathe, but there was nothing she could do. Her head began to cloud, her eyes starting to close as she slowly suffocated...

Fight.

It was a distant voice, but one she recognised.

You are the one with the power here. Fight.

Closer now, more of an order than a request.

If you give in now he will win. There will be no vengeance, and we will both be lost. Fight.

Adaali screamed in defiance. Her blade came up in an arc, its tip catching Egil's cheek, and he reared backwards, clawing at his face, screeching like a cornered animal.

She staggered back, the sound of his voice booming in her ears. Dantar still knelt trembling on the floor, but he managed to look up, eyes locking onto hers before he uttered a single word: 'Run!'

Gasping for air she stumbled to the door, feeling relief as she broke through into the bright corridor beyond. She felt shame at leaving Dantar behind but her head rang with the effects of Egil's sorcery and all she could focus on was getting as far away as possible.

Adaali staggered across the landing, almost falling down a staircase at the end. The sword was still gripped tight in her hand as she forced one foot in front of the other, emerging into a wide vestibule. Archways led out to the north-east courtyard and in the fugue of her mind Adaali vaguely remembered there was a way out of the palace across the open space.

As she stepped into the fresh air she was enveloped in moonlight, feeling relief as she breathed in deep, but before she could make her way across the ornamental garden there was movement to her right.

She stiffened, adopting the Mantis stance Dantar had taught her. As she watched, wide eyed and fearful, a hulking figure stepped from the shadows.

'We had bets on whether you would return here,' said

Manssun Rike, huge sword held loosely in his right hand. 'You've just won me some silver, girl.'

'Shame you won't get to spend it,' Adaali spat.

She knew she should have fled, run far away from here and left the fight to another day, but her pride would not let her. Tonight she had failed to find justice for her mother and brother, but here was a chance to snatch one victory. Here was her chance at a little piece of vengeance.

The Suderfelder strode towards her, fearing nothing. His blade still hung limp from his hand. He was underestimating her and she would show him the foolishness of that.

She struck, darting forward, blade flashing. Rike raised his own broad blade and parried her sword with ease. Adaali danced back before he countered, but the attack did not come. Instead he just laughed at her.

She wasted no time, striking in again, but again Rike blocked her attack, seeming to know what she was about to do before she did it.

'Too slow,' he said. 'Just like the old weapon master I killed.'

Adaali knew he was goading her, trying to enrage her into rushing at him headlong, and she tried to keep her focus. She struck again, this time low, but Rike sidestepped effortlessly.

'He wept at the end. A coward like all you Cordral bastards. Craven to the last.'

Adaali screamed, leaping in, sword high. Rike parried the blow, brought his foot up and kicked her square in the chest.

The air was smashed from her and she fell back sprawling. Her sword was gone now, her eyes bulging as she tried to squeeze some air into her lungs.

Rike stood above her. It would have been so easy for him to kill her but instead he gloated, not saying a word, simply taking pleasure in seeing her writhe in pain.

'Don't kill her.' Egil's shrill voice pealed from across the gardens.

Adaali was vaguely aware of more figures rushing towards her. From the corner of one eye she saw Egil Sun, still half-dressed and clutching a bloody hand to his face. At least she had one small triumph tonight.

'Don't let her get away,' the vizier said. 'And be careful – she has power.'

Adaali looked up at Rike standing above her. The last thing she remembered was him lifting a heavy booted foot, before he brought it down on her head.

18

JOSTEN reined his horse in as dawn broke over the eastern horizon. The beast was breathing heavily and it would be stupid to run it into the ground. He had no idea how much further he'd have to travel on the road eastwards, and he didn't fancy walking the rest of the way. It was leagues back to Shengen lines, and all of it enemy territory.

As the sun came up, his head only just started to clear. The ghost of Innellan was still in his mind, his encounter with her leaving a dark stain on his memory. He'd had his chance to kill her, to end all this in an instant, but he'd refused it. When he had looked into that sleeping face he'd seen Livia. As much as he knew she was gone, it had given him enough pause to stay his hand. But was she really gone? Even after all this time could he still save that girl he'd made a promise to so long ago?

No. Livia Harrow was dead, and had been replaced by Innellan. He could never have killed a goddess, even if he'd had the balls to try. Silver was the only one who could defeat her now. One way or another Innellan had to be destroyed, which meant the last vestige of Livia Harrow would be wiped from existence. It was the only way, and yet still Josten harboured doubts.

He shook his head. No point worrying on that now. If he didn't get back to Silver and her army it didn't matter a shit what he might do.

The road was well used. Josten guessed it was a supply line to the east and since Innellan had united the cults there was a lot more travel on these dusty old highways. It wasn't long before he could make out travellers in the distance and he slowed his horse to a walk, thinking about how he should handle this. He could turn off the road, give them a wide berth, but then he might end up lost in the desert. Josten had a disguise and a horse – there was no other way than to bluff it. He'd just have to keep his mouth shut and not give himself away.

As he got closer he saw it was a single supply wagon with a broken wheel, probably part of a convoy that had been left behind. There were two cultists just sitting there gazing into the desert. Josten approached, as nonchalant as he could, pulling the mask of his headdress up over his face. When his horse drew level the two cultists regarded him with little interest and he raised a hand in greeting. One of them waved back, his eyes blank, the reaction an instinctual one. The other just looked wistfully into the distance. Neither of them moved to stop him.

Josten gave his horse a grateful pat when he'd put some distance between him and the cart. It looked like his disguise was good enough, at least for now. The rest of the day went by without incident and he only passed a few supply wagons on the road. It wasn't until night fell that he saw there'd be a real test up ahead of him.

Campfires were winking into life up ahead. As dusk fell over the desert and the temperature began to drop, the fires shone like beacons. Again, he thought about taking the long route around them – he wouldn't get lost with the fires marking his position – but his horse was tired and they both needed food and water.

There was little else for it, just ride right in and act like he belonged. It had worked before, what would be the problem now? Josten knew well what the problem would be – hundreds of angry cultists desperate for blood. But what choice did he have?

Night had fallen by the time he reached the perimeter. He nodded at the sentries on the edge of the camp and they barely paid him any mind. Whatever Josten had expected from a camp full of raving cultists, this wasn't it. The place was just like any other encampment he'd been in. Men joked and laughed, food was being cooked over spits, here and there was gambling, singing, and any number of things that might have put Josten right back in a Suderfeld mercenary camp. As he rode his horse right through the middle of it, he began to relax a little.

'Ho, you there!'

But of course his luck couldn't hold out forever.

A man approached and Josten reined his horse in, trying not to panic. Desperate not to set heels to the beast and ride out of here as quick as he could.

'What's your business?' the man said, coming to stand close to the horse, the opposite side to Josten's sword arm. Shrewd or just lucky. Time to find out.

'I've come from the west. Byram has a message I'm to deliver,' Josten said. For a moment he thought about putting on an accent to match that of the cultists, but he'd always been a shit mimic and it would have given him away in an instant.

'What's the message?' asked the cultist. He stared up with dark-rimmed eyes, furs set about his shoulders, an axe at his belt.

'The message is none of your business. It's for...' Josten wracked his brain. This had to sound convincing. *Think.* 'Kraden's ears only,' he said, gripping tight to his reins.

'Sounds fair,' said the man. 'You'll be needing a fresh horse then.'

'That's the plan,' Josten replied, hardly believing his luck.

'See the horse master, Whiteback.' He gestured towards the edge of the camp. 'You should be able to get some food as well, while you're at it.'

The prospect of food made Josten's stomach rumble. He could only hope it wasn't more of the shitty gruel they'd given him back at the fortress.

With a nod of his head, Josten left the man behind and made his way towards the edge of the camp. A dozen horses were corralled in a makeshift pen. Whiteback, the horse master, was brushing down one of the mares and Josten could see by the firelight why they called him that. His bare torso was covered in thick wiry hair from the nape of his neck to the top of his arse. Josten dismounted, and approached warily.

'I've been sent for food and a fresh horse,' Josten said.

Whiteback nodded, taking the horse's reins. 'There's some food over yonder.' He gestured towards a nearby fire.

'Best be quick afore it's gone. I'll prepare another horse. Won't be long.'

Josten nodded his thanks and made his way towards the fire. There were three figures sitting around it and a large pot glowed atop it. Josten could smell something cooking within and his stomach growled in anticipation.

He sat on one of the rocks surrounding the fire, keeping his head down, trying to size up who he was sharing the fire with. One of the cultists had similar desert garb, his head lowered as though he were asleep. The other two were women, one with eyes bright as they reflected the light of the fire, the other sharpening a blade. Josten slowly rose and approached the pot, hoping none of them would speak. He picked up a bowl, filled it with bubbling stew, then took his place back on the rock. At first he resisted the temptation to down the bowl of broth in one, blowing it to cool it, but eventually his hunger got the better of him and he drank it down. It burned his throat but he didn't care – it beat slimy gruel any day.

'Come far, traveller?' said the girl who'd been gazing into the fire.

Josten looked up from his bowl, seeing the girl staring at him. She was young, but there was a hard edge to her.

'I am heading to Mantioch,' he replied without thinking. 'Bearing a message.'

'A dangerous task,' the girl said. 'The enemy surrounds Mantioch as we speak. It would take a brave or foolish messenger to even attempt to enter.'

'I have my orders,' he said, trying to think like a twisted

servant of a murder cult. 'How I feel about it matters little.'

'Of course,' said the girl with a grin. It gave her a mischievous aspect in the light of the fire. 'We are all servants of Innellan now. We live and die for her glory.'

'Sicabel,' said the woman cleaning her blade. 'Enough.'

The girl called Sicabel lowered her head, but gave Josten a knowing wink before she did so.

'Curious accent you have there,' said the woman, still sharpening her knife.

Josten felt a little fear creep up the back of his neck, and resisted the temptation to move a hand to his knife.

'I have lived in the south for some years,' he replied. 'I was a spy. Bringing news of the Suderfeld back to my masters. I never lost the tone of voice.' That seemed enough for the woman and she nodded knowingly. 'Now, I have to be back on the road.'

'Good fortune,' said Sicabel.

Josten didn't reply, making his way back to the corral as quick as he could. Whiteback was as good as his word and had a fresh horse waiting. Before he could take the reins, someone moved from the night and grabbed them from the horse master. Josten took a step back, recognising the other cultist who had been sat by the fire.

'Some spy, telling anyone who'll listen what he's been up to,' he said.

'It was a long time ago. And I am among my brothers and sisters. What harm in telling them?'

'None,' said the man. 'If indeed you are who you say.'

'And how would you have me prove it, brother?' Josten said,

conscious that the horse master was watching his every move.

'For a start you can tell me who you reported to in—'

Josten launched himself forward, forehead connecting with the scout's nose before he could finish his sentence. Fuck talking, fuck subterfuge, it was time to get out of here.

The reaction to a headbutt never failed to thrill Josten, but he had no time to gloat as the cultist fell backwards. Whiteback started hollering to the moon as Josten grasped the reins of his horse and leapt up into the saddle.

He could see figures running towards him in the dark and all he had at his side was a knife – not much use as a weapon on horseback. The only way out of this was to run.

Kicking the horse, he left Whiteback and his shouting behind, heedless of who was coming after. A quick glance at the stars set him roughly eastward, and he was relieved at the speed of his mount. Whiteback had done his job well, just a shame there was no time to thank him.

Josten couldn't hear anything other than the incessant drum of the horse's hooves as he made his escape. A glance back over his shoulder and he saw the cultists had been quick to rouse themselves. By the light of the campfires he could see two steeds were following. They'd be armed too, and there was no way he could take them on with nothing but a stubby blade in his hand.

He urged the steed on faster, seeing a line of hills rising in the distance. Perhaps if he could make it that far he could lose his pursuers in the rocks, or at least find somewhere to stage a decent enough ambush.

Josten barely had time to formulate the plan before he

saw torches planted in the ground, and beyond them the desert dropping away into a wide gorge. He yanked on the reins, feeling the horse protest as he forced it to a stop. The gorge stretched away into the night to the north and south and there was no way to cross. Glancing back he could hear the sound of hoofbeats in the distance.

With a curse he urged the horse on northwards. There would have to be a way across eventually.

He patted his steed's neck, urging it on with encouraging words. The fresh horse was in excellent condition, which was a surprise in itself. These fanatics knew their farrier-craft if nothing else.

As the dawn began to turn the dark skies red, Josten could see that the gorge ran on for miles to the north, but there was something up ahead that filled him with hope. He urged the horse into a gallop as he spied a bridge that spanned the chasm. It didn't look much but it was the only chance he had.

When he eventually reached the bridge, his brief excitement waned as he saw it was nothing more than a rickety footbridge.

'Fuck this place,' he muttered. There must have been a properly constructed crossing to the south, otherwise how would the cultists supply their forces to the east? Damn his luck. Was nothing going to go right?

A quick glance to the south and he could see those riders still coming after him, and by the plumes of dust in the distance they were coming at quite a pace.

'Come on then, friend. Let's go,' he said encouragingly, nudging the horse towards the bridge.

It took a single step then faltered, unwilling to move out onto the poorly constructed wooden planks. The horse wasn't as stupid as it looked.

But no one had ever said that about Josten Cade.

He kicked the horse again, but it was a stubborn beast. There was no way he was going to get it across the bridge. Jumping down from the saddle he saw the riders coming after him no more than a hundred yards away. Turning, he stared out across the bridge. It stretched away for fifty feet, an ancient jumble of rotting rope and wood. Only an idiot would have risked it, but then Josten was just that kind of idiot.

Gingerly he stepped out, feeling the wood give a little under his weight, but it held. Grasping the rotted ropes on either side he started to make his way across. He'd only gone halfway by the time the riders reached the end of the bridge. Josten glanced back, seeing both of them jump down and come after him, neither of them seemed mindful of the drop beneath or the poor state of the bridge.

This was no time for caution. Josten moved faster, the timbers cracking beneath his feet as he went. Ignoring the danger he raced to the other side, desperate to make it before the armed cultists caught him. Just before he reached safety he pulled the knife from his belt. The cultists were almost upon him.

His knife sliced easily through one of the support ropes. The bridge lurched to one side, and Josten felt a cold chill of satisfaction at the sudden look of panic in the first cultist's eyes. The man behind turned, desperate to make it back to the far side before the bridge collapsed, as the one at the front took the only chance he had and came at Josten, sword raised. His blade slid through another frayed rope and with a straining of fibres the bridge collapsed, pitching both cultists into the dark.

Josten didn't want to watch as they plunged to their deaths, but some things you just couldn't drag your eyes away from. Neither of them made a sound as they disappeared.

He stood for a moment, glaring across the ravine at the three horses. Each one was a beautiful beast, and would have fetched a fine price at any Suderfeld market. With a sigh, Josten turned and started the long walk eastward.

19

*S*HE *ran through the dark, only able to see a few feet in front of her. This was a maze, corridor after corridor, each one leading off into the black and her only companion was panic; a wave of dread engulfing her, forcing her onwards into the never-ending labyrinth.*

She stopped at a door, a twisted barrier of rotting wood and peeling varnish. Tentatively she reached for the handle, her short sharp breaths the only sound. She opened it, feeling a wartm welcoming wind blow into her face. The room was wide, opening out onto blue skies. Above her a high vaulted ceiling, the marble tiles beneath her feet felt cold to the touch. This would have been a serene place had it not been for the towering figures staring at her accusingly. They were titans all – an ancient man glaring from beneath a brow steeped in a thousand years of care, a beautiful albino seraph with the eyes of a demon, a carrion bird with the torso of a man, a woman in stunning garb fit for a queen. Each one regarded her with judgement, silently accusing.

Under their gaze she began to falter, wanting to retreat, but the door she had entered through no longer existed. She wanted to tell them she had made a mistake, that she would leave, but the words would not come. Though they made no move towards her she knew she was in grave danger.

Before panic could overwhelm her senses she noticed a huge diamond pulsating nearby. It seemed to welcome her, giving off a warm glow. As she approached it the immortals raised their hands, expressions changing from disdain to fright as she got closer to the gigantic jewel. She knew it was the only way. This jewel was her only salvation.

Before they could stop her she rushed to it, opening herself for its inevitable embrace, letting it consume her in a tumult...

She landed heavily, the dust getting in her eyes, in her mouth, up her nose. When she shook her head and dragged herself to her knees she saw she was in the palace training yard. It was night, crickets calling from the surrounding dark.

'What are you doing down there?'

She turned at the voice, feeling her heart leap at the sound of her teacher. As he appeared from the shadows she rose to her feet quickly, feeling her stomach lurch.

Musir Dragosh stood at the far end of the training yard, a giant in the shadows. She could see his face was bloodied and torn, his mail shirt split across the chest, his flesh open, ribs exposed.

'Choose a weapon,' he said, taking a step towards her.

All she could do was stand and stare at the walking corpse.

'Are you stupid, child? Take a weapon.'

Still she stood, unable to move.

Dragosh sneered, his back teeth visible through a gruesome tear in his cheek. 'This is why they died. Because you failed them. They are dead because of your inaction.'

She shook her head, wanting to protest, wanting to tell him that she'd done everything she could to protect them, but again the words would not come.

'Worthless creature. I wasted years on you. I should have smothered you the minute you were born.'

Dragosh took another step forward, eyes burning with evil intent. She darted towards the shadows, heedless of the dark. Let it take her, let the night consume her; it was a better fate than facing the chastisement of her dead master.

Her flight was halted by another door in her path. Wasting no time she wrenched it open, heedless of what might lie beyond. Closing her eyes tight she barrelled through, coming to a sudden stop, still listening with her eyes closed. There was no sound of crickets, no more accusations from the dead – just the noise of the wind in the trees.

She opened her eyes, feeling a cold chill of autumn against her flesh. Everywhere was green fields, the leaves on the trees turning brown. This place was alien to her but familiar all at once. In front of her was a small wooden cottage, the front door open.

Slowly she walked towards it, stepping up onto the porch and into the house. She found herself in a kitchen – every aspect of it familiar from the basin to the table to the little kettle that sat next to a wood-burning stove. In front of her was another door, this one ajar, and she opened it onto a small garden. Kneeling among a freshly turned patch of earth was a girl tending flowers. Her hair was dark and she hummed a sweet tune as she tended to the yellow hawkbit, pink foxglove, red poppy, blue cornflower. All these blooms she recognised, though how she did not know.

The girl looked up from her garden and smiled. 'Hello,' she said.

'Hello.'

It was the only reply she could muster despite all the questions she had.

The girl stood up and dusted down her skirt. 'I am Livia Harrow,' she said.

'I am...'

What was it? It was so close. She knew the answer, it was there lying just beyond her reckoning.

'It will come eventually,' said Livia Harrow. 'But we do not have time.'

'I am in danger?' she asked.

'Great danger,' Livia replied. 'But do not fear. I am with you.'

She shook her head, uncertain. 'Can I trust you?'

'Always,' Livia replied.

Before she could ask any more, Livia slapped her hard across the cheek.

The lacerated face of Egil Sun leered at her from the dark.

Adaali was in a candlelit chamber, the smell of incense so sweet it turned her stomach.

'There she is,' the vizier said. 'I was beginning to grow concerned.'

Adaali tried to move, to attack Egil before he could speak further, but her hands were chained above her head, her feet barely touching the floor.

'I will kill you,' she spat.

A smile crept onto Egil's face but was quickly gone. He raised a hand gingerly to the stitched wound on his cheek, and Adaali took some bitter satisfaction from the fact she was the one who had put it there.

'That would be a terrifying threat indeed, were it not an

212

empty one,' he said, glowering at her.

'I mean it,' she said, all fear gone from her now. 'I will kill you.'

'I'm sure you mean every word. But as you can see,' he gestured to the manacles binding her to the ceiling, 'you're in no position to make threats. You'd be dead already if there weren't questions that needed to be answered.'

'I will tell you nothing.'

'We shall see,' Egil replied. 'We shall see about that.'

He took a step back from her. Adaali could see there were others in the room; Egil's bonecasters, watching impassively from the shadows.

'How did you resist me?' he said. 'Who do you pray to?'

Adaali had no idea what he was talking about. 'Damn you!' she screamed. 'Damn you all. I will send every one of you screaming through the Bone Gate.'

Egil nodded, knowingly. 'That's what I hoped you would say.'

He turned to his men waiting in the shadows and gave them a nod. At the signal they left the chamber. Adaali caught a glimpse of darkness on the other side of the door as they left.

'Believe me when I say, you are about to experience much pain.' Egil didn't even deign to look at her as he spoke. 'That is because I want something from you. But you should also know, I want to hurt you because it will bring me pleasure. For decades I served the crown of Kantor. First your grandfather, then your father, then your mother after him. And every day I grew to resent it more and more. Your mother was a particular burden to me. Patrician, some might have said, but I always found Suraan to be… arrogant. She was dull-witted, did you know that? Poorly read, often disdainful of knowledge. It was painful for me to speak with her.'

He moved closer to Adaali, addressing her directly. His eyes burned with malice and there was spittle at the corners of his mouth.

'So many years I hated that bitch. If she had only listened to me this could all have been so different. I would have made her mine. She would have been my concubine. It would not have been pleasant for her but she would have lived, at least. So would your brother. But no. She had to defy me, even at the end. Her death was all too quick.' He reached a hand out as though to touch Adaali's face, but stopped short. His unwashed stink turned her stomach. 'Rest assured yours will be much slower.'

The door opened behind him and the bonecasters entered. They bore a casket with them – a plain wooden thing. Adaali realised it looked just the same as the coffin one might bury a pauper in.

Behind the bonecasters followed two more men Adaali recognised. The first was the envoy: the one they called Bertrand, the man with the eye patch. He looked uncomfortable, as though he would rather have been anywhere else. In contrast, Manssun Rike looked as though he were relishing what was to come.

'Ah, thank you for joining me,' Egil said.

'What's this about?' said Bertrand, looking at Adaali chained to the ceiling. She could sense his disquiet, but it was perhaps too much to hope he might try and help her.

'I thought a demonstration might be in order,' Egil replied.

'A demonstration of what? Your cruelty? Rest assured, Egil, we don't need you to prove yourself on that score.'

Egil Sun raised a finger at Bertrand, wagging it as though chiding his impudence. 'None of us are innocent, Duke Bertrand. You least of all. But no, this is a demonstration of an altogether different kind. One that I would have you communicate to your masters back in the Suderfeld. I understand they have power. I understand that the Suderfeld has... assets with particular talents. Skills of an altogether unearthly nature.'

'Yes,' said Bertrand. 'We've already shown you what powers we can summon if we so wish.'

'You have.' He signalled to his men to open the casket. 'Now allow me to show you that here in the Cordral we too have power. Let me show you that I am no mere puppet to be used as you see fit.'

Adaali could only watch as the bonecasters wrenched open the lid of the box. She stared through the gloom as its contents were revealed. Lying there in her finery was the body of Queen Suraan. Her cheeks had hollowed, her flesh gone deathly pale and she clutched dead fingers to her chest.

At the sight, Adaali wanted to scream. Something tightened within her heart, fury and sorrow burning in a tight ball, threatening to rise up into her throat. The need to bellow, to rage, rose like bile but she fought it back, keeping her silence. She would not show Egil Sun or these foul foreigners that she was in pain. That was the last thing her mother would have wanted.

'What is this?' Bertrand snapped, taking a step away from the casket and raising a hand to his mouth at the stench emanating from it. 'If you must torture the girl get on with it, but this is just—'

'This is just the start,' Egil said.

He positioned himself at one end of the casket, reaching down and placing his hands to either side of Suraan's head. As he did so, the bonecasters fell to their knees, heads bowed as they recited a whispered incantation.

Egil closed his eyes, reciting some foul litany, and the air turned colder. Bertrand and Manssun backed away to the far end of the chamber, but neither averted their gaze as Egil enacted his rite. Adaali wanted to close her eyes, to hide from the unholy ritual being performed before her, but she could not. Instead she stared in terror as Egil spoke his foul sacrament over the body of her poor dead mother.

The candles dimmed and Egil's voice grew louder, more urgent. Then Suraan's body moved.

Adaali wanted to scream, but still she forced herself to watch in silence as her mother's glassy eyes flickered open. Egil continued spouting his enchantment as the desiccated hands clutched together at Suraan's chest suddenly gripped the side of the casket.

Egil stood back in satisfaction as the corpse heaved itself out of the wooden box. The body of Queen Suraan stood, dead eyes staring blankly at nothing.

'What have you done?' said Bertrand, unable to look away from the scene. Beside him Manssun stood motionless, transfixed by the sight.

216

'You have your power, Duke Bertrand. And I have mine. For the longest time my prayers were never answered, but still I observed the rites and rituals of my faith. Not too long ago, my diligence was rewarded. The sorcery of my ancestors was bestowed upon me. And as you can see, I wasted no time in learning how to harness it.'

He came to stand next to Suraan, reaching into his robe and producing a curved knife.

'Take this,' he ordered.

Without looking, the corpse reached out and took the blade from his hand. Adaali felt the cold fingers of dread gripping her heart now. This was how Egil would have his vengeance. This was his ultimate revenge on both Queen Suraan and her wayward child.

Egil pointed at Adaali hanging there, helpless. 'Take a piece,' he said. 'A small one.'

Suraan stepped out of the casket, almost stumbling on those rotten legs before she approached. Adaali wanted to scream at her mother, to beg her to stop, but even she knew there was nothing of Queen Suraan left within this walking corpse.

Bertrand babbled something unintelligible. Adaali didn't hear what it was, she was too busy trying not to vomit at the sight and stench of her mother's rotting body bearing down on her. Those blank eyes stared vacantly as she reached out with a decaying hand and took hold of Adaali's upper arm. The knife moved slowly as she cut a slice of flesh away.

Adaali screamed. It was a cry of anguish more than pain, but one she could no longer quell. It was not just the stinging sensation of her flesh being cut but the heartbreak that it was her mother, or at least her mother's corpse, being made to torture her.

Use this.

The voice cut through her mind, through the pain, louder than the sound of her scream.

Do not give in to the fear. Harness the pain.

It was a voice she recognised. One from her dream. A name she knew. Livia Harrow.

Do not fear. Resist.

Suraan cut away the flesh, holding it high, that dripping piece of meat, as she stepped back from Adaali. Egil Sun's eyes burned with satisfaction.

'I trust this is a worthy demonstration?' he said to the two Suderfelders. Manssun nodded his satisfaction while Bertrand simply stared, hand over his mouth.

Adaali looked to her mother. The corpse was staring at her now, still holding up the sliver of meat in her hand. For a moment, Adaali was sure she saw a flash of recognition, a moment of doubt flit across the cold, white face of her mother's corpse. As Egil spoke further to Bertrand, Adaali concentrated, willing her mother to recognise her, to help her in this moment of direst need. Suraan's brow furrowed for a moment, her eyes swivelling to regard the knife in her hand. Then she looked directly at Adaali and her lips moved. There was no sound, but it was obvious she could see, could recognise her child hanging there waiting to die.

'Now,' said Egil. 'If your stomach is not strong enough, I suggest you wait outside. You won't like what's next.' Bertrand was about to answer, but as Suraan turned, all eyes were suddenly upon her. Egil held up a hand, his face contorting in confusion and fear.

'What are you doing?' he said as Suraan took a step towards him. 'Stay where you are.'

But Suraan was under his control no longer. The corpse moved with inhuman speed, no longer shambling like a marionette. The necromancer gave a cry of alarm as Suraan fell upon him, knife hacking down.

Egil let out a high-pitched wail as he was slashed again and again. Blood sprayed across the room and Adaali watched her mother cut down the vizier. She took some sadistic pleasure in those screams as they reached a crescendo then slowly died away. One of the bonecasters grabbed Suraan about the neck but he was thrown aside with such strength he hit the wall with a crunch. Another drew a blade, stabbing deep into Suraan's ribs, but she ignored it, lashing out with the knife and opening his throat.

The corpse of Adaali's mother might have cut them all down, but Manssun Rike had other ideas. Drawing his huge broadsword he strode forward, lifting the weapon high and hacking down to split the corpse from shoulder to waist. Suraan fell for the last time.

There was silence. Egil's body bled from a dozen wounds, the blood seeping across the floor as his dead eyes stared at the ceiling. Manssun breathed heavily, glaring down at the corpse in front of him.

'Witchcraft,' he said. Then he looked up and regarded Adaali where she hung from the chains. 'You did this.' He took a step towards her. 'You have to be—'

'No!' said Bertrand, moving into Manssun's path. He seemed tiny in comparison, but his feet were planted, chin raised in defiance of the giant. 'We are done here. Clear these corpses out.' He gestured to the surviving bonecasters. They obeyed without question, but then with the death of Egil Sun who else would they follow?

'She is dangerous,' said Manssun.

'That's what I'm counting on,' Bertrand replied. 'Now help clear up this mess.'

Reluctantly Manssun left as Bertrand turned to regard Adaali. They were alone in the room now, and Adaali could not help but feel like her troubles were far from over.

'Listen to me closely,' said Bertrand. He still seemed shocked at what he had seen, but he was doing his best to stay in control. 'There is much at stake. Do you want to survive this?'

'What kind of question is that?' Adaali blurted. 'Of course I do.'

'Good. Then if we're both going to live you need to help me.'

'What are you talking about?'

'I'm talking about an alliance. We both have enemies, but an alliance will see us survive this. It could see you back on the throne.'

'You think I would join with a man who helped murder my family?'

Bertrand considered that for a moment. 'I had nothing to do with their deaths. If I could have saved them I would have.'

'I will die before I help you,' she said, not quite convinced by her own words.

Bertrand sighed. 'Please, listen to me. Do you remember when we first spoke in the gardens? Remember when we spoke of duty and masters? Well, my master is coming. And he will want to use you for his own ends. There will be no resisting then, Adaali, I can promise you that. There will be no offers of alliance. There will be no second chances. You will obey or you will die. So you need to make up your mind quickly – help me or be a slave to him.'

She didn't answer. Whatever was coming, whoever Bertrand's master was, she would face him the way she had faced everyone else. Even if it meant her end.

When it was clear she was not going to answer, Bertrand left her alone in the chamber. All she had was the blood still staining the floor, and the memory of her dead mother. There was no one to help Adaali now.

20

THERE were distant screams in the night. Rising from her bed, Siff stumbled from her tent. All was quiet, nothing was amiss.

Looking over the darkness of the desert, she realised it had not been anyone within earshot. It was someone else, someone far away across the deserts.

Siff gritted her teeth against the pain of her injuries as she wandered out into the night. She could see everything, hear everything. A sand fox ran from her path as she moved, spiders slid back beneath the sands at her passing, a desert owl peered at her from half a mile away, but she was not concerned with creatures of the night. She had heard a cry across hundreds of leagues, a voice that could only have belonged to another of her kind. Whoever it was she had to find them.

The thought cut her deeper than any of the wounds she had sustained in battle. If more Archons had entered the realm of mortals it could spell doom for this place. It would mean she was too late, that the war raging across aeons would now be played out here. Millions would suffer, but perhaps there was still hope.

Siff knelt down on the cold earth. It teemed with life just below the surface and she placed her hands to the ground, palms pressing into the soft sand. Closing her eyes she began to explore with her senses. If another Archon had come through the Heartstone she would know where they were.

The cry had come from the south, and Siff reached out with her consciousness. Her essence travelled on the wind and through the earth, riding upon the life force of the vermin beneath the ground and the creatures in the sky, her spirit riding on everything that lived and breathed. Her mind flew through the desert, eating up a hundred leagues in the blink of an eye until she finally reached the walls of a city.

Here she paused, probing the city's aura, searching for her prey. If there was another Archon there their presence would be obvious – the fledgling host would stand out as though they were aflame. There was nothing.

Then Siff heard that cry again, a wail of grief and pain calling out across the city. This was no Archon, but a mortal stricken with fear like a beast caged and waiting for the slaughter. But how had a mortal managed to reach out to her over miles of endless desert? With some effort, Siff was able to convene with other Archons, but how was it possible with an ordinary human being?

She pressed further, moving like a phantom over rooftops, passing every mortal sleeping in their beds, sensing every innocent dream and forbidden yearning, ignoring the lovers and the killers, the debauched and the saintly, until she reached a dark tower at the city's furthest extent.

The screaming had ended now. There was nothing but

the dull hum of life emanating from the tower's summit. Siff moved up towards it, her essence scrambling along the dark façade like a bloated spider until she reached the top and crawled in through an open window. She slithered along filthy broken tiles, winding like a nebulous serpent until she reached a candlelit chamber. This place had seen torment. It had seen death, and only recently.

Siff entered, seeing a single figure chained in the centre. A girl, young but strong. Helpless but defiant. She was everything Siff admired about these mortals and more. So much more.

This girl had power. Siff could see it burning within her soul, glowing like a fire at the core of her being. She was no Archon, that much was for sure, but in time she might be as powerful as one.

Siff's first thought was how great an ally she would make. With a mortal like this among her army, Siff could destroy Innellan and end this war, but the thought immediately shamed her. This girl was already suffering, and all Siff could think was to embroil her further within this game of the gods. Besides, the girl was miles away, and though Siff could project her spirit across vast distances there was little she could do to influence events here. She could only hope the girl would survive long enough for her to send help.

Leaving the prisoner to her torment, Siff retreated, back across the city, back across the desert, through the night, retreating at the speed of a sunbeam until she opened her eyes with a gasp.

Siff still knelt in the desert. Her breathing was laboured, and as she raised a hand to the wound at her side she realised it had opened up, a fresh patch of blood having seeped through her tunic.

She stood and headed back to her tent, and in the dark she took a knife and cut out the old stitches before taking needle and thread to reseal the wound. With every prick of the needle she felt the pain intensely and there was a foreboding stench about the festering lesion. There was not much time before this mortal body succumbed to its many injuries.

It would be so easy to remedy this, and with every wince of pain she felt the pull of the souls surrounding her in the camp. How she yearned for it more every day; to walk out amidst the thousands and demand their worship. Every day the temptation grew stronger and every day she had to summon the will to resist it.

When dawn finally broke over the desert, Siff left her tent. The Shengen and auxiliaries had already risen. Many were wounded from the recent battle but their victory over Innellan's cultists gave them the strength they needed. It suddenly made her own wounds seem insignificant. These mortals endured as they always did. At least, Siff knew, no matter how intense the pain of her own injuries, no matter how gravely this mortal body suffered, she would live on. All her army had was its faith.

As she wandered, she saw a group of Shengen legionaries kneeling in mass prayer. They offered their benefaction to gods that were no longer listening, asking for deliverance in their time of need. Siff could only envy their ignorance, but she knew the truth of it – there was no one watching over them. No one but her.

When eventually she reached Laigon's tent she found him reclining in a chair. He looked more exhausted than she had ever seen him, but still he stood when she entered.

'You should be resting,' he said, guiding her to his chair. She gratefully took the seat, no longer feeling the need to appear strong.

'I am not the only one,' she replied. 'Have you slept?'

'Some,' he said, but she easily saw through the lie.

'What about the men? How do they fare?'

Laigon tried to put a brave face on it, but it was obvious things were grave. 'They will fight when asked, but they need time to recover before we demand more of them.'

'Then I am sorry,' she said. 'Time is a luxury we do not have.'

'Mantioch is not going anywhere,' Laigon replied. 'What does it matter if we wait another few days?'

'Innellan only grows stronger while we grow weak. If Mantioch falls, its populace falls with it. All we need do is force the city's surrender and her people will flock to our side as they have all across the desert.'

Laigon let out a long sigh. 'My people need to rest. But I understand we are running out of time.'

Siff struggled to her feet, laying a hand on his shoulder. 'If there was another way…'

'I know,' Laigon said. 'I will prepare the men.'

Siff followed him out as he went to gather the centurions of the Standings. As he left to give them the news, she carried on westward through the camp. In the distance, over a few scant miles of desert, lay Mantioch. It had to fall before they could travel further west to face Innellan. Ignoring it would be disastrous, effectively trapping her army between two hostile forces. Despite the risks there was only one choice.

As she gazed out west she saw someone approaching. For a moment she wondered if it might be an envoy sent by Innellan, someone come with a message, but the White Widow would not send someone else to do her dirty work. If she was going to demand Siff's surrender she would come herself.

As the figure drew closer through the haze, Siff got a familiar feeling. She began to move, her walk turning to a run as she recognised the man who approached. Josten was staggering, his clothes shoddy and covered in dirt, but still he marched inexorably onwards. When eventually she reached him he fell into her arms.

'You're a sight for sore eyes,' he said wearily.

Siff laughed, surprising herself at her reaction.

She helped him the rest of the way to camp, the sentries rushing to help when they saw she had returned with one of their own. Josten had a thirst that was hard to slake, and as he sat drinking a third waterskin she asked him what had happened.

'Innellan happened,' he replied.

'You saw her?' Siff replied. 'And yet you live?'

Josten nodded. 'No one's more surprised about that than I am. She wanted me to be her assassin. When I refused she wasn't too happy about it.'

'You managed to resist her?'

'I did. And I think I have you to thank for that.'

It made sense. Though Josten was no worshipper, he was still in her thoughts and under her protection. Perhaps despite her struggle to resist accepting the worship of her troops, Siff still held some power over them. Maybe Josten was just strong-willed enough to resist the lure of an Archon.

'So what now?' Josten asked, looking around at the busy encampment. 'We're mustering for an attack?'

'Mantioch has to fall. And soon. We lay siege in a matter of days.'

Josten rose to his feet. 'I'll get back to it then. I imagine Laigon's missed me since I've been away.'

'We all have,' she said, and she meant it. Josten was one of her most faithful and having him back soothed a wound in her heart. It made what she had to do that much harder. 'But you will not be coming to Mantioch.'

'What do you mean?'

'I have a different task. One more difficult than any siege.'

'What could be more difficult than attacking an impregnable fortress city?'

'I need you to travel south. There is someone in Kantor you must rescue and bring back to me. I can trust no one else with this.'

'I'm not sure that's true, but all right. Who is it?'

Memories of that dark cell came back to Siff. A vision of that young woman chained, tortured, in pain. 'Her name is Adaali. She is the rightful heir to the throne of the Cordral. And if you do not find her quickly she will perish.'

'Great,' Josten replied. 'You know I don't have the best track record when it comes to rescuing helpless damsels in distress?'

'This is no helpless maid. She could be a powerful ally in our fight against Innellan. Will you bring her to me?'

'Do I have a choice?' Josten asked. 'Don't answer that. I'll do it.'

Before Siff could thank him, someone called Josten's name. She turned to see a young Cordral soldier approaching, the only survivor to return from their failed ambush.

'Eyman,' Josten said, before the young militiaman gripped him in a tight bearhug.

'Good to see you alive,' Eyman said. 'I was certain you were dead. How did you manage to escape?'

Before Josten could answer, Siff placed a hand on both their shoulders. 'He can tell you on the road.'

'Road?' said Eyman. 'Where are we going?'

'You are both headed south. To Kantor.'

'Wait,' Josten said. 'This is a dangerous mission. One we might not come back from. There must be a legionary or scout who is better suited. Eyman isn't right for this.'

'He is perfect for this,' said Siff. 'You need someone loyal to watch your back. Someone who knows the land and who knows Kantor.'

Josten looked at Eyman. 'Well, the last time Eyman watched my back I was captured by the enemy, but I suppose you're the one in charge.'

Eyman seemed crestfallen at the remark until Josten clapped him on the arm and began to laugh.

They never failed to surprise her, these mortals. Their capacity for finding hope where there was none seemed infinite. And where they were going, hope was something they would need to cling to.

21

JOSTEN caught a few hours' sleep before they left at sunset, walking two horses through the desert as they headed due south. If there were any cultists lying in wait around the camp they slipped past them unseen. Laigon had been reluctant to let them leave, he would need every available sword for the siege of Mantioch, but Siff had explained the importance of their mission. Josten still wasn't sure. What help could one girl be, after all? Josten had seen the devastating power of two children at the siege of Dunrun, but could this young princess wield similar magic? Josten knew it wasn't his place to ask; he'd trusted Siff so far and he couldn't see any reason to doubt her now. He just had to keep the faith.

That one almost made him laugh out loud. Keep the faith? He'd never had any faith and he knew it. But then he'd never needed it. Now though, he was beginning to have his doubts. Had it not been for Siff and her influence, chances were he'd be a dribbling idiot locked in a cell somewhere. Or worse – he'd be Innellan's willing assassin.

He didn't really understand any of this, but he knew damn well not to question it. Gods, magic, whatever, this was too real, and if he didn't follow the path he was on, chances were he'd end up lost. One thing was for sure; Siff had to win. And if he could help her do it by saving this one girl then that's what he'd do. Not that the irony was lost on him. He'd tried saving Livia Harrow all that time ago, and where had it got him? Maybe this was a way he could make amends. Josten knew chances like that didn't come along every day. Whoever this girl was, he'd do his best to get her out of trouble and this time he'd die before he failed.

As the sun came up over the desert, he and Eyman were on horseback. They'd made good ground overnight and now there was nothing to see but open desert in any direction.

Looking over he noticed Eyman's tight-jawed resolve. The lad was nervous, and why wouldn't he be? This was dangerous, chances were they'd both be killed. He could only admire the lad for accepting the task.

'Thirsty?' he asked, offering him a drink from his waterskin.

'Thanks,' Eyman said, downing some of the warm water within.

'It's all right to be scared,' Josten said, thinking it the right thing to say. 'If we stick together we'll come out of this in one piece.'

He knew that wasn't true, but hopefully it would help settle Eyman's nerves.

'I'm sorry for leaving you behind,' Eyman said, handing back the waterskin. 'I should never have left you back in that quarry. I was a coward.'

'Don't be sorry. If you'd stayed you'd be dead. You ran and survived. That's always the best option.'

'You didn't run.'

Josten shrugged. 'And I'm lucky to be alive.'

'I wouldn't blame you if you thought ill of me.'

'You've done your job without question. Everything that's been asked of you. We all have regrets in this business so don't doubt yourself. That's as likely to get you killed as anything else.'

'I won't,' Eyman said, though he didn't sound too sure about it.

'I know you won't.' Josten replied. 'There's no one else I'd rather have watching my back.'

That wasn't true. He could have thought of a dozen, but most of them were dead. And besides, it was what Eyman needed to hear.

As they made their way south they could see a vast lake to the west. Their journey brought them almost to its shore and the calm surface of the water made a welcome change from the endless desert.

'Demon Sound,' Eyman said.

'Aye. Not far to the Cordral border, I reckon. It's a grand sight, still as a millpond.'

'I've heard dark tales about what lies beneath the surface.'

'You're not the only one,' Josten replied with a grin. 'So let's agree not to go swimming, shall we.'

They continued their journey, taking some relief from the cool breeze that blew across the lake's surface. Following the shoreline of Demon Sound, the two of them eventually turned southwest until they could see a small habitation squatted on the edge of the lake.

'There are people down there,' said Eyman. The tiny

port had a jetty and boats were moored there. Josten could just make out people at the makeshift harbour. 'Maybe we should go and see if there's any fresh water to be had?'

'All right, but be on your guard. It might look innocent enough but this is still the Ramadi. There's always something dangerous lurking round the corner.'

They rode into the port where they were looked upon with some curiosity by the inhabitants, but nobody challenged them. Children ran around in barely any clothes, their mothers busying themselves with fixing nets or gutting fish. The stink of the place was tremendous.

At the port a group of men were preparing to set out on the lake. As well as nets, they carried sturdy harpoons rather than line and rod. Josten could see the hull of their boat was reinforced with iron plates.

'That thing looks like it would sink like a stone,' said Eyman.

'I guess an ordinary boat's no good if the catch of the day has a habit of biting you back.' He regarded the calm waters of Demon Sound, remembering the tales he'd heard of the vicious creatures within.

When they reached the bay they saw what passed for a well standing just to the north, though it was more a bucket next to a hole in the ground. It didn't matter what it looked like, the thing was dried up anyway.

'No water,' said Eyman sullenly. 'What do these people drink?'

Josten scrutinised the twitchy collection of fishermen. 'Seawater by the looks,' he said.

Eyman's gaze rested on a larger boat at the southern end

of the bay. It had a furled sail and looked more like a trade ship than a fishing boat.

'Maybe we should pay for passage,' he said. 'Might save us a day or two.'

'Let's stick to the plan,' Josten replied. 'Besides, I've had my fill of boats.'

The memories of his time under Mad Vek came back to him in a rush. It had been the best time of his life in some regards but in the end, like most other things, it had turned to shit.

With no reason to linger in the place, they left the little port and struck out south, leaving Demon Sound behind them. Night fell and they made camp, Josten taking first watch by the fire. It was an eerie place to be alone at night, but there was little prowling in the dark to be concerned with. Josten knew the real predators were to the north. There was nothing in this desert more dangerous than Innellan and her fanatics.

They rose with the sun the next day and carried on. With nothing to mark the border with the Cordral Extent, Josten had to assume they'd left the territory of the Ramadi behind them. His guess was confirmed when they came across the ruins of an old farm, half eaten by the desert. The place looked as though it would have been magnificent once. The main farmhouse was more a mansion than the shacks he was used to in the Suderfeld, though now it was just an empty skeleton.

Surrounding the main buildings were broken pieces of machinery Josten didn't recognise, and the shell of what must have been irrigation equipment long forgotten. The broken system left a trail of piping all about, an intricate network that had once fed the land for miles around. Now it was lifeless, just like the rest of this place. Dead for a hundred years.

'This must have been fertile land in its day,' Josten said.

'It was, or so they say,' Eyman replied. 'Crops as far as the eye could see, before the Fall. Magic made this place green and full of life. When it disappeared…' He gestured to the arid landscape.

'Well, now it's back,' Josten said. 'But it hasn't brought the green with it.'

'What was it like growing up in the Suderfeld?' Eyman asked. 'I heard there used to be fields and pastures. Were they not destroyed in your wars? From the stories I've heard I imagine it must look much like this.'

Josten shook his head. 'No, it's still as beautiful as it's always been. It's not the land that's the problem, it's the people in it.'

'You speak that way of your own countrymen?'

Josten laughed. 'Every country has its share of bastards.'

'There's truth in that,' Eyman replied. 'But still, I would like to visit the Suderfeld one day. Just to see for myself.'

'If we live long enough, I'll take you there,' said Josten.

'I would like that.'

Josten found himself liking Eyman more and more. The men of the Cordral had a casual way about them he had grown to admire. Eyman reminded him of Ctenka – well-meaning but naïve.

'Do you have family back home?' Eyman continued. 'A woman waiting for you? Children?'

'No, I've never been wed,' Josten replied.

'But you must have had a woman. Someone special.

Someone your heart aches for?'

Josten's thoughts turned immediately to Selene and he regretted encouraging Eyman to speak so candidly.

'I had a woman once,' he said. 'But she wasn't mine to love.'

'So you admired her from afar.'

'If only,' Josten said. 'I admired her from far too close. It's what started all this in the first place. If not for that, I'd still be in the Suderfeld.'

'And you regret it?'

Josten could see Ermund's face. The old friend he'd betrayed. He could have beaten himself with the guilt of what he'd done, but guilt never did anyone any good.

'No point in regretting,' Josten replied. 'It won't change anything. Life has a way of pushing you in a certain direction, and sometimes there's not a thing to be done about it.'

'Agreed,' Eyman replied. 'Look at me. Last year I was posted in the arse end of beyond. No prospects other than to be slaughtered by invaders. Now look at me. I'm on a mission to rescue a princess. What could be better?'

Josten could think of plenty.

'As much as I admire your zeal, you might want to calm it with the enthusiasm. This mission isn't some boy's tale of daring adventure. It might end with us both dead and buried. And if we're lucky we won't be tortured first.'

That quieted Eyman. It was clear he hadn't considered the fact they might not succeed.

Josten perhaps felt a little guilty for that, but as he said: no point in regretting. He just hoped he could avoid any regret when they finally reached Kantor.

22

THE assault on Mantioch began at dawn. Volleys of arrows were fired at the battlements, the defenders firing back in return. From the rear of the Shengen lines, trebuchets lobbed boulders at the walls, having little effect against the impregnable fortifications.

Siff waited as the order was given for the frontal assault to begin. Two thousand Shengen legionaries charged, carrying a ram in their midst, shields raised in a defensive block. Laigon was front and centre, the plume of his helm just visible above the advancing ranks.

They reached the base of the main barbican, the sound of the ram hammering against the gate rising above the din. The defenders of Mantioch rained more arrows and fire down upon them, but the Shengens held, drumming that ram against the massive gate, not relenting nor giving an inch. Bodies piled up, screams filling the air as more missiles clattered against a wall of shields.

Now it was her time to act.

Silently she broke cover. The eastern wall of the city was relatively unprotected as Mantioch's defenders concentrated at the main gate. Her men carried ladders, each one fifty feet long. If they could make it over the wall and fight their way to the front, opening the main gate would be easy. Or at least that was the plan.

Siff sprinted towards the base of the wall, her men at her side. They were twenty yards short when the shout went up from atop the battlements that they had been spotted.

Heedless, her men ran on, bracing the ladders and pushing them against the curtain wall of the city. An arrow whipped down past her head.Siff lifted her shield as she planted a foot on the first rung and made her way upwards. She ignored the screaming pain of her wounds, ignored the cries of her men as they were hit by yet more missiles. All she could focus on was reaching the top.

How many times had she done this over the millennia? War after war, battle after battle, leading her forces into the fray. And every time she had felt the thrill of it. But not today. If she failed she knew there would be dire consequences. It would see this land in ruins. The sacrifices made today might yet save this world, and Siff knew she could not allow herself to be stopped.

She reached the top of the ladder, leaping over the rampart, smashing an archer from the summit with her shield. Dropping it she drew her twin swords, hacking her way across the gangway, clearing the path for her warriors to climb in safety. At her ferocious attack, the rest of the archers fled, calling for more troops to help repel the invaders. A glance down into the courtyard below and she could see cultists rallying to intercept.

Siff tried to control the bloodlust, tried to stay focused,

in control, but it was all too much. She knew this was no time for restraint. This was time for slaughter – she had to reach the gate. No one could stand in her way.

She fell amongst the cultists. Her swords flashed crimson. She was caught in a tumult of spears, twisting past every sweeping blade. The enemies that came for her were of every stripe, gathered from each of the blood cults of the Ramadi. Where before each cult had been loyal to a different Archon, now they were gathered under Innellan's banner, united in purpose. It would be their folly.

As she was caught up in the ecstasy of battle her men joined her. They fought together, caught up in the rapturous splendour of violence, and with Siff at their head they were invincible. In no time they had routed the defenders and were left alone amongst the corpses. Without a word, Siff led her troops north through the city.

The sound of battle echoed from the main gate and through the narrow streets. Distant bellowing rose over the rooftops, the sound of clashing steel and dying men. Siff raced through the winding streets until eventually they led to a long plaza, the path blocked by Mantioch's ancient temple. It was a gloomy edifice, all dark stone and weathered gargoyles that would once have leered but now were expressionless golems. Siff paused at the huge iron door. They would have to pass through to reach the gate, and there was no knowing what they might face within.

'Let nothing stop you,' she said before they entered. 'We may have to fight our way through.'

One of her men pushed the door open, and it creaked

ominously revealing darkness within. As Siff led the way through, the sound hit her – a hushed and monotonous prayer, countless voices joined together in worship. She was struck by the eternal sense of longing it imbued, but this prayer was not for her. It was for Innellan, and those kneeling by the score could know no better than to worship their witch queen. Almost every inch of floor space was taken up by kneeling children. Their heads were bowed and they made no move as Siff and her warriors entered the temple. The invaders could only stand and watch as these innocents prayed for victory. Even now their parents were fighting and dying in the attempt to hold back Siff's forces.

She could see the doubt on the faces of her troops, their previous determination faltering at what they saw. Many would have their own children, many would have lost them to the cults. For Siff, it only served to reinforce her determination.

'Keep moving,' she said. 'Use this. Feed on it. This is why we are fighting – to stop this. If we do not succeed, if we do not take this city, then every child across the land will become a slave as these children are. They will all be in thrall to the White Widow.'

Slowly, her warriors made their way through the temple, picking their way past the kneeling infants. Not one of those youngsters looked up or paused in their prayers and Siff passed in silence until they reached an archway at the far end of the temple.

It led out onto the streets beyond, where the sounds of violence were louder, more intense. The gate was not far ahead and Siff led her troops on. She could see the top of the gate, the great bastion rising above the rooftops, but she had not moved more than a hundred feet before she was brought up short.

Barring the way were a host of men and women, none of them warriors. For all intents they looked like normal city folk – servants and slaves to the cults – but their eyes betrayed their zeal. They were blind in their service to Innellan, and despite Siff's small force being heavily armed they charged, heedless of the danger.

Quickly, Siff looked for another way to reach the gate, but she saw no other path as the crowd fell upon her. On instinct the swords sang in her grip, slashing right and left as though of their own accord, taking down men and women. They fell silently, and Siff could see the doubt on her own troops' faces as they were forced to defend themselves against the attacking rabble.

'The gate!' she shouted above the din, trying to focus her warriors on the task at hand, but their enemies were too numerous. Some of her troops could not fight against such a pitiful foe, allowing themselves to be dragged down and torn apart by the bare hands of the horde.

Siff cut her way through the crowd. She had to forget her troops now, there was no way to help them. Though it wounded her to abandon them, she had to open the gate or all would be lost.

Eventually she fought her way through, finding herself at the base of the wall. The armoured defenders of Mantioch had manned the ramparts and she raced past them, keen to reach the gate. If she could fight her way to the summit of the bastion she might yet be able to open the gate and save the day.

There was nothing but the frenzy of battle surrounding her now, nothing but the gate and its defenders. Arrows streaked past her, blades lanced into her flesh, but she ignored each blow. Her swords were slick in her grip, two slashing steel blades, delivering death to all who stood in her path.

She took the stairs two at a time, an inhuman growl issuing from deep within her. Before her stood more of Innellan's followers. These cultists did not fear death and they did not fear her. All they wanted was to obey the word of Innellan, to defend this place to the last. They were filled with the strength of their devotion and would fight on even if it meant facing a god and falling at Siff's hand.

An arrow pierced her ribs, tearing Siff from the reverie of battle, and she screamed above the din. Dropping one of her swords she wrenched the arrow free, casting it aside. She was almost at the summit now, the main gate tower just ahead. If she could reach it, if she could release the main mechanism holding the gate shut, her army would pour into the city and victory would be hers.

There was just a short walkway to the gate tower, but it was heavily guarded, a cluster of spearmen stood before her. Siff raced at them, but it was difficult to breathe now. The puncture wound in her side made every step agony.

A spear flew past her head, another clattered into the wall beside her. She raced forward as another spear was thrust at her, opening up a wound in her shoulder. Weakness and agony began to consume her senses.

No, not now. Not yet.

She had to win. Had to overcome—

The spearmen charged. Siff hacked at them, and though weak she still managed to cut one of them down. Another spear was thrust into her thigh, and she cried out in pain once more. From the corner of her eye she could see the Shengen warriors below, fighting on, attacking the gate with all their might, and she knew in that instant that she had failed them.

Siff was not strong enough. She had never been strong enough. Innellan was right – without the devotion of her army, without accepting the worship they could offer, she would never be powerful enough to defeat her sister.

A spearhead lanced her shoulder, driving her back. Siff dropped her one remaining weapon, grasping the spear shaft, but it was no use. The impetus of the attack pushed her to the edge of the battlements, and though she tried to grasp one of the merlons, fingers tearing at the stone, she could not find purchase.

The fall was mercifully brief, the air punched from her lungs as she hit the ground. In a daze she raised her head, seeing she was surrounded by a legion of Shengen troops, shouting under the tirade of arrows that rained down on them.

Siff tried to rise to her feet, but something inside her body was broken. Despite her weakened state, she could already feel her bones trying to knit themselves together, but not fast enough.

'Silver!' one of the Shengen shouted.

Siff was barely aware of something on fire as she was helped to her feet. She could taste blood in her mouth, feel a pounding in her head. It took her some moments to realise that the huge ram they'd used to batter the gate of Mantioch was in flames. Scores of dead legionaries lay around it, their mission to breach the gate long since failed.

'We have to retreat,' said a voice she recognised. Laigon was at her side, helping to bear her away from the wall as more missiles rained down. 'Form rank.'

Siff was powerless to resist as Laigon handed her over to his men. They raised their shields against the deluge and Laigon bellowed for the rest of his troops to retreat. He stood tall and proud even in the face of defeat, even under the hail of enemy fire.

It was his undoing.

Siff saw an arrow strike the emperor as she watched from amidst the shields. She was powerless to stop it piercing his neck above the gorget, driving down into his chest. Even then he did not fall, standing tall, defying the mortal injury as his men grabbed him and bore him away.

She cried out in anguish then, or it could have been a whimper, Siff could not tell. She was too weak to know. Time passed in a vortex as the Shengen retreated, leaving the burning ram behind them. Leaving the city of Mantioch undefeated.

When they were far enough away she managed to find the strength to push her way past the Shengen shield bearers. The rest of the army were still retreating, looking sullen, broken. The last of them came carrying their emperor, bearing him on a shield. As the cries of victory rose up from the walls of Mantioch, the legionaries laid Laigon down before Siff.

She knelt, grasping his bloody hand, feeling the weakness in his grip. He stared at her but could not speak and she sensed his life was ebbing away.

'Laigon,' she said. But words were useless now. Siff could only watch as the light left his eyes and what strength remained in his hand ebbed away.

He had come here to serve her, to help defeat a great evil, and now he had perished. Just as she had with Bezial, she knelt over him and wept.

Was it her stubbornness that had brought them to this? Her pride? If only she had accepted the worship of her men she would have had the power to heal him. Now it was too late. Laigon was the best of them and he was gone.

Siff let go of his hand and stood, staring at the impregnable gate and the huge ram beneath it wreathed in flames. Defeat was no easy thing to swallow. The shame of it began to burn within her. She knew now that there was only one way she would defeat Innellan. No matter how much she wanted to resist, she knew she could fight it no more.

Night eventually fell but Siff did not move, standing like a statue in the dark, watching the city of Mantioch as it rejoiced. The Shengens finally bore their emperor away, but still she stood as the flames of the ram died and the sound of the cultists died with it. Only one sound remained as the night encroached.

Beyond that wall a thousand children knelt in quiet prayer. Siff stood for long hours and listened to every word.

23

THREE days of hard riding across the arid landscape and they finally saw Kantor in the distance. After such a journey, seeing any shithole town at the back end of nowhere would have been a relief, but Josten had to admit Kantor was a sight to behold. He would have been more impressed if he wasn't heading straight into a snake's nest of trouble.

'What do you think?' Eyman asked proudly.

'I think I've been to worse places,' Josten replied, not missing an opportunity to dampen Eyman's enthusiasm.

'Ha! There are no *better* places, my friend. Kantor is the seat of civilisation. Science and learning were born in this place. More great philosophers were struck with illumination in Kantor than any other city in the world. A bolt of divine inspiration emboldens every man who enters through its hallowed gates.'

'And yet it managed to miss you by a country mile.'

Eyman gave him a disconsolate look, then a grin broke out across his face.

'My talents lie elsewhere,' he said.

'Let's hope we live long enough for you to show me,' Josten replied, kicking his horse on down the road.

When they drew close enough, Josten could see the guards at the gate were vigilant, questioning everyone who entered, though it was obvious more people were leaving the city than arriving.

'Let me do the talking,' said Eyman.

Josten had no problem with that as they reached the gate. As they were confronted by the guards he couldn't help but feel nervous. There was no reason for it – they were just travellers after all. No one would have any idea what they were here to do. Even so, he couldn't shake the feeling that this was all about to go wrong at any moment.

'Greetings, friend,' said Eyman to the guard. His countryman didn't seem particularly friendly but he continued nonetheless. 'We've come a long way. I hope the city's hospitality is as warm as ever?'

'What's your business?' the guard asked, uninterested in Eyman's small talk.

'Just passing through. We were working a farm on the northern frontier but the crop has failed. Now we head to the Suderfeld. To greener pastures.'

The guard seemed to believe Eyman, but his look turned suspicious when his gaze fell on Josten.

'You've got the look of a southerner to you,' he said. 'What brings you north? Can't be the work.'

Josten just looked back, unsure of what to say. The silence began to grow uncomfortable until Eyman leaned in.

'Forgive my uncle. He is deaf and dumb. Emphasis on the dumb, but he is a hard worker. You obviously have a keen eye, too. There is Suderfeld blood in his veins, but we

247

don't talk about it much in our family, know what I mean?'

He winked at the gate guard, who gave him a knowing nod.

'All right. On you go,' he said.

The two of them passed through with no further delay. They hadn't left the gate more than fifty yards behind them before Josten leaned over.

'Emphasis on the dumb?'

Eyman shrugged. 'Just a cover story. I meant no offence.'

They made their way along the roads of the city at a slow trot, but Josten was well aware of the urgency of their mission. On the surface, everything seemed normal, but an undercurrent of tension could be felt on the streets. Everyone went about their business, but there was no laughter, no children playing. It was a city on edge.

'Where are we headed?' Josten asked.

'I know a hostel. A quiet place. Discreet. We can rest there after our journey.'

'Discreet sounds good but we don't have any time for resting.'

Eyman nodded his agreement and they continued through the city until they reached a quiet avenue. Josten could imagine it had been a busy promenade once, but now it was all but deserted.

'Discreet is the word,' he said.

Eyman seemed confused. 'I've never seen it this quiet.'

'Let's not question it. We could do with some luck right now.'

Both men entered the hostel. Their horses were stabled and they were shown their small but clean rooms. When the innkeeper offered them warm water for a bath and some food, Josten was sorely tempted, but there was a job to do.

'Where do we begin?' asked Eyman as they made their way out of the hostel and along the abandoned street.

'Palace is the best bet,' Josten replied. 'If they're holding her anywhere, that'll be it.'

'We would need the luck of saints to break in there. It's the most heavily guarded redoubt in the city.'

'If we don't take a look we'll never know. Are you giving up already?'

'No, but—'

'Then lead the way.'

Eyman walked ahead, leading them through the streets towards the palace. Josten didn't want to admit that the lad was right – the palace would be all but impossible to break into – but they had to remain positive. They had a job to do no matter how difficult. When they finally reached the place, even Josten's faith started to wane.

'Those aren't Kantor militia,' Eyman said as he saw the Suderfeld knights patrolling the outer perimeter.

'No, they're King Stellan's personal retinue,' Josten replied, pulling up the hood of his cloak. Though the prospect was small, the last thing he needed was to be recognised. There was every chance he'd fought alongside – or worse, against – one of these men over the years.

'So what's the plan?' Eyman asked.

Josten surveyed the grounds in front of them. The wall was sheer, the gate impenetrable. There was no chance of bluffing their way in and if they managed to make it to the other side he was guessing the patrols would pick them up in no time.

Before he could even start to think about what to do, he

noticed there was someone else at the far end of the plaza. The man was standing casually enough, minding his own business, but Josten noted a couple of furtive glances in their direction. He was dressed like any other man in the street, hood drawn over his head hiding his face, but by the way he held himself it was obvious he was more than an ordinary city-dweller.

'Don't look,' Josten said. 'But we're—'

'Yep, already spotted him,' Eyman said.

Josten was impressed with the lad's vigilance. Perhaps there was hope for this mission yet.

'Let's go,' he said, and the two of them walked away from the palace.

Josten made his way towards the nearest alley. Once they were in the shadow of the narrow street he signalled for Eyman to hide in one of the many doorways.

'Let him get past you, then follow.'

Eyman obeyed without a word – another feather in his cap – as Josten walked on. He could only hope the man who'd been watching them would follow. If they were being tailed he wanted to know why.

As he turned the corner at the end of the alley, he gave a casual glance back, seeing the man was making his way along behind. Once out of sight, Josten waited, pulling his knife clear and hiding it in his cloak.

Then there was the wait. He could hear the footsteps coming along the alley, closer and closer. That old feeling of anticipation crept up in him – the one he always got just before he stuck a knife in someone's guts.

Josten braced himself as the cloaked figure turned the

corner. He must have been confident he'd not been spotted, because seeing Josten there made him almost jump out of his skin. He was up against the wall, knife to his throat, before he'd even had a chance to cry out. Eyman raced around the corner, knife in hand, ready to join in, just as Josten pulled the hood from the man's head.

'You stupid bastard!' Josten barked. 'I could have fucking killed you.'

Ctenka stared back at him, eyes wide. Then he smiled.

'Josten. Eyman. My old friends!'

Josten stepped back, breathing out in relief as Eyman and Ctenka embraced one another. When they'd finished, Ctenka opened his arms, offering Josten a similar greeting.

'Fuck off, will you,' Josten said. 'What the bloody hell are you doing here?'

'Following you,' Ctenka replied. 'Have been since you got here. But the question is, what the bloody hell are *you* doing here?'

'Silver sent us. There's a girl she needs us to find. Someone who—'

'Princess Adaali?' Ctenka said.

'Yes. How did you know?'

'Because we are on the same mission, my friend. But the princess is not at the palace. Come, we shouldn't discuss this on the street.'

Ctenka led them through the back alleys of the city, which seemed all but abandoned, even the rats had scurried into hiding, and before long Josten found himself in a cellar beneath some grimy building. Ctenka lit candles and poured wine for Josten and Eyman. As much as this was a time for keeping a clear head, he didn't refuse it.

'We helped Adaali enter the palace some days ago.'

'Who's we?' Josten asked.

'I am not alone in this. The resistance is small but determined.'

'Resistance? To what?'

'You don't know about the coup?'

'We don't know about anything,' Josten said.

Ctenka told him a grave tale: of men from the Suderfeld coming to bargain with the queen; of the vizier, Egil Sun, staging a coup that saw the royal family dead; of Ctenka finding Adaali in the streets of the city and helping her and a companion enter the palace to exact revenge. Of her failure.

'Five days ago she was taken from the palace under cover of night. Egil's bonecasters took her across the city.'

'So where is she now?' asked Josten.

'Egil has a tower to the south. It was one of Kantor's most prestigious libraries but now the vizier uses it as his private manse.'

'That's good. It won't be as heavily guarded as the palace.'

'I wouldn't count on that. But don't worry. I've sent men to every corner of the Cordral to gather soldiers loyal to the crown. In a few days I'll have gathered enough men to stage an assault on the tower.'

'That's no good for us. We don't have a few days. This has to happen now – tonight.'

Ctenka shook his head. 'Tonight? But there'd just be the three of us. I can't gather any men in that time. It'll be a suicide mission.'

Josten shrugged. 'It won't be my first. Are you in?'

Ctenka looked forlorn. Then slowly that grin spread across his face. 'Damn right I'm in.'

'That's the spirit.' Josten rose to his feet. 'Now lead the way.'

Lamplighters were igniting braziers on every street corner and a strange calm had fallen over the city. Ctenka led them to a nearby stable, opening the door to reveal an open-topped wagon. Two horses stood in their pens, munching hay in the shadows.

'Don't tell me,' said Josten. 'This is part of your cunning escape plan?'

'Have you got a better one?' Ctenka asked.

Of course he didn't.

They yoked the horses to the wagon and set off across the city. Eventually they reached the southern extent of Kantor and Josten could see the tower they were to assault. It stood away from the other buildings, a monolith rising up above the streets, ancient stone weathered and dark.

'There it is,' said Ctenka. 'Adaali is somewhere inside.'

Josten looked around the perimeter. It didn't appear guarded, but that didn't mean a thing. There might be a dozen armed men waiting inside.

'How do we get in?' Eyman said.

'Front door looks inviting enough,' Josten replied. They all looked at one another, realising the madness of it. Ctenka had been right; this was suicide. 'Who wants to knock?'

Together, all three of them climbed down from the wagon and made their way across the plaza to the tower.

24

LAIGON'S body lay within the command tent. It had been adorned with sweet-smelling flowers, a rare find in the desert, but those auxiliaries that knew the land had gladly gathered them for the Shengen emperor.

Siff laid a hand on his breastplate, fingers tracing the gilded pattern that adorned it. A memory came back to her then, of Bezial, of her tracing a furrow in the blood that spattered his armour, of cradling her faithful servant in her arms and weeping a river. She had no tears left for Laigon. He had been as faithful a servant as Bezial and his death cut her more deeply than a physical wound, but Siff had run out of grief. Now there was only anger, a need to reap vengeance on those who had done this.

But how? She was weak, this body almost ready to go back to the dirt. Her flesh had been pierced by a dozen blades and she had not been able to summon the will to sew them up. Her clothes were sodden with blood, but still she had refused the attentions of the surgeon. Such was her penance for failure.

Siff stood gingerly. She felt tired, as though she could sleep for a century, but still she managed to walk from the tent. It was some time before dawn, and in the turbid light she could see the mournful army she had led to its doom. The sullen mood that hung over the camp was not just a result of its defeat. Each man was grieving for an emperor he had followed on a crusade far from home. And now that emperor was dead.

There was no way Siff could launch another attack, not with these warriors. They were beaten, as was she.

Perhaps she should let them travel back east to their homeland. Release them from their bonds now their emperor was dead. Not that she would have much choice in the matter. If the Shengen Standings wished to leave what could she do to stop them? Maybe it was for the best that they return to their homeland, at least then they would live... for a time.

And what then for Siff? Should she continue west to the city of the White Widow? Should she face Innellan alone, weak and beaten, in a last desperate bid to halt this endless slaughter? The temptation was strong, but Siff knew what the outcome would be. Innellan would crush her easily, destroying her mortal body and sending her back through the Heartstone. It would mean more war. More devastation the likes of which this mortal realm had never seen.

Siff could not give in. She could not condemn this land after coming so far, could not abandon these people to their fate. There was only one way, and that was to continue the fight with nothing more than a defeated army at her back.

They would not stay defeated if you were to give in. You know what must be done.

It was the only way. To listen to that inner demon, that

voice always testing her, that temptation at the back of her mind. If she was to gain enough power to defeat her sister she knew she had to succumb to the one thing she had resisted for so long.

Now their emperor was defeated, it was *she* alone that could unite them. Her broken body had to be restored, Innellan had to be brought down. The only way to do that was to become the thing she most hated. To embody the beast she had travelled so far to stop.

To become the Archon she had always been.

Siff limped past the silent army. Mantioch stood in the distance, silent and looming in the gathering dark. The Shengen camp sat in the shadow of a rocky crag which she struggled to climb, slipping as her blood dripped from her wounds, making the ground slick. Once she reached the top she looked down, taking a deep breath, preparing herself for what had to be done.

Fires burned hereabout. She could see piles of the dead being prepared for the pyre. A pall of doom had settled over the camp, a battered army preparing itself for the final defeat. It would not stay defeated long.

'Hear me,' she called out to them. Her voice was weak. No one was listening. 'I said hear me.' This time stronger as she called upon her last reserves of energy.

A few of the Shengen legionaries looked up at her. Some of the auxiliaries stirred themselves from their despair.

'Come closer,' she called. 'I would have you listen. I need to speak.'

There was a ripple of chatter as they considered whether

to heed her words. Some of them came a little closer, others chose to stay where they were, huddled by their fires.

Siff closed her eyes. This was her final chance. The path she was on could lead to her destruction. What she was about to demand could be the end of her. She might so easily fall to the corruption, the temptation of worship twisting her into something worse than Innellan. But to do nothing was to hand her sister a dynasty that could never be ended.

'Listen to me!'

Her cry echoed across the camp and stirred the army from its brooding reverie. In ones and twos they began to come, moving past the fires, gathering together below the rocky outcrop. Every eye was on her, every face upturned to listen to her words. Before long, the entire camp had risen, had walked to the foot of the rock to stand in wait.

'I loved your emperor, as you did,' Siff said. 'Laigon was mine as much as he was yours. He came north with me because he had faith. As you have. He knew our path was the right one. That defeating our enemies was the only way this land could be spared from perpetual misery.'

Through the gloom she could see they were listening with rapt attention. All eyes were on her, an entire army hanging on her every word.

'I understand your grief at his passing. I feel it too, and I am truly sorry. I was the one who brought him here. I was the one he followed. Who *you* followed into this forsaken place to fight a war that was not yours to fight. But I promise you, if you stay with me, if you follow me, I will show you victory. Our enemies will not stand a chance against us.'

'You will just lead us to our deaths!'

An anonymous voice from the darkness, but it stirred a wave of discontent through the crowd. Siff realised her words were not enough. She had their attention, but she had lost their hearts. There was only one way to show them, only one way to instil faith into this army of hers once more.

She closed her eyes, spreading her arms out to the dawn. The air and the earth were filled with life and she consumed what she could, drinking in the latent energy of this place. It imbued her with a fleeting burst of manna. Enough to restore her faculties, enough to allow her to reveal her true form.

There were gasps from the gathered crowd as Siff began to glow with power, an aura that burned through the darkness. Vast feathered wings sprouted from her back and she clenched her teeth at the transformation, her mortal body wracked with the pain of it as her flesh cracked and tore, bones stretching, breaking, creating a new form. Her hair grew long and dark, hands stretching into talons as she rose up from the rock, looming over the army like a new-born saint.

'I will give you victory,' she proclaimed, her voice echoing like a clarion call. 'I will lead you to glory. And all I ask in return is that you have faith.'

Her eyes burned with fire as she looked down at the crowd. One by one the Shengen and the slaves fell to their knees, mouths open in awe.

'Urelia,' shouted one Shengen centurion. 'Urelia the Wise has come to lead us.'

It was an ancient name she recognised. One she had used in millennia gone by. It seemed fitting enough.

Even as her last reserves of strength ebbed away, and she thought she could maintain this ethereal form no longer, Siff was suddenly filled with the power of their belief. They began to pray, their disparate voices joined as one in their worship of her. Each spoken word filled her with more power, feeding into her core as a trickle at first, becoming a stream until it was a river, a torrent burning within her Archon's soul.

It was a blessing she had not felt for so long. A gift she had spurned for centuries for the good of this mortal realm. Now she would feed on it. Now she would use it. Now she would show her faithful what she could give them in return.

Siff rose, her wings beating, whipping the still air into a maelstrom.

'Come,' she called, her voice booming like thunder. 'Take up your arms and follow me.'

Without waiting for her army to respond, Siff soared towards the gates of Mantioch. At the foot of the barbican the ram still sat, battered and burned, and she streaked forward like a comet. The gates exploded inwards, sending burning shards of wood and iron in all directions.

She landed beyond the gate, seeing the shocked army that awaited her beyond the city walls. Siff waited for a moment, a god among men, giving them the chance to surrender themselves, allowing them the opportunity to fall to their knees and forsake Innellan in favour of a more benevolent deity. It was not to be.

When they refused to fall prostrate before her exalted

visage, Siff was thankful. They had made their choice and she would punish them for it. The justice of a god.

The army of Mantioch, the gathered soldiers of a dozen desert cults, charged as one at the Archon who faced them. Siff swept forward on white wings. Spears, blades and axes hacked at her, but none could make a mark on her flesh, a body that was armoured in the faith of thousands. With every sweep of her arm Siff laid low the host that charged at her. For every dozen she slaughtered, a score would charge forth and she faced them in the joyous rapture of battle.

For how long she fought she could not tell, but the resolve of the horde eventually broke before her fury. When she had destroyed the strongest, the most zealous, all that was left were the weak of mind and body. As she towered above them on a pile of corpses, the defenders of Mantioch began to fear her, to regard her with the awe she demanded.

They knew they could not win. They knew that no matter their faith in the witch queen Innellan they would not be spared. There was no deliverance from Siff, and the only choice they had was to crawl on their bellies and beg for mercy.

At first she considered withholding it. So caught up was she in the joy of battle that she forgot who she was. Forgot why she had come here – to deliver these mortals, not to destroy them. That thought was gone in a fleeting moment as she rose above them, glaring down with eyes that burned like a sun.

'That is the way,' she said, voice booming throughout the city. 'Bow down. Abandon your false idol. Innellan cannot save you, but I will grant you redemption. For I am merciful. Pledge your allegiance to me. Put your faith in me and be born anew.'

She could hear their voices raised in a single prayer as she rose above them, the blood of the slain still dripping from her body. She had been anointed by her enemies and now she would bathe in their worship as only an Archon could.

The power was exquisite. She had never felt stronger, never felt such an intensity of faith.

Her army of Shengen warriors flooded through the gates, but they stood back in awe. She could see pride in their eyes, an admiration... belief.

Siff came to land in between the people of Mantioch and her army.

'Come,' she called. 'Gather to me.'

They obeyed, and she was soon surrounded by a crowd of thousands. In her new form she towered above the throng.

'From this night you are all one. Those who have been loyal to me, and those liberated from their shackles. Now you are family. Brothers and sisters united in faith. Rest. Feast. Rejoice. For tomorrow we strike west to face Innellan. And nothing will stand in our path.'

A vast cheer rose up, resounding throughout the city, threatening to shake the walls of Mantioch to their foundations.

Siff rose up once more, wings spreading, bearing her to the summit of Mantioch's highest tower. There she landed, taking a moment to gaze down on the crowd as it celebrated its union. The entire city was held in the reverie of worship, pledging their faith in her.

Dragging herself from the seductive sight, she entered

the temple at the tower's summit. It had been abandoned, every priest of Katamaru's Faithful having flocked to join the mass communion below.

At the centre of the vast chamber she saw it sitting there, calling to her like a beacon. The relic she had fought so hard to claim. The Stone of Katamaru was a simple artefact; an egg-shaped jewel no bigger than a man's hand.

Siff picked up the Stone and gazed into it. This was the key to another realm. It would be so easy for her to harness its power right now, to forget all this and slip through a door and back to her rightful homeland. But that would give her no peace. Across a sea of time and space the other Archons were preparing for war. Soon they would come through the Heartstone and wreak havoc on this place. The slaughter Siff had committed today would be nothing by comparison to the apocalypse that would follow.

Now she had to face Innellan, and find the strength to force her back home.

25

ADAALI was still chained to the ceiling, the flesh of her wrists torn and covered in sores, arms feeling as though they had long since split from their sockets. She fought against the delirium, but it was impossible to focus.

Candles flickered in their sconces, the wax having burned down to drip onto the bloodstained floor. In the shadows knelt bonecasters, heads bowed as they murmured their dark prayers. The air hung thick with magic, Adaali could feel it like a heavy pall, choking her with its intensity.

Lying on the floor of the chamber, arms spreadeagled, was the corpse of Egil Sun. He was naked, two black stones placed over his eyes. In the dim candlelight Adaali could just make out black necrotic veins standing out all over his body. She could guess the purpose of this ritual – the bonecasters were trying to raise their master from the dead – but after days of praying over his rotting corpse it was clear they did not share his gift for necromancy.

Despite their failure to raise the dead, Adaali could feel their evil rite's effects on her own soul. Whatever unholy magic they were summoning was dragging her into a torpor; even without the manacles holding her fast she doubted she would have been able to move. Their squalid words leached her will, pulling her into a lake of despair. She was drowning in it. There was no escape; there would be no victory. This was her fate, for as long as they willed it.

Memories came to her in brief flashes and it was impossible to discern what was real and what was a construction of her bewildered mind. Visions flashed before her eyes, too fleeting to grasp.

Adaali shook her head, sweat dripping from her brow. She tried to clear her mind, tried to focus through the miasma. There was no hope of rescue – she would have to make her own way out of here. No help was coming, no one even knew she was imprisoned in this place.

You are stronger than you know.

Was that her own mind telling her to resist, or was it that voice again? The one that belonged to…

No, the name was gone, but the sentiment remained. She was chained, but she was not helpless. A memory came to her, horrific and hopeful all at once. They had displayed her mother's corpse and brought it back through the Bone Gate with the intention of slaying her, but she had resisted. Adaali had made the wraith obey her will, had reached out and touched the wayward soul of her mother and resisted them. Could she do so again?

Adaali closed her eyes, trying to block out her surroundings, trying to drown the sound of the bonecasters' chanting with her own strength of will. There had to be a way to stop them, had to be a way to counter the vile rite they were performing. In all her life she had seldom prayed, but if ever there was a time to start surely it was now.

She opened her eyes, looking up to the dark recesses of the chamber's ceiling. There were only shadows, but her eyes penetrated deeper. Adaali reached out, for the first time in her life hoping, yearning for there to be someone watching over her. If there had ever been a god above this earth then surely they would be looking down on this, seeing this blasphemy being enacted. If she were to ask, would it not be the time for them to listen?

'Help me,' she whispered to the shadows. 'Please help me.'

I told you, I am with you.

It was a distant voice but one Adaali recognised. Though she could barely hear it, she already felt that little trickle of hope.

'Will you release me?' she asked.

I cannot release you. But you have the strength within yourself. All you have to do is find it.

It seemed impossible. Adaali was weak, bound, there was nothing she could do to get herself out of this.

I told you to trust me. And you must trust me now. Do not despair.

It was easy enough advice to give to someone, but Adaali wasn't in a trusting mood. The chain bit into her wrists and the droning sound of the bonecasters' prayers was driving her to the edge of sanity. She was thirsty, hungry, her grief ready to boil over into endless tears, and she was angry...

So use it.

Adaali gritted her teeth. In that moment she knew, of all the emotions coursing through every fibre, the most prominent was rage. All that pent-up hate, fuelled by her

265

grief and helplessness… it was there, ready to boil over, ready to be unleashed in a storm.

For the first time in days she felt strength returning to her limbs. Her muscles clenched, her atrophied fibres coming back to life in an instant. She pulled on the chains binding her to the ceiling, feeling them give, dust falling in motes from the rafters. For so long the monotonous prayers of the bonecasters had held her in bondage, but they no longer affected her. Their words were empty now, meaningless prattling. The manacles that secured her wrists no longer felt constraining. By the sheer strength of her belief, she knew that they were brittle as glass.

Adaali's voice had been hoarse, her throat parched, but the bellow that welled up from her lungs filled the chamber in a cacophony of rage. As she spread her arms wide the chains snapped.

She fell to her knees, feeling the cold floor beneath her. The bonecasters retreated in fear as she stood. Her legs trembled, not from lack of use but from the burning rage that fuelled her.

As the first bonecaster tried to make his escape, Adaali flung herself across the room, falling on him like a striking lion. She gripped him below the chin, wrenching his head back until she heard his neck snap, the body going limp beneath her.

When she stood she saw a second bonecaster staring in terror. Her swift blow turned his head around with a crack and he collapsed in a heap. Behind her, another drew his weapon, striking at her. Adaali caught his arm, the blade inches from her flesh. Twisting his wrist she heard the crack of bone, his scream high-pitched. She flung him aside, where he hit the wall with a sickening crunch.

There was only one of them left now, and he had fallen to his knees in fear, hands clasped together, praying to whatever gods might deliver him.

'No one is listening,' she said, grasping his head in both hands and lifting it until his fearful eyes regarded hers. 'No one is listening!'

She screamed, squeezing his head in her hands, hearing it break, seeing the blood begin to stream from his eyes. Adaali kept crushing his skull until his body went limp in her grip. As she dropped him to the floor she felt the reverie of her kill, the swell of victory within her. But she was not done yet.

The door to the cell was locked and there was no key, but Adaali would not let that stop her. She shoved at the heavy wood, hearing the frame crack and the ping of the bolt as it collapsed before her. The corridor outside was well lit and she could see several sentries waiting in an anteroom beyond. They were dressed in the uniform of the city militia, the same men who had betrayed her family. Men who had allowed her mother and brother to be killed. She would punish that complicity.

Before the militiamen could react she had charged at the nearest one, wrenching the spear from his grip. Adaali was acting on instinct now, stances and forms flashing through her mind as the spear swung left and right, thrusting and parrying, piercing throats, finding gaps in armour. Each of them died quickly, too quickly, but Adaali knew there would be more.

She left the corpses behind her, dashing down the

corridor, her body filled with a burning energy, fuelled by her hate and the thirst for revenge. Before she could find her next victim a sudden thought halted her slaughter.

Dantar.

They had taken him too. He must be here somewhere, perhaps suffering as she had suffered at the hands of the bonecasters. But where could he be? This was a vast building and he could be anywhere.

Adaali closed her eyes, gripping the spear tightly, willing a vision of him into her mind. She calmed, breathing deeply, reaching out with her consciousness. It was a strange sensation, an action alien to her, but she performed it instinctively. Her senses opened up, her mind probing the area, feeling rather than seeing. As she concentrated on Dantar her consciousness searched yet further, feeling with wraithlike fingers, easing through walls and down flights of stairs all at once. Eventually she sensed him. Though she could see nothing she knew it was Dantar, and she felt his rage at being bound like an animal.

Her eyes flicked open and she was moving once more, down through the tower, down through the dark, taking the stairs three at a time. There were no guards in the lower levels but that was better for them, anyone who got in her way now would regret it.

Eventually she reached a dark corridor in the lower dungeon. As she padded through the cloying tunnel she could hear the sound of a man in pain, grunts of agony echoing from the cell at the far end. The door was ajar, the chamber beyond illuminated by the light of a brazier. Adaali could smell the hot stink of burning meat and she gritted her teeth against the bile that rose in her mouth.

Dantar was chained, as she had been. His naked torso was drenched in sweat as he hung from the ceiling, mouth bound with a rope, skin striped with black burns. Beside him stood a torturer, stripped to the waist, rolls of fat fighting one another for space on his hulking body. The brute was heating an iron brand in the coals of the brazier, the metal burning white hot.

Adaali entered and the torturer looked up as though he'd been expecting her. There was no surprise, no emotion at all, but then she guessed that was necessary for a man in such a grim line of work.

The torturer lumbered towards her, raising the burning shaft of iron. Adaali knew she should have struck first, thrust her spear deep into those rolls of flesh to halt his attack, but instead she stood and waited, savouring each moment of this.

As the iron brand came down at her head she raised a hand, catching the shaft in her fist, holding it tight. There was a hiss as her flesh momentarily cooled the white-hot metal and she saw the flicker of doubt on the torturer's face – the realisation that he would not win this. That he was about to die.

Her spearhead pierced him below the jaw, driving up through his skull to protrude from the top of his head. Those emotionless eyes went wide, then dimmed as the torturer dropped to the ground in a heap, leaving her with the iron brand still clutched in one hand.

Adaali dropped it, glaring at her palm, expecting to see

it reduced to a blackened ruin. Her flesh was unharmed. She had no time to wonder about the miracle of it. Instead she moved towards Dantar, uncoupling the chain that secured him to the ceiling and letting him down gently. There was a ring of keys on the torturer's table and she grabbed them, trying one after the other in the manacles at Dantar's wrist. He groaned as she managed to find the right key on the fourth attempt, gently releasing his chafed and bloody wrists.

'Are you all right?' she whispered as she untied the rope from his mouth. 'Can you hear me? Can you walk?'

Dantar raised an eyebrow at her flurry of questions. 'I'm confident I can walk out of this place,' he replied.

She helped him to his feet. His legs were unsteady but she managed to bear his weight as they struggled out of the cell. The corridor was still empty, but from somewhere in the tower she could hear shouts of alarm.

'We have to move faster,' she said, practically carrying him on her shoulder.

Her anger was ebbing now, her body beginning to ache from its ordeal. Whatever magics she had manifested were receding fast. Her wrists were raw from the chains, the sting in her arm where the corpse of her mother had taken a slice of flesh intensified with every step they took.

They came out on a landing with three corridors. Adaali could hear more commotion, but couldn't tell where it was coming from.

'Which way?' she whispered.

Dantar shook his head. 'I don't care, just pick one.'

Struggling down the middle corridor, Adaali cursed as

they came to a closed door. The only other way was back, and before she could turn she heard a shout of alarm from behind them.

Quickly she tried the handle, expecting to find her way barred, but the handle turned with a click of the latch and she pushed the door open. Adaali barely registered the flickering candlelight or the bulky desk in one corner as she bundled Dantar through and closed the door behind her, bolting it hastily.

Dantar rested against the wall, his breathing heavy, as Adaali turned and surveyed the room. It was a study with books on the shelves, scrolls on the desk beside an inkwell and discarded quills. In the candlelight she could see one of the parchments was half finished and only recently abandoned.

Someone was standing in the shadowy recesses of the chamber. Adaali silently cursed herself for leaving the spear buried in the torturer's skull.

'Come out,' she ordered, desperate to sound more confident than she was.

Duke Bertrand stepped forward into the light. He was smiling, confident as ever, but Adaali could see a shadow of doubt marring his arrogant brow.

'So good to see you alive, Adaali. I was hoping we would meet—'

'Shut up,' she said, in no mood to listen. 'I think you've said enough, don't you?'

He spread his arms showing his empty palms. A gesture of peace perhaps? Or surrender? 'I can understand why you're upset. But I did try to help you. Surely you remember that?'

Adaali was unsure what she'd have done if there was a weapon in her hands. Would she have stuck it in this simpering bastard? Or would she have spared him?

'I remember you offered me an alliance. You offered me my own throne. What do you offer now I am not in chains?'

'My offer still stands. I didn't want any of this. I only want—'

'I should kill you,' she hissed, stepping forward.

He lurched back, cowering behind his shaking hands. 'I never wanted any of this,' he sobbed, the façade gone now. 'It was never my idea. I told you… I told you when we first met I have a master. I don't have any choice.'

He fell to his knees, tears streaming from his one good eye. Adaali knew this was no act. Bertrand was no schemer, despite appearances. He was just a pawn; somebody else's tool in a deadly game.

She walked towards him, so close she could smell the musky perfume he wore. 'Tell your master I am not finished here. When he comes he should not rest easy. I will find him. I will kill him.'

Bertrand nodded, unable to look her in the eye. That was enough for Adaali, and she helped Dantar to his feet once more.

There was another door from the chamber, leading out into a stairwell that twisted downwards. More noise echoed from below, a violent commotion barring their way. Someone was fighting in the depths of the tower.

She had no idea who they were, but it was clear they were no friends of the militia. Perhaps they were even here to help. Had there been an uprising? Had the people of Kantor finally realised the crimes committed against their royal family and risen up against the conspirators? Adaali was too desperate to worry about that now. She had to get out of there before Dantar passed out from his injuries.

They both struggled down the stairs, the sounds of battle growing louder. At the bottom she saw a fierce scene that brought memories of the battle in the royal palace back to her in stark reality.

Half a dozen militiamen fought against three intruders. In the torchlight of the entrance hall there were already three bodies on the ground, two in militia uniforms, one in the robes of a bonecaster. The door out to the street gaped open but the way was blocked by the battle. Two of the intruders Adaali didn't recognise but one of them she knew. Ctenka defended himself desperately against the militia, sword sweeping to left and right. At his shoulder was an older man, a southerner, staring at the enemy with a grim look of determination. The last one was as young as Ctenka, handsome but for the wild look of fear on his face.

Retreat appeared to be the last thing on their minds, despite the desperate situation, but without help they would surely be killed before they could make it to the stairs.

Adaali felt her anger well up once more. It overtook her fatigue, and she helped Dantar slump at the bottom of the stairs to lean wearily against the wall. There was a spear on the ground not ten feet away, the militia had their backs to her, no one even knew she was there.

She darted from the shadows, rolling, swooping up the

spear and rising to her feet in a single motion. One deft thrust and a militiaman went down. Rage burned within her, threatening to overwhelm her senses as another foe turned to face her. He hacked in with his curved blade and she span aside, sweeping the tip of her spear across his throat. She darted back as the rest of the militia broke their line to face this new enemy.

No sooner had they turned than the man from the Suderfeld barged in, shouldering one of them aside, his sword sweeping to hack into the arm of another. That was enough for the remaining militia and they broke, running in a panic for any exit they could find.

Adaali was left with her three rescuers, though who had done the rescuing was up for argument. As she regarded them, the world began to swim at the periphery of her vision. She staggered, the spear falling from her grip, but before she hit the ground the Suderfelder had caught her.

She gazed up at him, her head swimming with confusion. It was a face she recognised, a name coming to her from the dark void of her memory.

'Josten?' she asked, before her eyes became too heavy to keep open.

26

'Sнe's met you before?' asked Ctenka.

Josten shook his head. 'I've never laid eyes on her.'

'Then how did she know your name?'

'Trust me I'm as curious as you, but if we don't get out of here we're going to get butchered.'

That was true enough. The guards had run, but he was pretty sure as soon as they'd gathered reinforcements they'd be back.

Josten picked Adaali up. She hung limp in his arms, hardly weighing a thing. This girl he'd come so far to find, who was so important to Silver, seemed like nothing but a lost waif. But Josten had seen how she wielded that spear, how she took down her enemies so mercilessly. It was obvious she was more than just some innocent child.

'What about him?' Eyman said, before Josten could reach the door.

There was someone lying in a heap by the stairs. He looked like he'd been through it. Josten was only here for the girl, but as he glanced over he couldn't help but think he'd seen that wounded man somewhere before.

'Bring him,' he said. 'And hurry the fuck up.'

Josten carried Adaali across the square to the waiting wagon. Ctenka and Eyman dragged the other prisoner behind, one under each arm. As they bundled him into the back of the wagon, Josten scanned the area. He could hear the militia shouting in the distance but no one was running after them... yet.

Ctenka jumped into the seat of the wagon and took the reins as Josten sat beside him, blade at his side in case they met any resistance. Eyman crouched in the back with their unconscious load.

'I can't believe we're gonna make it,' he said, eyes wide as relief took over from panic.

'We're not out of the city yet,' said Josten. 'Stay sharp.'

The wagon trundled on through the streets. Ctenka took them on a circuitous route and Josten could see the sense in it. If the militia were after them they'd never be able to follow along the maze of twisting back streets. The road was barely wide enough in places, but that didn't seem to bother Ctenka as he guided them along in the darkness. Eventually they came out of a side street onto one of the main thoroughfares and Josten could see the city gate ahead of them.

He glanced into the back of the wagon. Eyman had covered the princess in a sack and draped a cloak over the other man's shoulders. With luck it would just seem like he was sleeping, and hopefully Ctenka could bluff them past the gate.

'Don't want to speak too soon,' Ctenka said in a low voice, 'but I think Eyman's right. I can't believe how easy that was.'

'If it's all the same I'll save the celebrations till we're miles away,' Josten said.

They should all have just kept their mouths shut. Before they were within a hundred yards of the gate someone shouted ahead of them. Josten's hand went to the hilt of the sword beside him, but instead of the militia running at them, spears at the ready, they began to open the gate.

It yawned wide, as though beckoning them through, but in the bright streetlight, Josten could see someone was entering. Men on horseback paraded through, two abreast, pennants held aloft. As they came closer, Josten could see the horsemen were armoured, the flags flying the golden lion of Canbria.

'What now?' Ctenka whispered.

'Just keep going,' Josten replied. 'And try not to look like we've just kidnapped the heir to the throne of Kantor.'

Not much of a plan, but it was the only one they had.

The wagon trundled closer to the gate, the procession of knights getting ever nearer. Ctenka pulled the horses to the side of the road, nodding respectfully as the knights reached them and began to ride past. Not one of them acknowledged him as they went, but then they were an arrogant bunch as a rule – none of them would have deigned to exchange pleasantries with some common-as-muck foreigner.

Josten kept his head down as the knights rode past, hand on the hilt of his sword, not that there'd be any fighting his way out of this. Thankfully not one of them stopped to check what they were doing or to have a look in the back of their wagon, and once the last of the knights had ridden past, Ctenka flicked the reins and set the wagon trundling towards the gate once more.

The sentries on the gate were still moaning about the knights as they rolled up. Ctenka stopped the horses and Josten held his breath, ready to strike if either of the gate guards took too much of an interest in the wagon's contents.

'Fucking foreign bastards,' Ctenka said, before the sentries could even acknowledge him.

'I know,' said one of them. 'Bloody cheek of it. Riding in here like they own the place. But what you gonna do?'

'At least they're on our side, right?' Ctenka continued. 'Wouldn't want to face any of those bastards in battle with nothing but sacks of grain for ammunition.' He gestured to the back of the wagon.

The sentry nodded. 'Yeah, damn right.'

'Anyhow. Soon be sun up, and this wagon won't deliver itself.'

The sentry nodded, waving him through. Ctenka even offered a wink and a wave to the other guards at the gate. Josten guessed there were some advantages to being a local.

The wagon bounced along until they'd reached a ridge to the north, then Ctenka opened the horses up. He flicked the reins, barking at the team, urging them on along the road. Josten looked back at the city, lights twinkling in the pre-dawn, expecting riders to come galloping after them at any second, but no one was in sight.

'Where are they?' said Eyman. 'They must know she's gone by now.'

Josten glanced down at the girl, who was still passed out in the back of the wagon. She looked little more than a bag of bones. 'Maybe she's not as important to them as we thought.'

'She's the princess of Kantor,' Eyman said.

'Josten could be right,' said Ctenka. 'Whoever holds sway in the city now has more important things to worry about than a troublesome heir. The Suderfeld presence in the city increases every day. And rumour has it there will be an invasion from the north.'

'Not if Silver can help it,' Josten replied. 'She should have defeated Mantioch by now. She's most likely on her way to face Innellan as we speak.'

'Then we had best hurry, if this girl is important to the cause,' said Ctenka, not allowing his horses any respite.

They travelled well into the blistering heat of the next day. Josten was worried about their lack of supplies, but Ctenka had made sure the wagon was laden with water and dry food before they set off. Josten didn't want to admit it, but the lad had come a long way since Dunrun. He seemed much more capable than the green recruit he'd said goodbye to a year before.

Eventually, as a rare bank of cloud cooled the afternoon, they stopped their wagon. Josten jumped down. The girl had still not regained consciousness, though Eyman was sure she was simply asleep, her breathing strong and regular. Their other passenger had seemed to recover a little too, and Josten offered him water and food.

'Thank you,' the man said, taking the dried meat.

Josten watched him, trying to think back to where he knew this man from. Those eyes, like an animal's, were the most familiar thing of all. Where had he...?

'You were at Kessel,' Josten said, as he thought back to

the day he and Randal had been set free. The man stopped chewing and looked up at him gravely. 'You... you spared us. Me and Randal. You were supposed to kill one of us in the desert, but you just walked away. You're one of the Sword Saints.'

The man carried on chewing the tough meat. When he'd finished he didn't have anything more to say.

'How did you get here? How do you know her?' Josten asked, gesturing to where Adaali lay in the wagon.

'I found her in the desert,' he said. 'I was protecting her.'

'Great job,' Eyman said as he cradled the girl's head, mopping her brow with a damp cloth.

Josten gave Eyman a sharp look, but he couldn't argue with the sentiment. 'What's your name?'

'I am Dantar.'

'And you were one of Innellan's?'

Dantar shook his head. 'Never. I left her behind. As you did. I am loyal to no one.'

'Not even to her?' He pointed towards the girl.

'Only to her,' Dantar replied. 'I was in the desert alone, and she came to me. I thought I would never be loyal to anyone, but I willingly pledged myself to her.'

'So what changed your mind?

'She seemed deserving of it. I was a man who tried to believe in nothing. But we all need someone to have faith in.'

Josten thought about Silver for a moment. 'Yeah, I guess you're right.'

He had Eyman see to Dantar's wounds. The burns looked painful, and had to be treated before infection set in. Eventually the time for resting was over and they carried on into the night until the desert air grew cold, and Josten ordered a camp be made. Ctenka saw to his horses as Eyman built a fire, and for the first time since they'd left the city Adaali stirred. Josten watched as she came to, recognising Dantar and surveying her surroundings with a confused expression.

She sat up in the wagon, and Josten offered her a skin of water. She drank deeply, then sat in silence, weighing him up.

'You're safe,' Josten said. 'Do you remember us?'

'I remember him,' she said pointing at Ctenka. 'You I'm not so sure.'

Her eyes twinkled in the light of the campfire, and though he'd never seen her before today he felt there was something in them he recognised. Perhaps it was her bearing, perhaps the way she spoke, but he couldn't shake the feeling they'd already met.

'I feel it too,' she said suddenly.

'What?' he replied.

'That we know each other. I realise it is impossible. I have never laid eyes on you before, but I feel I know you.'

Josten shrugged. 'The world is full of mysteries.'

'It is,' she said. 'Like why you came to rescue me. I know why he would come,' she gestured to Ctenka. 'But not you.'

'I fight for a woman in the north. Her name is Silver, and she is...'

What was she? A witch? A god?

'Fighting a war she must win,' Adaali finished.

'How do you know?' Josten asked.

'I wish I could tell you,' she replied. 'All I know is that

281

we have some kind of link. I also know she wants something from me, or you would not have been sent all this way to fetch me, and you would not have obeyed at such risk to yourself if it were not important.'

'She sees something in you. I don't know what and I don't know how, but it's important. There's a great evil in the north. Innellan threatens all the lands south of the Ramadi and if she's not defeated we will all be slaves, or worse. I can't force you to come with me, but I hope you'll help.'

She regarded him sceptically. 'You can't force me? But if I refuse to come, I think you'll try anyway.'

'I'd prefer it if you came of your own free will. I've been ordered to protect you and bring you safely to the north, so you've got me whether you like it or not. I don't have any choice in it.'

Adaali laughed, holding out her hand to him. 'Very well. Then we are stuck together. You and me against the world.'

Josten froze. He'd heard those words before, what seemed a lifetime ago. Livia Harrow had said the same thing to him just before they'd been separated. Just before she'd been taken by cultists and he'd followed her to the desert in the north.

'You and me against the world,' was all he could think to say as he took her hand. She had a surprisingly strong grip.

He left her in the wagon while he tried to get things straight in his head. No amount of thinking could make any sense of it though, and later he and Ctenka found themselves alone by the fire. It had been a long time since he'd had a chance to talk to the lad.

'You don't need to come with us,' he said.

'I know,' Ctenka replied, staring into the flames.

'We can take her the rest of the way, you've done enough. You should go somewhere safe.'

'Are you asking me or telling me? I know what you think. I remember what you said – *don't be a soldier, it's not for you*. Well I'll make my own way, if it's all the same.'

'You can do what you want, it's just—'

'This is my fight as much as it is yours. I returned to Kantor to protect my country. To serve the royal family. I failed them.' He glanced over to the wagon where Adaali slept. 'Now is my chance to make amends.'

'I understand. But you should know, it won't be safe where we're headed. There's a war, and your princess might end up in the middle of it.'

'Then where better for me to be?'

Josten patted Ctenka on the shoulder. Maybe he'd been wrong about him, maybe Ctenka *was* cut out to be a soldier, but then, who was he to decide? After so many years and so many mistakes, Josten Cade knew better than anyone that you should never judge a man until you'd seen him tested. And soon enough, they'd all be tested like never before.

27

THE wagon trundled on through the desert until there was little of the path left to follow. Despite being with men she barely knew, Adaali felt safer than she had in a long time.

Her head was clear now, and all she had left were memories, some distant, some stark and frightening. It was not just the thought of her mother's walking corpse, but what Adaali had done.

She'd acted as though someone else was controlling her faculties. An unseen hand filling her with power and fury and might. It was terrifying to know she had lost control in such a way, but at the same time she yearned to feel that sensation again. If she could harness the power within her she felt as though there would be no one who could stand against her.

Adaali shuddered at the thought. Dantar gave her a concerned look. She raised a hand to signal she was fine, and he went back to gazing across the endless desert. He had recovered quickly from his wounds, the burns were livid on his flesh but he gave no word of complaint. Of all the men who accompanied her north she trusted him the most. It was ridiculous that she would choose this mad hermit from the desert as her bodyguard, but he held no other allegiance but to her, and that was just the kind of man she needed.

Ctenka was trustworthy enough. He had proven himself loyal when he helped her enter the palace, and there seemed no pretence to him. Whistling as he drove the wagon he appeared to have not a care in the world, even making the occasional joke. There was something of the likeable buffoon about him, but Adaali did not know if she could rely on him fully. His companion, Eyman, was equally unassuming. He and Ctenka talked openly on the journey about their old days in the militia, and she was sure they were loyal enough. Harmless was the word. That was not the kind of man she needed right now.

The man Josten was far from harmless.

There was a haunted look to his lean face. Adaali had never seen a visage so grim, and yet she could not shake the feeling that she knew him. Deep in her heart she sensed she could trust him, but still her head told her to be wary. He was dour, taciturn and beside all that he was clearly a killer. Add to the fact he was from the very country that had plotted to usurp the throne from her mother, and everything told her she should hate this man. By rights he was her enemy, but she just couldn't regard him as such. Her only option was to give him time to prove himself.

On the second day they skirted the shores of Demon Sound and left the border of her homeland behind. They did not see another soul on the journey until the third day when Ctenka warned them of a rider approaching in the distance. Craning her neck, Adaali saw a far-off cloud of dust.

Josten ordered them to be on their guard, and his companions took up their weapons. Dantar grabbed a sword from a pile of supplies at the base of the wagon and Adaali placed the only spear across her lap. It felt good to have the weapon close.

As the horseman reined in before the wagon, Josten raised a hand in greeting. The man wore a unique style of armour Adaali recognised from a book she had read of foreign armies. This man was from the Shengen Empire far to the east, a scout by the looks of him.

'I am glad I found you,' said the scout. His face was filthy but he still had a noble bearing.

'Lucky you did,' Josten replied. 'This is a lot of desert to get lost in.'

'I was told where to you would be. Urelia Reborn sees everything. She is my guide.'

Josten gave a furtive glance at the other men, unsure of what the scout was talking about. 'Good for you. Did Silver send you?'

The scout suddenly looked confused. 'The one you call Silver is no more. She was but the vessel from which our goddess sprang like a fountain to smash the gates of Mantioch. It was she who sent me to find you and to bring the girl west. I will lead the way.'

'So Mantioch has fallen?'

'It has. Urelia defeated the forces of Innellan with nothing but a gesture, and brought the survivors over to our cause. Our lady leads the united army to Kragenskûl now. The final battle awaits.'

With that he reined his horse around and led them through the desert.

'What was that about?' Ctenka asked, when the scout was some distance ahead.

'I've got no idea,' Josten replied. 'Who the bloody hell is Urelia?'

'She is a Shengen goddess,' Adaali cut in. It was a random detail of theology she had been forced to remember during dull lessons with her history tutor. She had always wondered if such information would ever be useful, and now it appeared she had her answer.

'A goddess?' Ctenka said. 'We have a goddess on our side now?'

'Unless he means Silver,' Josten replied. 'But why would—'

'Who is this Silver?' Adaali asked. 'You speak much of her as though she is your leader. You say she needs my help. Who is she?'

'I guess she is our leader, of sorts.'

'And she is a goddess?' The notion seemed preposterous.

'Well… yes and no.'

'Which is it?' she asked, growing frustrated. 'Do you know this woman or not?'

'I do, but…'

'But also you don't? I can't wait to meet her. It seems she is something of an enigma.'

Their journey wore on. The men continued in sullen silence as they followed the scout over miles of barren terrain. Another day and Adaali saw what they had been journeying towards.

A vast encampment came into view. With the prospect of her journey's end, Adaali felt butterflies dancing in her stomach. This was what she had been waiting for, the woman who had ordered her rescue was here. Now she would find out just what kind of 'goddess' she was here to help.

Ctenka pulled the wagon over on the camp's periphery and Josten jumped down. They were greeted by more of the Shengen warriors and it seemed that Josten was well respected, despite his Suderfeld blood.

'Let's go,' Josten said, offering his hand to help Adaali from the wagon.

She jumped down herself, spear in hand.

'You won't need that,' Josten said. 'Silver's no threat to you.'

Reluctantly she laid the weapon back in the wagon as Dantar struggled to climb down.

'He can stay here,' said Josten. 'We have surgeons who can better see to those burns.'

Adaali shook her head. 'He comes with me.'

Josten shrugged. 'Suit yourself,' he replied, before leading them into the camp.

There was an array of people throughout the place. It was packed with Shengen warriors, cleaning weapons and armour, but there was also a variety of other warriors from foreign cultures Adaali did not recognise. Some wore armour of bone or red plate, others had savage markings on their flesh and faces; tattoos, bone rings and all manner of other adornments. Despite their differences they all seemed united in purpose, mingling as one people. It was an odd sight to behold.

'This is the strangest army I have ever seen,' Adaali said.

'If it helps, it's the strangest army *I've* seen,' Josten replied. 'When I left we had a legion of Shengen warriors and a few auxiliaries. Now it looks like Silver's recruited half the cults in the waste.'

Before she could ask any more, a tall man in the garb of a Shengen centurion approached Josten and they clasped arms in a warrior's way.

'Good to see you in one piece,' the soldier said.

'It wasn't easy staying that way, but it never is. Has anyone informed Laigon we're back?'

The man's expression turned grave. 'They didn't tell you? Emperor Laigon was killed during the assault on Mantioch.'

Josten merely nodded.

'All right,' he replied. 'Guess I'll go straight to Silver. There's someone she needs to see.'

The man nodded, motioning across the camp. As Josten followed his gesture, Adaali noted he had barely acknowledged the death of this Laigon figure. Whoever he was, Josten must have known him well, but he gave no expression of grief. Whether this was an old friend or a comrade, it appeared Josten was immune to the loss.

They moved through the camp to a tent larger than the rest, but it bore no flag or pennant to mark it as important. Neither were there any guards posted outside it. Whoever resided within must have been powerful, or supremely confident they needed no protection.

Dantar was growing wearier, and he leaned heavily against Adaali. Perhaps she should have let the surgeons see to his wounds, but something inside her didn't want to be apart from him.

'Are you all right?' she whispered. 'Should I have them take you—'

'No,' said Dantar, trying his best to stand on his own feet. 'I am with you.'

Despite his poor physical condition, he still gave Adaali the confidence she needed.

'Are you ready?' asked Josten.

She nodded, as he opened up the side of the tent and stepped in. She followed him with an overwhelming sense that she was stepping through some kind of void – as though once she entered things would never be the same again.

The woman Silver knelt in the centre of the tent. It was empty of any adornment, not even a pallet bed or a sconce for a candle. Josten left the flap of the tent open so the bright sunlight gave them some light to see by.

They stood in silence as the woman knelt. Silver looked as though she were at prayer but she made no sound. Adaali glanced at Josten, seeing by his expression that he was as discomfited by the silence as any of them.

'Thank you for coming,' the woman said finally.

She stood and turned to face Adaali. Her face was serene, hair falling in blonde rivulets to the shoulder. Her body was bedecked in silver mail, a plain white tabard covering her torso.

'I was not given much choice,' Adaali said. She could barely speak in the presence of this woman. There was an aura about her, something ethereal. The scout who met them on the road had mentioned they followed a goddess and now Adaali could see why.

'I am sorry for what has happened to you. Everything that has happened to you.' Adaali heard sincerity in her words. They had never met before, but it was clear this woman felt Adaali's pain and grief as though it were her own. 'I would have reached you sooner, but I was...'

'At war?' Adaali said. 'I understand.'

'That is good. I was hoping you would.' Silver took a step forward, reaching out and taking Adaali's hands in her own. They were smooth but strong and Adaali got the feeling that had she wanted to crush a man's skull in them it would have taken little effort. 'Then we are allies? Friends? I was hoping you would join me in the battle to come.'

'Why?' Adaali asked. 'I still have no idea why you had me brought here. I can fight, but you have warriors here with more experience than me.'

'I must face a great evil. I have to destroy Innellan – it is my purpose. Neither of us belongs in this place and to defeat her I must have help. There is much power within you, Adaali of Kantor, you must have realised that by now. Even I do not know where that power comes from, but it is clear you are a part of this.'

'How? This has nothing to do with me. I am nothing special.'

Silver regarded her closely, staring into her eyes as though searching for something. After a moment, she smiled. 'I understand why you would think that, but believe me when

I say you are much more than you know. Your fear is natural, but I will make you a promise – join me in this, and when Innellan is defeated you will have an army at your back when you return to claim your throne.'

'You would help me take Kantor? To face the army of the Suderfeld?'

'When this is over, no one will stand against you.'

It seemed too good to be true, but what dangers might she face if she joined this woman on her crusade? Then again, what did it matter? Without her aid, Kantor and the whole of the Cordral Extent was lost. She would be exiled to the desert forever. There was no choice to make.

'Then you have my help, for what it's worth.'

'It will be worth more than a thousand legions. You will be by my side when we take Kragenskûl. Josten.' Silver regarded the man who had brought Adaali here. He still seemed overwhelmed by what was happening, but he listened intently to her every word. 'You will lead the frontal assault. Adaali and I will face Innellan and banish her back from where she came.'

'But how?' Josten asked.

Silver retrieved something from a shadowy corner of the tent. In her hands she held a huge jewel, every facet glistening in the sunlight.

'With this,' Silver said. 'The Stone of Katamaru. It is an ancient key that links this world with another.'

She seemed proud of her plan, but despite her confidence, Dantar took a step forward, shaking his head.

'No,' he said, his dour voice cutting through the sanguine

mood. 'It's too dangerous. You cannot take this child into battle, I will not allow it.'

All eyes turned to Dantar now. He stood as tall as he could, though he was obviously still in much pain.

'But I need Adaali,' Silver said. 'She is the key to defeating Innellan. I know it.'

'Adaali would be in much danger. I will not allow it.'

As much as Adaali appreciated his concern, she would not have him speak on her behalf in front of such a powerful woman.

'I can fight,' she said, laying an arm on Dantar's shoulder. 'I can take care of myself.'

'No,' Dantar said. 'There is another way. I was raised in Kragenskûl. I know its secret paths and entrances. I can get Adaali inside the city, but far from the fighting.'

'No,' said Adaali. 'I want to fight. I need to be a part of this.'

'Dantar is right, of course,' Silver said. 'It was foolish of me to think I could take a child into battle.'

'I am no child,' Adaali said, biting back her anger as best she could. 'I am the rightful queen of Kantor. If I wish to march into battle then that is what I'll do.'

Silver smiled, laying a hand on her arm. Despite her annoyance, Adaali could not help but feel placated by the gesture.

'Yes, you are a queen. And I know you are brave. But I am asking much of you. If Dantar can get you into the city free from danger then that is what we shall do. Now, go. Rest and prepare yourself. Soon we will see victory over our enemies, and I have much to plan with my general.' She gestured at Josten.

Adaali bowed before she and Dantar left. In the bright sunshine she felt foolish.

'What has just happened?' she whispered to Dantar as they made their way back through the camp.

'I think we joined a crusade,' Dantar replied.

'I guess she's right then, we'd better get some rest.'

Dantar did not argue.

Later, after she had slept, Adaali sat at the edge of the camp as the sun dipped beyond the horizon. In the gathering dark she watched over Dantar as he slept. His wounds had been treated by an old apothecary and now he slept soundly.

It was silent across the camp as night fell, until someone raised their voice in song. It took Adaali a few moments before she worked out it was one of the Shengen. The song was rousing, the kind of thing you'd expect before battle.

Before long, another voice joined the first. Together they sang a strange lament, both melancholy and guttural. Then another song was struck up to the rhythmic beat of a drum. With different voices singing so many different tunes Adaali would have expected the result to be discordant, but no – the song they made was beautiful. All these disparate groups, united together behind a single overarching tune, made her feel like she belonged here. That for the first time ever she was on the right path.

As Dantar still slept, Adaali rose, picking her way through the camp to look out west. Somewhere in the distance was the city of Kragenskûl, wallowing in the desert, waiting for them to come.

And I shall be waiting. Come to me, child.

Adaali staggered back, clutching her head. The words had been like a physical blow and she reeled from it.

Before Adaali could begin to wonder what was going on, there was another voice, this one familiar and in no way malevolent.

Oh, I am coming, the voice said. *I am coming.*

Adaali heard the sound of distant laughter as the first voice drifted away on the breeze. Of the second voice there was nothing more. As night fell Adaali shivered, and it was not only the chill of the night air that blew through her bones.

28

KRAGENSKÛL was shrouded in darkness as Josten stood before it among the rest of Silver's army, waiting for her order to attack.

She was much changed since he'd left for Kantor. Gone was the warrior from the desert, and in her place was a queen every bit as alluring as Innellan. Though he hadn't seen it with his own eyes he'd heard tales about her growing wings, rising up as a goddess, eyes burning with fire as she slew an army. It sounded like madness, but he believed every word.

Silver had risen to take on the mantle of general and queen all at once, and now she had reached her endgame. One way or another it would all be over tonight.

As Josten bid goodbye to Dantar and Adaali he wondered if they'd make it. He would have been afraid for the girl as that wild-eyed warrior led her off into the dark, but truth be told Josten was too worried about himself to care. The girl was brave, no doubt about that, and she had Dantar to keep her safe. The Sword Saints were legend, and Josten would never have wanted to get on his wrong side.

Once they had disappeared into the night, Josten moved to the front of the Shengen line. He'd been given a decent sword and it felt comfortable on his hip. He placed a thumb beneath the cross-guard, flicking it up so the blade was an inch clear of the sheath, then let it slide back into place.

They stood for what seemed an age in the cold night, but no one was shivering. Every warrior was focused, driven, instilled with belief. Not a single one had any doubt they would be victorious, not even when the main gates to Kragenskûl yawned open. As the entrance gaped wide, everything about it screamed 'trap', but Josten didn't feel any fear.

Fires burned within the city, illuminating their path like a beacon. In that light, Silver was standing, waiting. The solitary vanguard of her vast army.

She turned to face her troops, and as one they fell to their knees. Josten couldn't help but join them. He'd never worshipped, never followed a general blindly in his life, but for Silver he would have walked into hell. There was a strange kind of purity in this, a relief in unburdening himself. He didn't have to make a choice... to doubt. Following Silver was the only path and he would walk it gladly.

An aura grew around her, a light that burned like a flame. Silver did not need to speak to inspire loyalty in her followers – seeing her there, radiant in the night, was enough. White wings sprang from her back and she rose up, spreading her arms in a final symbolic embrace, before she turned and swept towards the open gate.

She was a true goddess – Josten realised that now. He had fought beside her, followed her across endless desert and faced death for this woman despite his misgivings. It all made sense. Any doubts he'd had were gone with one graceful unfurling of wings. For the first time in his life he was a believer, instilled with an unshakeable faith. He knew in that instant he would never doubt again.

Josten rose to his feet, pulling his sword free of the scabbard. To either side of him the Shengen legionaries lifted their shields and spears, an army advancing to war, faithfully following their leader into battle. There were no shouts of fury, no growling herald of the battle to come, just disciplined ranks advancing, the righteous ready to take down their enemy.

As he entered through the gate, Josten was struck with how different this place was from the last time he had been here. Every building had been reduced to rubble, intentionally collapsed to make a desolate landscape within the city walls. The only edifice was Innellan's vast tower, still standing at the city's centre, and barring the way to it was an army. Siff had come to a halt, her body hovering above them all.

'Innellan,' she cried, her voice booming throughout the decimated city. 'There is no need for further bloodshed. These people do not have to die. Come out and face me. Let us end this now.'

Atop the tower a single fire burned, and from that summit ascended a dark silhouette. She too was borne on ethereal wings that shone in the moonlight, but where Silver's were bright white, hers were black as a cormorant's.

'This is the way it should always have been,' said Innellan. A shiver ran through Josten as she spoke. Her words echoed around the city, filling every mortal with dread. 'You have accepted their worship. An army at your back. Warriors come to die.'

'It is time for this to end,' said Silver gently.

'Yes,' Innellan replied. 'It is.'

Innellan's forces bellowed into the night as they charged in unison. Their devotion was unquestionable and their goddess would never give up without a fight.

Josten raced forward to face the charging enemy. The Shengen spearmen were at his shoulder, their armour clanking as they moved.

Before he was within a hundred feet of Innellan's army there came the sound of a thunderclap above him. He glanced up to see the gods at war; Silver and Innellan attacking one another with unmatched ferocity, each one wreathed in flame. He had never witnessed such an awe-inspiring sight, but he barely had time to acknowledge their battle before the enemy were upon them.

All thoughts of righteousness vanished in that first clash of steel. Josten's faith and the virtue he had felt in the charge was replaced by a snarling rage. The two armies began their slaughter, and there was nothing holy about it.

Josten's sword hammered in and he was quickly lost in the crowd of bellowing fanatics. This was worse than Kessel, worse than any battle he'd ever fought in the Suderfeld. Never had he been caught in a melee of such single-minded butchery.

Blows hammered in, and within moments his shield was battered, a hunk of dented metal in his hand. The Shengens kept their line, relentless in their advance, spears driving into Innellan's army. Screams pealed out, long and loud, and before he knew it Josten had raised his own voice to join them. He grew hoarse as he searched eagerly for the next enemy, breath coming fast and cold in the night.

Bodies began to litter the open ground and he stumbled, falling heavily to one knee. Someone grabbed his arm, dragging him to his feet. He didn't know whether it was friend or foe, but before he could strike he saw Ctenka, holding tight to his arm. Eyman was by his side and they were both wide-eyed – that mix of fear and shock and elation that afflicted every man who had to fight or die.

'Are you all right?' Ctenka shouted above the din.

'Do I look all right?' Josten replied, he didn't really know himself.

Ctenka laughed, his teeth shining white from a bloody face.

Josten risked a glance into the sky above. Silver and Innellan were still battling, feathers flying, inflicting grievous wounds on one another that would have floored a bull. They were oblivious to the fight raging below them – gods at war, focused only on defeating one another.

'We have to get to the tower,' he said to Ctenka. 'We have to help Adaali, that's where she's heading.'

Ctenka and Eyman nodded their assent and the three of them formed a tight formation, rushing at the enemy, battering their way through. A spear lanced towards them. His shield useless, Josten tried to turn the blow with his sword but he wasn't quick enough. It took him in the side, his mail cushioning the spear tip, but the force of the blow cracked his ribs and he was driven back. The sword fell from his hand, his feet giving out beneath him.

As he foundered, Ctenka and Eyman fought to defend him, pushing back the oncoming cultists. While they fought,

Josten struggled to his feet, gripping his ribs, but before he could continue towards the tower there was another almighty crack, as though lightning had struck in the midst of the battle.

Innellan lay in the centre of the battlefield. Her warriors fell back, watching as Silver gently landed beside her. The White Widow looked beaten, bleeding from a dozen terrible wounds. She stared up with those black eyes, regarding Silver with hatred. All had gone quiet now, and Josten was struck with awe as he watched these two inhuman avatars face one another.

'You cannot win,' Silver said. 'I have recruited an army, but you have gathered slaves. While you hid here like vermin, plotting your schemes, I was earning their respect. Where you demanded loyalty, I merely had to ask for it.'

A leering grin twisted across Innellan's face. 'You think that's where your power lies?' the White Widow laughed.

'I know it,' said Silver through gritted teeth. 'I have always known it. You can make as many demands as you wish, but unless you hold the hearts of your followers your power over them is built on a foundation of sand.'

Innellan laughed again, her body wracked by a fit of coughing. Blood spewed from her mouth and she spat black bile onto the ground.

'You think loyalty makes you powerful? Then let me show you loyalty.'

Innellan struggled to her feet, raising her arms, those black talons of hers clawing at the sky. Then in one swift movement she brought her arms down to her side.

As one, every warrior in Innellan's army fell to his knees, placing sword to belly or spear to throat. They fell on their weapons in a single act of mass sacrifice.

There was a deafening scream, as Silver bellowed in rage and anguish. Before her, Innellan stood triumphant, her wounds already healing, her body growing in stature as though every suicide were an act of worship dedicated to her.

Siff screamed. She could feel the dread and fear of every warrior as he gave his life, but they had no choice. Innellan's will was irresistible and they obeyed without question. Thousands died in the blink of an eye, each life granting Innellan more infernal power.

There was a surge of raw energy as Innellan drew in their benefaction. Their act of sacrifice filled the Archon with life, restoring her, invigorating her.

Siff clamped her eyes shut, grasping her spear tightly, funnelling what strength she had into the haft. It glowed red, then burst into flames. When she opened her eyes she saw her sister was restored, her body armoured in bronze, two smouldering swords manifesting in her grip, dripping with black venom.

With a beat of her wings, Innellan took flight, and Siff went after her. She thrust at her sister with the flaming lance, but Innellan easily parried the sweeping blow. Black tears of unholy joy began to cascade from Innellan's eyes as she rejoiced in the fight, sweeping her black blades at Siff, who was hard-pressed to block them. She could feel the fell energy of sacrifice emanating from them, the dark power that had granted Innellan such rejuvenation was fuelling those unholy weapons. Thousands of dead souls permeated those foul swords, and Siff had to face them and somehow overcome their terrible power.

She turned defence to attack, soaring in with her flaming lance, screaming, raging against her sister. The spear struck true, ringing against Innellan's breastplate, resounding with a fiery explosion. Both Archons reeled back from the blast, but as the flames subsided, Siff could see that her lance had not even left a dent in the bronze breastplate.

Now it was Innellan's turn to strike, and Siff barely had the chance to raise her lance before she was subject to a flurry of sword strikes. The black weapons came at her in a torrent, leaving dark rents in her armour. One of them cut into her arm and she screamed in pain, feeling the unhallowed venom course through her every fibre. With a last mighty blow, Innellan struck with both swords, hacking down as Siff raised her lance. The weapon shattered in her grip, searing metal flying in every direction.

She was unarmed and weakened now, but perhaps there was one last chance to bring her sister low. Reaching into the sack at her belt she grasped the Stone of Katamaru. It pulsated with power, and she could feel the artefact's yearning. It existed to breach the gap between worlds, to return the Archons whence they had come. If Siff could harness that power…

…but no, it would not answer her. Even as she held the Stone aloft she could already tell it would not respond to her command.

Innellan laughed. 'Why do you think I gave such little thought to that trinket?' she said, taking pleasure in Siff's failed attempt to harness its power. 'It was never meant for us. It is a mortal tool. No Archon can wield it.'

Before she could react, Innellan plunged one of those black blades into Siff's stomach. She tried to scream but every part of her was transfixed, poison coursing into her core, tainting her essence, driving the power from her.

Siff fell from the sky, landing in a heap on the cold, bloody ground. She tried to rise but the poison had leached the strength from her limbs.

Innellan came to land gently beside her, bare feet stepping through the rivers of red. In one hand she held the Eye, and with the other she took hold of Siff's throat, lifting her high into the air.

'Behold, sister,' she breathed, those dark eyes staring intensely, two rancid pools of hate.

As one, Siff's army dropped to its knees – Shengen warriors, freed slaves, converted cultists. To the last warrior they bowed their heads in supplication. They were Siff's no more. Now they belonged to Innellan.

29

THEY'D entered through an ancient sepulchre, half a league north of the city. In the moonlight, Adaali could see myriad tombstones dotting the flat landscape that stretched off into the night. Interspersed were larger tombs erected to more of the dead, perhaps kings and heroes exalted by these northern cultists. Dantar paused at one of the monuments, as though unsure of whether he was in the right place. When he pushed aside a huge stone covered in ancient carved script, it revealed a tunnel leading down into the black.

A foetid plume of stale air wafted out of it, but it did not seem to deter Dantar as he led Adaali inside, down ever deeper into the lightless tunnel. Reaching out through the blackness she felt him just ahead of her, and when they were far enough inside he paused. She heard a clack of flint, and with the third strike saw the flaring of a torch igniting. Firelight brightened the tunnel as Dantar held the torch high, and by it Adaali could see the walls were covered in ancient sigils, alcoves cut into the stone housing ancient skeletons, eyeless skulls gawping at the shadows. Had Adaali been alone she might have been unnerved by the sight of so many corpses, but there was nothing to fear from the dead. Once they reached the city she would face the real threat.

Dantar led on through the winding maze of catacombs. Adaali became completely lost, but her guide knew exactly where he was going, and eventually they came out into a vast subterranean crypt.

In the light of Dantar's torch she could see huge sarcophagi carved with the images of ancient warriors. A long row of monuments to the fabled Sword Saints ran off into the darkness, too many to count. As they pressed on she saw that the tombs diminished in age, each one less corroded than the last until they passed graves that were almost new, the marble shining in the torchlight, the sigils and carvings pristine.

Dantar suddenly paused, laying a hand on one of the tombs. He traced the inscription with his fingers, a look of loss on his face.

'A friend of yours?' Adaali asked.

Dantar nodded. 'My brother, gone to the eternal rest.'

'I'm sorry,' she said. 'I'm sure he died bravely.'

'He did,' Dantar said with a sigh. 'I was the one who killed him.'

What madness had led him to murder his own brother? And what must Dantar have gone through to be brought up in a place like this, where brother would be forced to fight brother?

Before she could think to console him, Dantar moved on through the cavernous interior. She followed in silence until they eventually came to a passage leading upwards. As they mounted a vast staircase that led out of the tomb, the sounds of fighting echoed from above.

The stairs emerged beside a vast plaza. It was covered in rubble, the surrounding buildings having all collapsed. Dantar discarded his torch and led her out through the debris.

Within the city walls, a battle raged. Adaali could barely make out what was going on in the gloom, but above the slaughter, two gods fought. She watched in awe as the winged seraphs attacked each other, one dark and terrifying, the other borne on white wings, flaming lance flashing in the night.

Dantar grabbed her arm. 'We have to get to the tower. There is no time.'

Adaali nodded, seeing the vast spire that rose in the centre of the city, the only monument left that had not been levelled. They moved quickly over the wreckage, picking their way nimbly as the battle was fought a few hundred yards away. Dantar paused as he reached the bottom of the tower, drawing his sword. Adaali expected such a place to be guarded, but it seemed every armed man in the city had thrown himself into the fight that raged not far away.

Dantar dashed through the arch at the bottom and she followed. The base of the tower was lit by dim torchlight and a vast staircase wound its way to the summit. As they made their way up, she couldn't shake the sense of unease rising inside her. It was like every brick of this place had been shaped from pure evil. Still she pressed on, following Dantar, determined to reach the top.

At the summit a huge window opened out onto the city. Adaali rushed to its edge to see what was happening below. All had gone silent now, and in the light of the moon she saw the fighting had stopped. Bodies littered the ground and among them the survivors knelt in supplication.

'You have to come and look at this,' she said to Dantar.

When he did not answer she turned to face him. There was a change about him, his face hanging slack, his eyes regarding her strangely as though he had never seen her before.

'What's wrong?' she asked.

Dantar shook his head. 'Kill me. Quickly,' he replied.

'What?' Adaali had a spear in her hand, but the suggestion was absurd.

'Do it. Now.' Dantar raised his sword.

A voice screamed at her from inside, bellowing a wordless warning. She brought her spear up in time to block the sword as Dantar leapt to attack. Despite his injuries he was still swift as an arrow, lithe, strong. He twisted in the air, blade striking twice more as Adaali barely managed to parry, skittering back from his attack.

'What are you doing?' she demanded.

But Dantar was gone now. All that remained was a wounded Sword Saint determined to murder her. And a wounded Sword Saint might well be the most dangerous foe she had ever faced.

She glanced back towards the staircase, thoughts of escape fleetingly invading her thoughts, but the chance was gone when Dantar rushed in again. Adaali tried to adopt the forms he had taught her, but she was facing a master. For every move he knew a counter, with every tactic he outmatched her.

Before she could even try to defend herself, Dantar struck her hand with the flat of his blade. Her spear fell and she

308

yelped in pain as he stepped in, grabbing her hair, spinning her around and pressing the blade of his sword to her throat.

There they stood, facing the window as a dark form drifted in. Innellan was a formidable sight to behold, eyes black as night, white hair billowing atop a body bedecked in bronze and scarlet. In one dark talon of a hand she carried Silver by the throat. The woman looked dead, blood covering her white tabard, the mail on her body shredded and broken.

Innellan unceremoniously dropped Silver's body in a heap as her bloody feet touched the floor. The dark wings at her back drifted away into ash, and she fixed Adaali with a fearful grin.

In her hand she held the giant jewel that had belonged to Silver – the Stone of Katamaru. Adaali could feel the power pulsating from within it, filling the room with an oppressive haze.

'Is this the girl?' Innellan asked of Silver. The woman lay at her feet, unable to speak. The magnificent white wings that had borne her aloft were now tattered and shredded, and she could barely raise her head. 'Is this the mortal with such overwhelming power you thought she could defeat me? Me!'

The last word echoed throughout the chamber so loud it made Adaali's ears ring.

Innellan held the Stone of Katamaru aloft. 'Such an insignificant trinket,' she said.

The black claw she held it with began to tremble. It was obvious she was trying to shatter the jewel in her grip, but it was too much even for her unearthly strength. With a growl she cast it aside, where it bounced to the corner of the chamber.

'I have won,' she gloated over Silver, taking sadistic pleasure in her victory. 'And this land will now fall. You were foolish to have even tried, sister. I was destined to win, but then it has always been thus, from the first wars to our last.'

As Innellan spoke, Adaali concentrated on the Eye. It lay a few feet away, discarded and forgotten, but she could still feel the energy thrumming from within it. That jewel was her only hope. It could open a gateway that would send Innellan back from where she had come, and as Adaali stared at it she felt a connection. The Stone of Katamaru called to her, yearning to be used. It was a door only she could open; the key to a lock only she could turn.

Dantar still held the blade at her throat as Innellan spoke. There was no hope of him overcoming the bewitchment that afflicted him, not with Innellan so close. Adaali would have to find her own way.

Heedless of the pain, she grasped the blade at her throat with her bare hand. She could feel the razor edge open the flesh of her palm, biting into the skin and muscle of her fingers. Rage built within her as she felt Dantar struggling against her. He tried to press the blade home but she was too strong and the steel bent in her grip. With a final scream of defiance she flung him aside.

Dantar span in the air, smashing against a column and coming to rest on the ground in a heap. Innellan had finished her gloating tirade now, focusing on Adaali, who was already darting across the chamber towards the Stone of Katamaru.

With a billow of black wings, the White Widow came for her, moving to intercept her before she could reach the

Stone. Adaali halted, staring up at this goddess, this dark unholy vision.

'Mortal,' she said, words dripping with spite. 'You still hope to win? I see what Siff admires about you, but it is useless. There is nothing you can do to stop me.'

Adaali wanted to spit in her face but she was stricken with fear. Despite the power she could feel burning within her, despite the voice screaming at her to resist, all she could do was watch in awe as this divine being gazed down at her.

A ragged roar thundered through the chamber. An animal cry of hate as Silver leapt at Innellan. Though her body was torn and broken she somehow managed to call on a last reserve of strength.

Innellan barely had time to raise her hands as Silver fell upon her and they continued their fight, clawing at one another like bears in a pit. Despite Silver's fury, Innellan was the stronger – the fight would not last long.

Adaali lunged for the Stone, grasping the jewel in two hands, feeling it throbbing with life. In that instant the ancient artefact cast visions in her mind, showing her a thousand scenes from a thousand souls. Adaali stood frozen, weathering the rush of information, feeling it threaten to snap her weakening grasp on sanity.

Then all at once it ended. Adaali could barely hear the gods battling nearby. There was but one voice. A voice she recognised. Livia Harrow.

Use it, she said. *Use it now and end this.*

Adaali held up the Stone of Katamaru, channelling its power. She could feel the jewel trembling, sending shivers down her arms, filling her with its incredible energy. She gritted her teeth, emitting an animal whine from her throat as the Stone burned with the light of a hundred suns, filling the chamber with its energy.

As the Stone of Katamaru imploded, Adaali screamed. All she could see was white light, all she could hear was a thunderous chime, as she was condemned to the void. She span amid the emptiness, consumed by the heat. Every fibre of her being was torn apart in an instant – flesh, bones, organs – split asunder and knitted back together faster than she could snatch a breath…

'Adaali?'

It was a distant voice. She still could not see, the blinding white light slowly turning to black.

'Adaali?'

There was the voice again, but this time it was closer.

'Adaali, are you all right?'

It was a voice she recognised.

As a hand gently touched her arm, Adaali opened her eyes to see a face she knew, a girl she had met in a dream. Though she bore Innellan's face, Adaali knew the White Widow was no more. Livia Harrow looked down at her, a kind smile on her face.

'Am I dead?' Adaali asked.

Livia's smile turned to a laugh. 'No,' she replied. 'We are alive. We are very much alive.'

Livia helped Adaali to her feet. The room was silent now as they both surveyed the scene. Livia was dressed in red, as Innellan had been, but the bronze breastplate was gone. Her hair was still white as a summer cloud but her face held none of the witch queen's malice.

Silver stirred, then rose to her feet, regarding her surroundings with confusion.

'Hera?' Livia asked, moving over to the woman and helping her to stand. As the two of them embraced, Adaali rushed to Dantar's side. He knelt against a pillar, gripping his shoulder.

'Are you all right?' Adaali asked.

'I've been better,' Dantar replied. 'But I'll live.'

Adaali breathed a sigh of relief as she stood. Looking down at her hand she expected to see it ripped and torn, but the flesh was unblemished. Dantar's blade had left no mark.

The night was silent, as Adaali moved to the huge window. From the balcony she looked down at what had been a battlefield of the gods. Where before had been thousands of kneeling supplicants, now stood an army. They had come to defeat an Archon, and they had won. She breathed deeply, but felt no sense of victory. The fight was not over for her.

Now Adaali had to ride back to the south and reclaim a kingdom.

30

*T*HEY *fought, spinning in infinity, riding an endless void that only existed to be their battlefield. The gods clawed at one another, rending and tearing, snarling their hate, baring teeth and parting flesh.*

As they fell through empty space, Innellan abandoned her earthly form, sloughing off her human guise to become a demonic creature of hellish proportions. Horns grew from a leathery skull, jaw distending, razor teeth probing for flesh.

Siff adopted her own alternate form. Where Innellan was demonic and unholy, she became angelic, her seraph's wings spreading wide. Against the wicked claws of the demon her body became armoured in a coat of silver mail, all but impervious to the infernal attacks of her sister. Still they fought with inhuman ferocity, rending, tearing, their only purpose to defeat the other. As they span through the void, howling their hate, it transformed around them.

The gods smashed into the earth. A blasted landscape surrounded them: deep gullies ran far into the ground. Nothing grew, for no flora or fauna could survive in this nightmarish land. The air itself was a cloak of poisonous vapour.

The gods rose, facing one another across the dead ground.

'I will have my vengeance,' spat Innellan, hot venom bubbling

from her lips. 'You may have won the battle, but I will lay you low.'

Siff did not answer. She had heard enough threats spew from her sister's mouth. Instead she waited for the inevitable attack.

Innellan charged, churning up the black earth, running on all fours to quicken her advance. As she did so, the demonic visage melted away to be replaced by serpentine features, hide scaling over, legs growing thickly muscled, leathern wings sprouting from her back as she transformed into a great wyrm of war.

Siff likewise began to shift in form, mane sprouting as her features became more leonine, body dropping to all fours, claws springing forth. A tail grew from her shanks, a hissing serpent's head at its tip.

When they met, it sent a sonic wave across the earth, the toxic gases billowing in their wake. Dragon and lion fought violently, their roars would have terrified anything within earshot, had there been anything alive to hear. Their battle took them to the edge of a great ridge. Such was their determination to destroy one another absolutely that they toppled over the edge, falling a mile or more, until they smashed into the ground. The brittle earth gave way beneath them, and the gods crashed through an ancient mine, long dried up and forgotten.

Further and further they fought, deeper and deeper their brutal conflict took them, until eventually they smashed through the side of a mountain and out into a new realm.

A black sun hung in a yellow sky. They fought on, crashing down the mountainside, toppling over black cliffs to plunge into the sea. Innellan's draconic form was already morphing, those scales shed to become the smooth hide of a shark.

As Siff hit the water she became human once more, but her legs became sleek, fins propelling her through the water as though she were born to it.

The shark homed in to attack, but Siff was too swift, avoiding those gnashing jaws with a deft flick of the tail. Down and down into the depths they went, twisting and spinning around one another, creating a whirlpool around themselves. When the great shark began to tire, Siff went in for the kill, that sleek form breaking apart to become myriad piranha, teeth attacking with ferocity as they swarmed over their enemy.

They began to shred the shark's hide, blood billowing through the water, blooming all around, but they could never consume the aspect of a god.

Innellan burst from the crimson vortex, now a huge serpent, diving to the bottom of the ocean and burrowing into the ground. Deeper and deeper the serpent sank, and Siff followed. She took on her godlike form once more, a seraph pursuing its serpentine prey to the centre of the world. There in the burning core they battled on – Innellan becoming a great beast wreathed in fire, Siff blossoming into a thousand white raptors.

Around them the fabric of reality began to crack, their fury breaking time and space itself. The very essence of these gods began to crumble, as did the reality they inhabited, until the tumult ended in a white blooming supernova…

Siff was spat out onto the cold floor. Her body was covered in ichor, her limbs weak from what seemed an eternity of endless battle.

Beside her, she saw Innellan, flailing on the ground. She was wrapped in a gelatinous membrane, her body weak but her eyes aflame with hate.

Their bodies were identical – hairless hominids with no discernible features. Each was as base and embryonic as the other, as though spawned from a mind with no imagination. Still they were fuelled by raw emotion, and Siff moved forward at the same time as Innellan. They flailed on the ground, trying to carry on their battle, squirming in a stinking puddle until they were eventually wrenched apart.

Durius held Siff about the neck and she was unable to do anything but flail helplessly, her fledgling body too weak to resist him. She panted, sucking air into her bantling lungs, still staring in hatred at Innellan. Mortana held her sister in a steely embrace. It seemed their fight was over.

'Let me go,' Innellan raged, her voice gurgling as she spat the foul ichor from her lungs. 'I must go back. I have to finish what I started.'

The Heartstone was standing but a few feet away. Siff could feel its call and she too yearned to pass back through the gate to the mortal realm, to once more feel the euphoria it would bring. But no – she had to overcome that desire. She had almost achieved her goal, she could not allow her baser instincts to ruin what she had struggled so hard to achieve.

Siff had to destroy the thing, now, once and for all. But how could she ever achieve that? She was too weak, she didn't know if she could even stand on her own.

'Let me go,' she said to Durius.

Gently, he released her, and she stood on trembling legs, still staring at the Heartstone.

'It won't be long before they return,' said Hastor in his ancient voice. 'Our brothers and sisters are coming. They will not be stopped. We have to destroy the Heartstone. Siff, you must do it.'

'I cannot,' Siff replied. The words came to her before she even considered what they meant. Was her refusal from a lack of desire, or

317

because she was simply not strong enough?

'You have to,' Durius said. 'We have run out of time.'

Siff moved towards the edge of the tower, away from the Heartstone. Already she felt her strength returning, and soon she would need it — on the northern horizon a host was approaching. Kastion and Badb led a flock of winged warriors that blackened the sky like a thunderhead. Out across the plain marched Ekemon, leading his swarm towards the Blue Tower.

'Don't do it,' Innellan pleaded, still in Mortana's grip. 'You will destroy us all. We were spawned from the earth to rule the mortals in their realm. If you destroy the Heartstone we will be condemned to rot in this place for eternity.'

Siff knew the Heartstone could sense her intention as a dark mist billowed behind each one of its gleaming facets. She had to destroy it, to end this, but she didn't know how. Could it even be destroyed?

And even if it could, would it end all this? Would millennia of conflict be stopped by one simple act of violence?

Perhaps she should abandon the notion. The Archons had been created for war, their sole purpose to harness the worship of mortals and to elevate themselves as gods. What right did she have to stop this and could she do it, even if she wanted to?

Through the Heartstone, she saw the world on the other side spinning at a frightening rate...

31

LIVIA Harrow walked through the silent city. They called it Kragenskûl, a name she had heard in another life. She had to admit – as far as cities went, it wasn't much. The place had been levelled but for a single huge tower, which might once have been an imposing monument but now merely looked like an empty shell. If there had ever been anything to marvel at within this city's white walls it was gone now.

People were still lighting the funeral pyres and everywhere she looked the bodies burned. The smell was rank, and the sensible thing might have been to burn the dead outside the walls of the city, but there was nothing left there now. The place was a monument, a sepulchre. What better place for these bodies to burn?

As she made her way past the rows of corpses awaiting the torch, she had never felt more alive. Being trapped on another plane of existence had been strange enough, like a distant dream, but being trapped inside Adaali's mortal form had been much worse. It had been a cage, her incorporeal body lost in a void, a purgatory of sorts. But when she had come to the fore, when she had risen up to empower the girl, she had felt like a god, like she could supplant that body and with it rule the world.

And of course she had resisted the temptation. No matter how trapped she felt inside Adaali, as though she could only view the world through the bottom of a glass, she had refused to take over. It would have been tantamount to murder, and Livia Harrow was not about to sink that low. Not yet.

Now she once more saw the world as it should be, and she didn't like it overmuch. Her hair had turned white as winter, hanging long and straight where before there had been a wave to it. Though now she looked more an old maid than a woman in her youth, she was sure she'd get used to it. Other things she would never get used to.

The red gown that had clung to her like a swarm of ticks hung limply over her arm. It stank of Innellan, her aura clinging to the fabric like an evil stain. Livia paused by one of the pyres, enduring that burning meat stink long enough to cast the gown into the flames. It burned quickly, and Livia paused to watch it turn black, before she went on her way.

As she moved away from the fire, she saw Hera waiting patiently for her. The warrior woman was a welcome sight. She had been gifted a coat of mail and a sword by the Shengens and looked more magnificent than Livia had ever seen.

'You seem sullen,' Hera said. 'We have won, Livia Harrow. You should rejoice.'

Livia turned to regard the bodies burning in their thousands. 'Some victory,' she replied.

'It has come at a cost... for all of us. But with the death of Innellan there are no more enemies.'

'This is not over yet,' Livia said, thinking about what Adaali had told her. 'There is one last fight to the south.'

'Then I am with you,' Hera said.

She placed a hand on Livia's shoulder. After all they had been through, Livia just wanted to embrace the woman, but she doubted the taciturn warrior would have appreciated the gesture.

They walked together through the open gates of the city, leaving the stench of the burning dead behind them. The army was camped beyond the walls, the mood buoyant despite the losses they had suffered. As they made their way past the Shengens and the freed slaves, Livia was aware that they viewed her without suspicion. Despite the fact that a day before her mortal body had been inhabited by the witch queen of the Ramadi, they now regarded her as she was – a farm girl from the south who just wanted to return home.

Josten wasn't hard to find, she could hear his voice rising above the sounds of the camp, a profanity-laden rant she remembered well. When eventually she reached him a surgeon had finished re-dressing his wounds and he sat with a glum expression. He brightened when he saw her approach, and she couldn't help but smile back at him.

'Feeling better?' she asked as she took a seat next to him.

'I've seen brighter days,' he replied.

Since last they had been together, Josten had gained a huge tattoo of a kraken across his back. She didn't want to pry, but Livia imagined the story behind that would be one she'd want to hear.

'I still haven't...' She stopped, unable to think of the

321

words. For what he had done for her, the lengths he had gone, there were no words.

'You don't have to,' he replied. 'You don't have to say a thing. I'm just glad you're… well, you're you again.'

'Will you be travelling south with Adaali?' she asked.

Josten nodded. 'Silver made a bargain. She pledged her army to the Queen of Kantor and my loyalty along with it. Besides, it's the right thing to do.' He struggled to his feet, wincing at the pain in his ribs. 'Shall we go and see our new queen?'

Livia nodded, following him through the camp. She was apprehensive at the thought of seeing the girl again – she and Adaali had spoken little since Livia had split from her host and been returned to her own mortal body. There was awkwardness between them. They had gone through so much together, experienced something no two mortals ever should, shared thoughts, hopes, fears. It was an intimacy beyond even lovers, and now that their bond had been sundered there was an unspoken rift between them.

All thought of that was gone as they reached Adaali's tent. It was at the centre of the camp, the tent Silver had taken and Emperor Laigon before that. Though Livia had never met the dead Shengen emperor she knew he was still mourned by his men. It was his legacy, his dedication to Silver's cause that kept them loyal to Adaali.

Following Josten inside, Livia saw Adaali kneeling beside the single camp bed. Upon it lay the warrior Dantar. His breathing was shallow but he was conscious. Adaali gripped his hand, dabbing occasionally at his brow with a damp cloth.

'Princess Adaali,' Josten said once they were inside.

The girl turned, nodding in acknowledgement. She ignored Livia completely.

'You have come to ask what I intend to do now?' she said, still kneeling at Dantar's side.

'I know what you have to do now,' Josten replied. 'It's just a matter of when. The longer we wait, the harder the journey south will be and the stronger Randal's grip on Kantor becomes.'

Livia found herself clenching her fists. From what she had gathered, Randal was in control of the Suderfeld. His children and their magical gifts had sealed the throne for him and now he had turned his eye further north. Adaali's family had been slaughtered, her throne stolen. Randal had acted ruthlessly to get what he wanted, but Livia knew his methods all too well. Now she wanted to strike south and take vengeance almost as much as Adaali.

'Dantar is still too injured to move,' Adaali said. 'I cannot just leave him here.'

'No you can't,' Josten replied. 'But neither can we wait. We have to go south.'

'No,' Adaali said. 'He might die if we move him. I cannot...'

Livia understood Adaali's reluctance, but she had to be persuaded.

'I know what you're feeling,' Livia said. 'I know your guilt. I feel it too. But Dantar was under Innellan's enchantment. Had you not defeated him, he would have killed you.'

'You mean *us*,' Adaali replied. 'He would have killed us, and so *we* had to do this to him.'

'We cannot leave him behind,' Livia said. 'We cannot

leave anyone behind. The cults have been defeated but they will rise again. They may rally and return within a matter of days. We must all travel south.'

Adaali stood, fists clenched to her sides. 'Don't you think I know that? But I...'

Dantar groaned behind her. Then he struggled to shift his battered body and sit at the edge of the bed. 'I can travel,' he said. 'I can come with you. They are right, we have to leave now, before it's too late.'

Adaali shook her head as though overwhelmed by the decision. 'Just like that?' she asked. 'I command and everyone obeys.'

'You have to lead us now,' Josten said to her. 'Silver gave you her army. You have to be the one to take us south.'

'How?' Adaali asked. It was like a plea. 'I have no power any more. Whatever Silver saw in me is gone now. You know that.' Her last words were said to Livia.

'You do have power,' Livia said. 'You always did. You might not be able to conjure magic but you are strong. You are the true queen of all the Cordral.'

'But why would the army follow me? I am nothing to them. How do I prove myself?'

'Show them,' Livia replied.

She stepped forward, grasping Adaali by the arm. Adaali took a deep breath, glancing back to Dantar who simply nodded. She knew there was no choice in this.

Adaali strode from the tent, Josten and Livia following close behind. They made their way through camp and Livia was heartened to see many acknowledge the young princess with respect. But what of the Shengen centurions? They had come north with Silver, but Silver was no more. Adaali could never hope to defeat Randal's army without them, but the question of whether they were still loyal hung in the balance.

When the three of them arrived at the centre of the Shengen camp, they saw the legionaries were already breaking their tents. There were three leaders left alive, each discussing their next move as Adaali approached. Livia wanted to speak for her, to help her as she had done these past months, but the girl was alone now. She had to show them she was a leader to be respected.

'I would speak with you,' Adaali said.

The three centurions turned. They looked grim, war weary. After months of campaigning it was clear they were ready to return to their homes.

'Princess,' said the tallest of them. His dark hair was tied back in a topknot and he bowed low on seeing her. A good start.

'You are clearing your camp. I hope you are not returning home before the fight is over?'

The centurion glanced at his fellows, and neither of them seemed willing to speak. With a sigh he continued. 'We have done enough, princess. Our men have pledged their lives to this and now the fight is over. We will return to the Shengen in the morning.'

'You are aware of your leader's pledge to me?' she asked, unintimidated by the huge men. Livia began to feel her own faith growing in this girl.

'Silver is dead. Emperor Laigon is dead. We have done enough.'

'Enough?' Adaali said. 'Do you think this ends here?'

'For us it does,' the centurion replied, turning his back on Adaali.

She looked crestfallen, but what could a girl do to persuade these seasoned warriors if their minds were made up? She was nothing to them.

'No,' said Livia. 'Your fight is not over.' She hadn't wanted to speak for Adaali, but there was no other way for it. 'The Suderfeld army has taken the Cordral. It eyes the north. Once it has conquered the Ramadi it will not stop there.'

'We have heard as much before,' said the centurion. 'That this Randal is as ambitious as the White Widow herself. How would you know all this?'

'Because I know Randal. He is the true ruler in the south. He controls the army, and he has power none of you can comprehend. He is as ambitious and ruthless as any god and he will stop at nothing. You think you'll be safe in the Shengen? I promise, you will not.'

The centurion looked at Josten. 'And you, Josten Cade? You would follow where these women lead?'

Josten shrugged. 'I would follow these women anywhere.'

The centurion did not seem surprised by Josten's words. He didn't even have to confer with his fellows before saying, 'Very well. You have the Standings. May we all die with honour.'

'Let's hope it doesn't come to that,' Livia said.

As they left, the Shengen centurions began to relay

orders to their men. Livia felt Adaali move close by her side.

'Even now, you still see fit to act in my stead,' said the girl.

Before Livia could reply, before she could explain or try to apologise, Adaali stormed off towards where Dantar still lay injured.

'Don't take it too hard,' Josten said. 'You've both been through a lot.'

'We all have,' Livia replied. 'And it's not over yet.'

They struck camp overnight and at dawn headed south. Livia found herself riding beside Josten. He didn't have to say anything, but it was obvious he was doing his best to protect her. Perhaps to make amends for failing her so long ago.

'You are not beholden to any promise you made,' she said eventually.

'I know,' he replied. Then there was silence. It was good to see he was as conversational as ever.

'It was a long time ago. A lot's happened since. You don't owe me.'

'You were the one who said we were stuck together,' he mumbled.

'And you've certainly taken that to heart,' she replied. 'How long have you been trying to save me? Even after I was…'

'After you were possessed by the spirit of an ancient god?' he asked.

'Look, we've both been through a lot. You don't owe me anything. If you ever did, you're released from any bargain you might think we made.'

'And what if I don't want to be?' he said.

'I appreciate what you've done,' she replied. 'I really do, but you're not in much of a condition to protect anyone, Josten. You have to get rest. Stay out of the fighting. There are plenty of men ready to put themselves in the vanguard when we face Randal.'

Josten barked a short rasping laugh. 'I don't give a fuck about Randal. You think this sorry bunch are going to be any match for the might of the Suderfeld? They don't stand a chance.'

'If you think that, then what are you even doing here? You're a mercenary. You don't owe these people. Why not ride away?'

'I guess I just need to see this thing through to the end,' he replied. 'Same as you.'

He was right. Livia didn't need to be there either and they'd both been through enough. No one would have blamed them for disappearing into the sunset, but that simply wasn't an option and they both knew it.

'It would have been nice to get back to the farm,' she said. 'It must be in a poor state by now. Fields will all have turned fallow. I reckon there's a lot of work to be done.'

'This might surprise you, but I picked up a thing or two about farming while you were… well, while you were away.'

Livia laughed at that. The thought of Josten Cade as a farmer was just as strange to her as anything else that had happened over the past year.

'I'll make you a promise then,' she said. 'If we make it through this, there's a place for you on my farm.'

She took Josten's silence as an acceptance of the offer. Not that it would matter anyway – if either of them were going to make it back to that farm it would take a miracle.

32

THE journey south seemed longer than the last time he'd made it, but then Josten hadn't been nursing a couple of broken ribs back then. Livia had been right – he wasn't in much of a condition to fight, but that had never stopped him before and it wouldn't stop him now. As for him protecting her, Livia said he didn't owe her anything. Josten took the hint, there was no point crowding her like a jealous lover, and he let her ride alone. She'd been through a lot, and Josten knew better than anyone she had wounds you couldn't see. Healing them was a fight you had to face your own way, and if she wanted his help all she need do was ask.

They'd crossed the border with the Cordral the day before. The road was empty of other travellers and both Ctenka and Eyman had taken to riding alongside him. They talked endlessly about all manner of nonsense, but Josten could tell they were both scared, despite the bluster. He didn't blame them – there'd be more pain once they reached Kantor, and they'd already suffered their fair share.

No one more than Josten, though. His ribs were killing him, and as much as he tried to hide the fact he was in agony, it wasn't easy. Besides his chest feeling like it was being crushed he had bruises and lesions all over his body and he ached from neck to knee. No matter how much he wanted to give in, just to climb down from his horse and go to sleep on the sand, he knew he had to press on. The end was in sight, just one more battle and this would all be over, one way or the other.

One way or the other? Who was he trying to kid? There was nothing waiting for them in Kantor but death. Randal had an army, and as tough as the Shengens were they just didn't have the numbers. Besides that, Randal had those children. Josten had met two of them at Dunrun, seen what they could do to ranks of disciplined soldiers, and by all accounts Randal had a lot more in his army. Josten could be leading a dozen Standings and they still wouldn't be enough.

But he'd faced bad odds before. Faced them and lived and come out the other side laughing. Why should this be any different?

He looked along the column of riders, seeing Adaali at their head. She acted confident – every inch the queen in waiting. Whether it would be enough to reclaim her crown was anyone's guess. She was determined, and if she could persuade her own people to rise up and expel Randal and his Suderfeld knights who could say what might happen? Maybe they'd even win this.

Whatever lay ahead, Josten had made his decision. He was with Livia and Adaali to the end. He'd always wanted that one cause, that something special to fight for, and now he had it. Everyone gets what they deserve, he supposed. Even if it gets you killed.

He'd have laughed at that, but his damned ribs hurt too

much for that shit. Instead he rode on, trying to look like he wasn't in pain. It was going to be a long fucking ride.

Two more days on the road and Josten saw the city of Kantor across the dry plain. Someone must have warned the city that an army was on its way, because outside the northern gate they could just see a small contingent of riders sitting there waiting.

'What should we do?' Adaali asked.

'That looks like a trap,' Josten replied. It was the most obvious bait he'd ever seen.

'I am not afraid,' she said.

'That's what they're counting on,' Josten replied. 'They're hoping you'll be so angry that you'll ride down there and confront them. Then they can kill you easy, like wringing a chicken's neck.'

Adaali glanced over at Dantar, who had managed to sit himself atop a horse for the past few miles. He shrugged his shoulders in agreement.

'And you?' Adaali said to Livia. 'What do you think?'

'I think you're going to do whatever you want, no matter what anyone says,' she replied.

That seemed to satisfy Adaali, and she nudged her horse forward. Dantar rode ahead beside her and the two struck out towards the gate of Kantor.

'For fuck's sake,' Josten breathed, kicking his own horse.

When Livia made to join them he held up a hand. 'No. You wait here,' he said.

The girl fixed him with a determined look. Her white hair was tied back in a knot, making her look much older than her years. She had changed so much, she was like a different person to the one he'd known so long ago.

'If you think I'm going to sit back and watch this happen you must be stupid,' she said.

Josten was in too much pain to argue. It was taking all his energy to stay upright in the saddle and he managed to shrug, following Adaali down to the gate. He couldn't have given a shit who else came too, but a glance over his shoulder showed it was just the four of them.

As they got closer, Josten could see there were only a handful of delegates awaiting them. Randal sat front and centre, that pointy hawk face poking from under his greasy mop of hair. He was surrounded by children, which would have seemed an odd thing, had Josten not known they were far less innocent than they looked. To his right was a man Josten didn't recognise; blonde hair, handsome, eye patch. He looked less of a threat than those youngsters. To the left was a figure he did know. Manssun Rike sat hulking atop his destrier, broadsword strapped to his back, arms bulging through the bronze bands that adorned them.

A glance at Livia and he could see she was burning with rage, her eyes fixed on Randal. And who could blame her? Everything she'd been through was because of that man. Everything she had suffered – and by the gods Josten didn't know half of what she'd suffered – had happened after Randal had murdered her uncle and taken her from her home. He just hoped they could all keep their heads and maybe this would end peacefully. Then again, maybe pigs would fucking fly.

'Princess Adaali,' Randal said, when they came to a stop. 'I have heard so much about you.'

He ignored the rest of them. If he recognised Dantar from the desert so long ago he didn't acknowledge it. It was obvious he would never have forgotten Josten or Livia, but he didn't even offer them a second glance.

'You are the one they call Randal Weirwulf?' Adaali said. Josten was impressed at the strength in her voice. If she was intimidated she was hiding it well. 'The one who holds the real power in the Suderfeld?'

'I see you're well informed,' Randal replied. 'And in no mood to bandy words. I like that.'

'Then perhaps you'll like this – I have returned to claim my throne. You have one day to gather your army and leave the city of Kantor...'

Randal was already smiling a wide grin. Josten wanted to leap at him and smack that grin right off his face but the way he felt he'd most likely end up face down in the dirt.

'This is just the beginning,' Randal said. 'The Cordral Extent, and every city state within its borders, belong to me now.'

'Let me guess,' said Adaali. 'Now you look to conquer more lands? To spread your empire north and across the Crooked Jaw? Are you a fool? We have just defeated a god. Stopping you will not be so difficult.'

Randal gazed northwards to where Adaali's army waited. 'Your forces are battle weary, and I'll take a guess that their numbers are severely depleted. I have taken this city without the loss of a single soldier. And I have other allies.' He gestured to the dishevelled children who surrounded him. 'You overestimate your strength, princess. Your legions will batter themselves against these city walls until they perish.'

Josten had heard enough. As much as he wanted to let Adaali say her piece he couldn't keep his mouth shut. 'Then maybe we should stop all the bloodshed. Maybe you and me should fight it out right now, you fucking arse.'

Randal turned his gaze towards Josten for the first time. 'I wondered when you'd speak up. It's been a long time, Josten. Good to see you.'

'Enough words, you simpering cock. Why don't you prove you're no coward. Me and you. Winner takes all.'

'You know, that's not such a bad idea,' Randal replied.

'What?' said Josten. He hadn't expected that response.

'I think you're right. There's been enough bloodshed. So we'll end this the old-fashioned way. Champion against champion.' He looked back to Adaali, sitting back smugly in his saddle. 'In the Suderfeld, when its kings honoured the Treaty of Iron, they settled royal disputes in the same way for a century. So why not now? Our champions will fight here at dawn tomorrow. The winner claims the throne of Kantor for their master.'

Before Adaali could speak Josten said, 'You're on.'

Randal grinned like he'd already won. 'Manssun? Would you be so kind?'

The grizzled king's champion leaned forward in his saddle. 'It will be my pleasure. See you in the morning, Cade.'

Adaali pulled on her reins and rode back up the hill. The rest followed, as Josten let what he'd done sink in.

'You have gambled my throne on a single fight to the death!' Adaali yelled.

Josten had to admit, her voice was getting more commanding by the day.

Livia rested a hand on her arm, trying to placate her. 'This is probably the best way. We cannot hope to defeat them in open battle. We don't have enough men for a siege and we don't stand a chance on the battlefield.'

That seemed to placate Adaali somewhat, but she was still furious. 'And what if, by some miracle, we win?' she said.

'Thanks for the vote of confidence,' Josten replied, feeling a sudden twinge of pain in his side.

'You are wounded,' Adaali said. 'Even if you do manage to defeat that brute, what guarantee do we have that Randal will honour the bargain?'

'We don't,' said Livia. 'But we have to give it a chance.'

Dantar rose unsteadily to his feet. 'I should be the one to fight.'

Josten shook his head. 'Look at yourself. You can barely stand.'

'One of the centurions then? Or a Shengen champion?' Adaali was clearly starting to panic.

'I know Manssun Rike,' Josten said. 'I know how he fights. I can beat that ginger-haired fuckwit with my eyes shut.'

Adaali stared at him, fury in her eyes. 'Tomorrow you'll

get your chance to prove it. For all our sakes, I hope you fight as well as you talk.'

'Guess I'll show you tomorrow,' he said.

Josten rose to his feet and left the tent; he'd had enough of being yelled at. As he looked down onto the city of Kantor he pressed a finger to his tender ribs. Even at full strength it was doubtful he was a match for Rike, and now he'd gambled this whole thing on beating him with broken bones.

'You're a fucking idiot,' he whispered to himself.

No one disagreed.

33

SIFF stared at the Heartstone. A hundred images flickered across the facets, every scene relayed to her in an instant. She watched warriors preparing for battle, children blessed with magical abilities sleeping soundly, innocents at prayer, schemers at play. All this she consumed in the blink of an eye.

There would soon be a fight for the throne of Kantor and Josten would lose. It would be so easy for her to return, to fight in his stead and end this, but Siff had already succeeded in her task. Now it was for these mortals to decide their own fate.

'Is this significant?' Mortana asked. She was standing close by, having released Innellan from her grip. Siff's sister now sat in a corner, weeping over an empire that could have been, the power she had lost. But of course she was; all she had ever cared about was herself.

'The end of something,' Siff replied. 'Of a war we started.'

'Between the mortals?' said Mortana. 'Then it is of no significance at all.'

Siff could not agree.

'They are almost here,' said Durius. 'It's now or never.'

Siff still stared at the Heartstone. She wanted to watch what was happening, needed to see how this would play, but she knew they were *out of time. The decision had to be made now — shatter this thing once and for all or return through it. All of them. Every Archon claiming an empire in the mortal realm that would eventually rip the land apart...*

Most of the camp were still asleep as dawn broke. Adaali had been awake for hours, kneeling at the top of the hill that overlooked Kantor. It was the very spot her brother had breathed his last, dying in her arms. She could still see his face. Still hear his last words: *I was silent. Just like you told me.*

The memory would have brought fresh tears, but Adaali was done weeping. Now all that was left were her prayers. She clasped her hands tight, bowed her head and pleaded. Over and over again she called on the goddess Anural to bring her champion victory. If the Cupbearer was listening, if she was even real, she must hear her now — a solitary voice in the desert. If anyone could bring Josten victory this day, then surely it was the goddess.

Manssun Rike was a formidable opponent, the man who had slain Musir Dragosh, but Josten Cade also had the bearing of a killer. If Adaali could grant him an edge by calling on divine help then it had to be worth a try.

Adaali prayed until she could feel the morning sun warming her back. It would soon be time and she stood, allowing herself a glance towards the gates of Kantor. They lay open, as though beckoning her to come down the hill. She would come all right. Only death would stop her.

Back in the camp, she saw Josten had already risen.

Ctenka and Eyman were helping him strap on a coat of mail. It looked like a struggle.

'Mind his ribs,' said Ctenka.

'I am fucking minding,' Eyman replied as Josten grunted in pain at their ministrations.

Her champion looked pale, dark shadows gathering beneath his eyes, a thick sheen of sweat on his brow. He looked just about ready to drop, rather than fight for her throne.

'Can you do this?' she asked, as they tightened the straps of his shoulder guard.

Josten rose to his feet. 'Just try stopping me,' he said, reaching for the sword Ctenka held out for him.

'The whole of Kantor is relying on you to deliver them from the yoke of t—'

'I know what's at stake, your highness,' Josten said, wrestling with the sword belt. 'I'll do what's needed. Let's just get on with it.'

He stormed past her, finally managing to secure the belt at his waist as he headed towards a row of horses. After selecting one he struggled up into the saddle, groaning at the effort.

'What are you doing?' he said, as Adaali climbed onto the steed beside him.

'You don't think I'd let you go alone, do you?'

'I'm—'

'You are about to fight for me. I will not wait behind like some coward. It is my throne that you might die for. I have a right to be present.'

'Suit yourself,' Josten said, clearly in no mood for an argument.

Before they could set off, Livia came rushing towards them. She was dressed in travelling clothes, her white hair flowing down her back.

'No,' said Josten, as she made to mount another of the horses. 'Not you as well.'

'Really?' she said, climbing into the saddle.

Josten sighed. 'As if I haven't got enough to fucking worry about.'

'Don't worry about us,' Livia said. 'Worry about killing the giant bastard waiting outside the city gates.'

Josten dragged on his reins, urging his horse down the slope. 'All right. No need for that kind of language.'

Ctenka and Eyman both climbed atop horses, making up the rest of the duelling party. As they made their way from the edge of the encampment they passed the Shengen centurions, who nodded their respect to her champion. Josten ignored each one, and focused on the task at hand, his eyes fixed on the gate below. There was already a delegation waiting for them. Randal was surrounded by his children – those prodigies she had heard such wicked tales about. Beside him stood Manssun Rike and Duke Bertrand. There were others too – helmeted knights in the red livery of the Suderfeld, along with prominent marshals of the Kantor militia.

Adaali's stomach lurched as they got closer. If this were some kind of trap they would all soon be dead, and she offered one last prayer to Anural as they came within a few feet of Randal's waiting group. He was smiling that detestable grin and Adaali could well understand why people loathed him so much.

'I'm glad you could make it,' Randal said as they pulled up their horses.

'I don't like to disappoint,' Josten replied.

'Oh, I know.' Randal turned his attention to Adaali. 'We can avoid all this,' he continued. 'No one has to die here today. Simply send your army home. Come with me and I will sit you on the throne of Kantor. There is no need for this unpleasantness.'

'There is every need,' Adaali answered, trying her best to contain her emotions. 'From the day you had my mother and brother murdered.'

'That was never part of my plan,' Randal said innocently. 'Egil Sun was the one—'

'Enough fucking talk, you whiny little pissant,' Josten barked. 'Let's get this over with.'

Randal shrugged, turning his head to Manssun Rike. The bearded warrior nudged his warhorse forward.

'I've waited a long time to take the head of Josten Cade,' he said, drawing his huge broadsword.

'And now's your chance, you pig-faced cunt.'

Josten drew his own sword, but as he pulled it clear of the sheath it fell from his grip and landed in the dirt.

He looked down at it in confusion, before suddenly tipping from the saddle. Livia reached out to stop him falling, but she couldn't grab him in time. Josten hit the ground with a thud, immediately trying to pick himself up, but he floundered like a drunk.

As Manssun laughed, Livia and Adaali climbed down from their horses. Josten was burning up, stricken by a fever. He tried to stand but he was too weak.

341

'It seems this fight is over before it has even begun,' said Randal. 'Perhaps next time you'll pick a more worthy champion.'

'This is not over,' Adaali said, rising to her feet, fists clenched. 'I will fight your man.'

That brought more laughter from Manssun Rike. Adaali could barely contain herself. This bastard, who had been welcomed into the queen's house, had led a revolt that saw her family murdered. He had killed her teacher, brought misery to her city. She would not be denied.

'Are you scared to face me?' she spat.

'Of course not.' Manssun Rike climbed down from his horse. 'I have killed men, women, dogs. What difference is a princess? If you want to die, I am happy to oblige.'

Adaali turned, holding out her hand to Eyman, who sat atop his horse carrying a spear. Reluctantly he handed over the weapon.

'You don't have to do this,' said Livia. 'We can find someone else to fight.'

Adaali shrugged her off. 'There is no one else,' she replied.

As Ctenka, Eyman and Livia helped Josten, Adaali stepped forward. Manssun Rike swung his sword, loosening up his arm, all the while staring at her across ten feet of dirt.

'There's not enough meat on you to feed a bird,' he said. 'It won't take long to bury—'

She darted forward, spear thrusting straight at Manssun's face. He ducked away, stumbling from the strike, but righted himself immediately. The giant adopted a defensive stance, taking her more seriously.

They circled one another as she looked for a vulnerability in his defence, but she could see no opening. Before she could plan her next attack his eyes widened in grim fury and he swung his broadsword. The weapon parted the air above her head as she ducked it by inches. Anticipating his backswing she rolled to the side, narrowly avoiding his second attack.

Adaali rushed back. Every one of Musir Dragosh's lessons came to mind vividly. She had to use the spear's range and stay out of reach of that huge blade.

Manssun swung at her again, the broadsword sweeping left and right as he advanced, closing the ground between them. Adaali dodged to the right, thrusting the spear at him, holding it at full reach. The spearhead dug deep into Manssun's thigh and he grunted in pain. Before he could grab the weapon, Adaali wrenched it free.

Blood ran in rivulets down Manssun's leg, but he ignored the pain, advancing on her once more, this time faster, instilled with a sense of urgency. His broadsword swept audibly through the air. Adaali timed her counterstrike to perfection, the spear jabbing in and striking Manssun's arm...

A dark shadow enveloped the summit of the Blue Tower. Siff turned to see that the gathered hordes had arrived. Swarms of fell beasts summoned by Badb, hosts of seraphs gathered to Kastion's call blocking the skies in every direction.

Ekemon appeared, heralded by a thunderclap. Kastion and Badb swooped down to stand beside him. At their arrival, Innellan rose to

343

her feet. *Already features were starting to develop on her face, a wicked visage summoned by her wicked intentions.*

'They wish to destroy it,' Innellan screamed.

Kastion ignored her, taking a languid step towards Siff. In one hand he gripped a huge spear crafted in bronze, golden vines etched in the haft.

'The wait is over. It is our right,' he said.

Siff glanced back at the Heartstone. Most of the facets had gone blank now, all but one showed her events in the mortal realm. A contest was taking place – two combatants fighting for a kingdom. Fighting for the future of their world. One of them was about to be defeated.

'I will take my rightful place,' Kastion continued, stepping forward again. He was almost upon her now.

Siff could sense the pull of the Heartstone, igniting the desire that lay within every Archon present.

'No,' she answered. 'We have no right.'

Before he could reach out to the Heartstone, Siff rushed forward, seizing the spear from his grip. She brandished it expertly, the tip almost slicing Kastion's perfect skin, but he darted away before she could strike.

'You would attack me with my own sacred weapon?' Kastion said. 'You think that will stop me?'

The bearded giant growled in pain, his weapon falling from his grip, but before Adaali could pull the spear free he grabbed the haft with his other hand. She tried to wrestle the weapon from his grasp but he held on tight, pulling the spearhead from his arm. With another feral bark he chopped the flat of his hand down, his immense strength snapping the spear in two.

344

Adaali was left with nothing more than a broken stick. Manssun glanced down to where his sword lay. As he lurched towards it, Adaali lunged in, seeing her only chance to stop him. She leapt, bringing the haft of the spear down across his head. The blow was a solid one and she felt it jolt through her arm. Manssun staggered, but he was within reach of her now. Before she could retreat he had clutched her by the throat, forgetting the weapon that lay on the ground.

'What did I tell you?' he snarled. Adaali felt all the air expelled from her lungs as Manssun punched her in the gut. It was like being hit with a battering ram.

'What did I tell you?' he repeated, this time smacking her in the jaw.

Adaali fell to the dirt. There was blood in her mouth, she couldn't breathe, couldn't see through the tears. She began to crawl across the ground, thoughts of escape flashing through her mind, but there was nowhere to go. Somewhere behind her, Manssun would be picking up that great sword and preparing to cleave her in two. She was beaten. She was dead.

Gritting her teeth she remembered her prayer.

'Anural,' she spat. 'Please help me. Do not abandon me now.'

She heard the heavy tread of Manssun Rike bearing down on her.

'Please, give me strength,' she begged.

Siff suddenly felt renewed power in her limbs, her body solidifying, evolving from its embryonic form. She began to glow with the energy of it. It was a strength that could only have been bestowed through

345

the purity of prayer. An entreaty from the mortal realm. A single voice granting worship through the Heartstone and in return begging for deliverance.

For the briefest of moments Siff closed her eyes, listening to the girl's voice calling across the void. She took the strength that lonely voice gave, and in return bestowed the power of a god.

Then it was over.

'Strike me down if you dare!' Kastion raged.

Siff raised the spear, hefting it to shoulder height, ready to strike. Kastion's eyes widened in surprise at her audacity. Then she span, striking the weapon into the midst of the Heartstone.

All she could hear were the Archons screaming as the ancient artefact shattered into a million pieces. It flowered in an explosion of light, shattering the essence of god and servant alike.

Their link to the mortal realm was no more...

A spark of vigour bloomed within her. Limbs that were exhausted came back to life in an instant.

Adaali pushed herself up, darting aside just as Manssun's broadsword hacked a divot in the earth where she had lain. He swung again and she dived to one side, rolling on the ground to come up in a crouch. Before her was half a spear lying within reach. She grasped it, rolling aside once more to avoid another sweep of the blade.

'Come here, you fucking bitch,' Manssun shouted.

'Hear me,' Adaali said under her breath. 'Anural, hear me.'

'Pray all you want,' said Manssun. 'There's no one to save you now.'

He charged, raising his sword high, ready to bring it down in a two-handed swing that would cut her in two.

Adaali had never felt so strong. Never felt so sure of herself. Her weapon was broken but it did not matter. She was not alone… she never had been.

She flung the broken spear, watching its trajectory as it soared and found its target.

Manssun's charge was halted in an instant, his feet slowing to a walk, then a stagger. The spearhead pierced his eye, the remaining one blinking in confusion. Adaali finally managed to take a breath as she watched the Suderfeld champion collapse to the dirt.

34

SHE *opened her eyes. The flat plain extended for miles in every direction. She could hear nothing, sense nothing. There was no voice from the beyond. The eternal call of prayer from the mortal realm was silent after millennia. But neither was there any desire to hear it.*

Siff dragged herself to her feet, breathing in the cleansing air. Surrounding her were her brothers and sisters, each one transformed, mundane and naked just as she was.

Ekemon was no longer godlike in stature or visage. He did not burn as he had done for as long as Siff could remember. Now he was a short insignificant man, slightly balding, his stomach burgeoning with a hairy paunch. Beside him, Mortana was no longer an alluring beauty. Now she looked as old as her years; her face wrinkled and slack, her hair lank, more grey than black. Badb had lost her corvid aspect and now stood as a young girl, red hair hanging in curling strands, a mass of freckles adorning her ruddy cheeks. Hastor was still old, but not the ancient thing he had been. His lined face was friendly, his matted beard curling about his jowly features.

He gazed at his body, then at Siff. 'What do we do now?' he asked.

Before she could answer, Siff heard a scream from beside her. It was the shrill rage of a petulant child, and when she turned she had to stop herself from laughing.

'What have you done?' screamed Kastion. 'You have damned us all to this place.'

He was a chubby little boy, his hair retaining its cherubic blonde style.

'Better that we are damned to our own realm than destroy the mortal one with our eternal squabbles,' Siff replied.

Kastion looked like he wanted to attack her, but instead he satisfied himself with stamping his feet.

Innellan stepped forward. Like Siff, her body was that of an ordinary woman, there was nothing remarkable about her at all. 'This will not stand,' she said calmly. 'We will find a way to return and claim what is ours. This is not the end. Durius, what say you?'

They turned to the trickster god. Of all of them he was the only one who still bore his Archon's aspect. He wore the same rustic garb he always had, his curly hair and mischievous grin unchanged.

'I say...' Durius flickered, as though he were lost between two planes of existence. His image winked back and forth, a projection, ephemeral and waning. 'I say it's been a pleasure, my friends.'

And with that, he melted away, his body breaking apart into tiny petals of spring blossom. Durius drifted away on the quiet breeze, leaving the rest of them watching empty air.

'What is this?' Hastor whispered.

'Where is he?' Innellan demanded.

The rest of them began to crow, bickering in the nothingness. What were they to do? Where were they to go? What had Durius done?

Siff laughed. It started as a giggle in her throat and turned to a bellowing guffaw.

'What's the matter with you?' Kastion shouted, his little face scrunched up in angelic rage.

'He tricked us all,' Siff said, trying to control her mirth. 'All this time we argued and fought over who would be the one to rule the mortal realm. In the end the only one of us to make it was the trickster god himself. But then, Durius always did have the last laugh.'

She started to giggle once more. Some of her brothers and sisters joined her. There were some who didn't, but she no longer gave a damn. Let them harbour their old resentments…

…Siff had long since ceased to care.

Livia watched with a mix of horror and awe as Manssun Rike collapsed to the ground, a plume of dust erupting around him.

Though Livia's eyes were fixed on the body, she was aware of a change in the atmosphere surrounding her. Something had shifted in the fabric of the environment, as though a cataclysm had occurred just beyond the realm of her understanding. A silent wind whispered across the desert, sweeping away any connection she might have had to the divine. When first restored to her mortal body, Livia had felt powerful, as though the latent energies imbued in Innellan's earthly form were still residually present. Now there was nothing.

The world was different, changed forever. Something was broken, but at the same time healed. The unseen rivers of magic flowing throughout the land had dried up in an instant.

The feeling overwhelmed her for less time than an intake of breath, and once it was over Livia was brought back to earth in a rush. Adaali had dropped to one knee, blood still pouring from her face, her hand gripping her gut where Manssun had struck her.

Livia ran to her, gently lifting the girl to her feet. 'Are you all right?' she asked.

'Better than him,' she said, gesturing at the Suderfeld champion's corpse.

She shrugged off Livia's arm and turned to face the onlookers, eyes burning into Randal.

'I have defeated your champion,' she proclaimed. 'I have shown you who is the rightful queen of Kantor. My throne is claimed. Now take your army and ride back to where you came from.'

Randal regarded the body of Manssun with a look of abject disappointment. Then he laughed.

'This means nothing. You never had any claim here, girl. Any power you might hold will be what I decide to give you. Do you think me some kind of fool? That I would hand you the Cordral for defeating a single warrior? I commend you for an entertaining display, princess, but this distraction is over. Now kneel, and I might let you keep your tongue.'

Livia and Adaali stood side by side. Neither of them knelt.

'You can't even talk some sense into this child, Livia?' Randal asked.

'Go to hell,' Livia replied.

'You've come a long way from the frightened little girl I remember,' Randal said. 'But playtime is over.'

He looked over at one of the children, the oldest of the bunch. An unspoken order was given and accepted and the boy slowly walked towards them. Livia looked down at him, seeing a sorrow behind those dark eyes.

Livia could hear Josten struggling to rise, shouting a word of warning, but there was nothing he could do to help. The boy simply stared, a growing expression of confusion crossing his face. Time went on, and Randal began to fidget atop his saddle. Whatever he had expected the boy to do had not happened.

Livia walked forward, kneeling down before the boy. There was a look of confusion on his face, and she offered a smile, raising a hand to touch his cheek.

'What's your name?' she asked.

'Hestan,' the boy replied in a tiny voice.

'Hello, Hestan. I am Livia. It's nice to meet you.'

'I feel… odd,' he replied.

'I know. But don't worry, everything will be all right.'

She stood, placing an arm around Hestan's shoulder and holding him close. She could feel the boy trembling against her.

'What is this?' Randal snarled. 'Hestan, what is wrong with you?'

'This charade is over, Randal. These children aren't your toys any longer – they're free of you.'

'Bullshit.' Randal looked down at a little girl beside him. 'Mabel, Olivar. Punish this bitch.'

The little boy beside him furrowed his brow in confusion. The girl looked up and simply shook her head.

'It's finished, Randal,' Livia said. 'The best thing for you to do is turn your horse and ride away as far as you can.'

That was the hardest thing for her to say. She had wanted Randal dead for the longest time – not just for murdering

Ben, but for everything else he had done. But Livia had seen enough killing. If this could be over without more bloodshed then perhaps she would be able to return home with some semblance of pride in herself.

'It's not finished by a damn sight,' Randal said. 'I still have the Suderfeld. I am still the real power. What do I need with children when I have King Stellan's army at my beck and call?' Randal didn't notice his armoured knights looking to one another uncertainly. 'I will defend Kantor to the last man. Bring your army. You will find we are not ready to give up the city so easily.'

A rider nudged his horse up beside Randal. He had an eye patch, blonde hair framing a pleasant face.

'It's over,' he said to Randal. 'I'm not sure what's going on, but it looks like these children are just that… children. You've had your day, Randal. Give it up.'

'Fuck you, Bertrand. It's over when I say it is. Now get back in line where you belong.'

Bertrand reached up and took the patch from his eye. Livia winced as she saw the hollow socket beneath, the skin around it torn as though it had been clawed out by a bird of prey.

'You don't have any power here,' he said. 'No one will follow you willingly. They never did.'

Randal regarded him with a contemptuous stare. 'You're a mewling prick, aren't you, Bertrand. Without me you'd be—'

Bertrand stabbed Randal before Livia even realised he'd been holding a knife. He drove it up to the hilt in Randal's neck.

Randal snatched Bertrand's hand before he could pull

the knife clear and they struggled for a moment. Eventually the one-eyed man wrenched his hand free of Randal's grip. There was a sickening choking sound, and Livia felt the urge to look away, but no – she would watch this. She would see it through to the end for old Ben's sake.

All eyes were on him as Randal fell from his saddle. He gripped the knife in his throat, eyes bulging. His children watched impassively as he struggled, fighting for air through a severed throat. It didn't take long for him to die.

Livia turned to Adaali. 'Time to claim your throne, my queen,' she said, breaking the silence.

The girl walked towards the gates of her city, not even giving Randal a second glance as she entered.

35

H<small>E</small> hadn't missed the grey skies. Nor had he missed riding a horse for mile after mile. A lot of travellers felt an affinity with their animals, but not Josten Cade. He'd grown to hate this nag over the past few days and he was pretty sure it had grown to hate him right back.

The wound in his side had healed pretty well but there was still a dull ache in his ribs. The fever had lasted a week, or so he was told. Josten couldn't remember much of it apart from the delirious dreams and the occasional lucid moment of vomiting. The court surgeons of Kantor had done a good job of nursing him back to health though, so he had no complaints.

He was weaker than he'd ever been, he knew that much. It was doubtful he'd ever be as strong as he once was, but that was the thing with age and sickness – they were inevitable. And inevitability was the one enemy you could never defeat. More than likely his fighting days were over. Or at least he bloody hoped so.

Once he'd recovered enough to walk, Josten hung around in Kantor long enough to see Adaali crowned. Eyman, Dantar and Ctenka had all remained by her side, each of them given positions of authority close to the new queen, but then she needed all the loyal friends she could get. Ctenka's face had been a picture as he'd pledged himself to that girl and had medals pinned to him. Josten had been offered a position of his own, but of course he'd refused it. She didn't need him anyhow. He'd seen first hand what she was capable of. Manssun Rike's rotting corpse was testament enough that she could look after herself when needed. Josten was sure she'd be just fine without him.

It felt strange being back in the Suderfeld. Everything had changed, not least Josten Cade. Maybe it was what he'd been through. Maybe it was what he had to look forward to. But then responsibility had a habit of changing a man.

Josten glanced back at the wagon. It was full of children, a good dozen of them. Livia had insisted on bringing them home, and who was he to argue?

Despite what they'd experienced with Randal as a mentor, they seemed surprisingly normal. Laughing, joking, throwing bits of bread at one another. It was enough to make a man…

Josten wiped the smile off his face. That was an odd thing – he'd never have credited himself with that kind of sentimentality. Things had definitely changed.

Even though he'd promised Livia to help see the children safely home, he knew there wouldn't be much danger on the road. Duke Bertrand had already led the armies of the Suderfeld back south, so the king's roads were protected well enough. How long that would last was anyone's guess, and with things returning to normal in Canbria he could only imagine what Stellan would be plotting. There was every chance the War of Three Crowns would start up again within the year. Then again, Bertrand had seemed determined that the alliance would hold. What he could do about it Josten had no idea, but he guessed time would tell if the Duke could achieve with diplomacy what Randal had managed with magic.

'We're almost there,' said Livia with a look of concern.

He'd told her a score of times not to worry and that he was pretty much healed, but she seemed to want the responsibility of caring for him. Not that Josten was complaining.

Livia Harrow looked more beautiful than he could remember. She'd been a girl when they first met and now she was a woman, and a strong one too. Determined, kind. He'd even got used to the shock of white hair on her head, but if it was going to suit anyone, it would suit her. Then again Livia could have been shaved to the scalp and she'd still have looked a sight for sore eyes.

'Maybe we should pull over,' she continued. 'Give you a chance to rest.'

'I can make it the rest of the way,' Josten replied. 'Stop fussing.'

She had acted like his nursemaid for most of the journey. With anyone else, Josten would probably have told them to mind their own business, but he let Livia do what she wanted. Not that anyone could tell her otherwise.

'So,' she said. 'What are your plans once we get back?'

It was a good question. Josten had to admit he'd given it some thought and not come up with much.

'There's always work for a man like me,' he replied.

'A man like you?' she said, looking him up and down as

though the sight were a disappointment. 'The great Josten Cade. Warrior and hero.'

'I'm sure something will turn up,' he said eventually. 'But I know one thing... I'm no hero.'

'They should be writing your name in the annals of history,' Livia said. 'Every man, woman and child in the land should be shouting your name in thanks.'

'You did see me fall off my horse, right? I was stricken with fever for days.'

'You're the bravest man I know.'

'I'm just a sell-sword,' he replied.

Livia shook her head. 'No you're not. You can be anything you want to be. And remember what you told me? Remember what I promised? If we made it through this there'd be a place for you on my farm.'

Josten laughed. The thought of it was ridiculous, but there was something tempting in it too.

'I was just talking. We thought we were going to die.'

'But we didn't.'

'No we didn't.' Josten looked about him at the Canbrian countryside, at the great oaks and the fields rolling off to verdant hedgerows that he'd not dared hope to see again. 'I never thought I'd live this long. And if I had I wouldn't have seen myself working on a farm.'

'What, you thought you were going to become a mercenary general? An officer in some king's retinue? Earn your fortune from the spoils of war? It never happened, Josten, and it's not going to happen now. The wars are over.'

'But who knows for how long?' Josten replied, a part of

him trying to cling to those old dreams. 'War could start up again any day now. Then I'll be—'

'We're here,' Livia said, pointing ahead.

In front of them, Josten could see the road leading down into a meadow surrounded by open fields. In their midst was a farmhouse – strong wooden boughs constructed around a solid stone chimney. A couple of barns stood close by, one of them burnt down to black ash.

Livia seemed to be in a trance as they rode down into the farm. She'd not been back there for a long time, and by all accounts the last she'd seen of the place they'd murdered her uncle and dragged her away like a piece of meat. It must have been hard for her, but Josten didn't have the words to console her. That kind of thing had never been his strong suit.

They stopped outside the farmhouse, and Hestan pulled up the wagon full of children beside them.

'Is this is it?' he heard one of the little ones say.

'Can we get out now?' whined another.

Livia just sat and stared. She looked like she might bolt at any moment; dig heels to flanks and ride away, not giving the place a second look.

'There's a lot of work to do, but at least the house is in one piece,' said Josten, doing his best to lighten the mood. 'That's good, right?'

Before she could answer, one of the little girls, Mabel, came to stand beside her horse.

'Can we go and play now?' Mabel asked.

Livia smiled down at the girl and said, 'Of course. You should all feel free to explore. This is your new home.'

As the children jumped down from the wagon, Josten climbed from his horse. He saw Hestan, the oldest of those youngsters, helping the others down. The boy had become their leader in a sense, their big brother, and Josten offered him a friendly nod of approval. Hestan smiled back, running a hand through the thick brown mop of hair he'd grown these past weeks.

Livia walked up onto her porch, looking into the house through the open door as though afraid to enter. Josten moved up beside her.

'You'll have this place up and running in no time,' he said. 'Most of these young ones are clever enough to swing a hammer and use a saw. They'll all muck in when the fields need planting and sowing.'

She didn't answer, stepping in through the door. Josten followed into a dark and dingy kitchen. The stove had long since gone cold, a table and a couple of chairs were in one corner. Livia stared at that table and he could see tears well up in her eyes. He stepped forward and put his arms around her. It seemed like the right thing to do in the circumstances.

'Will you stay?' she asked.

'Sure. I can help out until you get back on your feet.'

'No,' she said, looking up at him intently. 'I mean really stay.'

Josten shook his head. 'I'm going to need to get back on the road eventually. This farm life. This... family life, it's not for me.'

'All right,' she said. 'If that's what you want then I guess I can't change your mind.'

'No. No you can't.'

He held her close, feeling the warmth of her against his chest. Staying was a nice idea, but Josten Cade as a farmer? A father? Not a chance. He'd always been a mercenary, and never cared for anyone but himself. It would never have worked out, even if he'd wanted it, and besides…

…everyone gets what they deserve.

EPILOGUE

Canbria, 109 years after the Fall

SHE could hear the tinkling sound of laughter from outside and it never failed to bring a smile to her face. This place was once again filled with joy after so much sorrow.

Livia stirred the pan of broth, the smell of it filling the kitchen. The front door was open and it wouldn't be long before the aroma brought the children running. It was strange how the smell of good cooking could transform a room – just as her children had transformed this farm. They had chased away the ghosts of the past. Now all that remained was hope.

Hestan and Olivar had taken to this rural life as though they were born to it, and the rest had followed. With Livia and the boys in charge, the renovation of the farm and outbuildings had taken no time at all. All the children showed a maturity beyond their years, and it was hardly surprising after what they'd been through. But that was in the past now.

Of course, it had helped with them having a real father figure to look up to.

Josten had found it somewhat more difficult adjusting to

this life than any of them, but now he was a better farmer than Livia could ever have imagined. It had only taken him a season to stop saying he'd be leaving soon. Now, a year after her return, it was as though he'd been born to it. In the back of her mind she always wondered if he still hankered after his old life, but of course he would never leave now. Not when he had everything to stay for.

Livia took a step back from the stove, placing a hand to her belly. Before long she'd struggle to fasten the apron around her waist. Not long after there'd be another addition to this bizarre family of hers.

Thoughts of the future fled from her mind as she heard a tuneful whistling outside the house. She cocked her head at the sound. It wasn't one of the children. And Josten couldn't hold a tune to save his life. Before she could reach the back door to see who had come, the whistle turned into a song from a voice she'd never heard before.

'*Cormorant was quick at hand, a golden fish within its beak. Owl and falcon swept the land, their talons drawn for prey to seek.*'

Livia recognised the rhyme. It was common across Canbria and she'd often sung it herself, though she'd never known its meaning. She reached for the door handle as the singer continued.

'*Carrion crow and vulture soared, and stripped their meat from out the dead. Rook came hunting with its horde, a crown of blood about its head.*'

A feeling of apprehension fell on her as she gripped the handle. Surely this was just some passer-by? A tinker or a hermit or one of the village lads wanting some work in the fields. But Livia couldn't bring herself to open the door. Was she in danger? Were the children?

A dog barked outside, just beyond the door. When it barked again, Livia was certain she recognised the sound.

'Jack?' she called, wrenching the door open.

The sun beamed at her, and just a few feet away sat a small dog. On seeing her he padded forward, nuzzling into her hand with a whine.

'It can't be you,' she whispered, stroking his neck.

Jack had died years before, one of Randal's tallymen beating him to death out in the garden, but this mongrel looked so much like him.

Livia knelt, cupping his head in her hands. He looked similar, but this hound was much older, his hair flecked with grey, one of his eyes glassy and blind. The dog gave a whine and licked her face before turning over for his belly to be rubbed.

'They can always tell, you know.'

Livia looked up to see an old man watching her from a few feet away. She stood, regarding him from the doorway. His wispy hair blew in the breeze, two piercing blue eyes observing her from an old and wrinkled face. There was a familiar look to him, but Livia couldn't quite place it. Perhaps she'd seen him at Bardum Market.

'They can tell what?' Livia asked.

'Who has a good heart and… who doesn't,' the old man replied.

She looked back down at the dog. He was sitting at her feet now, looking up expectantly like Jack used to.

Livia shook her head. 'I'm sorry, can I help you?'

'Not really, I was just passing by. Met this little fella on the road and followed him back here. I'm guessing he's yours?'

'No, I don't think so...' The dog gave another whine. 'Can I get you some tea?' she asked, before she'd even thought whether this man might be a threat. But then how much harm could one old man and a stray dog do?

'That would be lovely,' the man said.

He followed her inside and sat himself in a chair next to the table. As Livia put the kettle on the stove the dog went and lay in the corner of the kitchen, right in Jack's old spot.

'Have you travelled far?' she asked as she took two cups from the cupboard.

'Oh yes,' he replied. 'Very far indeed.'

As he spoke the feeling she knew him from somewhere began to overwhelm her.

'Anywhere in particular?' The kettle began to boil.

'Nowhere to speak of, no.'

A curious answer, but then he was a pretty curious fellow. Livia filled the pot and set it down on the table alongside the cups.

'Do you have family nearby?' she asked.

'No, I have no family.' He gestured to her expectant belly. 'But I see yours isn't far away.'

'Yes.' She absently placed a hand to the bump. 'It won't be long now.'

'A new child is a joy to the world.'

Livia poured the tea into the cups and picked one up, blowing the steam away. 'I'm sorry, I haven't even asked your name.'

He didn't touch his cup. 'I've had many over the years.'

Livia felt there was something odd about the man, but she was not unnerved by it. In fact she began to think she would have been quite happy to sit and let him avoid her questions all day.

He was old, perhaps seventy winters, but those eyes of his were young, sparkling in the sunlight that gleamed in through the open window. There was also an element of whimsy about him,v like he didn't have a care in the world. The notion she'd seen him before simply wouldn't leave her. It was like they'd met, but perhaps only in a dream…

'So where are you headed?' she asked. 'Anywhere in particular?'

'Oh, I have much more travelling to do before I get to where I'm going. Much more travelling.' He picked up his cup and drank it in one, placing it back down and breathing in a deep satisfied sigh. 'Well, the road won't walk itself.'

The old man stood and Livia found herself rising and placing a hand on his arm. 'Won't you stay for dinner?' she asked from out of nowhere.

He felt like an old friend who she would miss once he had gone. Livia would have liked him to stay forever.

'No, I'm afraid I must go.' He lay his own hand on hers. 'But it's good to see you are doing so well. I'm glad you're happy.'

He made his way to the back door. The dog stirred, rising to its feet and following him out onto the rear porch.

'Looks like you'll have company,' Livia said.

'Looks like I will,' he replied, regarding her with those

366

bright blue eyes. 'You take care, Livia Harrow. Remember, you are special. You will always be special. And so will the child inside you.'

The feeling that they'd met before was stronger than ever. She wanted to ask who he was, but deep down at the back of her mind, in a place she hadn't gone for so long, she already knew the answer.

Livia watched as the old man and his dog walked the path away from the farm. In the distance she heard the sound of tinkling laughter once more, and by the time the old man was gone from view she'd forgotten he was ever there.

'May the gods go with you,' she said to no one.

Placing a hand to her belly, she felt the baby kick.

ABOUT THE AUTHOR

Richard Ford originally hails from Leeds in the heartland of Yorkshire but now resides in the wild fens of Cambridgeshire. His previous works include the raucous steampunk adventure, *Kultus*, and the grimdark fantasy trilogy, Steelhaven.

You can find out more about what he's up to, and download free stuff, here: www.richardsfordauthor.com/.

And follow him on Twitter here: @rich4ord